DEPTHS

DEPTHS

SOUTHERN WATCH
BOOK TWO

Robert J. Crane

DEPTHS
SOUTHERN WATCH
BOOK TWO

Copyright © 2014 Reikonos Press
All Rights Reserved.

1st Edition

AUTHOR'S NOTE
This book is a work of fiction. Names, characters, places and incidents are products of the author's imagination or are used fictitiously. Any resemblance to actual events or locales or persons, living or dead, is entirely coincidental.

The scanning, uploading and distribution of this book via the internet or any other means without the permission of the publisher is illegal and punishable by law. Please purchase only authorized electronic editions, and do not participate in or encourage electronic piracy of copyrighted materials. Your support of the author's rights is appreciated.

No part of this publication may be reproduced in whole or in part without the written permission of the publisher. For information regarding permission, please email cyrusdavidon@gmail.com

Acknowledgments

First thanks goes out to all who helped make the launch of Called: Southern Watch #1 in the Sinners & Sorcerers boxed set so successful. In no particular order, I owe gratitude to the great Daniel Arenson, Scott Nicholson, J.R. Rain and Phoenix Sullivan, who managed the whole thing with the professionalism and aplomb.

I owe the greatest debt to my friend S.M. Reine, without whom this series would not even be seeing the light of day until 2015. She convinced me to speed things up and gave me a damned good reason to do so, and for that - and much more - I owe her my thanks.

Gratitude also goes to Jerod Heck and David Leach, who read through the book in its first draft form to help me pin down major screwups. Thanks, guys.

Karri Klawiter once more did the cover, and she deserves extra mention this time for doing a second round cover on Called (which she totally knocked out of the park!).

Sarah Barbour pulled editing duty on this particular work, and gave me perhaps the greatest compliment of my professional career after remarking that the Gideon scenes were so disturbing she felt like she needed to shower afterward.

Nick Ambrose came out of retirement to format this book on extremely short notice. I'm dedicating Girl in the Box #9 to him, but he deserves extra special mention for this, too, because he's just such a standup guy. Without Nick, my publishing career would not be where it is today, and for that he has my thanks.

In the last roundup, thanks to my mom and dad as well as my wife and kids. 'Nuff said.

Chapter 1

Gideon could feel death when he listened closely to the stirring deep within. It was in the distance, maybe even miles away, but he could taste it when it came, and it was almost as good as if he were in the room while it was happening.

* * *

Jacob Abbott had saved for his divorce for years, and the bitch had gone and thwarted him two weeks before he had filed. He still felt sick about it, going on a year later. He'd paid a big shot lawyer down in Chattanooga with installment payments, one at a time, every payday for three years. It was some fucked up shit, too, Hayley going and dying in a car wreck before he'd had the satisfaction of seeing her fat face crumple when she read the papers. He'd planned to have them served while he was there, two weeks after his youngest daughter turned eighteen. He didn't want to miss it, after all. He'd paid for it, for fuck's sake.

But she'd gone and gotten herself ground up under the treads of an eighteen wheeler changing lanes on the interstate, and the goddamned lawyer had said that the retainer was non-refundable. He'd had some choice words for that cocksucker, but it still hadn't gotten him a dime back, which was a shame because he had a funeral to pay for. That was almost as much of a kick to the balls as not getting the money back from the lawyer.

It had turned out all right now, though. Jacob cracked open another beer, sitting in his underwear in the basement of the house they used to share. Back when Hayley was alive, he'd kept the basement as his domain, made it his own. After she died, he hadn't bothered to take the upstairs over again. The kids stayed up there when they were in town, which wasn't very often. Jacob just hung out in his basement after work, drank beer, ate his sour cream chips and watched SportsCenter. That suited him just fine.

When the first pains of the heart attack struck him, Jacob didn't have much time to ponder whether it was the beer, the cigarettes, the sour cream chips, or the last fifteen years in which the most strenuous exercise had been the one time a year or less that Hayley had let him fuck her that caused it. He just knew it hurt like a motherfucker.

It felt like someone had jabbed a flaming sword through his left arm and down into the center of his chest, and goddamn did it hurt. He wheezed and clutched at himself, gasping like he'd been run over by an eighteen wheeler. *So that's what it felt like,* he thought.

Jacob jerked like someone had run a hot poker up his ass. That caused him to swipe his hand across the end table at his left. He heard himself hit some things but barely felt them through the pain. He might have worried about what he'd knocked over, but he was too busy screaming between gasps for breath.

He slid out of his chair, spasming, and hit the floor, the agony searing through his chest. He could smell his sour cream chips, like a little taste of home as he lay with his cheek pressed against the tattered grey and brown rug. Chips were spilled all around him, the bowl upended in front of his eyes. Any other time it would have been a welcome scent, like a substitute for someone meeting him at the door when he got home from work at the plant. He loved those damned chips, didn't even mind when he beat off with the stuff still on his hand and it made his dick smell like them until he showered the next morning.

Now they were just in the way. He rolled, hearing them crunch as he broke them into tiny pieces. The pain had faded just enough for him to start thinking through what he needed to do, and finding the phone so he could call 911 was right at the top of his list.

Jacob had just enough presence of mind to realize that if the chips were on the floor, the phone probably was, too. His thoughts were spinning, the pain subsiding, creeping back to the center of his ribcage. Now it was like someone had left some embers alight in his chest.

He strained to recall if the phone had been sitting where it usually was, on the end table. The ebbing pain left him enough room to think that yes, it probably was. He stretched up, running his greasy, sour-cream-flavored fingers across the end table's pitted surface. It had a few burns from where he'd set cigs from time to time when the ashtray had been moved on him. He reached across, stretching hard, and the pain seemed to come roaring back, dropping him onto his side. He heard a whimper in his ears, and he realized it was him. It wasn't like anyone else was here with him, after all.

He made one last effort to raise himself up after he swept his eyes over the field of fallen and broken chips and didn't see a sign of the phone. 911. *Only hope.* The words buzzed in his head as he reared up, forcing himself off the floor one last time to look over the table edge.

He fell back, exhausted, a moment later after glimpsing the flat, barren surface of the end table, completely empty of anything. He figured it must have fallen on the back side.

Goddammit.

Jacob fell onto his back, the sound of crunching chips filling his ears, his breaths coming shallower now. For some reason he was reminded of the last time he'd gotten laid, a month ago now, at the whorehouse on Water Street. How that hot redheaded whore had felt as he'd sweated and rolled off her afterward like this, onto his back. He wasn't breathing as deep, but he'd made some similar noises, he was pretty sure.

The pain grew to an agonizing crescendo, one last swell, and he could have sworn he was screaming for Jesus, the devil, and anyone else in between to make it stop. He wasn't sure who answered, but they damned sure did.

And just like that, Jacob Abbott knew his ticket was getting punched. It wasn't an eighteen wheeler, either.

So that's what it felt like ...

* * *

Somewhere across town, Gideon could feel it, feel the life leaving Jacob Abbott. It was strong, that last whisper of agony, the cry of misery that no one could hear but him. It was like the sweetest candy, like the most exciting fuck he could ever imagine. It was a dirty little secret among their kind that demons fucked, just like the filthy humans. Sometimes even with the filthy humans. He didn't, but that was because he was a greater. He took care of his own needs.

The last echoes of Jacob Abbott's death sounded deep inside him, the whispers, the screams, and even lying in bed it was as palpable to him as if Abbott had died right in front of him. It was so beautiful, the closest thing he knew to sexy. He felt his hard-on and took it in hand when the feeling of death first came on.

It was tantalizing, that sense of death. Like he was standing beneath Abbott, his maw open and ready to devour him. The soul came down, and Gideon tasted it all—the fear, the misery—every drop of it came out as Abbott expired and he absorbed him, ate him up. The steady rhythm of his hand beat faster under the covers, moving up and down his own shaft as the sensation swelled.

Gideon could hear Abbott screaming, begging him to stop. He didn't. This was the best part, the man's essence being dissolved into Gideon's waiting self. It burned in such a good way, and Gideon stroked harder. The screams came louder in his head, and pleasure built to a climax and—

He'd finished by the time Abbott expired. The last bit of essence tore free and Gideon caught it, ingested it. It was a good climax, and little drops of Gideon's jizz seared holes in the sheets.

Gideon took long, deep breaths, lying on his back like Abbott had, just savoring the sensation. It was good, this feeling. He basked in his own particular kind of afterglow, took another breath, and hoped for another death. Soon.

His hand reached back down to his crotch involuntarily. Really soon.

Chapter 2

"A man moves into the hills of Tennessee," Hendricks said, looking around the table at the bar. He was up in the hills, coincidentally, at least ten miles out of Midian right now, and the guys sitting with him were hanging on his every word. The beer in his hand was cold but shitty. It had the smell of one of the generic nationwide brands, piss pre-bottled for ease of drinking. If it was up to him he'd just take it and pour it straight in the urinal to save himself the trouble, but it wouldn't give him the buzz he was after if he didn't drink it first. "He's there for, like, a day, before someone comes driving up in an old, busted-up pickup truck. Out of it steps this long-haired, overall-wearing, country-bumpkin motherfucker, the most backwoods son of a bitch you've ever seen."

Hendricks looked around at his audience while he was talking. There were three of them sitting with him, all guys, all dressed pretty damned natty—one in a suit and tie, another in a sweater vest. "The hillbilly comes up to the man and says, 'I wanted to come over and welcome you to our little corner of the woods. I wanted to invite you to a party, too, seeing as you're new around here. Give you a chance to meet some of the locals.' And the hillbilly leans close to the guy and says, 'But I gotta warn you, there's gonna be some drinking at the party. You don't have a problem with drinking, do you?'"

The guy directly across from Hendricks, the one wearing the sweater vest, kind of snorted. Hendricks smiled, took a long, sour pull from his beer and regretted it immediately. At least he could feel a faint buzz forming. He'd gone through half the beer just to get this far, though, and that was a disappointment. "So the new guy says, 'No, I don't have a problem with drinking,' and the hillbilly says, 'Good! There might be some cussing. You ain't got a problem with cussing, do you?' The new guy says, 'I might have used a swear word or two in my life; nah, I don't have a problem with cussing.'"

"Is this shit almost over?" The guy on the left asked, his beer sweating in his hand. He was wearing skinny jeans and a polo, collar up, to go with his thick-rimmed hipster glasses. Way too cool for this place, Hendricks figured. At least in that guy's mind.

"Shut up, I haven't heard this one before," the guy on the right said, tossing a nasty glare at his friend across the table. He was a wearing a full suit and tie, but he at least had the top collar of his white shirt unbuttoned. Hendricks had to wonder if he was a stockbroker or something, the way he was dressed. He damned sure looked out of place.

"'Well, there's bound to be some fighting,' the hillbilly tells the new guy," Hendricks went on, ignoring his heckler, "'so I hope you don't have a problem with fighting.' 'I've been in a scrape or two, the new guy says, 'so no, I don't have a problem with fighting.'"

Hendricks smelled the smoke in the air, from the regulars over at the bar pumping it out of their cigarettes like miniature chimneys. "'Well, this is my party, and there's always some fucking at my parties. I hope you don't have a problem with fucking.'" The new guy shrugs and says he doesn't have a problem with that. 'Well, good', the hillbilly tells him, 'I'll look forward to seeing you tomorrow night,' and then the guy starts back to his truck to leave."

"Heh," Sweater Vest said, staring at Hendricks from across the table. Like he'd just let out a preemptive laugh, thinking it was going to be good. And it was, really. Hendricks had told this one before, and it was always a crowd pleaser. He glanced over at the bar, and saw it was having the opposite effect there—that crowd did not look pleased. There were a half-dozen angry faces over there just staring at him.

"So," Hendricks went on, "the new guy calls out just as the hillbilly is getting to his truck: 'Wait a minute! What kind of party is this? I mean, what should I wear?' And the hillbilly just sort of stands there, truck door open, scratches his hairy chin for a minute like he's thinking it over, and then he says, 'Oh, I don't reckon it matters. You and I are gonna be the only ones there.'"

A low guffaw from Sweater Vest spread quickly to a roaring laugh from Suit and Tie. Hipster Glasses on the left sort of winced, throwing a nervous glance at the regulars over at the bar. They were all staring sullenly at the table in the corner, clearly with a bone to pick.

"Gah, that's probably so true," Suit and Tie said, picking up his beer for another drink. He wore an easy grin, but his glance over at Sweater Vest told Hendricks that he was looking for approval from his leader. Hendricks made note of the little co-dependent relationship between him and Sweater Vest and wondered how long that had been going on. "It's probably a true story."

Hendricks shrugged, keeping an eye on the characters at the bar. If one of them didn't start moving soon, he had another joke to tell, one that might get a little more provocative.

"Yeah," Sweater Vest said, nodding his head. "We've been down here for ... what? A week? Totally feels like that. Bunch of hillbilly fucks around here." He was talking loud, the booze letting his jaw run away with itself. Hendricks just sat back and let it happen. "It's all backwoods and backwater shit. Nothing to do—no theater, no culture, no decent restaurants." He looked around. "And the beer—"

Hendricks inclined his head slightly. "Well, that one I suppose I can agree with."

"It's like 1859 down here," Sweater Vest went on. "You lost the war, guys," he said, voice carrying. Hendricks watched as one of the boys at the bar who had previously remained facing the bartender turned around at that, bringing his chair around in a slow orbit. "Bunch of racists, just sitting around spinning their monster truck tires and slinging dirt—"

The bartender started over at a slow pace. He was medium-height fellow, a ball cap on his head and a windbreaker that read 'SM Lines' on the breast. It was zipped high enough that it revealed only a corner of plaid flannel beneath. He strode over to the table and Sweater Vest shut up, turning to look up at the guy, who didn't look altogether pleased.

"Yes?" Sweater Vest asked, staring up at him. None of the guys sitting with Hendricks looked like they weighed much over one-fifty. The bartender was a hell of a lot more solidly built than that.

"Sorry to interrupt you fellows," the guy in the hat said, "but I couldn't help but overhear you saying some mighty disparaging things about the folks around here."

"Nah," Sweater Vest, turning away to face Hendricks and the others at the table, "we were just talking about our experiences around here." He snickered and the other two followed right along.

"Well, boys, I don't think you've had those experiences around here," the man in the hat said, "I think you've seen *Deliverance* one too many times and it's stuck in your brain for some reason." He held up his hands in surrender. "I don't like to speculate on people's motives, and I definitely don't judge, but maybe it's because you've always had a yearning for a man to take you out into the woods and show you a firm hand."

"What the fuck?" Sweater Vest said, standing up so quickly he turned over his chair.

"Like I said, I'm not judging, but maybe you ought to control your derisive attitude a little while you're visiting our home," the man in the hat said.

"Your *home*?" Sweater Vest said, the scorn dripping off of him. Hendricks lowered his head, hiding his expression under the brim of his hat. This was going to be easier than he'd thought. "Your home is a rainy, backwards shithole where the attitudes are crap, your people are broke, uneducated idiots, and the culture is all about skinning things."

The man in the hat took it off, smoothed his thinning hair, and spoke again. "My name is Michael McInness and I've got a degree in French Medieval Literature from the University of Minnesota. I own this bar, and I only skin things during hunting season." He placed the cap back on his head and straightened it. "As evidenced by the fact that I'm not skinning you right now." He looked them all over. "These are people who have different interests than yours. Show some respect for them as fellow human beings. If you can't keep a polite tongue in your head while you're in my bar, I invite you to leave." He tipped the bill of the hat to them. "Good day, boys."

Sweater Vest just sat there sort of stunned, sputtering, not really sure what to say next. Hendricks watched, about ready to curse it. He needed a fight to break out, dammit, and polite, carefully thought out responses were not gonna do it.

"You think you're better than us?" Suit and Tie stood up, all uppity and filled with the sort of piss and vinegar Hendricks was looking for. Well, it might work out after all.

"I ain't better than anyone," Michael McInness said as he walked back to the bar. "But no one's better than me, either."

"I think I'm better than you," Suit and Tie said, and Hendricks watched him clench the beer bottle in his hand. He tipped it up and took it all down in one good drink. Hendricks was about ready to interject to say something to stir the situation up a little more when Suit and Tie smashed his empty bottle against the table and held it out in front of him. "I think I'm a hell of a lot better than you, you backwards fucking hick."

"You're gonna have to work to convince me of that from a rhetorical standpoint," McInness said. "A man who's got to break a bottle and threaten another man with it to prove his point seems like a man with a weak argument, like someone who just keeps repeating the same untrue shit over and over until he believes it's true."

"How about me and my buddies here just beat the shit out of you until you drown in a puddle of your own blood?" Sweater Vest said with a smirk. "I think that'd establish superiority."

"Not of intellect, that's certain," McInness said with a sad shake of his head. "I don't suppose you've noticed you're outnumbered."

This was the point where Hendricks started to get dry mouth. It was nerves, sure as shit. Trying to provoke these three into getting into a bar fight with the locals seemed like a good idea when he'd thought of it a few minutes ago. If it turned out they weren't actually demons, it'd be a damned stupid idea.

Upon further consideration he realized that if they did turn out to be demons, it might be even worse.

"Who have you got backing you up?" Sweater Vest said, nodding at the boys over at the bar. There were four of them, every one with a beard at least halfway down his chest. "*Duck Dynasty?*"

As one, the four men at the bar stood up, pushing their stools back from underneath them. McInness cringed. "I hope weren't being insulting there, because—"

"I was," Sweater Vest said, and Hendricks watched as Hipster Glasses stood, sending his wooden chair skidding back.

"That's a damned shame," McInness said, shaking his head. "Now, this is my establishment, and I'm asking you boys to leave."

"Make us," Suit and Tie said.

"That's a very kindergarten response," McInness said. He drew a stinging look from Suit and Tie in return. "You realize I'm going to have to call the law, since you've threatened me and failed to leave my property when I've asked you to. I even asked nicely."

Sweater Vest took two steps toward McInness and poked him in the chest with a long finger. "You won't last long enough for them to get here."

McInness gave Sweater Vest a slow nod. "I see. And you, Cowboy?," McInness looked past Sweater Vest at Hendricks. "Where do you stand in this whole thing?"

"Oh, I don't know these guys," Hendricks said, still sitting in his chair, beer in hand. "I was telling a joke, playing to my audience. Figured some shit-hot city wankers would get a good laugh out of the one I told. Turns out I was right."

McInness gave him the once-over. Hendricks was a little surprised Sweater Vest hadn't made his move yet. None of them had presented a hint of their true faces yet—if they had them—which was concerning. "So you came into my bar just to stir up shit."

Hendricks looked at Hipster Glasses and saw a twitch at the eye, a little hint of darkness within. He set his beer down, not taking his eyes off the guy as his hand crept slowly into his coat. "Sorry, but yeah. I did."

"Well, my patrons here enjoy a good fight," McInness said, nodding to the crew behind him. One of them was even wearing a bandana. Seriously. "But I think it's gonna end up causing some damage to my establishment, and I'm wondering who's going to pay for that."

Hendricks let his hand go inside his coat, felt the hilt of his sword and tightened his grip around it. "I think this one might have to go to insurance, sir."

"I'm gonna take it out of somebody's ass if my place gets torn up," McInness said. Now he was looking Sweater Vest right in the eye. There was a pause. "Son, you got something wrong with you? Been smoking the wacky tobacky?"

"What?" Sweater Vest asked.

"Your eye."

Hendricks caught the glimmer from Suit and Tie on the left. Shit.

Sweater Vest struck as Hendricks pulled his sword. McInness went flying through the air, shouting all the way. Suit and Tie went for the men at the bar on all fours, like a fucking wolf that had just been let loose from a kennel.

Hendricks buried his sword right in Hipster Glasses's gut. The resulting blaze of hellfire filled the air with the sharp stench of brimstone.

Hendricks coughed and stumbled back. Surprise attacks were the best on these motherfuckers. They were the only ones guaranteed to work, really.

Sweater Vest and Suit and Tie were tearing into the boys at the bar now, and Hendricks felt a tug of remorse. This was his fault. His stupid plan to get them to reveal themselves in a crowd so he didn't get blindsided had backfired on the locals. Guilt was gonna beat his ass down later, especially if any of these guys got hurt.

Hendricks threw himself forward with a recklessness that was probably at least partly the fault of the shitty beer's effects. He wanted to bury the sword in Sweater Vest's back, but Suit and Tie saw him coming and charged him. He took a shoulder to the midsection and all the air came rushing out of him. He felt it in the ribs and hoped nothing was broken.

They slammed into the floor. Suit and Tie moved a hell of a lot faster than Hendricks did. Hendricks realized his cowboy hat had fallen off in the scuffle as his head cracked against the floor of the bar. His eyeballs rattled in their sockets as the dirty, scuffed wood hit the back of his skull.

That wasn't enough for Suit and Tie, though. Hendricks's sword was out of position, his arms extended over the demon from where he'd gotten caught in the tackle. He couldn't reverse his hold on the sword quickly enough and a serious pain in his chest almost caused him to drop the blade. He was still injured from where another demon had done a number on him just a week or so earlier.

For a flash, Hendricks considered trying to stop the demon as Suit and Tie got up into a schoolboy position to start punching the shit out of him. That idea fled quickly and instead he tried to block. He caught the first punch with his left wrist and nearly screamed from the pain as it hit. His arm went numb from the wrist down, and it ached all the way up, like he'd gotten a shovel smashed into it.

"Get the fuck outta here!" Hendricks heard somewhere, and the heavy footfalls of boots fell around him. He dimly realized that it was the boys from the bar exercising the better part of valor. He wished he could join them.

The next punch from Suit and Tie caught him in the nose, and he felt the blood start running. His head got hazy. There were two of that fucker on top of him, weren't there?

Hendricks's eyes alit on Sweater Vest. He was standing just past Suit and Tie's shoulder, past the white shirt that was now a little spotted from blood. Hendricks knew some of it was his.

Hendricks's mind slipped back to him long enough to remember he had something in his hand. Something that might help. He looked over at it, blinking as the next blow descended.

Oh, right. A sword.

He jabbed up and poked it into Suit and Tie's ribcage. He put some power into it, like he needed to bury it up to the hilt to get the job done. It didn't go all the way in to the hilt, but he got it in a good three inches, and that was enough. Suit and Tie's bloody ensemble was engulfed in the shadowed fire that came from a demon's demise, and Hendricks felt the belching of the cloud of heat as he passed.

Hendricks wanted to sag to the floor and just wait, but McInness was in Sweater Vest's grasp. This was not going to end well, but still Hendricks could not compel his body to get off the damned floor.

There was a noise behind him, but he couldn't turn to look. Thunderous steps moved past him, heavy footfalls, like the boys from *Duck Dynasty* were back with friends, but—

No. That wasn't it.

A mountainous black man stood over him, wearing a sheriff's deputy's khaki uniform. He only glanced at Hendricks for a second before he grabbed Sweater Vest from behind and pulled him backward, throwing him out of Hendricks's sight.

Oh, thank God.

Arch.

* * *

Archibald Stan didn't like his first name, so he went by Arch. It didn't have the ring of a name to his ears, not a traditional one, but it worked. Easy to say, easy to remember, and distinctive. He didn't really care that it was distinctive, but it worked in his favor so he didn't dislike it.

Arch had seen the regulars go bolting out the door of the bar from where he'd sat in the parking lot, soaking in the silence in his patrol car. Rain tapped at his windows as the front door to the Charnel House Bar opened and men started spilling out. That was about as much signal as he needed to know that things inside had gone downhill. He'd been waiting for Hendricks to come out and get him once he'd confirmed that the out-of-towners inside were, in fact, demons. But the cowboy never did come out. If Arch had been any other deputy on the force, he could have just gone in with Hendricks.

But everyone in Calhoun County knew that Arch Stan didn't really drink, and if he did he wouldn't come to a backwoods joint in the south end of the county to do it. So instead he waited to charge in until the Charnel House had suffered a rapid exodus of its usual patronage.

Arch took one look around as he burst in the door. The bar in the corner was a mess of shattered beer bottles. One of the patrons was on the floor, bleeding from the mouth, and Mike McInness, the proprietor, was in the hands of a demon wearing a sweater vest.

Arch hadn't run into too many demons yet, but he'd seen one in a suit. A sweater vest? That was new.

Arch pulled the sanctified switchblade Hendricks had given him a week or so earlier and heard it click open before he stepped forward. He spared a passing thought for Hendricks and realized that the crumpled pile of black to his right was actually the man in question. He looked like he'd been roughed up good, but he didn't seem to be in immediate danger.

McInness, on the other hand, looked like he was about to get his head yanked off. That made him Arch's priority.

Arch moved to bury the switchblade in the back of the sweater-vest-wearing demon, but the guy moved at the last second. Arch caught the demon's shoulder with his free hand and pulled him back. The demon let go of McInness, who fell to the floor with a thud that echoed through the bar.

"Well, if it ain't another human," the sweater-vest-clad demon said with a wide grin, his true face revealed.

"Yep," Arch said, standing off with him. The demon was blocking passage through the door, not that Arch had any intention of walking through it right now.

"But you're not scared, are you?" The demon was still grinning. Like he didn't see the knife in Arch's hand. Or didn't know what it meant for him.

"Of a devil spawn like you?" Arch shrugged. "Can't see why I should be. You're just a little balloon of sulfur stink waiting to get popped."

"You think you got it in you to do it?" Sweater Vest leered at him. "Because I think you're gonna be dinner for me and my boys—" He looked left, then right, seeming to realize he was alone with Arch. "What the— Where my boys at?" He turned his fiery eyes to Arch.

"Seems like somebody let the fire out of them already," Arch said, trying to hide the switchblade, turning his body so the demon in the sweater vest couldn't see it. "But I'm sure you got nothing to worry about." Arch felt himself smile a little. "You're not scared, are you?"

Whether it was him turning the demon's words against him or just the accusation of being yellow-bellied that caused the demon to charge him, Arch didn't know. The demon came at him, though, and Arch jabbed him right in the heart with the switchblade. The air filled with the smell of brimstone and those hateful eyes just burned up right there. Arch had a hand on the sweater vest and felt the faint tingle as the black fire crawled over his skin while dissolving the demon.

Arch took a long look around after that, making sure that there wasn't another demon waiting to jump him from behind the bar or in the bathroom. Once he knew there wasn't, he checked on Hendricks, who was mumbling into the floor. "You all right?" Arch asked him, kneeling next to the man in the black drover coat.

"Feel like someone stomped my ass and then scraped me off their boot," Hendricks said, looking up at Arch with half-lidded eyes. "Gimme a minute and I'll get up. Check on McInness and the other guy, will you?"

"Yeah," Arch said and moved over to McInness. His steps creaked the uneven floorboards of the Charnel House as he went. The bartender was a little out of it, but Arch gave him a gentle slap to the face and his eyes flickered. "You in there, McInness?"

"Is it opening time already?" McInness said, his red face a little bloody. "Sweet Jesus, is that you, Arch?" The older man's eyes were open now, and when he parted his lips Arch noticed the upper one was split good. "What the hell are you doing in my bar?"

Arch stared into McInness's eyes and waved a hand over his face. "You might have a concussion, Mike."

"I think someone had a fight at my bar," McInness said. "I should probably check on the place before I go to the doctor."

Arch looked around him. "Uh ... you're in your bar right now, Mike."

McInness blinked, his expression perplexed. "I should probably go on to the doctor, then."

Arch couldn't disagree with that sentiment, but before he could voice it, he heard someone else grunt from the floor next to the bar. It was a guy he barely knew, Ellroy was the man's name, long-bearded fellow who worked a farm out near Culver, a little unincorporated town that Arch drove through every few days on patrol. He only knew the guy because he'd gotten flagged down once to help with some out-of-towner who was tearing up and down the man's road twice a day like a maniac. It had turned out to be a local high-school boy who'd been visiting a girl up the road. A warning had taken the lead out of the boy's foot, and Ellroy had been mighty grateful.

"What the hell ...?" Ellroy said, his lips oozing blood.

"You got in a bar fight," Arch said, watching the man struggle to a sitting position. Ellroy was wearing denim suspenders with a camouflage t-shirt underneath.

"Am I going to jail?" Ellroy asked. Arch could see the crow's feet at the sides of the older man's eyes as he blinked. He had the look of a man who laughed a lot.

"Not tonight," Arch said, keeping his eye on Ellroy. "I don't think you started it."

Ellroy nodded, seemed like he understood. "Did I win?"

Arch gave him a look. The good ol' boys did seem to enjoy a fight. "I don't think so. The guys who did it ran off, though."

"Aw, man," Ellroy said, holding his head. "How's McInness?"

"Needs to go to the hospital." Arch stood. "You sober enough to drive him?"

"I only had one," Ellroy said. He was a big son of a gun, not much shorter than Arch himself. The broken beer bottles left the place drenched in a smell that was more than a little disagreeable.

"Help me get him up," Arch said to Ellroy and gestured to McInness.

16 DEPTHS

The barman wasn't a small fella, either.

"Okay," Ellroy said, and on the count of three they each put an arm over a shoulder and lifted McInness up. The barman didn't say much about that, his eyes still fluttering. "Say, what about that cowboy?" Ellroy said, and pointed to where Hendricks lay on the floor.

"Oh, him?" Arch shuffled along as he and Ellroy dragged McInness out of the bar. He swung the door open and held it as they carried the big barman out into the night. Arch tossed a look back at Hendricks, who still lay on the dirty floor of the bar, hands holding his face. "I'll deal with him in a few minutes."

* * *

His name was Lerner, according to his driver's license, and that was what his partner called him as well. He tended to stick to suits, the blander the better; his color palette was admittedly not as creative as his partner's—Duncan, he was called. Duncan would have worn wild, lime-colored shit if he were allowed to. Lerner didn't let him, though; it just wasn't appropriate.

The humidity was thick in the air as Lerner stepped out of the town car. It was a rental, but they'd gone with it because it looked like a cop car, smelled like a cop car, and Lerner always tried to look like a cop, everywhere he went. Made his life easier. He sidled along through the sweltering night with Duncan at his side, ambling down a city street. Houses were lined up along either side, tall trees swaying in an ineffectual breeze. "Hot out tonight," Lerner said. Duncan just grunted acknowledgment. He was like that. The quiet type. Lerner made up for it.

The smell of someone's fried chicken was still hanging in the air, though Lerner couldn't imagine anyone wanting to cook with the windows open. "Like a fucking sauna out here," Lerner muttered to himself as he paused next to a white picket fence that ringed a white house. He sniffed the air; there was something under the fried chicken smell. "Here?" he asked.

Duncan nodded, his brown eyes narrowed under heavy brows, stray hairs jutting in all different directions. "You could fucking say something, Igor," Lerner said, but Duncan just shrugged. Lerner ran a hand over the gate of the waist-high fence, feeling the smooth, painted wood in his hand. "Even I can feel something amiss here." There was definitely some essence in the air, some hints of something that shouldn't be this strong.

They took the front steps off the walk, dress shoes sounding like the ticking of a grandfather clock. Same rhythm, too, Lerner thought, perfectly timed. He reached under his jacket, a nice little pinstripe number he'd picked up at Men's Wearhouse that came with matching trousers. When his hand emerged, he had a truncheon clutched tightly in it, a six-inch length of metal enclosed in a rubber grip. He could feel the checkering of the grip in his hand, and that little flutter within told him it was almost time. He stepped onto the porch and up to the front door where he stood in front of an oval window that was tinted with some crystalline highlights in a pattern. He could see a lacy curtain behind it.

Duncan was dressed in a cream colored suit for this. He looked like a damned pimp. "Stand off to the side," Lerner told him. Duncan did. He might not listen when it came to fashion, but when it was go time, he was all business. He had his truncheon out, too, in a waiting hand. He stood beside the door frame, the cracking paint peeling off on his shoulder.

Lerner stared at the front door for another second then delivered a heavy knock with his knuckles. He rapped hard and waited. He resisted the temptation to tap his foot on the grey floorboards of the porch.

"Who is it?" A male voice came from somewhere behind the curtain.

Lerner held a steady eye on the front door. "We're here from the First Church of—" He cut off, muttering something under his breath. "We're here to talk to you about our Lord and Savior."

A face appeared behind the glass, and it was just blank enough that Lerner knew on sight it was a demon. Just recovering from a ravening, his mouth probably watering at the "Lord and Savior" line. Demons ate up believers like they were candy, like they were a special gift from a divine they jerked away from in the light. Forbidden fruit.

It got 'em every time.

The lock shifted in the door with a loud clunk, then the door started to yaw open. A wretched smell poured forth when it did, something that might have set Lerner gagging if he was the sort who was disturbed by scents. Like the smell of rotting bodies.

Lerner took a step back. Gave him room, just like an evangelist might do. Polite. Lerner smiled, trying to look sincere.

"So you're here to convert me?" The man who was framed in the entry to the house stared out at Lerner. Duncan was out of his line of sight, just a step out of the way.

"Yes, indeed, I'm here to convert you," Lerner said, keeping the truncheon just behind his back. He kept his hands there like he was just maintaining a respectful distance and good posture.

"You might find that hard," the man said, and he just let it drip with irony. Lerner kept smiling. The guy in the door was wearing a suit of his own. Like he'd just been to church. Or had stolen it out of someone's closet, more likely.

"Well, sir, I think any change is bound to be somewhat disagreeable to one's natural constitution," Lerner said. "In fact, I've often wondered why people are so resistant to change." This was something he pontificated quite often. "I mean, there are obviously things that are good for someone—like eating vegetables, following a low-fat diet, obeying the law—that they just don't do, for whatever reason—"

Lerner saw Duncan roll his eyes just before stepping around the door frame and activating the spring on the truncheon. The point of the baton came rushing out and hit the man in the suit in the chest.

Lerner just stood there watching.

If the man in the suit had been a man, Lerner knew he'd clutch his chest, aching from the baton's spring punching the tip into his sternum. But the man didn't do that, not exactly. He clutched for his chest all right, but he did it while his mouth opened soundlessly, lit by a black hellfire that rushed out of his chest, his eyes and mouth, consuming him completely before he said a word of response.

"You could have let me finish first," Lerner said. He wanted to swat Duncan in the back of the head. His partner never listened to his deep thoughts, so it seemed only fair that their marks should have to before they lit them up.

"I'd have to hear it, then," Duncan said, crossing the threshold of the house.

"It wouldn't kill you to think a deep thought every now and again, Duncan."

"Let's not test it, though."

"All right," Lerner said once they were in the entry hall. It was white walls all the way back, opening into a family room or something toward the rear of the house. All the curtains were shut, darkening the place and filling it with gloom.

"Should we announce ourselves?" Duncan asked in a low mutter, hopefully too low for anyone to hear him.

"I think the element of surprise is going to be a nice thing to have working for us," Lerner replied. "Unless you like the idea of getting blindsided by a Tul'rore with a taste for flesh."

Duncan didn't have to think about that one for long. "I like quiet."

"Figured you would."

They crept along the old wood floors, a shiny, yellowed oak that squeaked occasionally as they went. Lerner grimaced every time it did. Duncan looked as indifferent as if he were choosing which bed he'd get at the motel.

There was a noise ahead and they both paused, truncheons up and at the ready. Duncan's was deployed still from impaling the first Tul'rore at the door. Lerner kept his finger hovering on the tiny button on the side of his. Having it spring-loaded was a nice advantage. It let him score at least one kill quick and easy. After that he'd have to work a little harder for it.

That was all right, though. Lerner didn't mind getting into a scrape here and there, so long as he and Duncan came out on top.

And they always did.

The noise turned into a crunching, like wood splintering under heavy pressure. He recognized the sound that followed, teeth rending flesh from bone. It took him only another second to realize the first noise was bone breaking. Getting crunched.

It wasn't a sound he loved.

Duncan came around the corner into the family room first. Lerner followed a step behind. It was a wide area, classic decor with cloth couches and a TV that took up half the wall. Lerner had given a lot of thought to the increase in television size, thinking they were getting bigger as people in society lost touch with themselves. It was almost like they had to expand the screen to fill the shrinking hole of self—

"There," Duncan grunted. There was an open door ahead, and the sound of the eating was coming from within. Red wallpaper gave the room a dim aura, the only light spilling in from where they'd left the front door open, the porch light sending shafts of illumination across the floor.

There was a dim light in the room ahead, too. Lerner looked at Duncan's shadow and gave him a quick nod. They both crept up to the door and Duncan stood behind the frame while Lerner looked in.

It was worse than he thought. Four Tul'rore were fully engaged, a body shredded on the kitchen table. Blood was dripping onto the oak floor. Three bulbs overhead cast the scene in a murky orange light. It made the blood look black.

There was an open chest cavity on the table, a naked figure that had been split right down the middle of the sternum like a surgery was being performed. No, not a surgery. Lerner had watched those on the TV when he and Duncan were staying in hotels. It was an interesting way to pass the time.

No, this was more like something from a slaughterhouse.

Lerner couldn't even tell if the corpse was male or female, such was the extent of the damage. The chest cavity was pretty damned empty, and the flesh was stripped off the legs, already sacrificed to the massive appetite of the Tul'rore. One of them could eat a whole human every twenty-four hours, and here there had been five.

"Fucknuggets," Lerner breathed.

The two Tul'rore on the opposite side of the table finally took notice of him. One of them got to its feet, overturning a chair in the process. Its real face was exposed and red eyes gleamed over the slick of blood that ran down its face and stained its cotton dress. It was ostensibly female, though Lerner knew that mattered as little with a Tul'rore as nipples on a man. It ate humans; it didn't fuck them.

"You need to sit your ass back down," Lerner said, holding up a hand. He knew even as he said it that it was utterly fucking pointless. Trying to get a Tul'rore to calm down was like politely asking a hungry lion to stop devouring you mid-meal.

The Tul'rore listened just about as well, too. The two closest to him turned to look at him now, too, and he imagined they didn't see anything but a giant flashing sign indicating he was another fine dinner waiting to be opened up. Like a fucking Happy Meal box for these bottom feeders.

Lerner wasn't stupid, and he didn't want to get tripped up, so he backed up into the family room. He passed Duncan flattened against the wall without so much as a nod of acknowledgment. Duncan was a big boy. He knew what to do.

Lerner made it about six steps back from the open door before the first one came charging at him. He let it come. Stuck out his truncheon when it got close, pushed the button. The bloodthirsty open mouth flared with black fire and the Tul'rore dissolved, sucked back into hell.

Lerner watched Duncan get the next one, jabbing out his truncheon as it came into the room. This one screamed before it burned, flesh cracking open in a fast-moving pyre. Lerner never got used to seeing them burn like this. It happened so quick it left an afterimage in his eyes, like looking at a bright light before walking into a dark room.

One of the last two Tul'rore burst through the wall behind Duncan as the other came through the door at Lerner. He wanted to shout *"shit!"* or *"fuck!"* but neither really fit the situation. It was all just local flavor anyway, stuff he'd picked up from the television. Those pay channels taught him all the nuances.

The Tul'rore were just too dumb to know that this time they'd bitten off more than they could chew.

Duncan flung the Tul'rore that was on his back through the air. It hit the ceiling and cracked the plaster. Lerner could see the dust fall in the faint light streaming into the room, like it was a little shower of powder dropping on him.

Lerner didn't even bother to hold up the truncheon as the Tul'rore charged him. He threw up a fist and caught it on the chin. It staggered, momentum completely arrested. Lerner followed with another punch and he heard the shell crack under his onslaught. "Do you have any fucking idea what you've done here?" he asked the Tul'rore.

The Tul'rore he spoke to was the one in the dress stained by blood. He brought the truncheon down across its face, whipping more than striking. It cut a dull gash in its forehead, exposing a little light of fire.

The light of the soul. The essence.

But it wasn't enough to kill it.

Not yet.

Lerner whipped the truncheon aside and leapt forward, grasping the Tul'rore around the throat and throttling its neck back. He could feel the fury creasing his face as he landed on his knees. He dragged the Tul'rore down with him and slammed its head on the oak floorboards. For good measure he slammed it down again.

That was pointless, too. It wasn't like there was a brain to damage on these things.

The Tul'rore looked at him with those hungry eyes, and he shoved it down to the floor and held it with one hand. He landed a knee in its gut and it reacted with a gasp. He knew it was like a squeeze, more shock than pain. They didn't have organs or guts, really. Just essence and energy swirling around in there. They could digest a human and add its essence to its own, could burn up all the flesh and blood. Other stuff would come out the other end eventually, waste processed by the essence. Compared to human digestive processes, it was fucking magic.

And fucking was another thing Lerner contemplated, because he'd seen demons have babies with humans. It was really a subject worthy of study—

"Are you gonna kill it or not?" Duncan asked from just above him. He was standing there waiting. His arms were folded. His truncheon was already collapsed, ready to stow. He wouldn't put it away until Lerner finished this one, though. Lerner knew that much. Duncan was a cautious bastard.

"Give me a minute," Lerner said.

"You start contemplating the wonders of human life, and I'll spike you and it both," Duncan said.

"You're such an anti-intellectuallist fucker," Lerner said, baring his teeth at Duncan. His real teeth, not the fake veneers he ate human food with. Lerner snorted and looked back at the Tul'rore. "You opened a can of fucking worms for us here. You left your damned essence trail all over the house next door, and the house before that, which tells me you've been feeding here for days, maybe a week. This shit where you eat a whole family then move to the next house in a line may fly in Detroit or New Orleans, but this is a small town, you numbskull dumbfuck."

The Tul'rore didn't answer in words. It made a snarling sound, the ravening still heavy on it. Lerner punched it in the nose and heard its head hit the floor. The boards cracked and the eyes flared wide. "Get that damned hunger out of your eyes when you look at me," Lerner said. "Aw, fuck it."

Lerner grasped the wound on the Tul'rore's face and pulled, ripping the faux flesh wide. He could see the black flames starting to escape, burning within.

"The sentence," Duncan said from above him.

"Oh, right." Lerner had almost forgotten. He looked back at the Tul'rore. "By chapter 8.14 of the Uniform Code of Daemonic Conduct, I hereby charge you with the crime of exposure for killing and eating multiple humans in a space of confined population. The sentence is carried out under the laws of the Pact, Occultic Concordance Officers Lerner and Duncan presiding over said sentence."

The Tul'rore seemed to be coming back to itself now, the ravening leaving it.

Too late.

Lerner ripped the flesh back from the wound and the flames escaped, rushing over the Tul'rore in one good burst. Lerner stood and watched it burn. It went quickly and slowly all at once. A moment and an eternity later it was done.

"Truncheon?" Duncan asked, and Lerner turned to see him holding it out. He had picked it up, the quiet bastard. What a time saver.

"Thanks," Lerner said, putting it back onto his belt. He looked down at the shadowed spot where the Tul'rore had been dragged back to hell and took a sniff. He kind of liked the sulfur smell they left behind. Most officers of the Occultic Concordance hated it. It was like a corpse stink to a human, he supposed.

Which was another interesting question, really. Why was the smell of rot unpleasant to a human while it was appealing to a maggot? Was it just an instinctual interpretation offered by their brains to keep them from eating something that would sicken them? Or was it something deeper, an intelligent reaction to their own mortality—

"You've got that look again," Duncan said, expressionless as ever.

"I was just thinking—"

"That's what I was afraid of," Duncan said, turning to leave. His cream-colored suit flapped from his turn.

Lerner ran to catch up, heard the squeaking of the floor as he did. "You ever eat a human?"

Duncan frowned as they reached the door. "Tried some one time. Didn't like it."

Lerner nodded. "I never have. Never saw the appeal. Steak, on the other hand, I love. Can't get enough of a good rib eye. What do you suppose is the difference—"

Duncan froze him with a good look that said, "Shut the fuck up." Lerner knew that look from Duncan, and he nodded. It was something he did out of courtesy. It had kept them as partners for over a hundred years, allowed them to tolerate each other.

Lerner took one last look up the walk when they reached the fence. He'd left the door open. He thought about going back and shutting it, but it was pointless. It'd only buy some time, and they might as well just get this out in the open now. It was already going to blow big in a town like this.

Duncan slipped behind the wheel this time, putting on sunglasses with exaggerated lenses that were too big for his face. Lerner didn't bother to say anything, but they were women's sunglasses. This was normal for Duncan.

Lerner looked back at the open door, thought about what was inside, what was probably waiting in the next two houses as well. "This is a fucking disaster," he said under his breath. He saw Duncan nod, those big-ass sunglasses bobbing along. "It's gonna blow this town wide open."

"Yep," Duncan said.

"Why couldn't they have stayed in a city?" Lerner said under his breath. He knew why not, of course. Because this was the place. The lights were on, the welcoming committee had rolled out the red carpet. There'd be more like this, more crazy shit unfurling in this small town than it could possibly handle.

"Nature of the business," Duncan said as he put the car in gear and pulled away from the curb. The nearest streetlight winked on, then off, cutting through the black night with intermittent illumination.

"Yeah." Lerner nodded then tapped his finger along the leather just below his window. He liked the feel of the town car interior. "You remember that town in Alaska we were at in … what, 1965?" He sniffed at the air-conditioned air blowing out at him. He saw Duncan nod out of the corner of his eye. "I get that same vibe here. Like it's gonna get out of control." Lerner put his hand over his head, pushing his comb over back in place. "How long did it take for them to tear that place apart?"

"Six weeks," Duncan said.

"I bet you it takes less time than that here," Lerner said as they turned back onto a major thoroughfare. There was a traffic light ahead, blinking a yellow warning, like it had been shut off for the night. "I give it a month."

Duncan grunted. "Maybe less."

"Yeah, maybe," Lerner said. "If someone gets fucking ambitious. Imagine the hell we'll catch if that happens again." He let out a ripping sigh. "Maybe it'll just dissipate. Back to business as usual." Duncan's grunt was less committal this time. "Yeah, fucking unlikely, I know. But I can hope."

They were passing through the town square now, full of boarded up windows and old shop fronts that probably hadn't changed since the fifties. It was kind of homey, Lerner had to admit. Too bad it'd be gone soon, in all probability. Even a couple officers couldn't hold back the tide rushing into this place and he knew it. Duncan too. He'd been around long enough to be pragmatic.

"Yeah," Lerner said, shaking his head as they rolled onto an old highway and Duncan gunned the car up to fifty-five. "I give this place—Midian, isn't it?" Yeah, that was it. "I give Midian, Tennessee, about four weeks before it's a fucking crater. Tops. There'll be nothing left but a bunch of body parts and wreckage."

Chapter 3

Arch waited to unload on Hendricks until they were back in the deputy's squad car, for which Hendricks was grateful. His nose hurt like hell, his head was still spinning, and he felt like his rib cage had been used as a piñata for a demon birthday party.

Other than that, though, he felt fine.

"You were supposed to identify them and then come get me," Arch was saying, his rich baritone still operating at a pitch that bothered Hendricks's aching head. "Not start World War D in a bar!"

"World War D?" Hendricks asked, leaning his head against the window. It felt oddly cool given how hot it was outside.

"Like the movie ... never mind," Arch said. The deputy was steering with his right hand at the top of the wheel, turning his body away from Hendricks. Hendricks wondered if there was some passive-aggressive shit going on with the man, but his head hurt too much to muster any give-a-fuck about it.

"I would have gotten you," Hendricks said, "but by the time I had them out in the open, shit was already going down. I couldn't just leave those guys in there to face down three demons while I ran for help."

"So instead you got two of the civilians beat up and got yourself whacked around like a heavy bag because you didn't get help," Arch said. There was a serious crackle of anger in the man's voice, and Hendricks did not care for the sound of it.

"I did what I could," Hendricks said. "I got one of the demons out of the way right at the start, and that helped limit the damage. I had all three of them between me and the door, so ..."

"So pick a better seat next time," Arch said.

"Well, I was kind of sitting at their table," Hendricks said, and he realized his lip was swelling, "so I pretty much had to take the last seat that was open."

"You, uh ... you sat down at the table with them?" The deputy's voice sounded more than a little incredulous.

"It's not exactly easy to make someone out as a demon an entire room away," Hendricks replied.

There was a seething silence in the car after that. Hendricks could tell that Arch wanted to let loose on him, but whether it was manners or a lack of a good angle of attack that prevented the deputy from battering away, Hendricks didn't know. Didn't care, either. The air conditioning was chilling the glass a little, and Hendricks had a bump on his forehead above his eyebrow. Pressing the bump to the glass was positively bliss for him, or as close as he could get right now without turning off all his nerve endings.

"You want me to drop you back off at your motel?" Arch asked, his voice echoing in the cab of the Explorer.

"Sure, why not," Hendricks said. He snuck a sidelong glance at the deputy. The man was physically imposing, but he still had his body quartered away from Hendricks. Hendricks had been trying to keep an eye on Arch, had been watching him as they'd worked together this last week. Some words were rattling around in Hendricks's skull, prophetic ones that had come from the lady who had told him everything since he'd gotten involved in this demon hunting gig. She hadn't been wrong yet that he knew of.

"Because you look like someone beat you bloody, then came back and did another round of it," Arch said. Hendricks hadn't looked in the mirror yet, but he suspected Arch was probably not understating it. "I'm gonna drop you off at Erin's."

"What the fuck?" Hendricks's head came off the window. "Why?"

Arch turned his body now, taking the wheel with both hands. The deputy paused a minute before he started to speak. "You're all manner of beat up. By all rights you ought to be in a hospital but failing that, you at least need someone to keep an eye on you. Make sure you don't have a concussion. Unless you'd prefer I drive you to the emergency room right now? Let them give you a clean bill of health."

"Showing up in a police cruiser wouldn't cause any headaches, I'm sure," Hendricks said, putting his forehead back against the glass. "I don't really have a lot of extra money lying around for medical bills, especially not so a doctor can tell me I've got a shit ton of bruises and cuts that'll heal in a few days."

"You could use stitches for a few of them," Arch said.

"I'm fine," Hendricks said. "I'm not even bleeding anymore, that means I don't need stitches."

"Now there's a sound medical diagnosis." Arch turned his body away again.

Hendricks sat there with his head against the glass. The rain started coming down hard as they drove through the hills, and he caught a glimpse of lights out his window, a strange pattern of them, like a square in a sea of darkness. "What the hell is that?" he asked, trying to make out the shape in the rainy night.

"It's the Tallakeet Dam," Arch said, matter-of-factly. "TVA project. Generates power for the whole area and holds back the Caledonia River."

Hendricks focused, trying to see it through the blur of the rain and one of his eyes swelling shut. "Looks big. Just a bunch of lights in the dark."

"That's just the top of it," Arch said, and Hendricks could tell he was not bothering to look for himself. "It's no Hoover Dam, but it's pretty big."

"Pretty dam big?" Hendricks asked with a wry smile.

Arch didn't smile, and for some reason that annoyed Hendricks even more. "I'm dropping you off at Erin's," the big man said again.

"How am I supposed to explain the state of my face and body, genius?" Hendricks said, tilting his head to look at the deputy. Dumb idea.

"Tell her you were in a bar fight."

Hendricks had to concede that would probably work, though it wouldn't make him sound too good. There was another problem though. "I don't ..." he felt his voice get involuntarily lower, "I don't actually know where she lives."

Arch whipped around again for this. "Haven't you been sleeping with her?"

"At my motel, yes," Hendricks agreed. "A few times, anyway."

"But you don't know where she lives?" Arch was staring at him, eyebrow cocked. It would have been an *are-you-fucking-kidding-me?* look, except Arch didn't swear.

"I don't know how familiar you are with the act of coitus," Hendricks said, "but it doesn't require you to know the person's address before you do it. Or even their name, really."

Arch made a sound like, "Gaaaah," a noise crossed with exasperation and possibly disgust.

"Don't get judgy," Hendricks said, putting his face back against the cool glass. "People don't like judgy Christians."

"Sorry if I'm reacting poorly to your revelation that you know very little about the woman you're sleeping with," Arch said. "I don't tend to hang around with people who have a lot of one-night stands. Or any at all, really."

"You don't have any friends your own age, huh?" Hendricks was just being snotty now, and he knew it.

"Not any like you," Arch said. "At least not until now."

"That's all right," Hendricks said, and he shut himself up before he could say, *I never knew any guys that were going to end the world until I started to hang out with you.*

* * *

Erin Harris wasn't at the bar tonight. It wasn't because she didn't want to be. It was because her rent check had just cleared and she was about fifty bucks short of broke with three days to go until her next paycheck. That wasn't a margin she was comfortable with, so she stayed in.

Some show was going on the TV, something she'd kind of stumbled onto by accident. It was a movie, maybe, something with a couple guys out after dark, walking a city street looking for trouble. It wasn't really that interesting, and she half expected a monster to jump out at them. She was sipping half-heartedly on a light beer, the last drink she could find in her fridge, but she wasn't really into it. The pungent smell of the weak ale was kind of turning her stomach, if she was honest about it. When she took a sip, she made a face. She took another sip anyway.

The TV was blaring, and she was on the verge of turning it off when there was a knock at the door. She got up and grabbed her pistol before she went to answer it, folding her hand around the Glock 19. The plastic checkering on the grip bit into her palm as she walked toward the door. Her career experience told her people who tended to knock on the door at eleven at night didn't always have pure intentions, even in little ol' Midian. Better safe than sorry.

Her apartment was small, a one bedroom with shabby carpeting that probably had been there since the nineties. She had minimal furniture in the main room, just a couch and a TV. The walls had a few pictures, and the whole place smelled of the Spaghetti-O's which she'd eaten earlier. It was the last thing in the pantry. Honestly, though, even if it had been the first thing in the pantry, she'd still have eaten it. She liked Spaghetti-O's.

She eased up to the door as another knock sounded. She looked out through the peephole, keeping the gun low at hand. She could smell the gun oil off the Glock, even at this range. She kept it pretty well maintained.

As she looked through the peephole, she breathed a sigh of relief when she saw the cowboy hat. Hendricks.

She pulled back from the peephole and frowned. What was Hendricks doing here?

She opened the door cautiously, peeking her head out. He looked up, raising the wide brim of the hat, and her caution was forgotten. "Jesus Christ!"

"No, I'm an atheist, remember?" Hendricks said, and he had a little hint of a smile on his beat-up face.

"What happened to you?" Erin felt herself sputtered, almost screaming.

"Oh, this?" He gestured to his lips, which were split. One of his eyes was blacked and swollen. "Apparently I got into a bar fight."

"Well, what the hell did you go and do that for?" She wanted to reach out to him, but she could almost feel her breath catching in her chest. He looked worse than that drunk that had smashed his car into a down by the square tree a couple months ago. Guy lost three teeth on his steering wheel, and his eye had popped out of the socket. By the time they brought him in to booking, the hospital had fixed some of it, but he still looked like a shit sandwich on crap bread. Hendricks maybe looked worse, she decided. His jaw line was bruised up, and he looked like he'd done some half-assed collagen injections, too.

"Can I come in?" Hendricks asked, slurring a little. "Arch was worried I might have a concussion, so he dropped me off here—"

"Why didn't he take you to a hospital?" In her horror it took her a moment to fully interpret what he'd said. "Wait, Arch saw you like this?"

"Well, yeah," Hendricks said.

"And he left you in this condition without taking you to the hospital?" She felt a mad-on building.

"I told him no," Hendricks said, shaking his head. "I'm fine, I just need a day or so to recover. I wanted to do it at the motel, but he said—"

She held out her free hand for him to stop, then put it on her head, which was now swirling with about a thousand thoughts. Her first instinct was to drive him to the hospital herself, but he'd already apparently put the kibosh on that. It took her a moment to realize he'd never actually been to her place, that this was something new, and a moment later that gave her a funny feeling of alarm. Which she would have thought would have taken a backseat to her concern for this human being all beaten to hell, standing on her doorstep.

Oddly, it didn't.

"I ... cannot believe this," she said finally, and it was all she could do to get that out. "You got in a bar fight."

"They started it," Hendricks said, almost plaintive. "Otherwise, Arch would have arrested me, you know that."

Well, that much was true. She put her hand over her face and peered at him through the split in the fingers. It didn't make him look any better, but at least one of her eyes was covered, so it made him look a little less worse. If that was a thing. He was a pretty handsome guy most of the time, and in good shape. Walked with a little swagger in his step.

Now he was hunched over, looking like an old man the way he was standing, and his face was swollen like he'd just gotten out of the ring with Manny Pacquiáo. "Jesus," she whispered.

"Can I come in?" Hendricks asked again. She felt sorry for him now; he looked like hell.

"Yeah, okay," she said, and stepped aside. The crescendo in her stomach grew, though, more than just nerves, and she let him in.

* * *

Gideon had felt the Tul'rore start on their meal. He'd felt the ones before that, too, and they'd been sweet. He'd savored every moment. He could taste the flesh and the terror as the Tul'rore went to work, could hear the screams echo in his ears as the victims began to die. He'd felt the last few that the Tul'rore had devoured, all of them since he'd gotten into town just a couple days ago, and they had been sustaining. A slow trickle of treats to keep him going.

Gideon slipped out of bed, the hotel sheets spotted through with burns like a thin slice of Swiss cheese. He knew others of his kind; death was a call for them. A yearning to be around the end of life, to feed on the misery of the souls leaving it. His kind gravitated toward wars, battlefields, and hotspots like carrion birds to the dead. He was the only one here, though. So far, anyway.

It had been tough to leave Chicago, especially with things going so well in the city. He'd had a steady diet there, enough for his needs. Some of the meals had been truly beautiful, moments of passion he would treasure for all time.

Gideon opened the curtains and left the sheer panel hanging over the window in place. He stared out across the dark parking lot of the Sinbad motel at the street. Rain was coming down, lit by the lampposts lining the roads. He could see the dark ripples hitting the puddles throughout the lot.

He wondered, with the Tul'rore dead, how long he'd have to wait for his next meal. He could sense it when demons got burned, but it was a blissless feeling. It didn't tantalize and thrill him the way it did when a human went. Demons simply passed through the veil and went back to the nethers; humans could be stopped, could linger and be savored. They had flavor, texture, misery.

He sighed and stared out at the motel parking lot, letting his hand drift lower. He could feel the pressure building inside, but there was nothing to do for it. Not yet. Not without death.

He sighed and went back to sit on the bed, cool sheets against his naked body, the smell of the singed cloth still hanging in the air. Somewhere in the distance, he heard a rumble of thunder and hoped it was a good omen.

* * *

The whole heavens had started to pour down on Arch just as he was pulling into the parking lot of his apartment building. The night was liquid and splattering across the windshield of the Explorer in thick drops, drenching everything around him as he stepped out of the car and slammed the door behind him. He took off at a run for the stairs. Then he cursed himself for a fool and altered his course, toward the ground-level unit on the opposite side of the building. His shoes splashed on the wet ground as runoff started to accumulate in shallow puddles.

He fumbled with his key as he reached the ground-level apartment. It was one of eight in the building, and not the one he'd been living in two weeks ago. Two weeks ago he'd been upstairs, in number six. But that had been before a bunch of meth-head demons had broken down his door and smashed the place to pieces. There were holes in the wall, a sink and countertop shattered. Basically an entire bathroom remodel already underway.

He'd been surprised at the grace with which the landlord, Gunther Sweeney, had taken the whole thing. Sweeney was an older man in his fifties, German, with a thick mustache turned grey. He'd looked around with Arch at his side, pronounced the whole thing *durcheinander*, and submitted the claim to insurance. When Arch had pressed, Sweeney let him move into the unoccupied unit without complaint. It worked.

Arch's key hit the lock and he turned the handle with gentle pressure. The door swung open and Arch stepped into a mirror image of his own apartment, everything a perfect opposite save for the missing wall hangings and the countless boxes that were still unpacked since the move. He shut the door behind him as quietly as he could, wondering if Alison was about. The lights were on, but that meant nothing; lately she kept the lights on when she slept.

He stood paused in the entry alcove, listening, to see if he could hear her. Nothing. After a moment he laid his keys on the small table in front of him and turned to look into the living room/kitchen area. He caught a glimpse of long blond hair on the couch, and realized she was just sitting there. The sound of the rain tapping at the windows was just background noise, and a peal of thunder crackled in the distance. The place smelled faintly of her perfume, but it was lingering and not fresh, a ghostly reminder of her getting-ready-for-work routine.

"Hey," he said as he entered the room. His khaki uniform was spotted with water and was starting to chill him in the cooler indoor air. The air conditioner, a small wall-mounted unit hung high on the wall, was humming faintly in the background,.

"Hey," she returned, but the word was as lifeless and motionless as the woman herself. Alison's blond hair hung limp and wet, and he noticed she wore a bathrobe as he came into the room. He gave her a kiss on the cheek and got not even a trace of a smile in return.

"How was work?" He laid a hand on the side of her neck, running his dark fingers down her tanned skin. He could see little goosebumps as he did it, pulling back the edge of the robe.

She adjusted herself on the sofa, pulling the neck of the white terrycloth robe tight. "Fine." She didn't sound angry or resentful, just flat.

He pulled his hand back to rest on the back of the sofa. She didn't turn to face him, just kept staring ahead. This was how it had been since the attack, since the demons had smashed into their apartment. She still had the barest discoloration on her neck where one of them had held her by the throat. He wanted to touch it, to touch her, but she always seemed to shift away.

"Going to bed?" Arch asked. He could feel the pull of the bed, the barely conscious realization that he had an early shift tomorrow. It was probably not going to be a very busy day, if tradition held. He hadn't really had a busy day yet, save for the ones where he was fighting demons after work.

And he and Hendricks had just killed the ones they'd gotten a lead on. It was all listening to rumors about strange out-of-towners so far, but it'd paid off a couple times. Arch enjoyed the scrapes, really, though he didn't necessarily want to admit it to anyone, least of all himself. He could feel it, though, the glow that came from knowing he'd punched the ticket of something really bad earlier in the night.

He stared down at his wife's exposed neck, wanting to let his fingers drift lower. The terrycloth robe was closed tight, though. He shrugged, though she didn't see him, and turned away to undress in the bathroom so he could hang his uniform up to dry.

Alison remained behind and made not a sound as he left. He felt the chill as he undressed and wondered if it was just the air conditioning unit fighting against the humid Tennessee summer, or if it was the wife who hadn't said more than a few words to him in a week that was causing him to shiver.

Chapter 4

If it was possible, Hendricks awoke feeling even shittier than he had when he went to sleep. His right eye was swollen shut, his ribs hurt like someone had kicked him while he was down, and his lips felt like they'd been transformed into Polish sausages filled with flaming, screaming nerve endings. He moaned and rolled over, forgetting that someone was in the bed with him.

His one good eye caught sight of Erin lying there next to him, her short-cropped blond hair more than a little tousled from the night of sleep. She was looking at him kind of pityingly, like she was uncomfortable with him being there or with the way he looked, or maybe even both.

"Good morning," he mumbled through his swollen lips. It came out more than a little twisted, and he wondered for a beat if it was even comprehensible.

"You look like holy hell, Hendricks," she said. She reached a tentative hand across the white sheets, and Hendricks caught a whiff of the flowery scent she wore on her wrist as she touched his forehead. Her thumb traced a delicate path around his eye, causing the pain to flare even so. "What were you thinking?"

"I'm asking myself that very same question this morning," Hendricks said and rolled to the side of the bed. His hip cried out in pain as he did, and he wondered what he'd done to offend it so. The bedroom was flooded with light, the carpeted floors and grey walls dimly illuminated in the light of the early morning sun. He placed a hand gently upon his eye and felt the pain radiate outward in waves.

"So you just walked into the bar and the fight started?" Erin asked over his shoulder as she got up, bed creaking beneath her. Hendricks ran a hand over his chest, feeling the curly hairs that sprang out of his skin and the bruises beneath.

"Kinda," Hendricks said. "Well, not really. I was there for a while, and this guy started some shit with McInness, the owner—"

"Oh, God!" Erin cut him off. "You were at the Charnel House? Why?"

"I dunno," Hendricks said. "I just was. It's where the road took me."

She closed her eyes tightly at this. She was standing at an angle, leaning heavily on one leg, face in her palm like she was trying to think of a way to ask what was on her mind but couldn't find a way to do it. She was wearing a thin wife beater shirt over her tiny frame, pink panties underneath it. If Hendricks hadn't been feeling like shit scraped onto toast, he knew he'd be trying to get her hair even more tousled than it already was.

As it was, she probably wouldn't have any of it. He was aching too much, anyway, and not in any of the right places.

"People do not just wander into random establishments in the backwoods and get into bar fights," Erin said finally, opening her eyes. "It's not normal."

Hendricks just stood there. "I wear a black cowboy hat and a drover coat everywhere I go. Where would you get the idea I'm normal in any way?"

She opened her mouth to respond but probably couldn't figure out what to say to that, so she shut it a moment later.

"Look," he said, "I didn't go looking for a fight." A blatant lie, but hopefully he carried it off well. "Some out-of-towners jumped McInness and the regulars, and I stepped in to help them when it went wrong. McInness got the shit kicked out of him, too, had to go to the hospital and everything—"

"Jesus," Erin said.

"Yeah, he didn't look too good," Hendricks said. "But Arch helped, and we ran the guys off. You can't expect me to just sit back while people are getting the holy hell hammered out of them. It's not who I am."

Erin had positioned her hands over her mouth while waiting for him to finish. She watched him through skeptical eyes, or at least that was how he would describe them. "And who are you, exactly?"

Hendricks stood there for a second. Wasn't it obvious? "I'm Lafayette Hendricks—"

"I know your fucking name, jackass." Erin wasn't too harsh with it, Hendricks reflected, but she also could have been gentler. "I'm asking *who* you are. Some cowboy drifter that blows into town, doesn't seem to work at all—at least not that I can see—just kind of hangs out, apparently jumps into bar fights from time to time." She ran a hand through her tangled hair. "I don't really know anything about you."

"Well ... I mean, you know a little bit about me," Hendricks said, and he felt heat on his cheeks. "We've been sleeping together for a couple weeks."

"We've been fucking for a couple weeks," Erin replied matter-of-factly. "We haven't exactly had deep and epic conversations." She changed posture, and he thought she looked a little more standoffish now. "Look, I slept with you because—I'll be honest—you really own that whole cowboy thing. It's a good look, and you wear it well, even with the coat, which *is* weird, by the way. Arch knew you, and he's about the nicest and most stand-up guy around, so I figured you couldn't be too bad. I mean," she said with a mirthless laugh, "I didn't even make you wear a condom." She blushed a little at this. "But I *don't* know you, not really. I know your name, I know you were in the Marines, but that's about it." She shrugged. "I know you get into fights, based on the bruises I've seen. So I guess I know you're not that good at fighting."

Hendricks frowned and felt his hackles rise. "You don't tell a Marine he's not any good at fighting unless you want an argument."

"Maybe I want an argument," Erin said, and he could tell by the testy way she said it that she probably did.

"Well, let me oblige—" Hendricks said, but the trilling of a cell phone cut him short.

She held up a hand palm out, like he was a kid on a trike and she was telling him to stop. She pulled the cell phone off her nightstand and answered it. "Hello?"

He stood there, kind of slack-jawed, wondering what the hell kind of argument this was. Wondering what kind of man he was, just able to be put on hold like this in the middle of what was kinda, sorta their first fight. He wondered if there would be another. He could feel his temper flaring, that sense of stubborn irritation and embarrassment, and he realized he was standing there in his boxer shorts while Erin was just listening to the phone.

"Fuck this," he muttered and started to pull his jeans on.

She walked out of the bedroom and pulled the door nearly shut behind her. He could hear her mutter, "Are you fucking kidding me?" into the phone as she went.

Hendricks pulled his shirt on, the cold chill of anger washing down into his guts. He tugged his shirt on, grimacing the entire time from the pain. He pulled on his socks as he heard a faint voice saying something indecipherable in the next room. He put on his cowboy boots one by one then pulled his coat out of the pile he'd made of it and put it on, careful to keep the sword hidden in its depths.

He grabbed his hat off the bottom post of her bed and put it on, checking himself once in the mirror. Yep, still looked like shit. There wasn't much he could do about it, though.

He walked through the apartment without bothering to glance at her. He saw her still on the phone, her mouth slightly open, out of the corner of his eye, but he didn't stop to say anything. She didn't get off the phone anyway, so he just walked over to the door, unlocked it, and left without saying a word.

She didn't say anything either.

* * *

Arch was on the scene less than ten minutes after Sheriff Reeve called him. He'd heard the basics from the sheriff, and it sounded like nothing he'd dealt with in his time with the department. Reeve was calling in everyone, Arch knew that for a fact, because that was what you did in a situation like this; you called for all hands on deck and got to work solving the crime.

Arch had gotten the thumbnail sketch from Reeve, but he still wasn't quite sure what to expect when he got there. It left him with a kind of nervous tension in his stomach, belly rumbling at him for leaving home without anything to eat or drink. He hadn't even bothered to shower, just tossed on his uniform and sprinted out the door without saying a word to Alison. He knew she was faking sleep, but he didn't have time to deal with it at the moment.

The Explorer's engine rumbled as he took it down a side street. He was only a few blocks from home, here in the heart of Midian. If there was such a thing. The town square was only a few blocks away also. He pulled onto Crosser Street and saw the squad cars. They were the older models, the Crown Victorias driven by Sheriff Reeve and the other deputies, three of them lining the road in front of a big white house. Arch flipped on his lights but not his siren. He hadn't even needed them to get here. Midian didn't exactly have a roaring rush hour.

The red and blue lights flickered in the dim early morning. Clouds covered the sky and cast a grey pall over the day. It was the kind of day that would be perfect for a funeral, Arch thought. The clouds were sapping all the joy and light, leaving nothing but a lifeless feeling over the usually vibrant town.

And as Arch stepped up to the white picket fence and opened the gate, he reflected that it would probably be an appropriate feeling.

He took the steps to the front porch in one bound, heard the squeak of the floorboard he landed on as he did so. The front door was open, and he could hear talk from inside. He recognized the voice of Ernesto Reines, the second-most junior patrolman in the department, one rung up the ladder from him. Reines was speaking in a low voice with Ed Fries, a portly officer in his early forties. Arch stepped in and saw them both, just off to the side of the dim entry hall.

Reines nodded to Arch as he entered, and Fries turned to him to do the same. Reines had a soul patch, a little growth of black hair just under his lower lip that was probably not department regulation, at least not the way Arch read the regs. Sheriff Reeve never said a word, though, probably figuring that in Midian, Tennessee, there were better uses of one's time than enforcing regulations about the length and location of facial hair.

"Man, Arch," Fries said in his low, drawling voice, "you better bring a damned plastic bag in there with you." Fries was looking unusually pale today, Arch thought, his chubby jowls bereft of their usual ruddy color. "I ain't never even seen anything like that."

"Reeve said on the phone it was Corey Hughes?" Arch had heard Hughes' name before but didn't really know the man. Worked at the paper mill, according to Reeve, just a single man living in a city house by himself.

"Yeah," Reines spoke up, his voice a little gruffer than usual. "But you wouldn't know it by looking at him."

"Right," Arch said. "The scene's a real mess?"

Reines and Fries exchanged a look. "You could say that." Fries shook his head, jowls flapping as he did so.

Arch walked on past them, taking his time, steeling himself. He'd seen photos of crime scenes at the academy, some videos where they'd gone in and catalogued evidence in some truly heinous murder cases. He came into a family room, the lights left off so as to avoid touching the switches and possibly disturbing whatever fingerprints might be resting on them. No, they'd leave the lights off and tread as carefully as possible until the crime scene unit from Chattanooga came and took apart the whole place, cataloguing all the evidence.

"Arch?" Sheriff Nicholas Reeve stepped into an open door to Arch's left. There was a light behind him, shining off his balding head. Reeve had short grey hair growing up from his sideburns that stretched around the back of his head in a strip, but the top of his skull was completely bare. The man had an open, earnest face that was creased with frown lines today. He was a little overweight but not too much. Certainly not as much as Fries. "Arch, you might want to bring a bucket with you in here. Ed already contaminated the scene by throwing up in the sink."

"Nice going, Ed," Reines said from down the hall behind him.

"Shit, man, you only just made it outside yourself," Fries shot back at him.

Arch felt the stale air in the house, warm and rank and humid. It smelled like when he'd visited the morgue during his time at the academy but fresher and more pungent. He could hear the faint hum of civilization somewhere in the distance, under the hushed voices of Fries and Reines. "I'll be all right," he told Reeve, and the sheriff stepped aside to let him pass into the kitchen.

The first thing he noticed was red where it shouldn't have been. The room was done in yellow tones, old wallpaper in amber and white that was faded with time, but there was red everywhere. It was on the ceiling, the oak floor, and it drenched the table. It pooled underneath on the floorboards, looking like black oil in the shadows.

The body was on top of the table, and Arch couldn't rightly recall seeing anything quite like it before, not even a post-autopsy corpse. He swallowed hard and then turned around, leaving the room before he could feel any more ill. He stood just outside, letting the smell of the scene permeate his nose. He didn't feel any sicker, but he didn't feel any better, either. He just stood there for a few minutes, trying to get his breath and realizing that what he'd just seen probably couldn't ever be unseen.

* * *

Erin drove along above the speed limit. She didn't have a police vehicle, just her old Honda, but all the cops in town were already at her destination, so who was going to stop her?

She hammered the accelerator as she went down a city street at forty, about ten miles over. Reeve had called, telling her to get her ass down to the crime scene immediately. She was a little excited and a little horrified, since she hadn't really been to any real crime scenes before. Most of her horror came from the fact that he'd told her to stop and get coffee for everyone. That stung. She tried to decide if he'd asked her because she was the most junior member of the department or because she was the only woman. With Reeve, it could have been either.

She took the corners with care, four Styrofoam cups on the seat next to her in one of those fancy holders they gave out nowadays. She was surprised that Pat at the Surrey Diner on the square had them, but she did. It was a little surprise, like Midian was slowly entering the modern world.

The prospect of what she was about to see, about to be involved in, was so overwhelming that it nearly eclipsed the thoughts still hanging around her head about Hendricks. She was still kicking herself over everything related to him. Sure, he was cute, and she'd thought because of his association with Arch it was like he came stamped with a personal recommendation. But that was kind of dumb, on reflection. She'd known all the other guys she'd slept with for pretty much her whole life. They were all local, and she knew through rumor and admission the people they'd slept with. The seedier ones she was careful with.

With Hendricks, though, it was like any good sense she might have had fled at the sight of his cowboy hat and lovely abs. And they were lovely. She liked to run a hand over them just to feel the firm ripples. She shook that thought out of her head.

He was a mystery, and who didn't love a mystery? Still, just because someone was mysterious, it didn't mean you had to sleep with them without a condom. Quite the opposite, in fact, because one of the secrets he could have been hiding under that coat and hat might just have been syphilis. At least she was on the pill; wondering what a baby cowboy would look like was one mystery she didn't want solved at present.

He'd showed up last night, beaten all to hell, then left this morning in the middle of a burgeoning argument. Didn't even say goodbye, and Erin had to admit that stuck in her craw more than a little. The next time she saw him, she wanted to give him a little hell of her own. The other part of her, the non-confrontational part, which was small but present, just hoped he'd pick up and leave town. Problem solved.

But most of her kind of hoped he wouldn't.

She pulled up behind Arch's Explorer on Crosser Street and killed the engine. She had to admit, she was more than a little envious of Arch. He'd gotten the last squad spot, the new car the department had bought last year, and he spent his days on patrol. Meanwhile she got stuck behind the desk working dispatch and filing and computer shit, had to drive her own personal vehicle, even on department business, and got stuck doing coffee and lunch runs (though she had to admit Reeve did split the lunch runs with her fairly often).

She didn't begrudge Arch any of what he'd gotten, but she did wish, as the sole owner of a vagina in the Sheriff's Department, that some affirmative action would kick in on her behalf. Maybe next year.

But probably not.

She made it through the gate and up the walk before she saw Reines and Fries just inside the door. It was dark and she nodded to both of them as she came in. Her khaki uniform was a little wrinkled because she'd run out the door without a chance to iron it, but she doubted that would matter here. She had the steaming cups of coffee in her hand, carrying the little Styrofoam tray. She wordlessly held it out and Reines and Fries each grabbed one, thanking her profusely.

She went on, listening to the squeak of the floor as she made her way down the hall. The crime scene unit from Chattanooga was probably still an hour out, which meant they'd all sort of stand around and try not to fuck things up until the pros got here. For her money, the best way to do that would be to get Fries and Reines outside, but she wasn't exactly in charge. Or anywhere approaching a mile of in charge.

She came around the corner into a family room complete with sofa and TV. The TV was half the size of the room, which screamed bachelor to her. Part of her wondered if that was because she knew Corey Hughes was a lifelong bachelor or if it genuinely was just because of the TV and the sofa.

The room was dark, the curtains pulled to. The day was gloomy anyway; it was doubtful that opening them would do much to brighten the place.

It took her a second to realize that Arch was standing against the wall to her left, just next to an open door leading into a lit room. Light was spilling out and she could hear someone moving in there. She surmised it was probably Reeve, since she knew he was on scene and she'd yet to run across him.

"You already go in?" she asked Arch, and he looked up at her. He looked like he'd been lost in his own little world before she'd said something, and she stepped over to him and wordlessly offered him a coffee.

"No, thanks," he said, shaking his head. "And yeah, I went in. It's …" Arch's voice got kind of choked. "It's bad."

She wondered at how bad it could be. Took a couple steps toward the door, but Reeve was there, holding out a hand and taking a coffee from the tray. "You don't want to go in there," he said. "It's just nasty. Ain't a fit way for anyone to die, and there's no reason for you to see it—"

"Sir," she said, and all the irritation she'd felt and bottled up at being asked to get coffee sort popped out, "please move aside."

Reeve cocked an eyebrow at her, and she could tell he was trying to decide whether or not to argue. He must have decided against it, because he shuffled left, leaving the door open for her to walk through.

She took a tentative step toward it, then another, wishing her pace was a match for the voice she'd just used to order the sheriff around. She stepped into the lit kitchen and the smell hit her.

It was like a memory she had of childhood, when her three brothers, all older than her, had conspired to drag her six year-old self out to the barn when her daddy was killing a hog. They told her it was something else, she couldn't remember what, that she *had to see it* and she went, dutifully, as though the three of them hadn't steered her wrong a thousand times before. She was naive like that as a kid. Thinking back to Hendricks, she wondered if maybe she still was.

She'd watched through a crack in the barn door as her daddy slit the hog's throat. She'd known the name of the creature at the time, though it escaped her now. Her brothers had stood behind her and snickered as she peered in. Their hushed whispers came back to her now, their excitement in the anticipation of seeing her reaction.

They were dreadfully disappointed when they actually saw it.

She remembered watching her dad raise the hog in the air once he'd gutted it, once he'd pulled out the innards and put them in a wheelbarrow. She could recall the smell of it, of the shit and piss and gawdawful rancid nastiness of the hog's carcass opened to the air. She just watched, though, not a word, not a sound, her brothers getting restless behind her. She watched her daddy crank the body into the air and she looked at that empty stomach cavity, saw the ribs from the inside.

And she never made a sound. Just watched while he cut it to pieces, reducing that hog to individual cuts of meat over the course of the next hours.

Erin looked into the kitchen of Corey Hughes's house. There was a carcass on the table, something that had been opened up. The ribs were cracked at the sternum and pulled back, and she could see that the heart and damned near all else had been removed. She took a step forward and peered in. The chest cavity was empty all the way to the spine. She took a sniff, and it was damned rancid, but it didn't bother her stomach. She heard Reeve catch his breath from the stench, a few paces behind her.

Just like slaughtering a hog all over again.

"I ain't never seen anything like this shit," Reeve said from behind her.

Erin didn't answer him. She looked into the open cavity, that empty space where life had mysteriously once existed. The thighs of the corpse were laid open, large chunks of meat removed by something. It was uneven, whatever had done this, not smooth like a knife. It was like teeth had come in and ground their way through one of the legs, even breaking the femur, which she knew wasn't a picnic. Which the rest of the corpse looked like, come to think of it.

A picnic for something.

Or *someone*.

"This place is a goddamned slaughterhouse," Reeve said behind her.

"Yeah," she breathed and tried to tear her eyes away. She couldn't, though.

* * *

Hendricks's long-ass walk was just about nearing its end. He was crossing the interstate bridge, the sky above was making noise like it might start dropping water on him again, and he was hustling to make sure he missed that. His stomach was rumbling but he had some snacks back at the motel. He wasn't in the mood for a greasy breakfast anyway, not even after walking for the last hour and a half, and that was just about all the diner across the interstate offered. Grease fried in grease, with some eggs possibly somewhere under the oil.

He wasn't really pissed at Erin anymore, not now. He'd walked it out of himself. Now he was just sullen and irritated. It's not like he knew her all that well, either. He'd never even asked if she was on the pill, just assumed it. Probably been too carried away with having sex for the first time in five damned years to even care. Like he forgot it could have consequences.

He'd got a little drunk on her, if he was being honest with himself. She was damned pretty, had a youthful cuteness about her that hadn't been part of his life over the last few years. She was cheery, that was it. Hendricks hadn't been cheery in a long damned time. Rueful, more often than not. Sarcastic, all the time.

Also, she had a body that didn't look like it had gotten any mileage on it since high school, and he liked that. She was a thin slip of a girl, and there wasn't any problem at all with that in his mind. She was proportioned just right for it, too, not comically exaggerated like she'd had surgery on her busts, as some did. No, her chest was pretty close to flat and for some reason it worked just fine for him.

He crossed into the parking lot of the Sinbad motel, bearing toward his room at little more than a saunter. It was about all he could manage, and it had taken him a while to get from Midian to out here. His hip was aching, and he figured he'd go in and sit in that ugly ass chair in the corner of his room, put his feet up for a spell. He might even need some more sleep, and he knew for a fact he needed a hot shower after the walk. Things were sticking together on him from the faint sweat generated by his activity.

He looked up in time to see a guy coming out of the room next to his. Kind of a middle-aged fellow, medium height, medium build, long hair around the sides but way bald on top. The guy was wearing—no shit—a t-shirt that said nothing but Nike, and a pair of khaki cargo pants. He had on a pair of white tennis shoes, and his legs were pale enough that Hendricks knew he was a northerner in a heartbeat. The legs looked just like Hendricks's when he didn't have his jeans on.

"Morning," Hendricks said, tipping his hat to the guy as he passed. He'd learned that this was the way things were done in the South, greeting everybody you passed. That shit didn't fly in the North.

The guy said nothing, just sort of nodded as he went by.

Hendricks didn't think much of it. Lots of people were unfriendly like that, and he ached too much to dwell on it or give a shit. He pulled his key and opened his door, disappearing inside to where slightly cooler air waited. And possibly a shower.

* * *

Gideon just nodded at the cowboy as he passed him. He looked back when he was sure the guy wasn't watching him, and saw him go into the room next door. Shit.

He knew the cowboy, had felt it when the cowboy had cut loose a couple of demons in a bar last night. That black hat and black coat. There was a sword in there somewhere; he remembered the vision of those Y'freiti demons getting stabbed right through. He'd filed it away at the time, indifferent, because demon deaths didn't do anything for him. He stared at the cowboy's back as the man retreated into his room and closed the door.

Still, a demon hunter in the next room? That was some nerve-racking shit for him to deal with. Gideon had no plans to do anything that would cross the cowboy, but it was still unnerving. Demon hunters and demons weren't exactly good neighbors, though apparently the cowboy hadn't seen his real face. Which was fortunate, because Gideon wasn't much of a killer. He was more of a voyeur.

Still, if the cowboy figured things out …

Nah. Gideon turned and kept on walking. He needed something to eat, needed to get out for a while and stretch his legs. Besides, if his nose didn't deceive him, he smelled death coming nearby. Really close, in fact. It was too tantalizing to pass up. And why not be deathly close when it came? He'd never really tried that before.

Gideon put thoughts of the cowboy out of his mind for now and turned to walk over to his rental car. He'd just head toward the death he felt coming for now and leave everything else to be dealt with later.

Chapter 5

Lerner stared out the window of the hotel and watched rain start. Again. Last night had been a downpour, the little Holiday Inn-style thirty-unit building buffeted by high winds and a hard rain all night long. He'd gone to sleep listening to it tap on the roof, the sound of Duncan's slow breathing in the bed next to his as familiar as eating. Not as enjoyable, though.

He put his hand on the glass and felt the slight chill from it across the tips of his fingers. He'd often given a lot of thought to the fact that the shell over his essence breathed the way a human did, could feel sensation and even had a sense of smell the way a human's did, but contained none of the organs of a human. No liver, kidneys, heart or lungs. On the occasions where they stumbled across dead humans and he had a few minutes, he liked poke around inside, see what was going on in there. Lerner thought being a doctor would have been a magnificent career, if only for the opportunity to poke around inside real, living human beings.

Of course, he didn't really care whether they lived or died, so that probably disqualified him.

Still, the knowledge was interesting. He remembered the smell of the kitchen in the house they'd raided last night. The corpse was so different from a living person. It wasn't better or worse, just different. The sight of a gutted human didn't offend him, really, it just bothered him from a job perspective. It meant paperwork. It meant headaches. When there were as many bodies as the Tul'rore had left behind, it meant an interdiction, possibly some expulsions from the plane. Which was what they'd done last night.

"You finish your Form S0-8T?" Duncan's tone was clipped, all business. He was sitting at the table behind Lerner, already trying to get his shit done for the day. Lerner was putting it off, and Duncan probably knew it. His gentle reminder was the same thing he always did, trying to push Lerner to get done, too, and Lerner didn't care for it. Still, he didn't feel the need to turn around and gnash Duncan's head off over it. Literally or figuratively. No, Lerner just kept staring out the window. Duncan would get the message in time.

The paperwork was probably the worst part of the job. Expelling pact violators wasn't a bad job. It didn't make him go sour in the stomach to crack open a shell and send someone's essence screaming back to the underworld. He didn't have a stomach, anyway.

Everyone knew the rules, and if they wanted to keep earth as a nice playground where everyone could feed reasonably, enjoy their desires in an orderly manner, and keep the humans from freaking out and staging a full-on anti-demon war the way they had in the past, the rules needed to be followed.

Lerner liked rules. Almost as much as he like pontificating.

Duncan cleared his throat, and Lerner felt his expression turn to an eyeroll. "No, I haven't finished my fucking Form S0-8T, and you damned well know it. Don't be a Mother Hubbard. I'll get to it eventually." The damned bureaucracy of the Office of Occultic Concordance was worse than the fires and freeze of damnation, honestly. "After all," he went on, "it's not like we've got anything else to do today."

Duncan made a sound like he was clearing the throat he didn't even have. "You know something could come in at any time."

"Yeah, well, let's hope it does." Lerner reached down and felt the truncheon on his belt. He kind of liked cracking open a demon, letting the essence pour out. It made him feel alive. He wondered if that made him like a serial killer among the humans, then realized he didn't much care.

After all, among his own people, it wasn't like murder was even a crime.

* * *

"What the hell is up with Hendricks?"

Arch got the question he'd been dreading the minute they were outside, out of earshot of Reeve, Fries and Reines. She asked as Arch was heading back to grab his raincoat, the big yellow reflective-striped one that he kept in the back of the Explorer as part of his standard gear. He fished it out and pulled it on as the first little droplets continued to fall here and there. He pretended to not hear her as he fished around in the back for the accompanying hat.

"Arch, don't even pretend you can't hear me," Erin's voice came at him again. "That crap might work on your wife but it doesn't work on me."

"Sorry, what did you want to know?" Arch said, forcing a smile as he came up with his hat. He put it on, adjusting the brim.

"What's up with him?" Erin didn't have rain gear on, and Arch cast a look skyward. He suspected it was about to open up, but she didn't seem concerned. Her khaki uniform was just starting to show the first signs of spotting from the raindrops.

"Well, he wears a cowboy hat ..." Arch started, a little tentative.

"I fucking know that," she said, not seeing the humor in it, plainly. Arch's stomach was a little unsettled yet from what he'd seen. He was glad he'd skipped breakfast. "What's his deal? Where's he from? Why's he here?"

"You could try asking him this, you know," Arch said, looking up and down the street. There were a few people out watching the cavalcade of police cars, but they were all safely under their porch awnings now.

"I'm asking you," Erin said with a seriousness he didn't usually see in her. "And I would hope, as my friend, you'll tell me."

Arch was caught a little off guard by that one. They were coworkers, sure, but he wasn't certain he'd have gone all out and called her a friend. Still, it made him feel a little bad about the whole thing. "He's from Wisconsin."

"If you're gonna be a kneejerk ass—"

"Whoa," Arch said, and could feel his eyebrow crank down. "Whatever problems you've got are between you and him, okay? Don't go dragging me into it." He slammed the hatchback of the Explorer down. "And clearly you've got a problem with him."

"I need to know some things about him," she said, unfolding her arms and seeming to spit fire at the same time. "He's like a damned cipher that got dropped out of the heavens onto my doorstep by you."

"I only dropped him on your doorstep last night because he needed someone to keep an eye on him," Arch said. He was still stinging from her swearing at him like that. "I figured that might be something you could do since the two of you were getting close—"

"We're not," Erin said, and a hand worked its way up to cover her eyes as she said it. "I mean ... we're ... you know ... but we don't really talk or know anything about each other like ..."

"Yeah, okay," Arch said, having heard more than enough.

"Look, I jumped all over him because he was a friend of yours," she said, peeking from behind her fingers, and for some reason that made Arch's stomach rumble again. "I figured it was as close as I'd get to my mom endorsing one of the bad boys I've liked. But without the creepy side effect of having her try and date him."

Arch started to say something to that, but gave up after a moment of trying to figure out what and coming up dry. "Um—"

"Do you even really know him?" she asked, and this time he felt the impact of her words like thunder on a clear day. "I need to know, Arch."

Arch tried to figure out what to say to that. "Not as well as you apparently think I do," he finally said.

Erin covered her face again, and he could barely hear her say, "Goddamn."

"Hey, y'all!" Sheriff Reeve's voice boomed out over the street, and Arch turned his head to see what was going on. Reeve was standing on the porch of the Hughes house next to Reines and Fries, gesturing to Erin and Arch with a hand to get on over there. Arch headed that way, listening to the tapping of the rain on the brim of his hat. It was getting worse, starting to open up on them.

Arch hit the front porch a few seconds later and looked back for Erin, who was not behind him. He caught sight of her rummaging in the back seat of her car and wondered if she might be heading out because of their conversation about Hendricks. She emerged from the back of the car a moment later with her rain gear. She slammed her door and it echoed down the street. The four of them watched while she ran through the increasing downpour to join them on the porch.

"All right, now that you're all here," Reeve said once Erin was there with them. Arch watched the water drip from her short blond hair. She wasn't wearing any makeup, which was probably fortunate for her given the wet conditions. Her khaki uniform top was now sported a dark brown, camo-like pattern from all the places it had gotten wet. "I need y'all to start canvassing the area, asking the neighbors what they've seen. If anything." Reeve pointed to the right. "Fries, you go that way, Reines, start across the street on the left, and Arch, go left. Take Erin with you and show her what to do."

Arch caught a flash of irritation from Erin, but she didn't speak up. "Yes, sir," Arch said.

"All right, then," Reeve said, his brow was puckered as if he was concentrating. "I'll keep watch here until the crime scene unit arrives. See what you can find out in the meantime." He waved them off, and Arch held up for a minute while Erin put on her raincoat and hat. Reines and Fries went scrambling to their cars to get their gear, the waist-high white gate slamming shut behind them with a rattling noise.

"Shall we?" Arch asked as Erin pulled her brim down low over her eyes. She didn't look up at him, just led the way down the porch steps as the rain pitter-pattered on the awning and the sidewalk. Heavy grey clouds hung low overhead. They walked under the shade of old trees that kept a little of the rain from falling on them as they went.

Arch was getting used to the freeze out, had become real accustomed to it lately at home, and it bothered him less with Erin than it did with Alison. They only had to walk one house down the street, anyway, and she was fit enough to keep ahead of him at a reasonable pace if he didn't try to run her down. Which he didn't, though his long legs would easily have allowed him to.

She did the knocking when they got up to the house next door. It was an old-style Southern house with a porch wrapping all the way around. She let her small knuckles rattle on the screen door, not bothering to open it. He just watched and said nothing; he could play this game as well as her or better.

When there was no response after a minute or so of standing in the rain-drenched quiet, she pulled open the screen door and laid a firm knock on the front door itself. It gave and creaked open an inch, a black line all that showed of the interior.

"Who lives here?" Arch asked, already rummaging through his mind for the details.

"Orin and Kim Hauser," Erin replied in a half second. "Older couple, in their sixties. He worked as a long-haul trucker until a few years ago when he retired." She looked back at him. "They've got a couple grown kids still in town, Jake and—"

"Lisa," Arch said with a nod. He stepped up next to her and pushed the door open slightly. "Mr. and Mrs. Hauser?" A stench hit him in the face as though he'd been punched in the nose, and he recoiled from it, drawing his Glock 22 as he did so. He could feel the weight of the plastic grip in his hand and heard the click as the metal barrel slid loose of the plastic holster. He kept his finger along the slide, off the trigger, and pointed the gun down at a forty-five degree angle. He pulled loose the little flashlight from his belt and threaded his left hand under his right. He pointed the flashlight in the same direction as the gun, and kept his eyes along the same sight line.

He saw Erin mimic his posture behind him, following along as he entered the house. His light illuminated the living room area ahead of him, shadows of the furniture cast on wallpaper checkered with blue dots or patterns too small for his eye to discern in the dark. A quick scan of the entry showed nothing out of the ordinary in the living room.

A wide aperture ran the length of half the room and entered a dining area of some sort. Arch could see the edge of a table beyond but little of the surface.

"Right behind you," Erin said quietly.

"We should have radioed Reeve," Arch said.

"He hears gunshots, he'll come a runnin'," Erin said.

Arch left his next thought unspoken—what if there was no time for shots?

Arch kept moving forward, each step throwing up a floorboard creak ominous enough to squeeze its way into any horror movie he'd ever seen at the drive-in theater near Whitsville. Any minute, he expected something awful to come crashing in through the window at him, claws and all.

He made the edge of the dining room entry and covered behind the wall. He caught his breath and felt Erin stack up behind him. He wanted to close his eyes for the next part, because the smell was truly awful and he suspected he knew what was coming next.

Arch turned the corner and pointed the gun into the dining room. There was a faint buzzing noise, a few flies that had made their way in somehow. They were sweeping in low circles around the dining room table, and the smell was dead obvious here.

Mostly dead.

There was a rib cage stripped of nearly everything, a skull cracked open and empty from what he could see, though the shadows hid the contents pretty well. Other bones were strewn about the floor and table. Lesser ones he suspected. He took another step and his shoe hit another skull; he only knew it because it skittered off and hit a table leg, then rolled back toward him. It came to rest in the glow from an uncovered window.

"Jesus H. Christ," Erin whispered from his side.

Arch didn't do blasphemy, but he thought about swearing here. Thought about it and swallowed it whole. Instead he reached up to his shoulder and cued his mike, radio formality all thrown out. "Reeve ... this is Arch. You're gonna wanna come next door." Arch took a look to his right, as though he could see through the wall and into the next house. "We're gonna have to search the whole neighborhood."

Chapter 6

Gideon didn't love the smell of the burgers frying on the grill, but it was what the diner served, so he was stuck with it. He actually preferred salad, which was a hell of an irony even for him to digest. The salad prospects on the diner's menu had seemed poor, so he just sat there, pondering the menu, waiting to see what happened.

He wondered, just briefly, if his reticence about burgers had anything to do with having "seen" and eaten so many heart attacks. He shrugged mentally and went back to studying his menu. If he was lucky, what he was here to eat would happen before he had to order, thus saving him both money and the prospect of eating something he didn't want to.

He glanced behind the counter as a waitress in her mid-fifties placed a little square of paper bearing an order onto a spike in the window that separated the area behind the lunch counter from the kitchen. He watched her, her grey hair tied back in a ponytail, her jeans a little too tight for what she was carrying underneath. She wore a peach blouse, and Gideon kept a close eye on her as she came back around the edge of the lunch counter, heading toward a booth in the corner.

He could feel it starting and knew she'd never make it. He watched her walk anyhow, caught the first hint of a stumble, and his hand went to his pocket immediately.

* * *

Linda Richards was in for a double today. She'd had a faint headache since she woke up that morning, but damned if that wasn't a consequence of waking up and forgetting to get coffee within the first hour of starting. The headache was in hour six of rearing its ugly head, though, and four cups of coffee hadn't done a thing to help.

The diner was buzzing like it always did during weekday lunch rush.

She was doing all she could to keep up, but she wasn't as young as the other waitresses. She'd heard 'em talk about her behind her back, but she was old enough to brush most of it off. She could still nail more orders than any of them could anyway, prissy little bitches. They wouldn't do half as well as her when their tits were sagging and their asses barely fit in their jeans.

She bumped an empty table mid-thigh as she passed, like it had just jumped out at her. She looked at it a little perplexed, and it blurred in her right eye. Not the left, just the right. Left was still clear. She tried to reach up to check her glasses, see if she'd gotten something on the lens, but her arms felt weak, like she couldn't lift them.

Her head was light, and she wondered if she could hear the blood rushing in her ears. She started to take another step, try to turn around to get back to the counter, but her legs faltered. The ground came rushing to her face, and she barely felt it when her cheek hit. The table she'd run into overturned, but she watched the whole thing like it was happening real far off.

She saw faint figures over her head, but they were out of focus, blurry. She couldn't move anymore. Not arms, not legs. Everything seemed to be drawing away.

The ceiling above was all white, lit by the grey day, and it blurred, bit by bit, until that color was all that was left of her world.

Everything else just faded away.

* * *

Gideon was out of his seat within seconds of her hitting the floor. It was so overwhelming, having her right there. It flooded his consciousness with the low buzz of what she was hearing, echoing as he heard it too. Her pain was sweet delight to him, all the better for his proximity. He got hard without prompting and jerked on the doorknob of the men's room with enough force to fling it open.

He could hear the cacophony of screams and cries behind him, the desperation of people unsure what to do next. Gideon knew there was no doctor that could save Linda Richards now, even if there had been one right there in the diner. She was past the point of saving, heading into

58   DEPTHS

death not twenty feet from where he was in the bathroom.

He shouldered into a stall, almost too overcome to bother shoving the lock into position. He whipped his fly down and started beating off, short strokes as the woman's last, dying senses came through to him in the bathroom.

He could feel her breaths coming slowly, her body fighting for the last ones, rasping for them ...

His breaths came in short gasps, hand working up and down in regular rhythm ...

He smelled the aroma of burning meat on the griddle as she smelled it ...

He tried not to breathe, the pungency of the old building's unclean toilet wafting up at him as he stroked his cock harder ...

The faint hum of people talking around her was like distant voices, whispering just out of sight ...

His breaths were heavy, in triumph, his essence threatening to explode out of his body the way he heard the heart pounding on some of those close to death ...

The bitter taste in her mouth was like acid working its way up from her last meal ...

He could taste the desire for it to finish, to come, to cum, to explode. It built inside, throbbing in his body. He looked down and could see through her eyes for one last second, the light fading into black. He stopped the movement of his hand and the shell of a penis ejaculated. It shot black fluid that spattered the white tiles, simmering as it hit. Drops fell on the toilet seat and sizzled, fell into the water and smoke wafted out.

He tried to control his breath, the steady, hard intakes of air that were just pumped into his essence and came back out again. It was pointless; he didn't need oxygen, but his shell made him breathe like a human, make the noise, take in the breaths, and his excitement caused it to speed up.

Gideon tilted his head back. He was still hard, still dripping. The sound of a drop spattering on the floor hissed and he shook his cock, trying to get the remainder in the toilet. He'd give it a few minutes, make sure it was all out before he put it back in his shorts.

In the distance, somewhere beyond the stall, he could hear the sirens coming. The sound made him hard again, and he took himself in hand and started to stroke up and down once more to the memory of what had just happened.

* * *

Erin was soaked in spite of her raincoat, drenched to the skin and surprisingly chilly for a summer's day. The summer had turned cold. Or maybe it was just what they'd found that morning.

Reeve called them all together inside the entry hallway of the Hughes house once they'd finished searching the street. They'd found one more house in the line that was filled with remains. This one was a house of bones, too, not a slaughterhouse like Corey Hughes's place. It still reeked, and she could smell it on herself through the plastic coat.

Or maybe it was just the smell of the Hughes house.

"This is fucking unbelievable," Reeve said as a member of the crime scene unit from Chattanooga went past them in a suit that was designed to keep the contamination of the crime scene to a minimum. Reeve seemed not to notice the stink eye that the guy gave them. "We've had more murders in this town in the last week and half than we've had in the entire time I've been alive." His voice quivered, his eyes were turned down in hard lines. "I'd give you all the 'not on my watch' speech, but the goddamned horse has already left the barn on this motherfucker, so instead I'm going to give you the 'find this cocksucker and let's pin their asscheeks to the wall' speech."

Erin looked over at Arch; he seemed desperately uncomfortable, like someone had put itching powder in his uniform. He shifted left and right, unable to keep himself still while Reeve was talking. She, on the other hand, felt no desire to do anything other than stand there frozen.

More dead than she could count. No clues. No sign of who could have even done such a monstrous thing.

"I want suspects," Reeve said.

"No one saw anything," Fries said with a shrug of his massive frame, jowls shaking as he turned his head.

"Don't give me that shit. Someone saw something," Reeve said, and put a finger up, pointing it Fries. "Something. A car. A person walking down the sidewalk. You can't tell me there's not some busybody in this neighborhood that didn't hear something." He turned and pointed toward the back of the house, where Corey Hughes was laid out. "You can't tell me he died without screaming while whoever did that to him … did it."

Erin had seen a bloody rag in Corey Hughes's empty, gaping cavity, and suspected he'd been gagged to keep him from making any noise while he was eaten alive or vivisected or whatever had happened happened. She'd seen similar rags in the other houses

It wasn't something she felt compelled to mention right now, though.

"I want suspects," Reeve said, a fury lighting his eyes. "We got a lot of new people in town lately." He turned to Arch. "What about that cowboy?"

Arch looked a little stunned. "He was with me last night until about nine."

Reeve leaned forward, eyes alight, jaw stuck out. "And after that?"

Shit. Erin coughed, and four sets of eyes came to her. "He was with me," she muttered.

"He's just an example," Reeve said. "Anyone else notice we got a shit ton of tourists in the last couple weeks?"

"Diner's been fuller than usual," Reines said, running a finger over his soul patch. "Thought maybe it was tourists."

"Tourists don't come to Calhoun County during summer," Erin said. It was true. They came during hunting season, hoping to get one of the wide-bodied bucks with a big rack that lurked up in the national forest around Mt. Horeb. "Not a damned thing to do here except hike, and most tourists go to the Appalachian trail for that."

"Well, there's sure as shit a lot of strangers here," Reeve said and pointed out the door, where the rain was still coming down. Erin could hear it on the roof. "And they ain't here for the weather right now."

"Maybe they're from England," Fries said with a low chuckle. His smile disappeared when everyone looked at him. "Sorry."

"Start shaking the trees," Reeve said. "Question everybody. Stop any cars that look suspicious."

"What if it's a local doing this?" Arch asked, and every head swiveled toward him. Erin had to blink a couple times.

"That's crazy," Reeve said. "We know everyone around here, and you'd think if someone was going to go around and completely eviscerate random people, we'd have had a hint of it before now—"

"Maybe not," Arch said, and Erin could tell he was holding his ground. His back was straight, his whole body was stiff. "Think of how many farmers we have around here. Serial killers often start with animals. Someone could have been practicing for years."

"What the hell are you saying, Arch?" Reeve was looking at him with narrowed eyes.

"I'm saying it could be anyone, so singling out strangers is kind of a futile strategy." Arch folded his arms, and Erin could tell by his posture he was done.

Reeve seemed to chew on this for a moment, looking at Arch in disbelief, like he wanted to say something but was holding back for some reason. Erin suspected it was because of race. If Arch had been a white deputy of the same age, Reeve would have taken his head off right then and there, called him stupid—to put it mildly. The problem was, the more Erin thought about it, Arch was right. She said as much.

"Corey Hughes looked like he'd been slaughtered, right?" she asked, and Reeve's red face turned to look at her, his eyes smoldering with rage. "Arch is right. We could have had a farmer ripping up his animals for years to practice up for this. It could be someone from here in Midian, or just the county. Or it could be someone from a neighboring county. Could be a total stranger from Colorado for all we know."

"Why Colorado?" Fries asked, his jowled face scrunched up.

"Just picking somewhere at random," she said. "Point is, we don't even know what we're looking for. This fucker, whoever he is, slaughtered three houses full of people. If he's some kind of cannibalistic sonofabitch and came for the meat—and the bones being picked clean mean he probably did—he's got a whole freezerful of it now, and we may not see him again for a while."

"Y'all been watching too many serial killer movies," Reeve pronounced, running a hand over his bald head. His face was lessening in its redness, expression softening. "I just can't believe anyone in Calhoun County would do something like this ... this ... atrocity." He said the word atrocity like it was worse than any curse he could have breathed. And since Erin had heard him casually throw out the c-word, he knew some pretty bad curses.

They waited in the circle until Reeve spoke again. "All right, fine. Maybe it is someone local. We need to keep an eye out for anything suspicious. We should troll through town on patrol at night, make our presence known. I want a light shined on every house. People are gonna go ape shit when they find out about this." He breathed out, almost sounded like he wanted to spit. "They may even send the news trucks from Chattanooga to cover this mess. This shit just doesn't happen around here."

"You know people are gonna be asking questions," Erin said.

"Yeah," Reeve said and ran his hand over his slick head again. "You're gonna be our department's official communications coordinator."

Bullshit, is what she thought, but caught herself before she said it. "That's not in my job description, and I'd be terrible at it." She saw him start to argue at the first part of it then deflated at the second half. Reeve knew she was a shitty liar. Couldn't keep a straight face during a poker hand for anything, they'd discovered that at the last department Christmas party. And that was without even any booze running through her.

"Yeah, you're right, dodging press questions ain't your forte," Reeve seemed to give it some thought. "Well, I'll have the wife handle it, maybe funnel the really important ones to me." He looked up at her. "I'll need you on patrol, then, helping pick up some of the slack."

She felt the rise of excitement. "I'll need a car."

Reeve scowled. "You can use mine. For now," he hastened to add.

"You need me to leave my keys behind so you've got something to drive?" Erin felt the rush of near-giddiness. Finally. One of the team, doing something other than answering phones, filing bullshit paperwork, managing time cards and fetching coffee.

"Uh ..." Reeve looked a little red in the face now, but for a different reason. "Nah, that's okay. I'll borrow my wife's car if I need to get around."

And he was calling her car a piece of shit. She sighed. At least she was moving up.

* * *

Arch hit the street as soon as Reeve was done with his inspirational talk. The direction he got out of it was basically to catch the guy responsible and keep an eye—and a lid—on things. There wasn't much more they could do, really, other than pull over anyone acting suspicious and look out for broken windows and such. It wasn't like they could go house to house, even in Midian. There were something like ten thousand people in the burg and surrounding area, after all, and that was a lot of doors to knock on. Even if they called in the cavalry and left the outlying areas of the county unpatrolled.

Which was a bad idea. Too much meth moving out there to leave it unobserved for long.

What he'd seen was still rattling in Arch's head, and the new car smell didn't come close to erasing the stink of what he'd gotten on him in those houses. He put the Explorer in gear and felt the pressure of the accelerator pedal as he pushed down. He took a breath and could almost taste the fetid, rotting smell in the back of his mouth. What he'd seen this morning was truly the sickest thing he'd ever seen.

He wanted to curse, but he didn't allow himself to say any of the ones that would have counted. To him they'd have been as rotten and unwelcome on his tongue as the smell of that house was.

Demons.

It all came back to demons.

He steered the Explorer along the rain-drenched streets of Midian. When he hit Old Jackson Highway, he took a right toward the Interstate. He needed to talk to somebody. It was pressing on him, Alison not really saying anything lately. Not that she would have been the one to talk to about this, anyhow. Demons were something so fantastical it was probably beyond his wife's comprehension.

There was no way in Arch's mind that what he'd just seen had been caused by a human being. Sure, people had done things like that in the real world, that and worse, he would acknowledge. But to come to Midian now? When it had just become a mystical hotspot and demonic tourist attraction? Surely not a coincidence.

He blazed past the Sheriff's Department office without even slowing down. He didn't habitually speed, but he suspected he would today. He'd need to hurry if he was going to squeeze this conversation in before he got back on patrol. Reeve probably wouldn't care where he was, so long as he was moving. Now wasn't the time to get caught taking a long lunch, that much was certain.

But there was a serial killing demon wandering the streets of Midian, eating its way through the populace, and that meant Arch needed to take action of a different sort than his standard patrols would allow. He needed help. An expert.

As he pulled into the parking lot of the Sinbad motel, part of him wondered why an expert on demon hunting would be staying here, but dismissed the thought without putting much into it. The sandy brown exterior of the motel wasn't much to look at and the inside was even worse, but it was almost all they had in this town. Almost.

* * *

Hendricks was lying on the bed, just savoring the pain that was racking him, when the knock came. He grunted and sighed, feeling his injuries come to him in an inventory as he rolled his way off the side of the bed into a crouching pose. He thought about answering with sword in hand, but it was daylight and unlikely that a demon was going to be attacking him now. He was more or less anonymous here, after all, having killed every demon he'd run across since coming to town.

Still, he pulled the chair his coat was resting on to within arm's length of the door before he even looked out the peephole.

It was Arch. He opened the door a moment later, not bothering to throw on a shirt. The sheriff's deputy made a low whistle that caused Hendricks to tilt an eyebrow at him. "You're all bruised up," the deputy explained.

"Though maybe you were admiring my physique," Hendricks said with a half-hearted smile as he headed back to the bed. "What's up?"

Arch's joviality disappeared like it was written in marker erased off a whiteboard. "We got dead bodies."

Hendricks cringed and not just from the pain. "Damn. Hazard of a hot spot, but I don't imagine it's ever easy to see people start turning up dead."

"We're not just talking normal dead," Arch said, and he crossed over to stand by the table. "We're talking eaten alive, nothing left but bones."

Hendricks nodded. No wonder the cop was a little touchy. That'd do it, all right. "There's a few strains of demons that like to eat human meat. How many dead?"

"Eight we know of," Arch said. "They got a whole family in one house."

Hendricks closed his functioning eye, racked his brain for what he knew. "They went from house to house?"

"Yep."

"Hmmm, eating their prey, hitting all in a line," Hendricks lay back on the bed and put his feet up. "Probably a pack of Tul'rore or a couple Spiegoth working in tandem." He opened his eye and tilted his head to look at Arch. "They weren't in the house when you got there?" Arch shook his head. "Probably the Spiegoth, then. They move around a lot, kinda strike a few targets of convenience, then they get lethargic for a while after that. Likely as not they're gorged, and they'll be under the radar for a few days."

"So ... what we do?" Arch asked. He was hanging on every word, Hendricks could see that.

Hendricks sniffed. His body smelled like the glue from adhesive bandages. He'd taped gauze over his eye, and the Plasticine smell of the adhesive hung heavy in his nose. "Well, we need to go hunting for their den. They're likely to choose something warm and damp." He looked toward the curtains, which were drawn, but he could still hear the rain outside and Arch was decked out in rain gear. "So, pretty much the whole area right now."

"Storm drains are starting to overflow," Arch said. "The Upper Caledonia River Valley is getting pretty wet. The reservoir up above Tallakeet Dam is probably pretty full at this point. That means the caves are probably beyond wet right now, probably getting to flooded. The water level is rising around here."

Hendricks stared at him blankly. "So?" he asked.

"It means that typical underground hiding locations, if you're talking about warm and damp, are out." The big policeman seemed overly stiff while pointing that out, like he was annoyed at being called on his explanation.

"Warm and damp doesn't mean underground," Hendricks said with a smile. "Caves are too cool. They'd hang out in a swamp, more like. Or a greenhouse, if they could find one to their liking." He glanced toward the closed curtains again, as though he expected them to be open or he could magically see through them. "The rain dropping the temperature?"

"Some," Arch conceded. "Probably low eighties."

"Yeah," Hendricks said, "they'll want somewhere hotter than the woods right now, then." He paused. "If it is Spiegoth."

"What do we do?" Arch asked.

"Come back when you're off work," Hendricks said, stretching on the bed. "Hopefully I'll be a little more mobile by then, because right now I'm having a time convincing myself to even go to the bathroom. Almost led to a tragic bed-wetting incident earlier."

"I probably won't be done until late tonight," Arch said, and Hendricks watched the deputy's face sag. "Reeve will keep us on until late. Probably even institute some overtime because of this, which ..." he flattened his lips and blew air between them, "... I always wondered what it would take."

"Okay, well," Hendricks said, trying to think it through, "I'm not gonna make it far without a car, not in this condition. Maybe we can go on your patrol together?"

Arch's face got rocky. "Probably not. If Reeve catches you riding along with me on a patrol right now, he'll throw a fit." Hendricks waited for the explanation and it came along shortly. "He thinks it's an out-of-towner that did this."

"Probably was," Hendricks said, trying not to take umbrage at the thought of a small-town sheriff taking aim on him or someone like him with an accusation like that. "But not a human out-of-towner."

"I tried to get him to look at everybody," Arch said. "Not get so myopic. Figured maybe if he'd broaden his search a little bit it might give him more opportunity to run up some blind alleys while we try and track down the real culprits, reduce 'em to a sulfur stink."

"Which leaves your cannibal serial killer murders unsolved. Might not be a bad thing," Hendricks said, focusing on the mauve/taupe wallpaper as he pondered it, "having people extra vigilant for a while. After all, depending on how long this hotspot lasts, they could be in for a lot nastier things than demons that want to eat them alive."

Arch's face twitched. "Worse? Worse than this? How?"

Hendricks told him. The big black lawman looked kinda pale when he was done.

* * *

Gideon walked through the rain, his skin still feeling like it was on fire, flush with heat of what he'd just seen. What he'd just done. It had been so close, so delicious. The cold rain battering him, soaking his t-shirt and cargo pants and chilling his skin, was easily ignored.

The taste of her death was just lingering on his tongue, like he'd gone out there and just licked her right in the middle of it. He could feel himself get hard as he walked, and he didn't care. That made it even hotter somehow. Being that close to the death drove the sensuality factor through the roof. He imagined himself walking out in the middle of the diner while it was happening. Fulfilling himself right there, his jizz spattering the checkered tablecloths and burning through them, smoke wafting in the air.

It was a pleasant fantasy, but that was all it was. The damp, humid air filled his nose as he walked over the highway bridge. Cars rushed past in the rain below, the noise of tires on a slick road reaching him far above. He looked over the side and wondered what it would be like to—

He'd forgotten his car at the diner. He looked back and could see it over there, the rental waiting in the parking lot. It was such a simple thing to drive a car, but he'd been so distracted he'd forgotten about it.

Gideon stopped and looked down to the interstate again. The traffic flow was steady. Semis raced past, minivans and cars in their wake. It was afternoon, and he'd seen the traffic level rise in the mornings with rush hour and in the evening as well. They were right there, traveling along at seventy miles per hour, a hundred lives a minute. So close he could reach out and touch them.

Almost.

A smile creased his face and he stared off the bridge then looked around. Cars were coming by only occasionally on the overpass. He had an idea. A solid idea, a good one. It maybe pushed the boundaries of what his kind normally did, but there weren't any real rules, right?

It wasn't like he was the first to cross this particular boundary, after all. He'd just never needed to in places like Chicago, or before that, Detroit. There were plenty of dead coming all the time in those places. Like New York in the seventies and eighties, before it got cleaned up. That had been like heaven. A handful of murders every day, plus all the deaths of natural causes. Now it was dried up and he was lucky to get one good kill per day. Chicago had been a boon for his kind the last few years. And it wasn't played out, but he'd fell the draw of the hotspot. Got sick of the snow, the summer, the streets.

The call of the hotspot promised something more. The Tul'rore that had blown into town after him seemed like they were going to deliver, too. It was entirely possible that other demons would come in, step things up, and turn it into a paradise like Chicago for a while, now that the Tul'rore were gone.

But until then, he was high and dry.

Watching Linda Richards die from a room away was a joy, and it had awakened in him a desire to experience it again. It was getting compulsive, and he wanted to reach down and take himself in hand, relive it—his most intense climax yet.

The rain kept coming down, though, and even though there was no traffic on the overpass, he knew better than to do it here. He didn't want trouble. Not the obvious kind, anyway.

It'd interfere with the plan he'd just crafted.

Gideon walked on, heading back to the Sinbad, back to his room. He'd go back to the diner and get the rental later. He'd need it around five o'clock.

A loud crack of thunder startled him, and he looked up. The rain was coming down in sheets, and the sky looked almost black to the east. Good. That'd be in his favor if it kept up like this.

He was so gleeful about his plan, about what was on his mind, that he almost didn't notice the Crown Vic with the sheriff's markings sitting just outside the Sinbad's parking lot. He tried not to be too obvious as he walked by, but he caught a glimpse of a blond woman watching the front of the motel. There was a sheriff's department Explorer parked in a space just outside his room, and Gideon started to get very, very nervous.

* * *

Erin was watching Hendricks's door. She hadn't followed Arch here because she'd made it away from the crime scene about ten minutes after he did, but she'd ended up in the same place as him, sure enough. She was just sitting outside the Sinbad's parking lot, waiting to see if he came out.

She asked herself again what the hell was going on, but no answer really came beyond the obvious. They were probably just talking about something or other. But what? It wasn't like Arch had run out here to tell Hendricks about her big promotion. Hell, she didn't even know exactly why she'd run out here to do it.

Okay, that was a lie. She'd driven out here because her BFF had left town before the curtain had even fallen on their graduation, and she'd done the slow draw away in the year since. Frequent texts became less frequent until they never really came at all anymore, and Erin had been left palling around with the other townies or her coworkers. None of them were really close. More like drinking buddies. Occasional fuck buddies, maybe. Very occasionally, lately.

Hendricks was the first thing to show up in a long time that had interrupted her monotony. This temporary field promotion or whatever was the second. Two breaths of fresh air in a stale town she had gotten a little bored of. So she was pissed at him for being all mysterious.

He was still the only person she could think of that she was actually excited to share this with.

What the hell was Arch doing in there? Why did he leave the scene of the most heinous murder in Calhoun County history and head immediately for a seedy motel to talk to a guy he had just professed not to know all that well?

Erin ran a hand over her face as the rain-streaked window of the Crown Vic blurred in front of her. What the hell was she doing here, anyway? Hendricks was just a guy she'd met less than two weeks ago. A guy she'd made some exceedingly stupid decisions with.

Still, she didn't put the car in drive and leave. She just sat there in the rain, watching the door to the motel, waiting to see if it would open.

* * *

Gideon circled around to the other side of the street where a gas station was damned near abandoned. He pushed in through the door and took a quick look around. Bored clerk behind the counter, not a patron in sight, no one filling up out at the pumps. The place smelled a little of mildew and the carpet squished faintly as he walked in. He went over to the candy, picked up something at random and went to pay for it. All the while he was watching the motel to see what the cop was up to.

She was just sitting there. He couldn't be sure from this distance, but it looked like she was watching the place. Maybe she was just watching the other cop car. Or maybe she was watching for him.

His mind reeled. What could they possibly be after him for? He hadn't committed any crimes, at least none anyone knew about. It seemed unlikely they'd already be on him for masturbating in the diner bathroom, even if someone had seen him. Besides, the cops hadn't even showed up to the diner, just the paramedics.

No, this was something else, and he was straining to think of what it could be. Maybe something to do with what the Tul'rore had done? They had left a hell of a mess, and surely someone had found it by now. Gideon frowned as he pulled out a dollar bill to pay for his purchase. Maybe they were going to try and pin it on him. He was new in town, a stranger, and didn't these small-towners like to do shit like that? Paranoid, xenophobic sons of bitches.

He stripped the wrapper off the candy bar when he was done paying, told the clerk to skip the receipt, and paused before walking out the exit door. "Hell of a storm," the clerk said to him from behind the red counter.

"Sure is," he agreed without thinking about it.

* * *

Arch left Hendricks a few minutes later, stepping back out into the rain from the shelter of the Sinbad motel's second floor overhang. It didn't help much because the rain was now coming sideways. It was a drenching downpour, absolutely soaking everything. The parking lot had been dusty before, the result of an abandoned construction dig just one lot over from the motel. They'd planned to build a restaurant there once, but that was before the recession caused the investment dollars to dry up. Arch didn't care much about that, except it might have been nice to have another place to eat in town.

He got in the Explorer and out of habit checked the rearview. There was a sheriff's car just behind him, out of the parking lot a little bit. He thought it might have been the sheriff's own and turned around to check.

It was. But Reeve had been back at the scene when last he saw him.

The answer took him only a moment to come to—Erin. He wondered why she'd come out here, but only for a second, because it was fairly obvious. Why she was waiting out here was a little more puzzling, until he thought about how things might have looked from her end. He'd taken off on patrol but ended up stopping off here first? He felt an uncontrolled grimace. This was probably going to require an explanation but not until later. He hated lying anyway.

* * *

Gideon watched the big Explorer pull out of the parking lot and head down the road back toward town. He waited, and sure enough, the Crown Vic pulled into the space occupied by the Explorer only a few moments later. The girl got out and knocked on the door that the other sheriff's deputy, the big burly black guy, had just come out of a minute before. It only took Gideon a second to remember that the cowboy had been in that room.

What the hell was the deal with the cowboy? He was a demon hunter but working with the law? Was he like a Texas Ranger? But for Tennessee, maybe? Was there even such a thing as a Tennessee Ranger?

He waited, staring out into the rain for a couple more minutes while he finished his candy bar. It didn't look like they were interested in him, in any case, so there was no reason to hole up over here any longer. He had some thinking to do, anyway. The rain was getting worse, and that was all to the better.

* * *

"So ..." Hendricks said as he sat back down on the bed. When he'd heard the second knock, he figured it was Arch coming back to tell him something else. It wasn't, and he couldn't decide if that made things better or worse. When he saw it was Erin, it sent a shot of butterflies right to his stomach, knowing he was going to have to answer questions he didn't want to. Her raincoat was filling the room with a mildew smell, like it had been with the department since the sixties and hadn't ever been cleaned. It wasn't making Hendricks real happy to be next to her.

"So ..." Erin said, and she sat down next to him. "What's the deal?"

Hendricks tried to figure out what he could evade on this one. "With what?"

Her eyes grew wider for a second before narrowing back down again, and her nostrils flared. He got the feeling this conversation might end up having to get cut short. It wasn't going to be pretty if it went that way. "What were you and Arch talking about?"

Hendricks laughed a little under his breath, and he saw her react again. Well, it wasn't like he could tell her the truth. His logical mind was shouting the answer to him, and he was connecting the dots pretty easily. She was pissed at him anyway, so she was going to have to go. "You're not my girlfriend, so don't go playing like you're a jealous one."

He could see that one land, like he'd slapped her, and he felt a hard stab of remorse that he fought to keep off his face. This was why demon hunters didn't get involved. He'd been stupid to get barnacled onto her as tight as he had so quickly. He wanted to kick himself, but her response did that for him. "Fuck you," she said.

It was simple, it was direct, and it was followed by her standing, turning her back on him, and walking out with a slammed door that echoed in the room. He stared at the closed door, a wet palm print from where she'd grasped it presenting a dark spot, like she'd bled on it.

He put a hand up over his mouth, clenching his teeth tightly shut, and rubbed his face. Like he could somehow compel the words he'd said back in there and replace them with something smarter, something that wouldn't have torpedoed the fuck out of the first real connection he'd felt with a woman in five years.

* * *

Gideon passed the blond sheriff's deputy as she stormed out of the room next door. She didn't even notice him, standing by his door, about to unlock it. She'd clearly had a tiff with the cowboy, and that made him feel even better. This really didn't have anything to do with him.

He smiled as he unlocked the door and strode into his room, dripping on the carpet. He didn't even bother to lock the door, just started stripping off his clothes. He kept his hands off himself, though, tempting as it was to relive the joy of watching that waitress die of the stroke again. He was going to save himself for tonight.

Because tonight was going to be even better.

Chapter 7

Erin raced down the road in the sheriff's car, sirens flashing. She didn't need them on, it was a violation of regulations, but by God, did it feel good. She could feel the anger burning through her, pushing her foot down on the pedal as she headed out of town. The Crown Vic smelled of fast food, like the thousand burgers probably consumed in it were still sitting on the back seat.

Erin was a little surprised she'd gotten that heated that fast with Hendricks. The bastard had pushed a button, though, and she'd let him have it and stormed off. She could feel the tension across her skull and back, a forming storm of a headache, maybe one of those migraines she got every now and again. It was hard for her to believe some drifter passing through and making a stop of her was worth that much aggravation.

She kept the pedal down, though, the rain coming down in sheets across the windshield, and headed back toward town. There were a thousand mysteries about Hendricks running through her mind, questions that she still wanted answers to even though she'd told him "fuck you" pretty clearly. It was itching at her, causing her stomach to rumble. Or maybe that was just the lack of breakfast combined with the coffee doing the talking.

She kept on into the rain, the trees barely visible on either side of the road, not really caring where she was going.

* * *

Arch had wanted to go home. Getting around two o'clock he started feeling the urge, like it was a normal day and a normal shift. He'd started around seven, but he wasn't clocking out at three this time around. He'd exchanged brief words with the sheriff a couple hours earlier, and it had been made clear to him that he was on a double today, straight through until eleven.

He'd left Alison a message telling her, but she hadn't called back. This was not a huge surprise, given how much talking she'd done of late when they were at home. She was clearly of a mind to give him the silent treatment, and he was not all that sure of how to deal with it just yet. It was tough for him to wrap his mind around the idea that she'd gone so cold so quickly. She'd always been the warm half of the two of them, always the lovey-dovey one, while he was the cool, collected, aloof one. It worked for them. She brought him out; he stayed pretty well clear of entangling with anyone but her.

He was sitting in his Explorer on the side of the road close up by town. He had gotten eight speeders in the rain so far today between patrols. The weather just pounded the Explorer, gusts of wind rocking it from side to side every now and again. Arch sat there, smelling the new leather with every other breath, fingers drumming on the center console, listening to the roar of Mother Nature's fury and thinking how it compared to Alison's.

They'd fought before, of course. They'd been together since high school, after all; it wasn't like they'd been perfectly happy every day of it. Usually it stemmed from Arch making some emotional misstep. Alison was sensitive, had lots of feelings and emotions. She was a songbird, shifting emotional states and making it clear by whatever tune she was warbling at the time. When she was mad, it came quick and obvious. When she was happy, the music was lilting, her affection was sweet and perfectly timed—and a little over the top.

But this dead silence for over a week? This was new.

Arch glanced at his dashboard clock for the first time in three minutes. He thought it had been an hour, but when he checked it was only three minutes. He sighed then wondered how quickly he could get to Hendricks and start hunting the things that had done this. They'd made a heckuva mess, after all, killed a lot of people. There was no way the sheriff's department was going to be able to stop these things, whatever they were.

Next to that, mending fences with his wife just didn't seem quite as important.

Or so Arch told himself as he kept thinking about what to do next, wondering if he should just go get Hendricks now. All the while, every here and again he felt the urge to drive to Rogerson's to see Alison, but he snuffed that thought like a curse word about to pop out of his mouth.

* * *

Gideon was done waiting. He'd watched the old clock by the bed, the jointed red numbers gradually creeping up. It was four forty-five and he couldn't wait any longer. It had been hours of anticipation stifled, of desire pent up. He hadn't gone this long without gratifying himself in a year, probably. And that was after an orgy of shootings had been followed by a serial killer torturing someone to death. He'd been exhausted.

The Sinbad's rooms were extra shitty, and it didn't take him long to change into some new cargo shorts and a fresh shirt. Lingering around on the bed in nothing but boxers hadn't made his resistance of temptation any easier. He liked to play with his belly a little, though, since it hung over his waistband some anyway. He pulled the cargo shorts over his hairy, spindly legs and zipped up, getting a little thrill at the thought of the zipper coming down again soon.

He walked out the Sinbad's door once he was dressed, pausing only to grab the short blade knife he kept in his luggage. He'd never needed it before, but he carried it just in case. He pocketed in his shorts and stepped outside, his shoes still squishing with wetness. That didn't really matter, though, because within a minute of walking out they were soaked through completely, and he couldn't hear the squishing over the sound of the rain pouring down anyway.

He headed across the parking lot, back toward the diner where he'd left his car. He was walking faster than usual and could feel himself twitch with anticipation.

Soon. It would be so good. Very, very soon.

* * *

Lerner was sick of sitting around the hotel room. It was nice enough, but he'd been staring at the white walls forever, taking only occasional breaks to look out at the rain. The whole place had the smell of a hotel, that scent of laundry done in bulk and the aroma of dry air recently run through a vacuum's filter. Lerner was standing, pacing, trying to think. "Any word of activity?"

"Nothing," Duncan replied, staring straight ahead at the wall. It's what he did. Like he was trying to somehow memorize the colors to add to his palette for later use in something appalling for his wardrobe. "All's quiet. Everyone's probably bedded down with this storm going. You know demons are like cats; they don't like getting wet any more than humans do."

"My kingdom for a Vernosh attack," Lerner mumbled under his breath. He glanced back at Duncan. "Anything, really. A Urunock infestation."

Duncan shuddered slightly. "You don't mean that."

"Probably not that one, no," Lerner agreed. Urunock were just nasty and could burn through even the shell of a demon in seconds. "Something, though."

Duncan just sat there. It's how he did what he did, Lerner knew. Communing. Taking messages. Sensing. It didn't make it easier on Lerner, though, whose mind cried out for someone to talk to, someone to spitball with.

"You know," Lerner said, "I've always wondered about hotel maid service—"

"No," Duncan said.

Lerner sighed. These days were the worst.

* * *

Gideon paused at the car. The sky was nearly black, like night had fallen early. It did that shit up north, in the winter, but this was Tennessee in summer. Dark clouds were blotting out almost any trace of light and the rain was falling in sheets, making it hard to see more than a few feet in front of him. He was buffeted by the wind, which had gotten much worse since he'd walked back to the motel earlier. There were even a few moments when he worried crossing the interstate bridge that it was just too nasty for him to pull off what he'd planned.

But then things would clear for a few minutes and he'd start to think he could pull it off again. It damned sure didn't hurt to try.

He approached his car from the rear. He thought about giving himself extra deniability, maybe stabbing the knife into one of the tires, but that meant he'd actually have to change it. What were the odds a rental car tire was going to get traced back to him anyway? They were all the same, weren't they?

He found he didn't really care. The cops had enough going on right now, probably still dealing with what the Tul'rore had left for them. They'd had to have found it by now, right? If things got too intense, all he'd need to do was to vanish for a while. He knew there were explanations, ways to get out of it, but he found the thought of what he was going to do way more exciting than what would happen if shit went wrong.

Planning was for other people. He needed to act, now.

Gideon got in the car, felt his wet clothes soaking the cloth seats. He started her up and wheeled around to make the left turn out of the parking lot. This part was something he'd thought about over and over.

He looked down the highway, saw traffic getting heavier. There was a break in the downpour, just enough to allow him to see a hundred feet to his left and right. Cars were moving slowly, the rain too much for their windshield wipers to handle.

He pulled out when he had a chance, and after about thirty seconds he hit his emergency blinkers. The steady clicking sound was drowned out by the rain hammering the roof of the car.

Gideon pulled onto the shoulder of the interstate bridge, taking care to position the sedan so it obstructed part of the right lane. He parked on the far side of the bridge, trying to place the car exactly where he needed it to be.

A semi roared by, heading toward the entry ramp for the southbound lane. Gideon's car shook, but whether it was from that or the rain, he didn't know. He held his breath and counted to five, watching his rearview mirror to make sure he didn't get blindsided by another truck as he got out.

He opened the door and the cold deluge hit him immediately. The temperature had dropped from the steady rain, and now that it was after five p.m., the sun was lower in the sky behind the clouds.

He was already soaked and not getting much wetter, though, so out he sprang and started walking around the car. When he reached the trunk he fought to put the key in and unlock it. The yellow hazard lights beat out a steady rhythm of flashes, occasionally coinciding with the lightning overhead.

Gideon smiled when he opened the trunk. He looked back as a minivan passed by on the highway bridge. He couldn't feel the people inside, but he knew they were in there. Just like below him. He couldn't see the cars traversing the interstate beneath him, but he knew they were there.

Gideon pulled back the matting in the trunk of the sedan, exposing the spare tire. It was bolted down, and he removed the tire iron that functioned as the crank for the jack as well as the bolt loosener and starting to unscrew the tire. The rain continued to douse his back, droplets rolling down his nose. He ignored them as he worked, wet shirt hanging off of him. He could feel it riding up behind him, exposing the small of his hairy back to the motorists passing by.

He didn't care.

When the bolt popped free, he lifted the tire and dragged it out of the trunk. He kept the tire iron in one hand and carried the tire in the other. He might need both. After a moment's thought, he put them both down, went back around and grabbed the jack and the restraining bar out of the trunk as well, setting them against the concrete barrier at the edge of the bridge.

When he came back around after shutting the trunk, he could barely feel the rain anymore. His skin was on fire with the anticipation. He busied himself while he waited for another semi to pass, the engine noises barely reaching him through the rain.

After that, he could see no one coming from behind him on the bridge.

Gideon took a breath of wet air and picked up the spare tire. He could feel the weight of it as he hugged it close, heavy in his hands. The treads pushed into his hairy arms, and he could feel the gaps with his fingers. He took one last look to make sure no one was coming over the bridge, and then looked down over the edge to the interstate below.

Cars and trucks whizzed by every few seconds. The rain was still pouring, but the visibility was good enough for him to see a couple hundred feet below. A Buick was emerging out of the curtain of rain just at the edge of his visibility, and he timed it purely by gut. He tossed the tire over the edge of the bridge.

* * *

Jerry Bryan was on his way home from work. He was just doing his shift down at the distribution center a few miles down the highway, passing through, one exit to go, and counting the miles till home. The rain was an absolute hell today, the blacktop on the interstate slicker than shit. Jerry knew a little about this stuff, and he would have sworn the oil and sediment that made it all so dangerous was supposed to wash off in the first half hour or so of a good rain,

But they were on day two, and it was still slick as hell.

Jerry had been on a couple long shifts the last few days. Lots of heavy lifting. Lots of carrying. Lots of packages going out the door. He had only had the job a month, the warehouse opening a boon to Calhoun County. Jobs were getting rarer out there, especially ones that paid eleven bucks an hour in this area.

The rain was just slamming down, running across the windshield like someone had poured a bucket over the glass. The wipers were at max but barely keeping up, giving him a clear view for a second before they got overwhelmed again.

He was trying to keep his eyes on the road, but his head was drifting to think about the baseball game he'd stayed up to watch last night. The Braves had taken the Phillies in the ninth, and there was—

Jerry saw a shadow overhead and then something hit the windshield. It shattered, spraying him with glass before whatever it was dropped in and bounced off the steering wheel to hit him in the face.

It was like he got smashed in the teeth and nose by a concrete block. The pain was immediate, and Jerry slammed his foot onto the brakes on instinct. His head was spinning and he could feel cold rain mix with warm blood on his face. The car jerked and locked into a spin.

Jerry felt the world shift around him as the Buick's back end swept around. The rain kept coming and he saw a faint shadow ahead of him through the blood that was dripping into his eyes.

* * *

Gideon listened as the tire fell. The sound of it hitting the Buick's windshield was like a gunshot. Like he was back Chicago again.

Gideon had already reached down and grabbed the jack. It was heavy, the steel edges biting into his eager hands. He was already shaking from the thrill of it. Now it wasn't just anticipation, it was the beginning of the stirrings. He could feel Jerry Bryan suffering down there, and he saw the semi truck emerge from the rain below and knew that the driver wouldn't have enough time to stop, even if he tried.

Still, he flung the jack anyway and waited with shaking hands and his breath held to see what happened.

* * *

Jerry ran a hand over his face to clear the blood, and that turned out to be a real mistake. He saw the black shape emerge from the haze of the downpour. It was just out his window, at a perfect forty-five degree angle to his left. He heard the brakes squeal and the engine make a noise like it was downshifting, but that stopped a moment later when something hit the truck's windshield.

He saw the spiderweb cracks like it was happening in slow motion, then the whole thing caved in like someone had chucked a brick through it. The next thing Jerry saw was the windshield of the truck disappearing as the front grill of it became his whole world, and he barely felt the impact when it slammed into his Buick.

* * *

Gideon could hear the collision, the semi eating the Buick with Jerry Bryan in it. He'd felt the trucker actually die from the jack hitting him, the steel edge catching him in the temple and breaking his skull open. It didn't happen immediately; these things never did, but he was rendered insensate and unable to stop the truck. Gideon knew that even if a paramedic had been on scene with a doctor, the trucker—named Jack Benitez, lately out of Miami, Florida—would still be dead in minutes.

It was locked in, now. Nothing to do but wait and savor that one. Those were the best, in Gideon's opinion.

82   DEPTHS

Of course, the one that Jerry Bryan had experienced, the mostly sudden type, those were good, too. Jerry Bryan was just barely dead now, splattered on the road underneath Benitez's semi. Parts of his brain were still working, even though they were spread out over several lanes of traffic. Bryan wasn't anywhere near conscious now, though, so most of the satisfaction was gone.

Gideon had the tire iron in his hand and heaved it over at a delivery van detouring below to avoid the accident. The left-hand lane was still mostly clear. Mostly. Gideon's throw ended that, though, as the delivery driver caught it right in the chest. Gideon had the demon strength, fortunately, though he rarely had cause to use it.

He chucked the last piece, the brace that kept the tire mounted in the trunk, and aimed it a little farther out.

* * *

Sarah Glass was in a hurry. She was supposed to start babysitting fifteen minutes ago, but her mom had been late in getting home from a shopping trip to Knoxville. They shared the car on days when Sarah had to work, like today. It was a tough gig, and Sarah knew she was in the shit as she drove along way faster than she should with the rain coming down like it was. Her fingers danced over the keys of her iPhone, tapping out a text message, a hurried apology to her boss, Anna, who was actually a very lovely lady to work for. Anna had given Sarah a fucking amazing bonus last Christmas, which she'd used to get her first tattoo, a little flower on her ankle.

Sarah was texting one handed, one eye on the road and one on the screen of the phone. The car was warm, the heater working overtime to banish the chill the rains had brought it. This shitty weather was going to totally fuck with her plans, because the kids she watched would be confined indoors tonight. On nice nights, she could take them out to the park near their house. On a night like this, it'd be episode after episode of *Bubble Guppies*.

Anna wouldn't get home until after midnight, because she was on a permanent hybrid shift at her job. That was the name of the game. Sarah would put the kids to bed at eight-thirty, work on homework until eleven and fall asleep on the couch or watch TV until her boss came home, and then she'd drive home to sleep a little longer. Anna had long offered for her to stay, but it was fifty-fifty whether Sarah would even get to sleep in the house. It was hard to sleep anywhere but her own bed, the smells of Anna's home just not-quite-familiar as her own. The couch was kinda shitty, too. It had a spring that always poked her in the back.

She sent the text and tossed her iPhone into the cup holder. Shit shit shit. Anna would be late to work, that was the bottom line. Fuck. She felt bad, but she didn't have her own car, and her goddamned mom just *had* to make a shopping trip to the mall in Knoxville today. Why? No reason, really. It's not like she didn't already have plenty of clothes. It's not like she didn't know the weather was going to be shitty. It wasn't like she didn't have plenty of warning that traffic was going to suck on the way back—

Her furious irritation with her mother was interrupted by something smashing into her windshield. It broke the glass and hit her in the arm, stunning her. The words, *did that just fucking happen?* ran through her head. She tried not to swear around the kids, but fuck, sometimes that was hard.

She was still processing what the fuck was happening when she realized that there was something ahead. It took her a second to realize that both lanes were totally blocked under the overpass at the Midian exit. A semi-trailer looked like it had smashed a car on one side, and a blue van with something written on the side had neatly smashed into the bridge support between the opposing lanes of traffic on the left. The van was wedged sideways and no more than three feet of space remained between it and the accident in the right lane.

Sarah hit the brakes but knew she was far, far too late. She slammed into the van with her mother's Subaru. There was no windshield to shatter now. As the hood of the car crumpled before her she barely felt the impact of her face against the side of the van, smashing her skull into oblivion.

* * *

Gideon staggered back toward the rental now. He checked to make sure no one was coming over the bridge before breaking into a run toward the driver's side door. He reached it and threw it open, yanking his pants down around his ankles the moment he was in. He could feel them, so close—Jerry Bryan, Jack Benitez, Sarah Glass. The delivery driver was still alive, barely, but there were other cars piling up now. The ones who were too dumb to slow down, driving seventy even with the visibility as low as it was, like they were fucking invincible. They caused the mess to grow by leaps and bounds.

Gideon's hand was on his cock and rubbing now, the desire and heat rushing through him. He'd been hard since Jerry Bryan had died first. Now it was just a ongoing rush of arousal, his ejaculations coming one after another with an intensity from the closeness of the deaths. He felt another car slam into the pileup and a family of three died nearly instantly. He exploded and felt the hot ejaculate splatter his legs and drip onto the floor mat. He could hear the hiss, the smoky smell of the plastic and carpet filling the car.

Another semi slid in below, a long-haul driver named Sam Worthen dying as his sternum cracked on the steering wheel. He hadn't been wearing a seatbelt. Worthen writhed in his cab in immeasurable pain. Gideon felt himself come again, his fingers sticky with the burning ejaculate, stinging his flesh as he continued to stroke himself to the feeling of the man thrashing around in the semi below.

Gideon was on fire now, his hand moving up and down his shaft in a symphony of pain and pleasure. There were voices crying out below him, souls leaving their bodies while screaming in agony and terror, and he was drinking it all in. The thrill was almost more than he could manage, and just when he'd catch his breath in his throat, another car would slam into the pile-up, another life would flee its earthly shackles, and he'd explode in an orgasmic burst that would send another ejaculation spitting from his tip.

He could smell the cloth seat burning, but his eyes were closed tight as Gideon savored the sensations around him. He was feeling those souls come through him. Their cries were like the sounds of his lover, their moans of pain as near to his lover's orgasm as he'd ever experience. They filled him up, these twenty dead and counting, and it was more powerful than anything he'd ever felt before.

The feeling started to taper off, this most intense of pleasures, this hottest fire of arousal he'd ever felt. His hand was covered over with his own expulsion, and the car stunk of sulfur and smoke. It was thick in the back of his throat. He could barely move his hand over his cock, it was so sticky and taxed. His wrist shook with the strain of what he'd been doing, and looked down at the clock.

Five fifty-four.

He felt a surge of panic and hurried to wipe his hand on the passenger seat. It burned and sizzled as he did so, and then he fumbled for his keys. He looked down and his seat was burned through, a clear swath of nearly two inches seared right through the cloth, then yellow insulation burnt black in the hole. He could see a little had even burned through the floorboard of the car, though the hole was small enough that it didn't concern him. It was maybe as wide as his pinky. Little spots of black on the steering wheel marked the places where particularly violent ejaculations had melted the pleather.

Gideon fumbled for his keys and felt the metal bend under his touch from the remnants of his ejaculate still on his fingers. He turned the key in the ignition hurriedly then removed his hand to see his fingerprints melted into the plastic head of the key. Fuck fuck fuck.

He looked back and could see some minor traffic on the bridge. There were lights flashing below, police and paramedics and firemen on the scene that he hadn't even noticed in his orgasmic engrossment. He hurriedly put the car into gear, feeling the metal of the gearshift melt beneath his touch. He looked down quickly and noted his pants and underwear were mostly intact; the instrument panel had a few spots where the plastic displays had melted because of his emissions coming to rest on them.

He put foot to pedal slowly, not wanting to arouse any suspicion. He was just a lookiloo, he told himself. Just someone watching the chaos. Or at least that's what they'd think at first. He'd need to be gone by the time that they realized otherwise.

Gideon steered the car over the bridge and crossed into the left turn lane. He got onto the freeway, heading south toward Chattanooga. He'd ditch the car somewhere down there, switch to a different rental company and get another one before returning to Midian.

Why come back? he asked himself. He'd done something new here, experienced his most intense session yet, better even than that one a year ago. But if he tried to replicate it again, it probably wouldn't go so well.

But the excitement! The raw excitement of moving from letting things happen naturally, lying back passively and expecting death to come to you, around you, from watching at a distance to being up close, right there, and even MAKING IT HAPPEN—

No, that was a rush he couldn't forget. It was a new high of arousal for him. He felt his hand shake as he guided the rental down the on-ramp to the interstate below. There was no traffic, none at all.

Gideon smiled wider as he cranked the car up to seventy. The rain hammered the windshield, but he didn't care. He had to come back. He was going to re-experience this moment in his motel room later tonight, over and over.

And then, after he was good and worn out, he was going to take some time to build his excitement again—and figure out a way to do it even bigger and better next time.

Chapter 8

This was a sick fucking day, Erin reflected as she stood in the rain, looking at the mangled pile of cars under the interstate bridge. She was still wearing her rain gear because the shit soup was still pouring down. She was the only one of the sheriff's department presently on scene, but there were a few Tennessee state troopers there and more on the way. She'd seen the latest one pull up a few minutes ago, siren blaring over the downpour and blue lights flashing, throwing up gravel while churning up the shoulder.

Erin was basically watching at this point, left to supervise the more prosaic of two evils that had happened in Midian today. It was a bitch of a coincidence that the largest multi-vehicular accident in Tennessee history should happen on the same damned day as the discovery of a mass murder, but she had only the barest of suspicions about that. It was something that was nagging at her as she stood there in the rain, waiting for the tow trucks to clear things out enough that they could divert traffic up onto the off-ramp temporarily. They'd closed the interstate an exit back and everything was flowing through Midian proper now. That'd make the downtown shop owners real happy and piss off the homeowners.

She felt a cold that went way beyond the chill the rain had brought as she stood there on the shoulder, the gravel crunching beneath her shoes as she shifted from left to right foot and back again. She studied the remains of the accident and tried to figure out how it had happened. It was enough of a jigsaw puzzle she honestly wondered if she'd ever be able to figure it out before conceding that no, she probably wouldn't. Maybe the brains at the Tennessee Highway Patrol or even the National Transportation Safety Board would figure it out.

But for now, she just stood there, watching them try and manage the scene. And it was a hell of a scene to manage.

Colonel Donald Ferris of the Tennessee Highway Patrol worked his way over to her as he had every few minutes in a more or less standard orbit. His wide-brimmed hat was state trooper standard, and he'd come from district headquarters to oversee the shit fall out from this wreck. He was an older man, grey shot through his hair, he carried a few extra pounds and seemed to be of the same stripe as Sheriff Reeve. He walked plenty upright and was doing his damnedest to be courteous, Erin could tell that much.

Whether that was because he was just wired that way or he was treating her different because she was a young woman, Erin didn't know. Didn't care, either, so long as he didn't cross any lines.

"Ma'am," Ferris said, doffing his hat slightly and getting himself wet in the process. Erin found a little amusement in that. Very little, but on a day like today she'd take it.

"Colonel," she said with a nod. She didn't bother to doff her hat. Not that it would matter at this point; her hair was soaked anyway.

"We found some … unusual things here," Ferris said without much preamble.

"How unusual?" Erin tried to keep her cool, but inwardly she could hear her heart thumping louder than the raindrops on her head.

Ferris gave a kind of shrug. "We found some things in places they shouldn't be. A spare car tire that we can't match to any of the vehicles in the collision. It's pretty mangled since we pulled it from under the semi at the head of the crash, though. A car's jack in the cab of one of the big semi trucks; kind of out of place there. A bent-up tire iron that looks like it might match the jack." Ferris's hat was sluicing water off as he talked to her, and she could tell he was raising his voice to be heard over the rain.

"So what do you think?" Erin asked, pretty sure she knew what he was going to say. It seemed obvious enough to her.

"I hate to jump to conclusions, but it looks like this might have been intentional," Ferris said, looking no more bothered by the news than if he'd just told her he had to pick up a gallon of milk on the way home. He pointed up to the highway bridge above them. "Someone may have thrown some things down to try and trigger an accident."

Erin wanted to be sickened by the thought of that, but she'd already seen much worse just today. "What do we do next?"

Ferris shook his head. His khaki shirt and green pants lost some of their luster under the clear plastic rain gear. He was one cool customer, Erin thought. "Nothing you have to worry about," Ferris said. "I've got my forensics people bagging evidence, and we'll get 'em back to our impound for investigation." He scratched his cheek with long fingernails yellowed by tobacco. "Department of Transportation and NTSB might get involved with something of this scale."

That sinking feeling in her stomach was getting worse by the minute. "You'll keep us in the loop, right?" Erin asked.

"Yes, ma'am," Ferris said, and doffed his hat again. She watched water drip down his collar and he made a face. Any other day, under any other circumstances, she might have found it amusing. Today was not that day.

* * *

Arch felt like he was snowed under. The call about the multi-vehicular catastrophe had come in a couple hours ago, and part of him wanted to rush right out there, but dispatch—played currently by the sheriff himself, still at the Hughes house crime scene—had told him to sit in town and keep writing tickets between patrols.

He was doing this now, stuck in place along Old Jackson Highway with about a million cars crawling along in front of him. The traffic shunted from the shut-down interstate was plugging Midian's main thoroughfare, a string of headlights that went for miles and miles, with very little movement.

Arch had the itch under his skin, sick of the smell of the Explorer's heater, tired of hearing the slow hum of the engine idling and the rain tapping on the roof. He'd heard of Chinese Water Torture and was sure as he could be that it had to be employed in some manner in Hades. He wanted to drive, but he was trapped in a parking lot on the side of the road, waiting for the mess to clear.

He wasn't likely to be writing many tickets here, either, unless it was for parking violations.

He considered riding the shoulder and probably would when the time came for his next patrol in a half hour or so. Until then he was stuck in place.

It only took a short time for him to connect the dots and start thinking of that as a metaphor for his situation with Alison, with the demon hunting he was undertaking and all else. By then the itch to move had settled into a slow, painful burn, and he just ground it out for as long as he could—another five minutes—before he flipped on the siren and lights and headed down Old Jackson Highway toward the Sinbad motel.

* * *

Hendricks was a little surprised at the knock on his door. He figured Arch would be a lot later getting there, taking at least a few more hours on patrol. That would have suited Hendricks just fine, because he was sleeping through the dulled sensation of pain racking his side and the ache around his eye. The good news was that he was able to open his eye slightly, and his vision was clear. Holding it open for long resulted in some discomfort, though, so he shut it until such time as he'd need it.

Hendricks made his way across the chill motel room, hip still bothering him. He rubbed his face as he got up, a bleariness settling into his head. The heater wasn't working; he'd already checked before he'd gone to sleep. Some kind of seasonal bullshit, he figured, to keep customers from cranking up something they shouldn't and letting it run all day and night. Probably affected the motel's narrow profit margin.

Hendricks opened the door and said, "Weren't you expecting you quite this early." He reddened after he said it, because he'd spoken without seeing who it was. It didn't occur to him—like he was some kind of moron or something—that it could be anyone but Arch. It could have been Erin, back to apologize for what she'd said, or to rip into him again.

It wasn't, though. It was a woman, but most definitely not Erin.

"You were expecting me?" She had her head cocked to the side, the very picture of curiosity. Her eyes were studying him fiercely. Her hair was long and red, not a hint of moisture on it even though she wore no raincoat. In fact she didn't seem to have much of anything on besides a tank top covering her small breasts and a pair of blue jeans that looked tight on her thin figure.

"Ah, no," Hendricks said, fighting for the words. "I was … uh … actually expecting someone else." The eyes were piercing, watching him.

They felt like they were boring into him, trying to drag out an explanation. "I thought you were Arch."

"No," she said, almost singsong, still staring at him, a little less blankly now. "I am not Archibald Stan."

"Well, yeah," Hendricks said at last, "I know that now, Starling."

Chapter 9

"What's going on here?" Arch asked as he strode up to the door of Hendricks's motel room. That red-haired woman, Starling, who'd saved his and Hendricks's bacon a week or so earlier, was standing out front, looking at him with those eyes. Arch found them kind of intimidating; it was like they anchored on to you and didn't let go. He looked and realized he couldn't tell what color they were even in the light.

Hendricks stood in the door, leaning against the jamb. The cowboy looked like he was still half-asleep to Arch. "I was about to ask her when you came walking up, actually." Hendricks was in a black t-shirt and jeans, and his face still looked like all heck, but his swollen eye was partially open, so that was an improvement at least.

"You got any idea what's going on out there?" Arch jerked a thumb toward the direction of the interstate, just a few hundred feet away. The rain had started to slacken, waning into a drizzle now. The parking lot of the Sinbad was under a good quarter inch of water even still, and Arch had passed more than a few drainage ditches on the way here that were full and still rising.

Hendricks looked past him and shrugged, looking surprisingly nonchalant for a man whose face bore all the signs of being caved in only last night. "Rush hour?"

"Murder," Starling breathed, and it really wasn't much more than a breath the way Arch heard it. It was low and throaty, hissed out as she narrowed those striking eyes. He watched her, and if he'd had to make a guess, he'd say she wasn't too happy about the whole situation.

"Murder?" Hendricks had a scowl in place now. "Not those Spiegoth again?"

Arch waited a second to see if Starling would explain. When she didn't he took a step closer. "What do you mean, murder? Last I heard it was a multi-vehicular accident—"

"Open your eyes," Starling said, and her face was back to the normal, placid expression now. "Too much death. Too much blood."

Arch let out a breath he didn't know he was holding and shot a glance at Hendricks. "It does appear awfully coincidental. Can you prove that something's going on with this wreck?"

Starling cocked her head at him, and Arch suddenly felt mighty small. "Do you need proof? Can you not find it in you to take such an extraordinary occurrence on faith?"

Arch looked back at Hendricks to find the cowboy looking back at him. "Don't look at me for faith," Hendricks replied quickly, his arms folded over his black t-shirt, "but that does seem like a big coincidence, this coming after those murders."

"What kind of demon would kill people this way?" Arch asked. It was a good question to his mind. "The ... Spiegoth?"

"No," Starling said, and she paused to look away as though she were sniffing the air. "There are no Spiegoth in this town. Yet."

"Yet?" Hendricks said, coming off the door frame. "Does that mean they will come eventually?"

Starling turned to look at the cowboy, and her answer was glacially cool. "All things will come here eventually."

"If it wasn't a Spiegoth that did this," Arch said, trying to wrap his brain around the whole situation as he leaned in to rest a palm on the facade of the Sinbad motel, "what did?" He wondered if he'd recognize the demon name were she to spit one out.

"Hard to say," Starling said after she appeared to ponder his statement for a moment. "Come with me." She turned without another word and began to walk through the parking lot. Arch noticed for the first time that she wore cowboy boots too, and then turned to look at Hendricks, who was still poised in the doorjamb, looking like he was still deciding whether to move.

"I guess we should go with her," Hendricks said as he met Arch's gaze. "You know, at least see what she's got to say." He waited a minute before saying anything else and Arch did too, trying to figure out what protest seemed reasonable under the circumstances. "We do owe her our lives."

"Yep," Arch said, but he could hear the resignation in his own voice. Nodding, he turned to follow the red-haired woman across the parking lot. She did not look back to see if they were following her.

* * *

Lerner was about to hit the breaking point when Duncan opened his eyes and finally spoke. "Something's going on. Something big."

That was music to Lerner's ears. A tapping noise in the depths of the motel's rank air conditioner was slowly driving him batty. Even the shade of the walls was violently disagreeable at this point. "What and where?" he asked as he grabbed his keys off the dresser at the front of the room.

"Toward the freeway," Duncan said, unfolding himself from the wood and cloth chair that was one of a matching set sitting in front of the motel's window. He gestured vaguely, pulling his suit coat off the back of the chair. It was one of the milder ones, a deep purple one that looked almost navy in low light. Duncan seemed to have made an effort to coordinate it with his tie. Lerner let it pass.

"I'll drive," Lerner said, shocking neither of them. He liked to be in control. Driving gave him time to think, which probably annoyed Duncan, but who cared? Duncan, probably, but Lerner didn't. He slapped the door with an overly enthusiastic rap of the hand as he passed through and held it for Duncan.

The rain was slackening off. This was a good thing. A sign of better days to come, hopefully.

* * *

It didn't take Gideon long to get another rental. He had a bank account with a lot of money in it, the byproduct of years of taking money from the accounts of people who didn't need it anymore. He waited until they were dead, and using that little bit of contact he had with them as they were passing him, took an ATM number here, a bank account number there, a passcode or credit card or social security number every now and again. He always got a complete sense of them as they passed through and him, so it seemed a shame to let their money go to waste when he was clearly in need.

And he was in need. In more ways than one.

The drive back to Midian was hell, a slow, dragging ride. The rain was starting to lighten up, for which he was thankful. He was still trying to figure out how best to top his last move, and it wasn't coming to him. Feeling the twenty-eight people who had died that afternoon had been the single most thrilling and satisfying experience of his entire earthly existence.

And it had been a long existence.

He'd lingered near wars before, but it was tough to predict a battlefield and get there quickly without exposing himself to danger. During most of World War II, he'd stayed in the U.S., just feeding off the slow misery and dying that naturally happened in the cities. Things had picked up in the sixties and seventies but had started to quiet down in the nineties. New York was boring now, so passé, and even some of the hotspots hadn't been very exciting over the last few years. Sure, New Orleans and Detroit could be counted on in a pinch, but where was the excitement in that?

No, Gideon needed something new. What he'd done this afternoon by spurring the accident, that had been new. That had been thrilling. That was still making him tingle in the right places. He fought to keep his hand off himself as he got a reflexive erection just thinking about it as he drove. He'd jerked off again and again as he took the rental to Cleveland to ditch it, making a bigger mess of the car. By that time, who cared? It was already fucked. And he needed to get it out of his system so he didn't fuck up the new car.

He figured he'd have some excitement reliving this one, but then he'd be spent. The urge would start rising. The thirst for something greater would start to build, and just jerking off to the same old souls spilling the same old blood would lose its thrill. He needed a new mountain to climb. Metaphorically, of course.

He just had to find a way to kill lots of people in a massive hurry.

And it was that thought he entertained as he kept driving down the interstate, back to Midian.

***

"Where the hell are we going?" Hendricks asked as he and Arch hurried to catch up with Starling. His whole body was still aching, in spite of having taken a couple Percocet that he had from the time when he'd broken his arm. He'd been holding onto them a year or so, knowing that, given his profession, he'd need them eventually. He didn't really like to take them unless he had to because they fucked with his body, making him sleepy and shit. He was probably at the tail end of the effect, but he still wanted to just sleep. Not much chance of that.

"This way," Starling said, just a little ahead of them. Hendricks watched her go and marveled at her ass. It wasn't bad, all out on display in her tight blue jeans. She hadn't been wearing those last time, had she? He didn't think so, but it was tough to remember. Seemed like she was mostly around in the darkness and turned up when he was in a scrape, which didn't exactly lend him to paying attention to her choice of wardrobe.

Hendricks shot a look at Arch and adjusted his hat, tipping the brim back and out of his eyes. He liked wearing the cowboy hat, liked the feel of it, liked the fact that he used to be able to hide the switchblade in it before he'd handed that off to Arch, but it did occasionally get in the way. Arch seemed not to notice, keeping his attention on Starling ahead of them.

There was a little bit of a scent trailing in Starling's wake, though, Hendricks had noticed. It wasn't exactly sweet, but it wasn't bad. Kind of nice, really. He'd been in a car with her the week before and hadn't noticed it. It wasn't like any perfume he'd ever caught a whiff of before. Maybe something new.

They headed on up the bridge over the interstate, following the slight grade up. Hendricks looked to his left and saw the road closed ahead, like they'd just shut the damned interstate completely down. What the fuck?

The whole damned bridge was shut down, actually, no traffic either way. Hendricks kind of boggled at it, and looked down the on-ramp again to see a shit ton of blue and red lights down on the interstate. His head involuntarily leaned forward, like he was a duck about to peck the ground. He could feel his jaw fall open.

It was damned mess of epic proportions. Ambulances, cop cars— mostly the multicolored mess of Tennessee Highway Patrol, he could tell at this distance, and wreckers, dragging cars away. "How did I miss this?" Hendricks asked.

"The painkillers coursing through your blood have dulled your senses," Starling answered without turning around. Her long, red hair swept as she moved, sashaying with the natural motion of her body. "I am surprised I was able to roust you out of bed."

Hendricks shot a look at Arch, who gave him a sidelong glare. "They're prescription," he told the cop.

"Yours, I hope," Arch said.

"They're mine," Hendricks replied. Arch looked a little put out, but then he'd looked like that a lot lately. That should maybe have worried Hendricks more, but he was still feeling drowsy.

"Over here," Starling said, approaching a yellow line of police tape. There was a man in a Tennessee Highway Patrol uniform covered by a rain slicker waiting there, eyeing them cautiously. Arch nodded at the man and the trooper lifted the tape so that Starling could pass, followed by Arch and then Hendricks. He didn't say anything, just followed Starling's ass in those tight jeans.

"Here we are," Starling said and stopped about a quarter of the way up the bridge on the shoulder. The ground was still damp beneath them, but at least there wasn't a flow of water running down the bridge.

Hendricks looked over and saw that all the police presence was down below, buzzing around like bees on a damned honeycomb. He could see a few stretchers covered over with white sheets and it stopped him. He knew all too well what that meant. "Damn," he breathed.

"What is this?" Arch asked, drawing Hendricks to look back onto the bridge instead of over the edge to the catastrophe below. He took a few steps closer to them. Starling was standing upright but looking down. Arch was bent over, his fingers extended toward the ground as he reached down to touch the road.

"Do not do that." Starling was bent double in a second. She caught his shoulder, pulling Arch back up.

Hendricks got over to them and looked down at a little puddle of black goo that looked like oil had fallen on the ground. He cocked his head and started to ask Starling what was so important when he saw it.

The goo was burned into the pavement.

"What the fuck?" Hendricks asked.

"It's oil," Arch said, frowning. Hendricks could hear it in the cop's voice.

"No, it's not," Hendricks said. "It burned into the pavement before it stopped." He squinted to look closer. "It's like an acid or something."

"It is an emission," Starling said.

"Seems like that'd be the sort of thing a carburetor is supposed to catch," Hendricks said. He tried to put amusement into the way he said it, not really sure if it came out like it was intended.

"It is an ejaculatory emission from a male demon who feeds on the death of humans for his own emotional and physical gratification," Starling said, and by the time she got to the end of what she was saying, her utter passivity was disturbing as hell to Hendricks. "A Sygraath."

There was a beat of quiet as Hendricks waited to see if Starling would say she was joking. He was pretty sure she wasn't the joking type, but ...

"Excuse me?" Arch asked.

"Was something I said unclear?" Starling was looking at Arch with a hint of curiosity, her head cocked at him.

"I think it was the part about a demon ejaculating," Hendricks threw in. He looked at Arch and shrugged. "Demons ... uh ... do that?"

Starling gave him a cool look, her head tilted at him. "Demons are fully capable of sexual activity and enjoyment and frequently partake in said activities with both their own kind and humans."

Hendricks looked up to see Arch holding his head, like he had a headache. Leave it to the puritan to get shut down when they needed to discuss something important. "So ... you said this guy—demon—Sygraath—feeds on death. But he had an emission—like, an orgasm emission, like a cumshot—here?" He waited for Starling's subtle nod. "So he was here ... uh ... beating off?"

"So it would seem," Starling said.

"And he killed these people," Arch said, finally getting his head back in the game. Hendricks had been ready to clap him on the back to get him out of it. "Killed them so he could get his ... kinky thrill?"

"That appears the natural conclusion," Starling replied, to Hendricks's mind still amazingly neutral, especially since she'd just posited a scenario in which a demon had killed people in order to get off. Then again, he wasn't sure he'd seen her express a single emotion yet.

Hendricks felt his stomach churn at the thought of that, and he took an involuntary step back from the demon's ejaculate. "So this guy jerked off right here on the side of the road? Like, out exposed, where everyone could see him?"

Starling shook her head, and her hair still looked lively, fire-red in the dull light. "He was most probably in a car. I would speculate that his emission burned through the automobile and came to rest here on the pavement before it lost its heat and settled." She looked from him to Arch. "It is, however, still highly toxic to humans."

"So," Hendricks asked, something tickling the back of his mind, "if you said that demons regularly have sex with humans, but his spunk is fatal to us ... how does that work?"

Starling cocked her head at him, and he realized it was her expression of choice. "You of all people should know that demons do not all care about whether their actions harm humans." Hendricks felt his gut clench tight when she said it, and he said nothing as she went on. "However, not all demons have such adverse effects in their sexual activities. Just some types."

"Okay, I've heard enough," Arch said, and there was a raw sort of disgust in the cop's voice. His body was held at an angle, like he was about ready to haul off and hit someone. It made Hendricks glad he was standing a few steps away. "So we've got a murdering bunch of demons slaughtering their way through town, we've got some pervert demon who's ..." he lowered his voice, "... pleasuring himself while causing massive accidents." His face was stern, angry. "This is out of control."

"Agreed," Hendricks said, and wandered over to look over the edge of the bridge at the chaos below again. "I've got work to do."

"Both of us do," Arch said from behind him. "We need to find these things and start putting an end to them now."

Hendricks looked back. "Don't you have a shift to finish?"

Arch let out a short exhalation through his nose that reminded Hendricks of a bull snorting. "I'm supposed to serve and protect, remember? Far as I'm concerned, fixing this list of problems is priority one. Pointless patrols through the community and traffic cop duty can wait. Let's go burn this scum."

Hendricks nodded and shot a look at Starling, who waited next to Arch. "You got any ideas where we can start looking?"

Starling walked toward him with slow steps, until she was standing beside him and looking over the bridge at his side. Her expression flickered as she looked down on the scene below, like the muscles in her face were twitching. "There are ... possibilities," she said.

"All right," Arch said and turned to walk away. He was walking back toward the motel, and Hendricks could already see there was an itch in the deputy's britches, a definite urgency to his step.

"Come along," Starling said. She started back toward the motel as well. Hendricks just followed her.

* * *

Erin saw Hendricks look over the bridge from where she stood below. It was getting damned chilly, and she was occasionally stamping her feet, just trying to keep warm. She didn't like to admit it, but she was a freeze baby and hated the winters in Tennessee. This was like a slice of autumn and it was way too damned early.

Still, the amount of chill she felt was doubled when she saw Hendricks look down and survey the scene. It was hard to miss his big cowboy hat, even if she hadn't recognized his face. She could see a couple other people with him—Arch, that was obvious. Even if the big black lawman hadn't stood out in a crowd because of his height and build, his skin color coupled with the uniform he wore would have given him away.

She wondered what the hell Arch was doing bringing Hendricks to a crime scene, and then she saw the redhead with them and it made her even more uneasy. The redhead was of a reasonable height, and when she sashayed up next to Hendricks, Erin felt her stomach drop. The woman was a looker, without a doubt. Pale as death itself, but pretty; high cheekbones, a well-sculpted face.

Erin wondered who she was. It definitely wasn't Arch's wife. Alison was all too familiar to her. She wasn't wearing a uniform, so it seemed unlikely she was with the THP. Not in that tank top. And why would she be hanging out with Arch and Hendricks right in the middle of a crime scene?

None of it made a damned lick of sense, not one damned lick.

Arch disappeared behind the bridge's concrete safety rail, hidden away from her sight. But Hendricks and the redhead stayed there until Hendricks came closer, looking over the edge of the bridge. The redhead joined him a moment later.

She didn't know if it was the burn of jealousy she felt, exactly, but there was a definite what-the-fuck factor to the emotions that were following her swirling thoughts. It wasn't like Hendricks was in town to work. He didn't have a job, she knew that. He didn't even have a damned car. He was like a bum, except he had money and smelled way better, most of the time.

Erin saw the redhead turn, and start off down the bridge, and Hendricks was just a step or two behind her. Any closer and if she tripped he'd fall right into her twat.

Which, for all she knew, he already had.

* * *

Lerner was waiting at the far end of the closed-off bridge, behind a police cordon. He usually didn't let those sort of things stop him, but there was a whole assload of Tennessee state cops in the area, and he wasn't looking for entanglements with the human world's version of a justice system at the moment. He had enough other shit to worry about, frankly, without antagonizing the Tennessee Highway patrolman standing guard just a few feet away from him.

The rain was gone but the clouds remained, the dark skies overhead hinting that there'd be more later. Lerner didn't care, really, other than he didn't like to get wet. He'd heard on the news earlier that the entire Caledonia River Valley—what he figured was this town and maybe the whole county—was at risk of a flood, the water getting high on some dam up the river.

Lerner had other problems. He sniffed and could smell it, even this far off. He could see a motel and a gas station on the other side of the closed-off bridge over the interstate and knew that what he was smelling was closer to that end of the bridge than the one he was on.

"Emission," Duncan said, and Lerner could hear him sniffing as well.

"What are you thinking?" Lerner asked.

Duncan shrugged. "Some type of soul-eater getting ambitious about drumming up more business. Probably a Sygraath, based on the emission." He sniffed. "A really horny one, judging by how much is on the ground there."

"How do you figure?" Lerner asked.

"I think it burned through a car," Duncan said, and Lerner could still hear him sniff. "Some traces of melted metal, cloth, carpet. Given the number of bodies visible over the bridge, number of cars, it was a hell of a lot of dead to feed on."

There were a few people past the line, a local cop from what Lerner could see, a tall black man. He had a redhaired lady and a guy in a cowboy hat with him. The wind picked up and Lerner could feel it tickle the flesh of his shell. Chilly. "What's up with them?" he whispered to Duncan.

"Hmm," Duncan replied, huddling beneath his navy jacket. He squinted in concentration as Lerner watched him. "Couple garden-variety humans, possibly of the demon-hunting stripe, and—" He stopped when he was looking at the woman. "Um."

Duncan didn't say "Um," at least not in Lerner's experience. "'Um,' what?" Lerner asked.

"She's ..." Duncan seemed like he was trying to hone in on her, closing his eyes. Lerner watched as his face squinted in concentration, like he was squeezing out a turd. His kind of demon didn't really do it like that, though, preferring to excrete through the mouth when necessary, and only every four to five days at that. "She's a blank. It's like she's not even there."

Lerner could feel his eyes widen, which was his customary expression of surprise. "What do you mean she's not there? I can see her."

"I can see her, too," Duncan admitted. "But I can't feel her. It's like she's hollow, or a dead zone or something."

"What does that mean?" Lerner asked, and he actually reached over and touched Duncan on the arm, felt the smooth fabric of the suit beneath his fingers. He could tell it was purple even in the low light. Dammit.

"I don't know," Duncan admitted. "I've never run across that before."

Lerner watched as the cowboy and the cop started walking away to follow the redhead. What kind of being would fool Duncan? They'd been around the block, hadn't they? They knew their shit.

Still, the redhead kept walking, and Lerner kept watching her. Duncan too, he saw out of the corner of his eye. Clearly they were onto something here. "Demon hunters," Lerner said, "and something else. Something that's got you confused."

"Yep," Duncan said. "Let's get back to the car. See if we can find a detour to the other side of the interstate so we can get a closer look. Maybe it'll help me figure her out."

"Yeah, okay," Lerner said, and they both turned to walk back to the sedan. "I don't like the sound of this, though. You're not getting a little addled by being here for so long, are you?"

"Dunno," Duncan said with a shrug. Taciturn bastard. Lerner cursed him for it as they got in the car.

"I've often wondered about the long-term effects of being on earth to our kind—" Lerner started.

"Just drive," Duncan said.

Didn't even want to talk about it. Annoying son of a bitch. Lerner put the car in drive and hung a U-turn back toward town.

* * *

Arch wasn't exactly stomping along, but he could feel the excess vigor in his step. He wasn't enthused, that was for sure, but he was moving with purpose. Each slap of his shoe against the wet pavement was like a thundering wake-up call. The cool breeze blowing in his face was almost like a reminder that he was heading into the wind—metaphorically speaking. Literally, too.

Which was something he should have been doing before now.

There was a smell in the air, too, like oil on pavement, maybe from the wreckage below. It was strong, and the low hum of activity from the accident was buzzing in his ears. Part of him wanted to feel guilty. The other part already did.

He heard the thump of boots behind him and turned to see Hendricks jogging to catch up. He was passing Starling now, and she barely gave him a glance as he went by to fall into step next to Arch.

"Something on your mind?" Hendricks asked.

Arch could feel the tightness in his arms as he swung them. He was feeling the urge to hit someone, right now. "Just a little upset is all."

"Not at me, though, right?" Hendricks asked. Arch caught the half-smile.

"Not right now," Arch said. "Gimme a few minutes, I might come around to you. Your coming to town hasn't exactly been a harbinger of the best of times for me." Which was true, Arch reflected, though he wasn't sure how much he blamed the cowboy for this. It wasn't like Hendricks had intended to turn his world topsy-turvy. Arch frowned. "Why would it matter if I was mad at you? We have a job to do."

"I don't know," Hendricks said with a shrug. "I don't like to go into battle with tension between me and a squadmate. Makes things damned uncomfortable."

Tension wasn't something Arch paid much attention to, but he felt his face turn sour as he thought of Alison. "Well, do me a favor," Arch said, "put your big boy pants on and deal with it. We've got bigger things to worry about than me hurting your feelings."

"I'll be fine," Hendricks said, and now Arch could hear the stiffness in the cowboy's voice. "Just trying to resolve any problems before they get serious." They took a few more paces and hit the thin patch of grass that separated the Old Jackson Highway from the Sinbad's parking lot. "So, what's in your craw?"

"I'm not really in a mood to be sharing feelings," Arch said with blistering impatience.

"Not now?" Hendricks asked.

"Probably not ever," Arch said and had to admit that was honest. Talking feelings was not his way. It was awkward enough on the rare occasions when he did it with Alison.

"Huh," Hendricks said as they crossed the Sinbad's wet parking lot. It was like walking in a puddle, and Arch could feel the water splashing into his socks. They were already wet, but this was just making it worse. "Seemed like back there on the bridge you made some kind of fateful decision."

Arch didn't give him a searing look but only because he was already focused on other things. "Just decided to start actually doing my job instead of worrying about whether my boss thinks I'm doing my job."

Hendricks was quiet for a pause, and Arch was happy enough with that. Then the cowboy had to speak again. "Well, okay, then. What are we doing now?"

Arch felt his whole body tense again as he paused next to his Explorer and hit the button to remotely unlock it. "There's a lead I've been thinking about but haven't followed up yet."

"No time?" Hendricks asked.

Arch looked back at him evenly, tried to keep from showing any irritation. He wasn't really irritated at Hendricks, anyway. "No. Just wasn't sure it was worth following up. Besides, until now it's not like we've had a shortage of demons to chase." He felt an urge to lean against his car, so he did, and then felt the water droplets resting there soak his shirt. He sighed. "Remember those demons that busted up my apartment?"

"Yeah," Hendricks said.

"One of them was a woman who I'd arrested before, named Amanda Severson." He tried to brush the water off his sleeve, but it was already soaked in. "I've got a last known address for her, just outside of town a ways. I figure we probably killed off all her roommates, if she had any—"

"But you don't know for sure," Hendricks said, and the cowboy was nodding. "Not a bad idea. Especially since we're out of leads. If nothing else, we might be able to catch a demon and get a line on what's going on around here."

"See, that's what I was wondering," Arch said, nodding along, starting to feel like this might not be as desperate of an idea as he'd feared, "the demons, they're social enough that they know what others are up to?"

"Some of them," Hendricks said, and the cowboy made for the passenger door. "But hey, if nothing else, we'll punch some more sulfur-stink tickets out of town, and that's never bad, right?"

"Well, if it doesn't get us closer to solving this problem, I'm not sure it's the best use of our time."

Hendricks seemed to think about that for a minute. "Well, let's ask—" The cowboy's head swiveled around, and it took Arch a second to realize he was looking around for someone. Someone with red hair who was nowhere in sight. Arch heard Hendricks swear and ignored it, just like always. What the cowboy said on a regular basis would have gotten Arch's mouth slapped until his jaw was broken when he was a kid. "She does that all the damned time," Hendricks said.

"Would have been nice to get a little direction from her," Arch said. "Seems like she knows what's going on here better than we do."

Hendricks frowned. "Seems like a lot of people do. Doesn't that bother you?"

Arch shrugged and headed around the front of the Explorer to the driver's side. "Could be worse."

"Oh?" Arch heard Hendricks say as he opened the door and got in the car, careful not to hit the door of the grey sedan parked next to the Explorer. It hadn't been here when he'd driven up, he was pretty sure of that. "How so?" Hendricks asked.

"We could be as in the dark as my boss," Arch said. "Or Erin." *Or Alison*, he didn't say. But he thought it.

* * *

Gideon was back in the motel. He was wheezing, lying on the bed, his gut out and heavy on him. It felt like it was squeezing his essence out from the sheer weight his midsection, but it felt like that all the time. The TV was on in the background, where some local weather forecaster was predicting more rain. Gideon thought about the sky on his drive back from Cleveland and didn't exactly die of shock at that.

The feeling of what had happened to him on the overpass that afternoon was still lingering. He was too exhausted to do anything about it right now—like relive it for pleasure—but it was a kind of euphoric afterglow that he could get used to. His head was filled with lightness, and so was that spot in his chest where he imagined a heart might be if he'd had one.

He was still thinking ahead, though, reaching his feelers out. This feeling wouldn't last, after all, and he'd need to be on to the next one soon enough. That was a problem, though, because he couldn't feel the next one anywhere on the horizon. And he was trying. Stretching his mind out, expanding the radius.

There had to be something out there. Anything. A coronary. This was the south; weren't people fat here? He knew he'd read that somewhere.

Someone had to be dying of a heart attack soon.

He stretched his mind along toward the hospital, like fingers dancing over a bedspread trying to get to a nightstand just out of reach. He did finally feel it, could get a basic sense of the souls there, but there was nothing moving. He knew they were there, but that was it.

No one was dying.

He took a ragged breath and rolled to his side on the scratchy motel comforter. It smelled like stale cigarettes even though he was in a non-smoking room. It had never been dry like this in any of the cities he'd lived in. It had occasionally been like this in the days when he traveled between cities, back when he did it by bus or even horseback, a hundred years ago.

The problem was the damned county was just too sparsely populated. He didn't know how many people were within his reach, but he knew the two biggest cities nearby, Knoxville and Chattanooga, were just too damned far away. They weren't even close to within his grasp.

He felt the first throbbing of pain in his head as he pondered this possibility. He could hear a noise outside, the first sounds of rain starting to come down again. Gideon crossed to the window and looked out at the parking lot. The cop car was gone, for which he was thankful. The sole lamp illuminating the parking lot showed nothing but a flooded puddle over the entirety of the pavement.

Gideon narrowed his eyes as he looked at it, something scratching at the back of his mind. He let the curtain fall back into place and grabbed the convenience binder that some maid had left on the dresser. He opened it up to the local map that they'd thoughtfully enclosed on page five.

Gideon scanned over it until he found what he was looking for and started to crack a smile. Maybe. Just maybe. If that was really set up the way he thought it was, it would surely let him kill people. A whole lot of people. Maybe more than anything else he could devise, short of a nuclear bomb.

But first he'd need to take a car ride to see if what he was envisioning was even feasible.

* * *

Erin was back in her car because the rain was fucking coming down AGAIN. The THP was sorting shit out anyway, and that colonel was already off the scene, presumably to file a report with his superiors. Erin watched the wreckers moving the cars out one by one, like they were deconstructing twisted metal sculptures. She shuddered when she thought about this particular statuary represented.

The morgue wagons were loading up the last even now, and she could see the bodies going into the bags in the rain, the steady fall of water wetting the ones still under white sheets. Red spotted the white, like paint splashed on pure canvasses. It had been unnerving enough when they'd just been shapeless things, but now that they were being drenched, they were looking like corpses under sheets again.

Erin hadn't seen any human dead bodies before. Until today, and suddenly she'd seen a mountain of them. The acrid taste of stomach acid reminding her she hadn't eaten was coupled in her stomach with the rumbling, churning feeling of disquiet. Part of her wanted to leave, maybe run up to the gas station or the diner up the ramp on Old Jackson Highway and satiate it.

But that other part of her—the one that remembered she was in the middle of her big chance—that part kept her ass anchored to the seat of the patrol car.

She tried not to think about Hendricks and the redhead, but it was defying her ability to keep it out. Like she was slamming the door on it in her head, but the thought was some abusive gorilla-sized offender, and it kept breaking though.

Well, okay, it wasn't really like that, but it wasn't good.

The thing that itched her the worst of all was that even though she knew she'd screwed up with Hendricks, even though she'd had it out with him, told him to go fuck himself, and was certain—to a T—that she'd massively fucked up by ever taking up with the cowboy—it STILL bothered her that he was wandering around a crime scene with some strange redhead.

And Arch. What the fuck was going on with him? Wasn't he supposed to be on patrol somewhere?

Erin was steaming and trying to figure out whether to just say fuck it and get something to eat when the radio crackled. "Fifteen, this is dispatch, what's your twenty, over?"

She started to reach for her shoulder mike. Fifteen was Arch's badge number, his call sign, and the voice was the sheriff's wife. Erin didn't say anything, though, and the same message was repeated twice more without a word of reply.

* * *

Hendricks was watching out the window with his good eye while Arch drove the Explorer. He had no idea where they were going, exactly, though it felt like they might have been following the interstate on a frontage road. He thought about asking, but Arch seemed more than a little touchy. Not that Hendricks could blame him; the sheriff's deputy had gone from a calm life one week to in-over-his-fucking-head the next.

Hendricks looked over and saw Arch with his cell phone in hand, the face plate lit up and buzzing. The deputy didn't make a move to answer it, though, and after a moment the light faded and then died.

Hendricks thought about letting it pass without saying anything, but his curiosity got the better of him. "Who was that? Your wife?"

"No," Arch said, and his voice was subdued. "My boss."

"The sheriff?" Hendricks asked, feeling a little bloom of nervousness. "Why wouldn't he try and reach you on your radio?"

Arch didn't react, just stared stone-faced at the front windshield. "Because I turned it off."

* * *

Erin's cell phone lit up in the falling dark and she scrambled for it, hitting the talk button almost before the caller ID told her it was Reeve on the line.

"Where the fuck are you?" Reeve barked.

Classy fucker. "Still out at the wreck," she said.

"Okay," Reeve's voice calmed down a little. "Thought the wife was having some trouble getting radio commands out. Did you hear that call for Arch a minute ago?"

"Yep," Erin said, and there was that itch again. She felt a desire to twitch, to bleed off some nervous energy somehow. "I heard it."

"Well, he's usually pretty quick to respond," Reeve said. "He's like our constant in that regard. You seen him?"

"Yeah," Erin said, and for a moment she pondered lying for him. Then she just figured fuck it. "He was up on the overpass here a few minutes ago with that cowboy friend of his and another woman—some redhead I've never seen before."

There was a full ten seconds of dead air. "Excuse me?" Reeve's voice was extra polite, extra condescending.

"You heard me," Erin said. It was probably the equivalent of spraying the man in the face with a cold hose, but fuck him too. "He was here, not twenty minutes ago. Looking over the scene."

"His ass was supposed to be on patrol in town," Reeve said, and Erin could hear his voice rise on the other end of the phone. "You see where he went?"

"Back toward the Sinbad," she said and felt that itch beneath the skin get a little worse, her face burning. With shame or something else, she didn't know. "That's where Hendricks is staying."

"Get up there and see if you can find him," Reeve said, and she could almost feel him reigning in some much harsher words. "Call me if you do. I want to talk to that—" Reeve cut himself off, she was pretty sure.

Just as well. Knowing Reeve, she could imagine what would have come next, and it was probably not anything that would have been flattering to Arch. Or his mother.

Chapter 10

Lerner had a few ponderous thoughts clicking through his head as they came around a bend in the road. They'd followed the frontage road down the highway for miles, watching the near-empty freeway through a wood and wire fence. One lane was moving just fine, heading north. The other was empty, presumably shut down by the Tennessee Highway Patrol. The rain was coming down lightly at the moment, which allowed him to see all that.

Really, though, to Lerner, it was like a perfect metaphor for life as a human. They'd be going along, and suddenly the road would be blocked. What would they do? Well, some would pull off and eat. Some would detour and hurry like hell to find the fastest way to get back on the road. Some would just pull off and give up.

No, that analogy didn't work. It was a shame, too; it had seemed so promising when he'd started it.

Lerner looked over at Duncan, sitting peacefully in the passenger seat, his hand resting on the handle that hung over the door. He'd never really thought about what that thing was called before. The emergency handle?

He started to voice this thought to Duncan when they came to a T in the road and his path ended at a stop sign. The car's headlights shone into a fence and an empty pasture beyond.

"Take a right," Duncan suggested.

"I'm not stupid, I know I take a right," Lerner said, giving Duncan a scathing look. Duncan just shrugged.

Lerner turned his head back to the road and his headlights illuminated a police cruiser as it passed in front of them. He caught a glimpse of the driver and passenger as they went by; it was the cop and the cowboy. "Hm," he said.

There was a pause. "Hm, what?" Duncan bit.

Lerner could feel himself smile. Duncan almost never bit on these sort of queries. "Is it serendipity that led us to the point in the road where we fortuitously picked that exact moment to argue, thus stalling us long enough to—"

"Shut up and follow them."

* * *

Erin slid a key into the lock of Hendricks's motel room door. She'd knocked and heard nobody, sitting there with the rain blowing in under the overhang and soaking her again. After that she walked in the seeping chill down to the manager's office, idling cursing the name of Lafayette Hendricks and wondering why she'd ever thought a man named Lafayette could even be attractive. The manager had been surprisingly compliant and quick to give her a key, which she'd dutifully taken and trudged back down to Hendricks's door. By this time, the hems of her pants were soaked again. Goddamned Lafayette Hendricks.

She pushed open the door and paused before crossing the threshold. She wondered a little idly why she was even going to these lengths; it wasn't like Reeve would have expected her to do this. Probably. She lived in the grey space between what she thought his expectations might be and what he'd told her to do. This fit neatly in there. Somewhere.

The room was dark, and the outside light didn't do much to help the situation. She fumbled to her left and then her right before finding a switch to flip. It made a crisp noise as it clicked up, and a light popped on in the corner.

What it illuminated wasn't much more than she'd already seen. Some ghastly red/purple/beige hybrid design on the wall that might have been wallpaper. Maybe. Beat-up furniture and threadbare chairs. A bed that hadn't been made. A bachelor pigsty with little in the way of possessions and even less in the way of cleaning. Didn't this motel have a maid?

She took a step, her wet shoes soaking the carpet. She closed the door behind her, taking special notice that her car was the only one parked in the entire front row. Wherever Arch had gone, it looked like he'd taken Hendricks with him. She nudged the door to the bathroom open when she reached it just to be sure.

It looked about like it always had, too. Towels on the floor, and one of them wasn't hers this time. Looked like Hendricks had declined housekeeping services for the day. Probably because he'd been hanging around for some reason or another. Nowhere to go, maybe.

His toiletries were pretty standard. She poked around in his toiletry bag but didn't see anything too outrageous. An aging prescription bottle of Percocet that was ready to expire, but otherwise just the normal Tylenols and ibuprofen one might expect from a ...

She picked up the bag again and rifled through it. Hendricks had ibuprofen, Tylenol and a couple other brands of over-the-counter pain relievers. She scrunched up her face as she looked at them then rattled the Percocet bottle before opening it. There were a handful left, which was odd on a prescription bottle nearing a year old. He could have just kept them in case he needed them at some point, or maybe he just forgot about them.

But why all the other pain relievers? She tried to probe her memory, see if she could recall him taking any. She came to the conclusion after a minute that he might have bought them today. He was in at least some pain, she had to concede. That bar fight didn't look like it had gone in his favor at all, no matter what he said.

She exited the bathroom, still frowning. The place had his smell, a kind of worn scent. Maybe a little bit of a hint of something from his boots, too, but it wasn't bad per se. Neither was it super attractive. He didn't seem to have much in the way of cologne, either, just his deodorant, which smelled all right. It didn't permeate the place like the smell of his boots did, though.

His duffle lay on the metal folding luggage rack in the open closet area. She gave it a quick rummage, but there was nothing save for a couple old, leather-bound books and a mess of clothes. She didn't spend much time on it and came to the conclusion that he was pretty boring in terms of his wardrobe. T-shirts and jeans, that was pretty much all he had. A couple of collared denim shirts for colder weather, with some flannels in there as well.

She was just about to put the books back in the bag when something stopped her. She hesitated and put one of them in the crook of her arm while she looked at the other. Neither was very big, maybe a little thicker than a Bible but smaller in overall cover size. She opened one of them and flipped to the front page, where her eyes felt like they were about to explode out of her head.

Disposition and Types of Unholy Creatures

She looked up, like she could just glance away for a second and come back to see the book was actually something totally normal, like *The Hunger Games*. In a leather-bound, super-old edition. She looked back.

It wasn't *The Hunger Games*.

She thumbed through the book, noticing the old paper pages and the even older-sounding way the book was written. Lots of "thees" and "thys."

When she got to the first illustration, that was when she really thought her eyes were going to pop out.

What the fuck was wrong with Hendricks?

* * *

Arch pulled the car off the road onto a moonlit country lane, the Explorer shuddering with every rut it hit. He had the window cracked just a little, cool night air circulating through the cab. The rain was coming in dribs and drabs, the windshield wipers slinging it off the glass every few minutes and giving him a clear view of the dirt road, grass growing up in the middle of it. He could hear the car whine as it bogged down on the loose soil. He squinted and saw that there was standing water in the tracks. Nope, that was not good.

"This road is all washed out," Hendricks said from across the cab. Helpfully, Arch was sure.

"I noticed that, too," Arch said, keeping a level tone. "The four wheel drive can handle it." He reached down and turned a dial on the Explorer's console, flipping it to "Snow, Grass and Gravel" mode.

They bumped along for another minute before entering a small copse of trees. The rain subsided as they went under the boughs, and appeared again on the other side as they pulled up to a trailer on blocks at the end of the road.

"A little slice of paradise," Hendricks muttered.

Arch nodded. The trailer was an older one, metal-sided and covered with rust. There was a place in the yard where it looked like there might have been a dog staked to a chain at one point in time, the ground torn up in a circle all around it. Grass had started to sprout there again, though, so the dog probably wasn't here anymore. Arch stopped the car and pulled the key out of the ignition, opened the door and let the overhead light blind him for just a minute.

The rain was down to just a patter now, and Arch could feel it sprinkle on his shoulders and head. The last embers of day were hidden somewhere behind the clouds, barely casting any light. A lone lamp hung from a wood pole out in the trailer's yard. Coupled with the headlights that were still aglow from Arch's cruiser, it shed enough light that he could see just fine.

The windows of the trailer were lit, like someone was home or had left a light on for themselves. Arch started to lead the way, but Hendricks ducked out in front of him, sword drawn. Arch started to throw the cowboy an ugly look but had to concede that might have been the right idea. "Be careful with that thing," he said.

"I've yet to stick a civilian with it," Hendricks said. His long, black coat fluttered behind him. The fluorescent light overhead gave it a greenish tinge.

They walked up the steps to the trailer together, the sound of the wood creaking into the night. Hendricks tried the door and it squealed, opening with a rattle.

Arch tried to look inside over Hendricks's shoulder, but his view was limited to a television sitting on an old table. His fingers clutched the switchblade.

The TV had a commercial on for some local dealership in Chattanooga, barking out its incredible deals. Hendricks swept through the door in a hurry, like his life depended on clearing through it.

Arch followed as the cowboy surged into the room. The smell of cannabis filled Arch's nose the moment he was inside.

"Clear," Hendricks said in a clipped tone, turning his body to the left. "Kitchen clear." Arch glanced over to see that in the direction Hendricks was facing there was indeed an empty kitchen, no lights on overhead within it.

Arch turned to look to his right and saw an empty room spread out in front of the TV. Hendricks had probably given it a once over when he came through the door, Arch decided, but it was definitely empty.

The hallway beyond the main room, however, had an open door that was moving slightly, like it just been thrown ajar.

"Hendricks," Arch whispered, triggering the switchblade and pointing toward the door.

"I see it," the cowboy whispered from at his elbow.

Hendricks took a step forward and the floor creaked like he'd put a thousand-pound weight on it. Arch wanted to shoot him a dirty look, but that really wasn't his fault.

The cowboy walked on, heading toward the narrow corridor that led along the right side of the trailer. It was dark back there, threatening to swallow the man in the black coat whole. Arch tried to follow a step or two behind, waiting to see if something leapt out at them.

Hendricks had to get all the way to the bedroom before something actually did.

Something hit the cowboy in the black coat just as he was coming through the door, slamming him into the wall with shattering force. Hendricks's sword was held high, and Arch knew he couldn't get it down to thrust it into the figure that had hit him.

The thing that hit him was a guy in denim shirt, as near as Arch could tell in the darkness. He hurried into the room to follow and something hit him in the ribs as he came through the door. He instinctively jerked the switchblade around and buried it into the flesh of the figure that had run into him.

A low stink of brimstone filled the room. A hiss of air and a dark flash illuminated a small bedroom, no more than eight feet squared. Black shadows lit around the edges by fire crawled over the shape that had hit Arch as the demon was ripped back into hell.

Arch started to fight his way forward to stab the demon that Hendricks was struggling with, sword still aloft, but another demon hit him in the side with a shoulder charge.

He knew it was a demon by the eyes. Even in the dark it was obvious, the glow. Like a red iris inlaid over blackness.

The demon had a shoulder buried in his ribs, and Arch could feel the ache from where it had hit him—same place as the last one had. He dropped his elbow on its head, landing it on a scruffy bearded jaw. He had a vague impression of long, raven hair that was curled. The smell of pot was thicker here than it had been out in the main room.

He could hear Hendricks fighting behind him now. Arch had fully turned to deal with his threat and tried to throw the demon off of him, but to no avail. He dropped another elbow and heard a grunt, but his arm with the switchblade in it was trapped low, beneath him. A strong demon arm had pinned his arm to his side, unable to move.

Arch drilled the demon with another elbow to the head, wondering if it was having any effect. He remembered the last time he'd wrestled a demon in close proximity. It hadn't been the most fun thing in the world, and he was doubtless overmatched.

The memory of his last time fighting one of these things triggered a thought. Arch sunk lower, dropping into a football stance. The demon still had a shoulder in his ribs and resisted.

Arch pushed down, hammering with his elbow, all he had available to fight with. Had it been a human, he would broken its jaw by now. The demon only grunted. Arch pushed down harder, buckling the demon into a ninety-degree angle. It tried to shove back, but its leverage was limited.

Arch hit it with a knee that caused it to make a grunt of pain. He could feel the balance shift and pushed forward like he was up against a practice dummy back in his football days.

The demon's footing was lost, and Arch came crashing down on him. He buried his knife in its ribs, over and over again until the black fire crawled over it and it disappeared with only a hissing sound.

Arch fell to the floor, the demon no longer holding him up. His hand reached out to touch a sliding closet door, and he struggled to his feet and turned around.

Hendricks was still grappling with the demon on one side of the bed. Grunts of exertion came from both of them, and the thump and bump of them against the walls of the trailer rattled the whole place.

Arch grimaced, catching his breath, and then sprang off the closet door and entered the fray.

* * *

Lerner and Duncan were watching the trailer shake on its foundation. "Looks like somebody's getting fucked in there," Lerner said. "Hard."

Duncan just shook his head. "It's a fight. Those two demon hunters up against two Acuspidas." He paused, and Lerner watched him think. "Make that one Acuspida."

"Sounds like our boys are making progress," Lerner said and turned back to the wheel. "How shall we handle this? Clearly the woman is not with them."

"Clearly."

"Someone who shows up as a dead zone to you sounds like it's within our area of interest, yes?" Lerner asked.

"It is," Duncan said, a little reserved.

"You don't seem concerned," Lerner said. He kept his hands pressed tight to the wheel.

Duncan shrugged just a little. "If we're trying to find out about the woman, we might have to ask them some pointed questions. Not sure we want to raise the stink messing with a local lawman would cause."

Lerner nodded. He had a point. "What if we could just get the cowboy alone for a while? Ask him some questions independently of the police officer?" Lerner thought about it for a minute. "You don't think the entire department is in on the hunt, do you?" Duncan just shook his head. "Of course not," Lerner said, and relief flowed through him. "That sort of shit doesn't happen, a whole department hunting demons." He laughed, but it was weak.

That sort of scenario was exactly what they were here to prevent. Humans turning en masse against their kind was bad for the status quo, bad for those who were living peacefully—or relatively so—on the earth. Big disruptions, huge body counts, these were the sorts of things that tended to attract attention.

And attention, for a demon, was a big no-no.

"What do you think they know about the Sygraath that's jerking off to traffic accidents?" Lerner asked, frowning.

Duncan shrugged again. His jacket looked black in the dark. "Probably less than us."

Lerner nodded, pondering it. "Have you ever seen a Sygraath jump the tracks like this? You know, start slaughtering people instead of waiting out their deaths?"

"Yeah," Duncan said. "Sometimes when they get desperate or blood drunk, they do crazy things." Lerner heard him sniff lightly. "After World War I, a bunch of them went mad and started doing things like this. They went through a kind of withdrawal after some of the major battles and couldn't handle coming down from the high. Tough to go from an orgy of slaughter to a few deaths per day."

"Huh." Lerner fixed his eyes on the trailer. The shaking had stopped. "If we're going to have a conversation with one of these boys—"

"Just the cowboy," Duncan said.

"If we're going to have a conversation with this cowboy, we probably ought to set ourselves up for it," Lerner said. "Get in the shadows, if you know what I mean." He waited to see what Duncan would say to that. Turned out he didn't say anything, but he gave Lerner a hell of a nasty look.

* * *

They had him overmatched. With Arch's help, Hendricks had overwhelmed the last surviving demon, and they had him on the ground, a sword at his throat. The stink of the weed that had been smoked in the trailer was nearly overwhelming, enough to take Hendricks's breath away, and he kept pushing the sleeve of his coat up to his nose to stifle it. Problem was, the drover was starting to pick up the smell.

"You got a problem?" Arch asked him, not taking his eyes off the demon.

"Stinks in here," Hendricks said. "Let's kill this guy and get out."

The demon's dark eyes widened, but the blade was at his throat and Arch had one of his hands pinned down with the switchblade at the wrist. All it would take would be a little poke ...

"Wait, wait," Arch said, and Hendricks could feel him picking up the hint. They exchanged a look, but it was almost unnecessary. He'd play good cop by default. "We're not going to just kill this guy." Arch stared down. "Let's burn him a little first."

Oh. So he wanted to be worse cop. Hendricks could play with that. "You want to torture him first?"

"Yeah, see what he knows," Arch said. "How do we do that?"

Hendricks pretended to think about it. "Well, fire doesn't rupture their skin on its own but hurts like hell, I'm told. Probably a lighter around here somewhere, based on the smell. Cook a little of his shell, I bet he'll be singing up a storm as his essence starts to get all hot and bothered." Hendricks paused. "Not THAT kind of hot and bothered, you understand—"

"I got it."

"Waaaaiiiit!" the demon said, eyes starting to return to human from the slitted, snake-like glowing ones he'd shown while fighting. "If you let me go, I'll tell you whatever you want."

Hendricks poked him in the neck with the sword, just a little. "And you end up breaking down my friend's door like your buddies did last week?"

"Oh ..." the demon's voice was subdued, kind of scratchy. "Was that you? I heard about that. Awfully sorry. I didn't have anything to do with that, really. I mean, I'm not into assault and murder type stuff—"

"No, you're into petty larceny and possession," Arch said, glancing back toward the living room. Hendricks caught his meaning; there had to be some paraphernalia out there, probably some pot as well. Maybe it was all used up, though. "I don't think our criminal justice system is quite designed for demons. It's supposed to be for people, not things."

"I'm ... I'm a people," the demon said, and his human-looking eyes were wide. "A person."

"Really?" Arch said. "Prick you, do you not bleed?" He made a move like he was going to stab the switchblade into the demon. "Let's find out."

"No, no, no," the demon said, shaking his head. "Look, I'll talk. Please, just let me walk away afterward. I won't be any trouble."

Arch and Hendricks exchanged a look. Hendricks could see the conflict in the cop's eyes and made a note to ask him about it later. "All right," Hendricks said, like he was resigned to it. "You talk, we let you go. Fair's fair. What do you know about these slaughters that happened in town?"

"Oh, yeah, righteous feast, huh?" The demon cracked a little bit of a smile that fast disappeared. "You know, if you're into that sort of thing. He rested his head on the dark, brown shag carpeting as they sat in the half-light of the trailer bedroom. "Uhm, yeah, it was a bunch of Tul'rore."

Hendricks nodded. "Not Spiegoth?"

"No," the demon said, looking blank. "They were eating and feasting. Moving from one house to the next, all in a row."

"Where are they now?" Arch asked, and Hendricks could see him tense as he asked the demon the question. The words came out pretty low and harsh considering the guy was cooperating.

"Dead, I think," the demon said. "Word was they got toasted in a raid by two OOCs." Sounded like moooo-k to Hendricks. Without the M.

Arch gave Hendricks the sidelong. "What's an ... OOC?"

"Office of Occultic Concordance. They ride herd on demons," Hendricks replied, mind racing. "Keep 'em from making too big of a splash. I've heard it's to keep things from getting out of hand, so humans don't get wise to the threat in their midst and start killing them off."

"Ever run across them?" Arch asked.

"No," Hendricks replied. "I've talked to other hunters who have. As far as I know, they tend to give us a wide berth."

"So if the things that killed all those people are dead," Arch said, focusing back on the demon lying upon the shag carpeting, "who caused that accident outside Midian earlier?"

The demon's eyes were blank, still wide. "That ... I don't know. I didn't hear anything about that."

Arch nodded. "I believe you."

He poked the demon in the arm with the switchblade, and the black fire crawled over the demon. He was gone within seconds.

"Why didn't you lie to him from the outset?" Hendricks said, sliding his sword back into his scabbard. "You start threatening them with being tortured to death, it makes them desperate. Might get us in a world of hurt."

"I don't like to lie," Arch said, pushing the blade back into the handle of the switchblade. "There's this whole commandment that tells you that you shouldn't."

"I don't think your God had talking to demons in mind when he scrawled that in the stone," Hendricks said, trying to be nice.

"It was on the tablet," Arch said, and to Hendricks's ears he sounded a little testy about it, "and I think if the good Lord had had a caveat in mind saying it was okay to lie to the servants of evil, he would have added it."

Hendricks chuckled. "I don't think these guys are serving much evil.

More like serving themselves."

"Serving none but yourself could be considered a very great evil," Arch said, and Hendricks felt the buzz of annoyance at the sanctimony.

"Whatever," Hendricks said and kept just this side of rolling his eyes. He turned and headed back toward the living room.

"Where are you going?" Arch asked as Hendricks hit the door leading outside and opened it.

"I gotta take a piss," Hendricks replied with a tight smile.

"They've got a perfectly good bathroom in here." Hendricks could hear Arch say it even with the door standing between them, blocking the passage to the bedroom where the police officers still stood.

"I've seen the rest of the house, I doubt it's anything approaching 'perfectly good,'" Hendricks said as he let the door slam shut behind him.

He wasn't even off the steps when he felt something hit him solidly in the back of the head. He was dimly aware of his hat tumbling off, of strong arms taking hold of him, but he never saw his attacker.

Which, he had just enough time to think, was strange, since the area around the front door of the trailer was awfully well lit.

Hendricks passed into unconsciousness, feeling the weight lift. His head throbbed in pain, not for the first time this day, as he faded away.

Chapter 11

"Heavy bastard," was Duncan's only comment as they loaded the cowboy in the back seat.

"Probably the sword," Lerner said, pulling the blade off the cowboy as he reached in. "Or maybe the gun." He pulled a black-steel pistol with wooded grips out of a holster on the man's belt. It looked vaguely familiar, like something he would have seen before in a movie, but Lerner didn't know guns. They were nearly useless in his line of work.

"Or it could be he's a solidly built guy," Duncan replied. Lerner heard him click a pair of cuffs around the cowboy's ankles. "Swords and guns don't weigh all that much." Their voices were hushed, and the rain had once more quit. Lerner was trying to keep quiet so as not to tip off the police officer in the trailer that there was something going on out here.

Lerner didn't respond to Duncan's observation. Instead he walked up to the left rear tire of the police cruiser SUV and jabbed the sword in delicately until he heard a hiss. Then he withdrew it, gently, and watched the black rubber deflate slowly to the ground. "Hope you got a spare, Officer."

"Let's get out of here," Duncan said from behind him. He didn't have to say it twice. Lerner got in the car, started the engine, then put it in gear, all very slowly, as though the cop could hear him from the trailer. He didn't switch on the lights, either, keeping them off and the engine low until after they were over the flooded tracks and back onto the main road.

* * *

Arch got outside just as a sedan disappeared onto the trail. He would have cursed, but he didn't allow himself to say anything strong enough to count in a situation like this. He'd wondered what was taking Hendricks so long, but he got a little caught up looking around the trailer. He'd forgotten how bad it smelled until he stepped out into the fresh air of the rain-cooled night. The chill, from the air and from what he'd just seen, ran over his skin, and he bolted for the Explorer.

He was just about to yank open the door when his conscious mind realized what was wrong with the scene before him. The left rear tire was flat, and the Explorer was sagging in that direction.

Hendricks was gone; somebody had probably grabbed him. Though he couldn't rule out the possibility it was someone like Starling, giving him a lift. No, that didn't fit.

His first instinct was to pick up his mike and call it in. Then he thought about the sweep pattern that was going on, the traffic diversion of the interstate, and hesitated. This would throw a wet clump of dirt right in the middle of the sheriff's plans, and he'd have some manner of explaining to do. Explaining that he couldn't do. And that'd be in addition to pitting unwitting sheriff's deputies against something they were absolutely unready for.

He sighed and hurried to the hatchback of the Explorer. It'd take him a while to change the tire and get in pursuit. Two questions bounced along on infinite loop in his head as he went.

Who had taken Hendricks? And why?

* * *

Erin was still up at midnight, pulling into the sheriff's station in the sheriff's own patrol car. She could see the lights burning within. Normally this would have been an all-hands-on-deck kind of meeting, but there wasn't really time for that. Not with everyone on patrol and Arch gone to God knew where.

She parked the car and walked stiffly across the parking lot, her head still reeling from everything she'd found in Hendricks's hotel room. There'd been one last thing that'd absolutely knocked her back, and she rubbed her hand over her hair, pushing it off her forehead.

She was glad the rain had stopped but was not loving the chill it brought with it. When she opened the station door, it only got worse.

She got hit with a blast of cold air that told her the ancient air conditioner wasn't working the way it was supposed to. That was no great shock; it only worked when it wasn't needed. There was a scent of stale coffee lingering in the air as she passed through the waiting area. All was quiet. As it should be.

Reeve was waiting in his office. His wife, Donna, gave Erin a faint smile as she passed through the area behind the counter where all the desks were lined up. The place was always quiet at this time of night, but something about the events of the day made it seem even grimmer than usual. Donna was a well made-up Southern belle, her hair steel grey and short cropped. She had the lines that Reeve wasn't showing yet but still had a stately look. She didn't wear any sort of sheriff's deputy uniform, because she wasn't deputized. She was admin when they needed the extra help.

"Come on in," Reeve called out as she passed his open office door. The man looked worn out, rubbing a hand over his bald head and down through the grey that remained on the sides. His eyes were normally clear, but she knew he'd been on overnight shift last night, and it showed. She suspected he'd be sleeping in his chair soon enough.

"Hey, Chief," she said and gave him a wan smile. She sat in the nearest chair to the door and looked around the office. It was usually in disorder, but today it was even worse. There were scrawlings on the white board near the door, new patrol schedules and phone numbers for crime labs, as well as for that colonel from THP.

"It's been a day, huh?" Reeve asked, leaning back in his wooden chair. This was how he usually looked, all leaned back, but not quite so tired.

"Yep," she said, not really sure what else she could add to that. It was cold in here, too.

"I got nothing on Arch," Reeve said after a minute, and he was looking down the whole time. "Talked to his wife, but she ain't seen him." He looked up, and his expression was a muddle. "Between you and me, she seemed a little too cool about the whole thing."

"Did you tell her that her husband was missing?" Erin found it hard to believe Arch was actually missing. Almost as hard to believe as him just turning off his phone and disappearing during a crisis like this.

"I stopped short of that," Reeve said. "I just said he was off the grid for a little bit, probably pursuing a lead on things, and that I'd surely appreciate if she heard from him first, that she'd tell him to call me."

Erin sifted that for a minute. "He ain't up in the hills, though, is he?"

"I don't know where he is," Reeve said, and it was the admission of a man completely perplexed, like he was ready to throw up his hands. "I don't know what the hell is going on here. I got eight people murdered this morning in some shit right out of a serial killer movie, I got a traffic accident this afternoon that wasn't actually an accident at all, and my best deputy has decided to turn off his radio and stop answering his phone even though he's on duty."

Reeve made a grimace, and he ripped a piece of paper off his desk and balled it up before throwing it, hard, against the wall. It made little noise as it fell onto the carpet. "Oh, and by the way, the TVA is calling me up to let me know that Tallakeet Dam is probably going to have water flooding over the top tomorrow, so get ready for the river banks to overrun if this fucking rain doesn't stop." Reeve put his face in his hands. "Like I don't have enough shit to deal with without having to sandbag the fucking Caledonia River."

"I've never even heard of anything like that happening," Erin said, frowning. "Don't they open the sluice gates to let more water out in case of something like this happening?"

"I guess they are, but the rain is just coming too damned fast," Reeve said. "As for hearing of this happening before on the Caledonia River, you wouldn't have. It's called a once-in-century flood, and you're not exactly close to a century of age, are you?" He ran fingers over his face, like he could just massage the tiredness away. "We're going to need to build a sandbag line along the most vulnerable flood plane."

"Sounds like fun," Erin said. "When do we start on that project?"

"Not until tomorrow. The TVA is working on putting a crew together."

Erin felt her face crumple in a frown again. "Didn't you say it was going to start flooding tomorrow? Shouldn't we start tonight?"

Reeve threw his arms wide. "No sandbags. I got nothing to do until they come up with it. And honestly, murderers and psychos slaughtering people and causing multi-car pileups on the freeway is more my area of expertise than flood control." Reeve's hands came back down to rest on the arms of his chair. "Which is a grim thought. Honest to God, it's like this whole damned town is just going straight to hell."

Erin felt a flash of discomfort at that turn of phrase, remembering

Hendricks's books on demons. "Sounds like we're just in the middle of a run of bad luck," she said, hoping that was really was the case.

* * *

Gideon knew he needed fertilizer. Tons of it, probably, though he'd need some other things too. He was spending his time splayed out on the bed, his tablet computer in front of him, just doing research. He couldn't sleep, not after today's excitement, and especially not with the prospect of what he might turn loose tomorrow.

So he just kept reading, page after page. Nothing about it looked too difficult, and after the scouting run he'd done earlier, he was excited. A couple of rent-a-cops were the only thing standing between him and his objective. He'd probably be able to just drive right in.

The even better news was that there was a fertilizer dealer right here in town. Set up for big accounts, too, according to the website. He'd just have to pretend he was a farmer, looking to set up with someone, and then he could get all the fertilizer he needed.

Then he got a little further down the page and stopped. He could feel the frown creasing his forehead.

Where the hell was he supposed to get THAT?

* * *

Hendricks started to come to, his head pressed against the hard plastic edge of a door handle. It took him a minute to realize what it was because it was dark, and only the sight of lights whipping by occasionally above him cracked through the blackness outside. There was a faint glow above him, over the seat, he realized after a minute. By that time he'd figured out he was on his back in the back seat of a car.

And his head ached like a motherfucker.

His eye throbbed as he started to sit up. He felt pressure on his wrists and ankles when he did, realizing that he was wearing handcuffs. That paused him for a moment, and a voice came from the seat in front of him.

"He's awake."

"Oh, good," came another voice, this one a little more droll. Sounded a little like a Boston accent. Or Jersey. Somewhere Northeast. "Maybe now we can get some answers."

"Answers to what?" Hendricks asked, shifting his body to try and sit up. He was in the back seat of a sedan of some sort, not exactly luxury. Cloth seats rubbed against his cheek as he dragged himself up. His ribs were still protesting against the rough treatment they'd received two fights ago.

"You'll find out," the guy in the driver's seat said. There was a shift as the car started bumping along, and Hendricks realized they'd left the paved road behind.

Hendricks's mind raced, feeling a little like he had to think while his heart was causing his brain to throb with each beat. He had a feeling he was heading into a torture situation, something which he hadn't really had to deal with before. There'd always been the threat, of course, when he was in the service, but it had never actually happened to him. He pulled on the handcuffs and heard them clink as the car hit a bump and his head whacked the door. Shit.

* * *

Arch thought he'd gone the wrong way the minute he got the Explorer out of the driveway, but he couldn't be sure. When he got to the point that he doubted himself enough to turn around, he drove a hundred miles an hour with his sirens and lights on back in the opposite direction only to find not a single thing. The road didn't exactly lend itself to tracking a car, not being a dirt path. And he wasn't supposed to drive that fast on a spare tire.

He slammed a hand into the steering wheel and felt the pain in his wrist. He'd pay for that later. He started to reach for the radio—again, for the thousandth time—and stopped himself. The only thing calling in would do was provoke a flurry of questions and land himself in hot water. He made a seething noise as he blew air out through gritted teeth and slapped the Explorer's plasti-leather interior panel next to the window. It rattled from the force of his strike.

Where to now? What to do? They were tough questions, and they weren't going to get answers by driving randomly down Lihue Lane, a winding road that stretched five miles in either direction. Hendricks could be halfway across the county by now, in the hands of the demons—whoever they were—and Arch had no one to ask for help.

Arch thudded his palm against the wheel again. The shock of pain ran up his wrist, but it put him back in the moment. It was the same feeling he got when he'd hit a guy playing football. He could be dazed, trying to think of the next move, but when that hit happened, it always woke him up.

The road he was on was taking him back to town. Where the sheriff was waiting, somewhere. Arch looked down at his phone and thumbed the faceplate on. He'd missed twenty calls, all from the same number. Whatever Reeve wanted to talk to him about—and he had a fair idea—he'd probably expressed it in the fifteen voicemails he'd left.

He hit the outskirts still without any idea. "God ... what do I do?" he asked.

He didn't expect a literal answer by any means, but he felt the tug of his heart guiding the wheel, and he steered himself down the familiar streets toward home.

* * *

They'd pulled off into a little wooded area, Hendricks knew, some copse of trees he could see by looking out the window on the other side of the car. His feet were visible, too, cowboy boots up against the opposite door's panel. He thought about busting up the door, but why? So some poor bastard cop would see it, stop them, and get killed? Pointless.

He'd probably need all his strength to endure what was going to happen next, anyway.

Hendricks heard the car stop, felt the subtle shift in momentum that threatened to roll him off his seat. The car dinged as one of the doors opened and the guy in the passenger side got out before it was even shut off. Hendricks heard the driver scrape the keys in the ignition as he pulled them out. Cool, wet air hit him in the face as the driver opened his door.

One of the seatbelt buckles was right in his bruised ribs, and Hendricks had a feeling it was not going to get any more comfortable from here, fuck it all. He could hear a muted conversation between his two captors just outside the car, but it was too hushed for him to make anything out.

He could hear his ragged breathing, and he tried to steady it. He tried to scoot, to bring his hands down and around his ass so he could get them in front of him, but the door opened before he could make any progress. Strong arms pulled him out, not even letting him get his feet underneath him.

They dragged him, one on each side, backwards into the woods. Hendricks wished for his weapon of last resort, the switchblade he'd fastened in his hat until just last week, but he knew that it was out there, somewhere beyond his sight—with Arch.

* * *

Arch paused outside the door of his apartment before letting the key hit the lock. A part of him resisted going inside. He thought about driving around, aimless. Calhoun County was only three hundred and fifty square miles. Sure, it would be utterly fruitless, but at least he'd be doing something.

He shook off that feeling like he shook off the chill as he opened his front door and stepped inside. Alison had turned the heater on. Not a big surprise there, she didn't do well in winter, except for fashion-wise.

"I'm home," he said. He didn't advertise it particularly loudly, but he didn't have to. Alison was sitting on the couch, staring straight ahead. She looked over at him as he entered, her long blond hair falling around her shoulders. She had changed out of her work clothes into denim jeans and a grey t-shirt. She looked good, he reflected as she stared back at him evenly.

"Oh?" Her voice was as flat as the look she gave him. "I thought you were going to be working late." She didn't seem to care either way, just going by tone.

"I just came home for a little bit," Arch said, and now he felt the chill in the room. He took a step toward where she sat in the living room, felt the tension in his body. "Couldn't, uh ... I don't know, I couldn't ..."

"Long patrol, huh?" She didn't sound particularly sympathetic. She didn't really sound particularly ... anything, lately. Just dull, flat, like she had no emotions left at all.

"Long day," Arch said and lowered his head. "Did you hear about the murders?"

"Yeah," Alison said, and he looked up to find her expression hadn't changed a whit. Her eyes were slightly narrowed, like she was tired. It wasn't a look he could recall seeing on her face before. She didn't look mad ... just different. "Never heard of anything like that before. Not in Midian."

"No one's heard of anything like that around here before," Arch said. "Let alone that thing this afternoon."

"Big crash," Alison said, nodding her head. "Not an accident either, I hear."

Arch shook his head. "Nope."

Alison looked away from him. "Quite a day."

Arch couldn't really think of much to say to that. "Yep." He wondered if it'd be capped off with Hendricks dying.

* * *

For Hendricks, being dragged by the demons was like what he remembered of being picked up by his parents as a kid. He was facing the opposite direction of the one he was being dragged, trying to crank his neck around to look.

"Little farther," the one on his left said. It was the guy from the passenger side. He was wearing a dark suit that looked like it was tinged with purple. Hendricks had to look twice to make sure. "We're almost out of earshot of the house over that hill there."

Hendricks didn't love the sound of that, either. He didn't love any of this. Not that he could think of anyone that would.

His heels were thumping with the natural curves of the ground. His shoulder was pissed at him, too, making a little racket, pain firing up here and there. He didn't know which fight that had come from.

The air was crisp, and he looked up to see a black sky above. The chill on his skin wasn't just from the weather, that much he knew.

"Gonna rain again," the guy in the purple suit said.

"I've been wondering about that," the other said. He was the one that sounded like he was from Boston. "When it comes to atmospheric conditions—"

"Not now," Purple Suit said. He talked softly, one of the gentlest voices Hendricks could recall.

They went quiet and stopped after another twenty yards or so. They tossed Hendricks to the ground like he weighed no more than a piece of firewood, and he rolled in a pile of dead leaves. He came to rest face down, hands still cuffed behind him, legs chained together.

"We're curious about that redhead," Purple Suit said abruptly.

"You want to know if she's single? Ask her yourself." Hendricks felt his head rock from a sharp slap from Boston. It stung more than anything. "I'm curious about her, too," Hendricks said, compressing his neck to look up. He rested his chin on the dirt, and started to roll over. "She's not exactly forthcoming with the details of her life, if you know what I mean."

"You look like you're cozy with her," Boston said. Hendricks couldn't see either of them; they were lurking above him and back a little ways.

"Not really," Hendricks said, trying to roll. "She showed up a week or so ago, saved my ass a couple times, then vanished until today." His shoulder was now super pissed at him for trying to roll.

There was a pause behind him. "Forgive us," Boston's sharp voice came back, "but we think there's more to it than that."

"I'm sure there is," Hendricks said with a grunt as he rolled onto his back. His arms were now pinned underneath him, but at least he could look the two of them in the face. Boston was watching him, just a few paces away. Purple Suit was a little farther back, standing off to the side, staring into the woods with his fingers on his chin. "But she hasn't shared any more with me. You got a real woman of mystery there. First time I met her, she jumped off an overpass and disappeared before she hit the ground."

"No shit?" This from Boston.

"No shit," Hendricks said, staring him down. "Makes me think she might be one of your people."

"'Our people'?" Boston's voice carried a note of offense.

"You know," Hendricks said, with as much of a shrug as he could manage with his hands behind his back. "Demon."

"Uh huh," Boston said, watching him with a thoroughly unamused expression. His lips were tight, eyes slitted. "'Our people.' Tell me something, demon hunter," and the guy said almost like it was a slur, "you ever meet any of 'our people' that you didn't kill?"

"Maybe a few here and there," Hendricks said, and felt the wet dirt against his hands. "Never met one who crossed me I didn't let the air out of, though."

"Oh, we got a feisty one, Duncan," Boston said, looking over at his partner, who was still staring off into the woods. Hendricks could hear the drip of water from the branches above in the gap of silence once the demon stopped speaking. "Kind of a loudmouth considering you don't have your sword or your gun." Boston took a step closer. "Don't know what 'our kind' does to 'your kind'?"

"Kills us," Hendricks said, trying to scoot his hands down his back. He rocked and brought them around his ass and started folding his legs one by one under the chain so he could bring his hands in front of him. Boston watched and didn't seem to care. "Eat us. Disembowel us for fun."

Boston shot a look at the one he'd called Duncan, then looked back to Hendricks. "I don't know any of our people that would disembowel just for fun. Maybe in the course of eating, or playful torture ..." He let his voice drift off. "Okay, I guess some would consider it fun."

"What about you?" Hendricks asked, steeling his voice, trying to keep it even. "What do you do with humans for fun?"

Boston took a step closer and peered down at him. His expression was almost totally cold, blank. "I don't have fun with humans. I tolerate humans. I go around humans. Avoid them. Try to ignore them when they inconvenience me." He knelt, and Hendricks noticed for the first time he was wearing some cheap looking loafers that were caked with mud. "Right now, you're inconveniencing me."

"I've told you what I know," Hendricks said, and held his hands up, still cuffed. "You can believe me or not, but I don't know that much about the redhead."

Boston narrowed his eyes at him. They became slits then glowed red with a dark fire. "Do you know her name?"

Hendricks felt himself tense. Unless his handcuffs were blessed by a holy man of some kind, they wouldn't do any damage to a demon. What was in a name, anyway? "She calls herself Starling. That's all she ever told me."

Boston settled back, then stood, looking down at him, his face bunched up pensively. The fire in his eyes was gone. "Starling? Like the bird?"

Hendricks shrugged. "That's what she said."

"Duncan?" Boston asked, turning to face his partner. Hendricks watched Duncan, who was still staring off into the forest.

"He's telling the truth," Duncan said.

"Well, okay then," Boston said and reached out for Hendricks in a flash, pulling him to his feet. "I guess we're almost done here."

Hendricks heard that and took note. "Oh, yeah?" Boston was way too casual about this. He braced himself to run for the woods.

"Yeah," Boston said and promptly hit Hendricks in the kidney, doubling him over. "Almost done."

Hendricks hit the ground and looked up. Boston stood over him and now so did Duncan. They were flanking him, and his back hurt like Boston had used a battering ram to bust him open. Hendricks just lay there, looking up at the two of them, as they both reached down for him, blotting out his view of the tree branches above.

Chapter 12

Gideon had tried to put it all together, tried damned hard. Well, he'd done the research anyway. Ammonia-based fertilizer bombs had sounded easy when he'd looked them up, but then things got complicated fast. Some of the materials would require serious effort to get hold of. And they assumed he'd be able to make a functional bomb out of everything once he was done, which was a big if.

It took him until nearly two a.m. to settle on what he was doing wrong. He was thinking like a human.

And he was not a human. He was better.

The rental car bumped along down a dirt road. He'd had to do a little searching to find what he was looking for, but he'd found it. The web was really a boon for their kind, if you knew what to look for. Need a live human delivered to your apartment in New York for fresh meat? There was a service for that. Funerary rites for a Du'clen'tau demon? All on a webpage, indexed somewhere on a server in the Ukraine for viewing anywhere that Wifi or 4G could reach.

And if you needed the services of a few of demonkind's more … elusive and mysterious purveyors, they were there, too. Fortunately for Gideon, some of them liked to follow the hotspots. And updated their web pages accordingly. Or blog, in this case.

The car smelled new, clean, like a rental should. The last one he'd ditched it wasn't smelling so good by the end. This one was blowing mildly warm air, which worked for Gideon because he was still in cargo pants and a t-shirt. He was starting to stink, he knew it. A few days of fevered pleasuring without a shower would do that, and he certainly hadn't had time for a shower.

No, he had plotting and scheming to do. Research. Shit to think up. Plans to execute.

He pulled off the road when he saw the mailbox. It was painted red, blending in with the flag that was on its side. It felt wrong somehow, like it was some sort of violation of USPS code, but Gideon just shrugged and turned because that's what the website said to do.

He felt the rutted road pitch the car, felt the heat blowing out of the vents on his face, smelled his own stink and the rental car's cleanliness mix in some perverse blend. He touched himself quickly, just a goose to remind him of what this was all about. Oh, yeah. He was hard again already.

He stopped behind a green pickup truck that looked almost black in the dark night. A porch light was the only thing illuminating the scene. Gideon pulled the keys out of the ignition and took another breath of himself before he got out. He kind of liked it.

His shoes squished in the mud and gravel of the road. This looked like it was on higher ground than most of the roads he'd seen. Lots of standing water after the rains. That was good. Lots of ground saturation.

He headed for the door to the house. It was painted red, too, and when he knocked—four times—he heard a voice within.

"Enter."

It was almost a whisper, but it resonated inside, touched his essence. He paused and let that feeling linger. It was like someone had run fingers over his deepest insides. It was not something that was done to strangers casually; it was awfully forward.

Gideon liked it. He took hold of the old copper handle and opened the door. What he saw inside made his head spin.

* * *

"What are you gonna do?" Alison's soft voice wafted over Arch with a seriousness that he still wasn't used to. She could pout with the best of them when she wanted, but she was a mostly chipper person. He tried not to let her change in personality get to him, even as he sat back on the couch next to her, sinking into the corduroy monstrosity. Her parents had gotten it for them when they'd moved into the apartment.

"I don't know," Arch said, leaning his head back and feeling the faint lines of the fabric against the back of his neck. He ran a hand over his short hair, then down the bristly stubble on his cheek.

"Are you coming to bed?" She asked this with as little interest as she asked anything else, but his ears perked up and listened for hints of something—anything—from her. Interest. Anything to hint she might be the same person who was so anxious to have a baby with him only two weeks ago.

"Not yet," he said. There was some pull in him to keep him from answering the way he knew he should, the way he wanted to deep inside. Some stubborn refusal to acknowledge that he maybe needed to bend toward her, even a little. His breath caught in his throat before he spoke. "I just … I think I'll stay up a little longer."

"All right," she said in a rough whisper. She stood and walked past him, pausing only to reach down and kiss him on the forehead. It was quick, perfunctory, and nothing but silence followed after it.

* * *

Hendricks was in the back seat again, now with his hands uncuffed. The last few minutes had been strange. He was sitting upright now, in the middle of the seat, his coat on the floorboard.

"What do they call these handles?" This from Boston, whose actual name, he had found out after he'd introduced himself and helped Hendricks out of the mud, was Lerner. Lerner pointed at the handle hanging next to Duncan's head. "You know, the ones on the roof of a car by the door. Lunkhead here doesn't know." Lerner waved at Duncan.

"I don't know their technical name," Hendricks said carefully. He was still walking on eggshells with these two, in spite of the sudden shift in their demeanor toward affable. "But I've always heard them called 'Oh shit' bars."

"'Oh shit bar'?" Lerner frowned and glanced back at him. They were heading back toward town, Hendricks thought, but he wasn't sure.

"Yeah," Hendricks said, staring back at Lerner. "Cuz when you need them it's usually at a moment when you're saying, 'Oh shit.'"

"Ha!" Lerner's laugh was a bark. Hendricks looked at Duncan, but he was silent, staring into the windshield. Hendricks was ready to write him off as fucking weird, but he had said something about Hendricks telling the truth about Starling. That was interesting. If he was a mind reader—

"Yes," Duncan said. "Not really mind, though. Essence reading."

"Bullshit," Hendricks blurted. Couldn't help himself. He had to think back, try and figure out if he'd been talking out loud.

"No," Duncan said. "You weren't speaking aloud. But everything you were thinking was written all over your soul."

Hendricks tried not to roll his eyes, but he didn't try very hard. "Whatever, man. I could accept you could read minds somehow. Souls are kind of a different story."

"Oh, now this is an interesting discussion we could have," Lerner chimed in. "About the immortal soul—"

"He's an atheist," Duncan said nonchalantly, like he'd just mentioned what he was having for dinner.

"Really?" Lerner said, and his face got flat around the mouth, like he was impressed or something. "Don't meet a lot of demon hunters that aren't of the faithful." He looked over his shoulder into the back seat. "What was it that brought you into the field?"

Hendricks glanced at Duncan, who looked back at him. The man's face was blank, but his eyes were peering right into Hendricks. "Personal tragedy," Hendricks said, knowing he sounded tense. He waited to see if Duncan would elaborate, but the demon said nothing.

"Met a few people in it for that reason," Lerner said, but he was back to the wheel now. "But usually they go toe-to-toe with a few demons and get religious real quick."

Hendricks shrugged his shoulders. "Don't know what to tell you. I've never believed in anything I can't see some scientific proof of."

Lerner laughed and exchanged a look with Duncan. "That's kind of funny, champ. How do you explain what you fight every day?"

Hendricks smiled. "Just another species of animal. Different basis of life, obviously, since carbon-based lifeforms don't go PFFFFFT when you stab them with a sword, but still a species of some kind. You can feel 'em, see 'em—"

"Not all," Duncan said.

"—smell 'em, hear 'em—" Hendricks went on, wondering a little what Duncan meant by that one.

"You can taste 'em, too," Lerner said with a smile and looked back at him again. "Though I don't imagine you've probably done that. A little too up close and personal, especially for a guy who's made this a vendetta."

"So, you're demons," Hendricks said. "And you're here to ...?"

"Keep things quiet," Lerner said, and now he was looking at the road again. Dark pastures and fences were passing them by outside the window. "Keep a lid on our peoples' activities. Keep humanity from getting all uppity and rising against us."

Hendricks thought about that one for a minute. "You kill demons?"

"I've let the brimstone out of more of 'em than you, sonny," Lerner said, like he was some kind of snappy used car salesman getting pissy with Hendricks over his territory.

"Humans?" Hendricks asked.

"No," Lerner said with a smile after a pause. "Most demons don't kill humans, by the way. They keep their heads down, blend with your people, live their lives. Eat food, work jobs, have babies—"

Hendricks blinked at that one. "Demons have babies?"

"You're a cute kid," Lerner said, laughing. "Yeah, demons have babies. Some of them are cute, too. Some of them ..." Lerner paused, "... not so much."

"So, what are you doing with me?" Hendricks asked, trying to bring things back around. He wasn't sure he entirely believed Lerner when the man—demon—had said he didn't kill humans, but he'd sounded convincing.

"Asking questions," Lerner said and then he sent a scalding look back at Hendricks, which was mirrored by Duncan. "And hitting you for probably banishing some of our kind without good cause."

Hendricks flinched. "Banishing?"

"Yeah," Lerner said. "You don't think you're actually killing them with that little pointy thing you swing around, do you?"

* * *

Erin was driving the patrol car around in circles. She'd been awake for close to twenty-four hours, and her vision was a little blurry at times. She pulled off and got a coffee at the all-night convenience station next to the interstate. Sat there for a while, drinking it in the parking lot with the car idling, watching the Sinbad motel.

She told herself it was because she needed to drink the coffee before she could safely drive around some more, but even she knew that was a lie.

* * *

Lerner took a left onto the main road. The cowboy demon hunter was in the back seat, Duncan was silent next to him now, and he was happy as he could be. The cowboy didn't seem bothered by his desire to talk, which was kind of like heaven—or some form of paradise, at least—after being stuck with Duncan's annoyingly reticent ass for so long.

"So if they're not dead ..." the cowboy said from the back seat.

"Back to the underworld," Lerner said. He wasn't a stupid one, fortunately. "Suffering down there together with their own kind. Probably trying to find a way back, which is ... problematic."

"Why is that?" The cowboy asked.

"You don't need to know," Duncan said, breaking his silence. Lerner looked over at Duncan, who was giving him the side-eye. It was annoyance combined with a dose of shut-the-fuck-up.

"So what are you doing here?" the cowboy asked after a moment's silence. Persistent, too.

"Keeping things on the level," Lerner said, letting the sedan glide smoothly along the highway. Much better than the bumpy dirt back roads. He cracked a window and listened to the rush, the cool night air catching him in the face. It had that damp, post-rain smell to it. Lovely. "Keeping our kind from crossing too many lines. I don't know how many hotspots you've seen—"

"I've been doing this for a while," the cowboy said. What was his name again? Hendricks, yeah.

"About five years," Duncan added helpfully.

"So you've seen a few," Lerner said. "But you've missed the really bad ones. The ones that vanish off the map. To say nothing of the places that aren't hotspots that just get hit with a wave of demon activity. Someone hangs out a shingle, says, 'Hey, we're open for demon business!' And it's a mad rush. Lost a town in Serbia like that last year. Ugly mess. Entrails everywhere." Lerner shook his head. It had been gruesome; he and Duncan got to bat cleanup on that one. And cleaning up had been all that was left when a family of M'r'kirresh had been done.

"So, you're demon hunters, too," Hendricks said. Lerner felt himself crack a smile. Yeah, talking to this human was all right.

"We're lawmen," Lerner said.

"Law-demons?" Hendricks asked.

"Whatever," Lerner said, shrugging. He didn't get caught up in semantics like that. He had the male pieces, after all, even if they didn't really get used. "We enforce the Pact, which set forth Occultic law on earth to govern everything non-human. Keep things from getting too heavy, make sure that when stuff gets out of control and loud somewhere, it gets stopped as quick as we can make it happen."

There was a silence in the back seat. "So you're ... I hate to use this term ... kind of like ... 'good guys.'"

Lerner sighed. "I hate that phrase, too. It shows such a lack of subtlety. Of complex thinking. So I'm 'good' just because I don't murder humans?"

"I don't ..." Hendricks was quiet for a moment. "It doesn't make you bad, I don't think."

Lerner shrugged. "I turn my back on the killings of humans every day, did you know that? If they happen in small batches, I remain unconcerned. My job is to stop the big ones, the ones that get attention." He grinned and turned back to the cowboy, who wore a little bit of a sick look now. "Am I still a 'good guy'?"

"Probably not," Hendricks said, and Lerner could hear the distaste.

"But you do the same thing every day," Lerner said, and his grin was just getting bigger. It was a such a joy to hammer home a rhetorical point. "Where was that place a few years ago where they had that ethnic cleansing?" He clicked his tongue. "South Sudan." He snapped his fingers a couple times, like it could help him remember. "Darfur! Yeah, that was it." He turned to the back seat. "Did you go to Darfur to help stop the slaughter?"

The cowboy's voice got quiet. "... No."

"Well, then welcome to the 'bad guys' team," Lerner said with a grin, steering the car along. They were almost there, he knew as they passed a diner on the left.

"I do what I can," Hendricks said, and Lerner could hear the fire starting in his voice. "Going in, me—one man—against an army? Suicide. I go to hotspots and try and stop demons there—"

"And kill some of them who have never hurt a human in their lives," Lerner said. He was enjoying this. "Yep, you are a hell of a 'good guy.'"

There was a sigh from the cowboy. "Where are we going?"

"Right here," Duncan said, speaking up, as Lerner turned the car into the Sinbad Motel's parking lot.

"You drove me home?" Hendricks asked from the back seat, and Lerner could hear that the boy was more than a little perplexed.

"As a good date should," Lerner said with the same grin. "But actually, we're not here for you. If we'd been heading the opposite direction, I would have left your ass on the side of the road." He wondered if the cowboy thought he was kidding. He wasn't.

"Why are you here?" Hendricks asked, remaining still in the back seat even though they were now parked.

"Now that is an interesting question," Lerner said as he pulled the keys out of the ignition.

* * *

Erin had seen Hendricks's cowboy hat in the back seat in profile as the sedan pulled into the Sinbad's parking lot. She thought about driving over right then but held back. There were two guys in the car with him. She felt her hand tighten on the hot coffee cup, heard the Styrofoam crack a little before she slackened her grip.

What the hell was going on now?

* * *

Gideon stepped into a world upside down. He'd seen farmhouses on TV; they were simple, quaint things, filled with homey samplers on the wall, quilts on the back of overstuffed furniture. For some reason he imagined the smell of gravy cooking, the smell of every greasy spoon restaurants he'd ever been to.

This was nothing like that.

Every wall was red. Deep red, not quite blood, but a heavy maroon of the sort you'd see on a weather map. The smell was all herbs and spices, or something of that sort. Maybe incense. Damned sure wasn't vanilla, though. And the furniture wasn't homey. At all.

There were cages to his left, animals within, but not a trace of the smell he might have associated with them. He could hear the rattle and noise of some of the chickens—and there had to be a half dozen of them alone. He could see some dogs below that, in bigger cages, staring out at him with hopeless eyes. Gideon had to concede that if he was a human, it might have moved him. But he wasn't, so his eyes moved on.

There were other animals, too, the cages stacked floor to ceiling on three sides of what had once been someone's sitting room. The last three cages, the ones closest to the open arch leading to the entry hall, had humans. The cages were kind of small for their occupants, heavy metal bars fencing in two men and a woman. They were dirty and naked and didn't project one third of the sad-eyed pathos that the dogs did.

"Come in," came the voice from ahead. Gideon stared forward, looking away from the spectacle of the cage room, and started walking down the hall. Every step in his shoes made a lovely, resonant thump against the hardwood floor that echoed through the quiet house. If the animals were making noise, it was masked by a conjuring of some sort. And that was fine with Gideon. If they were screaming toward death, he'd hear it anyway. If they were just screaming, he didn't give a fuck.

He walked down the long, red hall, keeping his eyes on the space ahead. The hall was longer than the house, at least as he remembered it from outside. The occasional shelf and end table that could be found along it was filled with curiosities, orbs, jars with light and darkness enclosed within and shelves laden with arcane, leather-bound books.

"Come further," the voice commanded. It was cold and clear, reminding Gideon of a winter wind in Chicago for some reason. It felt like it was blowing down the hall at him. He didn't shiver, but it was a near thing.

He could see the hall widen ahead, another room to his left, a stairway leading up to his right. It had an old wood banister with a thousand nicks in it that he could see even at this distance. The smell of incense was stronger here. It reminded him a little of an Indian restaurant in the neighborhood he'd lived in in Detroit.

"Ah, I see you now," came a voice from just around the corner.

Gideon entered a large dining room complete with an oval wood table and six place settings. A man sat opposite him, with a small smile, one that barely wrinkled the corners of his eyes. He looked small somehow, with greying hair at the temples, and solid, thick hair. There were no teeth in the man's smile, and he wore a Nehru jacket, which seemed totally at odds with his utterly Caucasian look. It reminded Gideon of the movie villain in Austin Powers.

Gideon halted in front of the table, staring at the man opposite him. "You could see me, huh? Like through a conjuring?"

"No," the man said, his smile widening. He put out a hand, open palm gesturing to the staircase behind him. "I have a mirror over there." Gideon looked and saw it, mounted just above the staircase—one of those distorted ones that stores put high up in their corners to keep watch for shoplifting. "No, you're not really the type that's within my power to keep an eye on easily, are you?"

"I guess not," Gideon said. He shifted on his feet, side to side. There wasn't much decor in the dining room; a couple paintings on the wall, a six-foot grandfather clock with gold pendulum halted in the middle of its chest in the corner. There were a couple incense burners, and the light was dim. "So."

"So," the man said and stood, pointing to the chair opposite him. "Have a seat?" He extended his hand as Gideon took a step forward. Gideon took his hand and found it cold, desperately cold. When Gideon looked up at the man, his smile was back to practiced and small, any hint of his teeth gone. "My name is Wren Spellman. And you are?"

"Gideon," he replied. It was an assumed name anyway. "Wren Spellman?"

"An appellation some locals gave me in Kansas once," Spellman said, taking a seat. That same, unmoving smile remained maddeningly perched on his lips. "I liked it so much, I kept it."

"Uh huh," Gideon said. He was itching to know Spellman's real name, but that was an itch one simply didn't scratch in their world. "I'm looking for some things."

"I see," Spellman said, and the smile was gone, replaced with all seriousness. "May I ask how you came to find us? Was it by word of mouth, an ad, our website—"

"Website," Gideon said, frowning.

"Ah, good," Spellman said, and Gideon realized he had a pad of yellow paper in front of him and was writing on it. When Spellman looked up and caught Gideon looking at him, he smiled again. "Just making a note; we like to make sure our marketing dollars are being spent well, you know. I had a man from Russia design the site and give it some SEO." Spellman laughed. "Oh, how things have changed since the days when you just hung entrails outside a tent. But in this modern world you have to adapt to maximize profitability, you know?"

"I guess," Gideon said, a trace uneasy. "Listen, I'm looking for ..."

"A conjuring? Some sorcery, perhaps?" Spellman said with that same false smile.

"Yeah," Gideon said and ran a hand through his thinning hair.

"I have many of those that might interest a man such as yourself," Spellman said and started ticking off his fingers one by one as he listed. "Glamours, potions, runes. Something to increase your potency, perhaps?" There was a twinkle in Spellman's eye at that one.

"My potency is doing just fine, thanks," Gideon said matter-of-factly. It was, after all.

"Sorry, that's the most popular request," Spellman said with a shrug of the shoulders. His Nehru suit was green now, though Gideon could have sworn it was grey only minutes ago. "And sometimes it takes people a while to admit it, so I like to just get that out there in the open at the outset." He steepled his fingers and leaned back in his chair. "So, what's it to be, Mr. Gideon ...?"

"Just Gideon."

"What's it to be, 'Just Gideon'?" Spellman wore a pensive look, like he was trying to stare down Gideon's eyes and look behind them.

"I need something ... really particular," Gideon said, and Spellman leaned forward. Gideon had a feeling the reaction would be good.

* * *

"We need to hold up here a minute," Duncan said as they got out of the car.

"Why?" Hendricks frowned at Duncan. The man in the purple suit was mysterious as all hell, and it was getting on his nerves. There was a chill in the parking lot of the Sinbad that was settling on Hendricks's skin, a chill he hadn't felt since he'd blown into town. Summer had been in full force when he arrived. Now it was starting to feel like autumn in Wisconsin.

"Because your girlfriend is in the parking lot of the gas station across the street, watching us," Duncan replied as neutrally as if he were reading a passage out of the car's manual.

"She— what?" He started to turn his head to look and sure enough, a sheriff's car was sitting across the street, lights off. He could see the exhaust puffing out of the tailpipe because of the gas station lights. Hendricks felt his stomach growl and realized he hadn't eaten in a long damned time. For a second he thought about going over there—to talk to her, maybe grab a hot dog afterward.

That thought got squeezed off when the cruiser's headlights came on and it eased across the street and into the Sinbad's lot. It rolled up real slow, like she was taking her time to build the suspense. Based on how their earlier conversation had gone, Hendricks didn't have high hopes for this one. "How'd you know it was her?" he asked Duncan, who stood with his arms folded, eyes closed. "Could you sense her when we were on our way here?"

"No," Duncan said, not opening his eyes but swaying slightly as a gentle wind blew through the parking lot. The cruiser eased closer, stopping in a spot just next to the sedan. "I can't read humans from a distance. There are just too many of you."

Erin stepped out of her car and had her flashlight out immediately. He could tell it was her in the instant before she clicked the light on just by the profile. He'd seen her in the dark enough to recognize it, though usually it was when she was astride him.

"Hey," he said, as tight-lipped as he could be. This had the potential to be a really awkward conversation, especially in front of Lerner and Duncan.

"Hey, yourself," she said, and she didn't sound any more pleased to see him now than when he'd seen her earlier. Plus she was shining the light in his eyes. He had a hand up to block her, but still, that maglite was damned bright. "Where have you been?"

He felt his face crease with annoyance. "Out. Why?"

She ignored his question and took her light off of him to illuminate Lerner, then Duncan, one at a time. "Who are your friends?"

"I don't have any friends," Hendricks shot back. He layered on the sarcasm nice and thick.

"They're not demons, are they?"

Hendricks felt his throat tighten, and his eyes felt like they were about to bulge out of his head. She still had the flashlight pointed at Duncan, who was staring back at her, cool as an icy spring, apparently indifferent to her jibe. Hendricks, for his part, was mentally scrambling to figure out how to answer that one when the light came back to him and damned near blinded him again. He got his hand up a little late and tried to blink the spots of out of his eyes.

"Demons?" This came from Lerner, chuckling. He came off folksy, even with the accent. "That's an unkind thing to say to a total stranger, ma'am."

Erin took a step toward Hendricks, and he still couldn't really see her. He held out his hand to try and block the flashlight's beam, but it didn't work. "Could you put that down?"

"No." Erin's voice came back at him, cold. She took another step and was within arm's reach. He just stood there, wondering if she was about to cuff him or something. Not that she'd have much on him, but he didn't want to give her a reason; his weapons were still in the trunk of Lerner and Duncan's car. She took one step closer and Hendricks felt something hit him in the gut, a light slap. It had some weight to it, and he lowered a hand to catch it by instinct.

It was leather, square-like, and took him a minute to realize it was a book. No, two books. He pulled them closer to his face and recognized the spines in the blinding light. "Hey, these are mine."

"Yeah, I took 'em out of your room earlier," she said, and there was more than a little growl to what she was saying. "Along with this." She held something out, something that looked a little like a piece of paper.

Hendricks took hold of it between his thumb and forefinger and blinked the lights out of his eyes as he turned it over.

He knew it by heart. It was a picture, and he was in the tux on the left hand side. He looked younger, a little better kempt. He should have been, he was only nineteen when it was taken. On the right hand side was her. The spots in his vision from the flashlight worked in his favor this time, because he couldn't see her face clearly.

Without the photo, though, he couldn't ever see her face clearly anymore.

"You're married," Erin said, in a low note of accusation. Hendricks didn't answer, just felt the sting, felt the blood rush through his head at the thought of her going through his room, searching his things. "Deny it."

"Why would I?" Hendricks said, and he did not even recognize his voice as he said it. "You've got photographic evidence to the contrary."

He could see the silhouette of Erin nod, felt the fury boiling off of her, but it was nothing—not a drop in the goddamned bucket—compared to his own. "Did you get a divorce?"

"Nope," he said, with zeal born of rage. He felt it coursing through him, wanted to stick it to her, make her feel the pain. He hoped like hell she was humiliated, at least as much as he was from the thought of her going through his things.

There was a pause. "So you've been cheating on her with me." This came out quiet.

"I've been fucking you," Hendricks said, and he felt the spittle fly from his mouth. "Like you wanted me to."

He could feel her tense, see it in her silhouette. His eyes drifted down to her other hand, the one not holding the flashlight. It was tough to tell with the maglite still shining in his eyes, but he was pretty sure it was on the butt of her gun.

"Lover's quarrel," Lerner's voice came over at him. "This is so cute."

"Shut the fuck up," Erin said, low and slow. He'd wanted to say much the same, but she beat him to it.

"Yes, ma'am," Lerner said and pretended to tip an imaginary hat to her.

"I trusted you," Erin said after another minute of unfiltered quiet.

"I'm a stranger that blew into town on the wind," Hendricks said, and he laughed, feeling a little cruelty come spitting out from that rage, from his sense of violation. Now he just wanted to hurt her so she'd get the hell away from him. The sooner, the better. "You were just looking for a good time. Something to cut the boredom, someone new to fuck—"

She stepped toward him like she was going to hit him with the maglite but stopped a foot away. He could smell the coffee on her breath, see her eyes. They weren't red. They were cold. Damned cold. "You're a fucking asshole."

"And you're a police officer who executed an unwarranted search and seizure of my property," he said and held up the books. "Which makes you a fascist and a—"

"Let's keep it polite," Duncan said, drawing Hendricks's attention to him for a second and breaking his train of thought off the blinding rage he was feeling.

"Remember," Lerner said, voice tinged with amusement, "even here at the lovely Sinbad motel, a veritable mecca of refinement, you have an audience."

Hendricks stared in her eyes, she stared back at him. It was cold fury on both sides, Hendricks realized, and he did not give a fuck. All he wanted was her to get away, now. He took a step back. "I don't have time for this shit."

Erin took a step back of her own. "Stay out of trouble, and stay out of my way, you crazy, cheating fucker."

Hendricks doffed his cowboy hat to her. "Your wish is my command, you possessive, sneaky bar slut—"

"Hey," Lerner said, and Hendricks saw his lips were pursed like he was shocked. "Why go there? Like it's some kind of mark against her that she was stooping to sleep with you?"

"Whose fucking side are you on?" Hendricks found himself asking.

"Not yours," Lerner said with a shrug.

"Stay out of trouble," Erin said again, and Hendricks looked back to see her almost to her car. "Stay out of my way." She opened the door to her cruiser and got in, slamming it behind her. She didn't click the light off right away, and Hendricks could see her face illuminated by it as she started the car and backed out. There wasn't an ounce of give in her expression; it was hard as a block of granite. She squealed tires at the edge of the parking lot, taking the cruiser back on the highway.

"Women, huh?" Lerner said. "And men, too." It took Hendricks a minute to realize he was talking to Duncan.

"Should have just told her the truth," Duncan said softly, and Hendricks looked over to find the demon staring at him, looking through him again.

"Fuck that," Hendricks said and thrust the books into the side pocket of his coat. "And fuck her, too."

* * *

Erin could feel her hands shaking as she drove away. She didn't cry when she got upset like some did; she just got more furious. The cabin of the cruiser felt hot and stifling, and she rolled the window down a crack to let the cool, humid night air come in. Motherfucker. Hendricks had used her, played her, made her a party to his cheating, and when she confronted him about it, he didn't even have the decency to lie.

What an asshole.

She pushed down harder on the pedal and the car gave back a satisfying roar as she headed toward the lights of town in the distance. Driving when she was pissed was a favorite activity. Doing it in a squad car was even better.

"Shit." Her voice sounded low and rough, even to her. She'd slept with a married man once before, and it pissed her the hell off in the light of the next morning when she'd found out. Cheating wasn't a thing she did. She just didn't do it.

"That motherfucker." She saw her knuckles turn white on the wheel, gripping it tight with every finger. She'd gotten played and it burned.

She kept the car going seventy in a fifty-five the whole way back to town. She'd slow down when she hit the city itself.

Maybe.

* * *

"I love you science guys," Lerner said as they stood in the parking lot of the motel, waiting for Hendricks to unlock his door. "I love your explanations for things. Like, for example—I bet you have a doozy when it comes to explaining what happens to our kind when you stab us with a sword." He loved the night air. His skin had a natural burn to it, so the cool was just fine by him.

"Yeah," Hendricks said as the lock clicked. The cowboy adjusted his hat and looked back at Lerner. "It's like popping a balloon, I guess. Or pulling the plug out of a drain."

"Oh, is that how you explain it to yourself?" Lerner asked, and he almost felt giddy. "Why does it happen, though?"

"I don't know," Hendricks said with a shrug, opening his door and gesturing for them to enter. "Because they don't belong here."

"That's probably true," Lerner had to concede. Not bad on Hendricks's part. "Try and figure this out, champ—you poke 'em with a pointy thing that has certain words and rituals performed over it, their shell breaks, and their essence gets a one-way ticket home." He felt the grin return. "Why is that? Why not with any pointy thing?"

He watched the cowboy's face as he struggled to find an explanation. Finally the man gave up and shrugged. "I don't know."

"You don't think it's because there might be something to this whole religion thing?" Lerner asked. He was loving this, twisting the cowboy's tail. Putting the spurs to him.

"Nope," Hendricks said. "It sounds a lot like 'correlation is causation' to me. So you perform some ritual on a sword—which I've never seen done, by the way—and it somehow makes it a holy instrument of," he rolled his eyes, "some almighty power. Who's to say that's what's causing it to send demons back?" He frowned. "Why? Are you telling me there is a G—"

"We don't really say that name," Duncan said abruptly, ending the fun.

"Awww," Lerner waved him off. "You could have let me keep going on him."

Hendricks paused, and Lerner could see him working through it. "So you're saying there is a—" He halted, and looked at Duncan, who was almost glaring at him. "... that guy?"

"We're not saying anything." Lerner grinned. Humans were fun.

* * *

Gideon stared across the table at Spellman. The red walls were making him feel feverish. Or was that just the desire rising? He took a breath of the fragrant air and realized it was more than a little hot in the house. "So … can you do it?"

Spellman still had his fingers steepled. His expression was even, and he gave a little shrug. "Easy enough. I can have it assembled by tomorrow before midday."

"Okay," Gideon said, running it through his head. It was after midnight. "You mean later today?"

"Eh?" Spellman seemed lost in thought. "Yes, sorry. Time zones are confusing to me. Later today. Midday."

That would work just fine for Gideon. He'd seen the clouds outside, and the weather reports. It was going to rain even more, and that wouldn't be a bad thing at all. He nodded absently while he finished his train of thought. "That'll work."

"Excellent," Spellman said with a long, slow inhalation that Gideon could hear from across the table. "May I suggest another item of mine?"

Gideon held up a hand. "I'm not really interested in—"

"Oh, this I think you'll find of interest," Spellman said with a grin. He put a hand under the table and came out with a little silk cloth bag, tied at the top. "This contains a rune that, when carried on the person, keeps you from being detected by anything other than the five senses."

Gideon could feel his face crease into a frown. "Why would I want that?"

"Oh, I don't know," Spellman said with a thin smile. "It could be those two Officers of Occultic Concordance at your hotel room right now. Maybe you'd want to avoid them?"

Gideon felt the world snap into sharp focus around him. "OOCs?"

"At your motel." Spellman looked pleased about it. Gloating. "Just thought I'd warn you. Find another place to stay."

"How did you know?" Gideon smacked his lips together. His whole body burned, but not from desire this time.

"I pay to know these things," Spellman said with a light shrug. "OOCs are bad for my business, it's why I keep my whole operation under this shroud. Dislocation conjurings, obscurement charms." He waved a hand through the air to indicate all that was around them. "I'll have your item ready tomorrow." He hesitated. "If you're going to use it to hurt a lot of people at once, I feel I should advise you that it's not going to be very satisfying for you." He ran a thin finger along the table. "It's all one rush, very immediate, not much pain or suffering ..."

"That's not a problem," Gideon said. "Know where I could stay for the night?"

Spellman gave a slight shrug. "They'll be watching the motels." He smiled a little. "There's a place on Water Street I think you'd like. I'll get you the address." Spellman hesitated. "I am strictly confidential with all my clientele, but perhaps I should ask what you plan to do with your item so that I'll know how best to structure the incantation?" He ended with a pleasant smile and folded his hands together.

Gideon told him.

"Holy shit," Spellman said, jaw slack, eyes wide. "I'll need payment in advance." Spellman's mouth opened and closed as he looked around the room like he was surveying it. "And some time to close my doors. Midday."

"Works for me," Gideon said. "That address?"

"I'll get it for you," Spellman said, getting out of the chair. He moved slowly, hesitantly.

"This isn't going to be a problem, is it?" Gideon asked as Spellman reached the threshold of the dining room.

"No, no," Spellman said, turning back. All the amusement was gone from him. "Just a little more trouble than I was expecting." He leaned closer to Gideon, like he was whispering something confidential. "You're a sight more ambitious than any of the Sygraath I've met in the last age."

Gideon watched his retreating back as Spellman walked toward the stairs and began to climb them. "Just got a taste for it now, that's all."

* * *

"You don't really believe much in having personal possessions, huh?" Lerner hit Hendricks with that as he was slipping the books back in his duffel bag. Everything was neat and mostly consigned to the bag.

Hendricks looked down at the duffel as he tucked the photo into the cover of one of the books, face down. He didn't want to look at it. "High speed, low drag."

He could hear the puzzlement in Lerner's voice. "What?"

"It's a saying in the Marines." Hendricks stood, cracking his back as he did so. He was making more popping noises now when he moved than he had before the fight yesterday. Also, his back still ached from where Lerner had given him that cheap shot for his brother demons or whatever. "In the infantry, you move around a lot. You don't want to carry a lot of shit with you. Makes drag. Slows you down."

"Huh," Lerner was nodding like it made some kind of sense to him. Hendricks doubted it. The demon was standing over by the table against the window. Duncan was paused just inside the door, and Lerner looked over at him. "Can we go in there now?"

Duncan's eyes were closed, and he was just standing there, still as could be. He didn't even wobble like someone trying to stand still would. "She's gone. We should be clear."

"I love the hint of chance in that," Hendricks said, "because keeping a clean criminal record this long hasn't been reward enough."

"Stop whining, you big pussy," Lerner said.

"I need my gun and sword back," Hendricks said.

"Yeah, yeah," Lerner said. "Now that your girlfriend's gone, they're all yours." He gestured toward the door, and Duncan stood back, opening it so they could leave.

"How are you gonna open the door?" Hendricks asked as he followed Lerner out and watched Duncan close it behind them. "Something more subtle than kicking it down, I hope?"

"Sure," Lerner said with a wink. "We have our ways, after all."

* * *

Gideon turned his car onto Water Street, which was just at the edge of Midian. It was ramshackle as all hell, a messy collection of old houses with peeling paint, white paneling falling off in great strips. Even at night it was obvious that the houses were just decaying away.

He checked the note Spellman had given him for the address again. He drove down the tree-lined road, figuring it wouldn't be hard to spot.

It wasn't.

Most of the houses were little shit, things you'd find in the first-ring suburbs of most major cities that had grown up after World War II. Tract homes. No exception here, except they might have been older. They were tiny, barely shanties in his opinion, save for the one he had the address for.

It stuck out in the middle of the block, probably once a beautiful manor house with lovely sculpting and a pleasant veranda to sip tea on as the sun went down.

Now it was a shithole, with the same faded wood paneling as everything else on the block, the warped floorboards visible even from the street. All the paneling from the gables of the roof had torn off, and what looked like mildew was growing beneath.

Gideon stepped out of his car as the rain started to fall again. He could hear it rattling the tin roof of the house as he made his way up the front walk. The lawn was overgrown, and a light burning in the front window was the only sign the house was occupied. The fresh night air was soured by the smell of some kind of smoke drifting off a porch down the way. Gideon could see the flare of someone lighting something up, but it didn't smell like tobacco.

He reached the front porch and avoided the most obvious of the warped floorboards. He stepped off track a dozen times before he reached the door and knocked tentatively.

There was movement inside that he could hear, and the door swung open suddenly to reveal a raven-haired woman in a white silk robe. Her skin was tanned, with spots here and there that showed hints of her age. He would have guessed she was on the late side of her thirties, but he wasn't all that good with human ages.

"Hello, darling," she said in a thick, husky voice. The accent wasn't Southern; it was almost more European.

"I'm ... uh ... looking for a room for the night," he said, hearing his voice change pitch through the sentence with embarrassment.

"Come right on in," she said, and her green eyes were lit with amusement. She was wearing a lot of dark makeup under them, and her eyelashes were black and prominent.

Gideon followed her into a foyer that didn't really match the exterior of the house. That was twice tonight. Inside it was decently maintained, with a placid blue wallpaper pattern highlighted by gold fleur-de-lis. There was a staircase just inside, and he looked at the white carpet leading up it as the woman shut the door behind him.

"My name is Melina Cherry," she said in that husky voice. He turned to look at her and she smiled. Her smile was about as real as her tits.

"Gideon," he said with a nod. He could feel the unease. "Like I said, I need a room."

"Well, Mr. Gideon," Melina Cherry said as she reached out and ran a finger softly across his face. "We don't just do rooms here, you must know. There are several lovely hotels here in the Midian area that would be more than glad to just let a room to you." She straightened up, stretching her long neck. Her robe fell open, revealing a bare breast. "Here, if you pay for the girl, the room is yours."

"Okay," Gideon said with a nod. "I'll take a girl—but only if I can have the room for the night."

She made a sound somewhere between a laugh and a snort. "We're not exactly set up for room service—at least not the kind you'd find in a hotel, but all right. I don't care if you sleep in the bed after you use it. Not at this late hour, anyway."

"Okay," he said. He didn't really want a girl, but it wasn't the end of the world. "How much?"

"A hundred," Melina said after a moment, running fingers through her thick, black hair.

Gideon nodded and fumbled into the pocket of his cargo shorts. He had it, it and plenty more to spare since Spellman was fine with being paid by bank transfer. He stripped five crisp twenties off the wad of money he carried and handed it over to Ms. Cherry—he doubted that was her real name—and she watched with patient expectation and counted as he went.

"Blond, me or the redhead, Mr. Gideon?" Melina Cherry asked once she'd slipped his money into the pocket of her robe. It was still open, and Gideon looked. He wasn't really into human bodies, but hers was not in bad shape. A little dappled on the skin. Age would do that, he knew.

"Uhm, blond," he said, picking at random. It mattered little to him.

"Interesting. Most people are asking for the redhead, lately. Colleen," Ms. Cherry trilled in a lovely tone. A whiff of strong perfume came from behind him and Gideon felt a hand tuck delicately around his waist.

"Show Mr. Gideon to a room, please."

"Right this way, sir," Colleen whispered in his ear. She walked at his side, and he glanced over at her. She was in her twenties, he figured, blond hair curled like she was a movie star. She sniffed a couple times, like she was trying to get a whiff of him. Her fingers were light against his back, and he could feel her tickling the flabby skin that he'd heard called a love handle. That was no big deal, either.

"Make sure you show our guest a good time, Colleen," Ms. Cherry said, and Gideon looked back to see her leaning against the banister, her robe still open for him to see. "Make him sleep soundly."

Gideon looked back to Colleen, who wore a smile that was fraught with tension. Her eye twitched and he wondered just what she was on. "Oh, I'm sure she will," he said aloud before Colleen could answer. "I'm sure she will."

Chapter 13

Erin had slowed down near town and let her thoughts catch up with her. She was almost through the town square when she thought of something and hit the next right turn.

The rain was spotting the windshield when she pulled into the apartment complex, the heat blowing so loudly that she couldn't even hear the rain. It gave off that smell, the one heaters had, and it felt like it was drying out her nose.

The Explorer was parked there, sure enough, just sitting in the middle of the parking lot. It had mud all over the back rear tires and covering the wheel wells. She stepped out into the freshly falling rain as the puddle just outside her door rippled from the droplets falling into it. The brick apartment was lit by a couple lampposts and lights outside every door.

She had been by Arch's old apartment once but knew that he had moved to a different one after some lowlifes had dropped by and kicked down his door. It had been the most exciting thing to happen in Calhoun County for years. Until today.

She stood outside her car and hesitated. Knocking on Arch's door at this hour felt strange. He was probably here, after all, since his car was parked outside. Why wouldn't he answer his radio or his phone, though? She bit her lower lip and chewed while she thought that over. The thing she least wanted to do was get into some sort of argument with him, especially about Hendricks.

"Dammit," she whispered, talking to herself, "his business is with the sheriff, not me." She started to turn and get back into her car when she saw someone move in the shadows.

* * *

Lerner let Duncan open the door because he had a subtle art with these things.

"Excuse me," Duncan said and gestured for Hendricks to move out of the way. The cowboy did, and Lerner felt himself grin. This was going to be good.

Duncan kicked the door open. The frame splintered around the lock and burst inward.

"Son of a bitch," Hendricks said, looking over his shoulder like the cops were going to descend on him at any minute. "I thought you said you had your 'ways'?"

"It's open, ain't it?" Lerner asked, grinning. "That's one way to do it." He gestured for Duncan to go in, which he did. Lerner started to follow but paused as he passed Hendricks. "Listen, kid, if you don't want to come in and see what it looks like when a Sygraath is nesting right next door to you, don't. Stand your law-abiding ass right out here and wait for us." He winked. "Won't be more than a minute or two."

With a pat on the cowboy's shoulder, which was covered with that black duster coat he wore, Lerner moved on in. Duncan was already standing in the middle of the room, feeling it all out. The place looked about like Hendricks's room had looked to Lerner—a complete and total shithole. The wallpaper was something between beige and reddish, but it looked brown—also, like shit—and the place smelled like someone had been whacking off and spraying their demon spunk all over the place. Which had probably happened because the inhabitant was a Sygraath.

Same bed in the same place, same shitty half-clean hotel smell that Lerner was used to. This one smelled like it might have been a smoking room at one point in time, the lingering aftereffects of cigarettes in the air after what had probably been years of absence. Or, hell, for all he knew someone had lit one up last week in the place. Lerner ran a hand over the wooden dresser and the TV as he steered past where Duncan stood. "Anything?"

Duncan was quiet for a beat before answering. "Nothing."

"What do you mean, nothing?" Lerner asked, frowning. It wasn't like Duncan to come up with 'nothing.'

"He's gone," Duncan said. Blank eyes turned toward Lerner. "Completely gone."

"What, did he leave and go back to Chattanooga or move out of range of your sense of him?" Lerner had seen that happen before. Wouldn't surprise him, either, if the Sygraath had gotten jumpy and bailed. It's what happened sometimes when OOCs came calling. The wise would pack up and leave rather than run into the storm that followed.

"No," Duncan said, and Lerner knew him well enough to recognize that look. It wasn't a good look.

"What the hell are you guys talking about?" Hendricks asked from the door. He was just leaning there, the cowboy, waiting outside the door frame looking guilty as a Frac'shaa with its hands in a baby carriage.

"He's disappeared," Lerner said, picking what Duncan was saying out of him without having to have him say it. "Which means he's got some black arts working for him." Before the cowboy could ask, he turned to head it off. "He wouldn't disappear if he didn't know we were on to him. Makes me worry he might have something in mind, something he'd like to be left alone to pull off. Something big." He could see the kid wasn't getting it, so he made it even more obvious. "Something that'll kill enough people to satisfy him."

* * *

The girl—what was her name again? Colleen—shut the door behind them. Gideon found himself drowning in her perfume, like it was sprayed on in a factory that made the stuff. The room didn't help; it had an obvious scent, too, like it was disinfected recently. It was a feast of red up here, the fleur-de-lis still present on the wallpaper, but everything highlighted in crimson instead of blue as it had been downstairs.

"What do you want to do, baby?" Colleen asked him, rubbing a hand across his shoulder. Gideon's t-shirt was still a little wet, and it was clinging to him in uncomfortable ways, especially around the gut. She leaned in close, and he could smell the gin on her breath, heavy as though she were pouring a glass of it right in front of his nose.

Gideon hadn't been with a woman before. It wasn't really his thing, wasn't something he was interested in. He knew other demons did it, but not his kind, not Sygraaths. They were self-gratifiers. He'd never even tried it with a human woman.

He felt himself smile. He hadn't tried a lot of things until lately.

Colleen lingered just a few inches away, and her hand made its way down to his cargo shorts and unfastened the button. He didn't need a belt, after all, and could barely keep the button fastened most of the time. It was just the shape of his body. It wasn't like he ate or anything. Just the way he was made.

He felt her hand slide down in there. She gave him a goose through the pants. He held his breath and thought of Sarah Glass and how she had died that very afternoon. How he'd felt it. He was hard when she put her hand on his cock, and he let his breath out in a gasp.

"I want you to blow me," he said before he even knew he was saying it. Her eyes were dull and glassy, but she nodded and slid down before he could say anything else.

She pulled his shorts down around his ankles and he felt her slide her lips around his tip. He gasped when she did, and closed his eyes. He thought of the afternoon, of what he'd done, and it made him swell. Every stroke of her lips up and down his shaft was twice as blissful as any time he'd ever touched it, the sensation of his own lack of control making everything a mystery and a surprise.

She stopped after a minute, and made a low, gagging sound as she pulled her mouth off his cock. He felt a rage fill him, the heat flooding his senses. He stood there, hard-on sticking out as she made a face then retched. "I'm sorry," she said at last, sounding a little choked. "I'm sorry, I think it's the cologne ... or whatever ... you put on there ..." She looked up at him. Her eyes weren't vacant anymore, but they were still glazed. "Can we switch to something else?"

Gideon could still feel the heat burning beneath his skin, but even with the desire fully engorging him, he still felt a little caution prickle at him. "Oh, I don't know," he said, lowering his eyes. "This was ... kind of a fantasy of mine." He didn't have much experience with lying, but he thought that came out all right.

"Oh, baby," Colleen said, and she cleared her throat. She slid up from her knees and took him in her hand, working him back and forth while she looked him in the eyes. "What other fantasies do you have?"

Gideon was smiling like mad inside, but he only inside. He kept his eyes down, only looking up at her every few seconds to gauge her reactions. "Well, I have this one ... but it's kind of ... kinky."

Colleen ran her free hand over the skin of his neck while she kept gently jerking him off with the other. It was keeping him hard, but that was about all he could say for it. "How kinky, baby?"

"Not too kinky," Gideon said, and kept his eyes downward. "I just always wanted to fuck a girl from behind ... while she was wearing a gag."

Colleen let out a little laugh, then pulled away from him to arrive at a wooden, mirrored vanity She slid open the top right-most drawer and her hand came back with something black and leather. Gideon had seen one of them somewhere before, in a movie. What was it called? Right. A ball gag. "I think we can handle that, baby," she said.

* * *

Erin saw the shadow moving out of the bushes over by the left-hand side of the building. She was already out of the car, so she started toward it. It was probably just someone walking a dog or out for a ... post-midnight stroll?

She kept one hand on her Glock in its holster as she made her way through the parking lot toward the shadow in the dark.

The air felt even cooler now after the heater in the car had warmed her up. The rain was starting again in earnest, switching from a drizzle to something more steady, and she wasn't wearing her rain gear. She could feel the droplets hitting the top of her head and her shoulders, falling onto the back of her uniform and seeping through to the skin. The world around her had a blanket of quiet dropped on it save for the sound of the rain and her shoes as she jogged across the pavement.

She edged closer to the source of the movement and saw the figure walking on the path along the side of the apartment building now. A lamp caught a flash of red hair and Erin hurried on, following behind.

Another few steps and she caught a glimpse of the profile—it was a woman. The same woman she'd seen on the overpass with Arch and Hendricks just this afternoon. She was pale like Snow White, her red hair glowed in the light of the lamps, and she was wearing too-tight jeans that were pretty much like something Erin herself might have worn. Except the redhead had on cowboy boots.

Erin started to freeze where she stood, one foot up the half-inch step over the parking lot's curb onto the sidewalk. She fumbled the step, though—probably from being surprised—and made a noise as she caught her balance. She looked back, like she was expecting to see something other than a curb she tripped over, and when she looked forward again, the redhead was gone.

"What the fuck?" she whispered to herself. There was a quiet hiss in the air as the rain picked up.

"Hello, Erin Harris." The voice startled her, made her jerk her head to her left. She kept herself from drawing the gun, but it was a close thing.

The redhead was just standing there, looking at her with a cold expression, watching her like she was some kind of animal to be studied. "Hello," Erin said. "How do you know my name?"

"I know a great deal about you," the redhead said, never breaking off her cold study of Erin.

"Oh, really?" Erin said and kept watch on her—on her hands. Like she could be hiding a weapon anywhere on that body. In those jeans. Yeah, right. "Well, I don't know anything about you."

"My name is Starling," the redhead said, still watching her.

"Great," Erin said, and tried to keep from making a sarcastic noise. "That's really fucking helpful. What are you doing here, Starling?"

"Very simple," Starling said, never once taking her eyes off Erin— which was fucking nerve-wracking. "I am here to speak to you."

* * *

The night air in the room was alive around Gideon, almost electric. It was dark, the lights off, and he was giving it to her from behind. Each stroke was almost as good as the ones he gave himself. Better in some ways. The smells of the act were something he was unused to, but they didn't bother him. He could hear her soft grunts muffled by the gag as he thrust into her and pulled back out again. So this was what he'd been missing.

He focused on the moments of the accident, the catastrophe he'd caused. He could feel their souls floating by him—Sarah Glass, Jack Benitez. Could touch them again, feel their agonies. It was bliss. He could feel something about to happen here, too. He was warming up to it, could feel his skin starting to heat up again. He exhaled, his breaths coming in light gasps. It was enjoyable, in its way.

His hands were on her hips, on her ass, pulling tighter to her, then away as he prepared for another thrust. He had a good grip and the pre-show was about to begin ...

He felt her jerk, saw her back tense in the moonlight that peeked between the red curtains. She made a noise but it was muffled by the gag. He could hear it in his head, though.

A scream. Of pain.

He gripped her tighter and clutched her close, felt himself grow stiffer within her. She was clawing at the bed, trying to reach the headboard. Trying to get away.

Silly bitch. No chance. Not against a demon.

She clawed at the sheets and he could hear her nails rip into the fabric. He held on, tighter, his fingers breaking the skin as he kept thrusting.

He grunted, as loud as he reasonably could. Moaned, louder still, to cover her noises. He could feel the desperation as she clawed to get away from him. Felt it. Fed on it.

The thrill overcame him and he finished, could feel the pulse of it, the discharge. He spurted for the first time in a live human being, and he could hear her scream in his head, even though it was muffled by the gag.

"Yeah, baby," he moaned as she struggled against his grip. His fingers tore into the flesh of her hips. He could feel the blood running down them. She didn't seem to notice. She had other problems.

The first sizzling noise presented itself to his ears. He could hear his ejaculate burning through her, out her belly. She went limp in his grasp, unconscious from the pain. He could feel himself still climaxing, the power of it stronger somehow, by the proximity and the act.

His breathing grew heavier and his discharge continued. He could feel it tunneling deeper into her now as she sagged limp in his arms. It had ruptured her intestines, her stomach. She was out from the pain, but he could still feel the agony tracing its way through her in her dreams.

He lay her gently upon the bed, facedown. He could hear the sizzle as his jizz burned its way through the mattress. And he did not care.

"There, there," he said and he stroked her ass. He stayed in her, though he could barely feel anything at all now. Everything close to his member inside had been burned away, seared into ash.

Gideon slumped on top of her, felt her clammy skin against his own warm flesh. He was still coming, her pain a fresh, delicious sweet for him to savor. Being in contact with her skin was like nothing he'd even felt. He didn't even have to touch himself to keep going. His ejaculations continued unabated, just by being this close to the source of the agony.

He felt his fiery emission creeping deeper and deeper within her, felt her nerves reacting even within her unconscious form. She was so close to death, so close ... and he was so close to her, he could feel it, taste it, touch it ... it was right there ...

When he felt her die, shuddering one last time beneath his fat belly, he came again, this time so hard he could hear it burning all the way up through her sternum and her neck.

When it was over, Gideon rolled over onto his back and fell into deepest sleep. The sleep of the utterly untroubled.

Chapter 14

"Beg pardon?" Erin asked. She was standing there, outside Arch's place, and the redhead was staring at her with those dead, dark eyes. Her hair looked like it was on fire in the light. Crazy shit. Some damned nice product at work there. "What the fuck did you say?"

"I am here to speak to you," the redhead said. The chill didn't seem to be affecting her, because she was wearing a tank top. A little too revealing for Erin's taste. It wasn't like she hadn't worn less, of course, but usually only at a beach or a swimming pool. Or in bed.

"About what?" Erin said, her hand resting comfortably on the grip of her pistol. She hadn't wrapped her hand around the Glock yet, but her palm was resting on the butt of the gun. It wouldn't take long for her to pull if something went awry.

Erin felt her face pinch as she frowned. Why was she even thinking about drawing a gun? It wasn't like this woman had done anything to her. She pulled her hand away.

"About the future," the redhead said.

"Oh, well that's exciting," Erin said. The future what? "First thing's first—what's your name?"

"Starling," the redhead said.

"Last name?" Erin asked.

"Just Starling," the redhead replied.

"Is that your stage name?" Erin said with a smile. "I bet the guys at Moody's Roadhouse just go nuts when you take your top off." Starling just cocked her head at her, looking bemused. It probably wasn't as cute as she'd thought it was. "What about my future or the future or … whatever? Make yourself plain, will you? And while you're at it, explain why you're sneaking up on Arch's door?"

"I told you, I am here to see you," Starling said in that same dull voice. "And I have no idea what 'Moody's Roadhouse' is, nor what sort of top I would be taking off there."

"I was calling you a stripper," Erin said. The shit she was saying did not seem to be dawning on this Starling. Maybe the girl was slow. "Get on with whatever you wanted to say about the future."

"Your future is not what you think it is," Starling said in a low voice, almost intoning.

"That's ... inspirational," Erin said. "My future is not what I think it is? Incredible. Say," she went on, "you're not one of those tarot card readers that hangs out back in the woods off Larren's Pike Road, are you? Because you hill folk really ought to stick to home; this town stuff really doesn't work out well when you—"

"Your future lies in a different direction," Starling said, and this time her voice seemed to come alive, stirring something in Erin. "You will protect the people."

"I'm a cop," Erin said, a little short. "That's what I do."

"You sit behind a desk," Starling said, eyes looking off into the distance. "You fetch coffee and sandwiches, answer radio dispatches. But you are called to a higher purpose."

Can I arrest her for lurking? That was the thought on Erin's mind after the last little gem came flying out of the redhead's mouth.

There was a clicking noise of a door opening and Erin turned her head to look. Arch stood framed in his doorway, gun in hand. "Erin?" His soft voice seemed to echo in the empty night. "What are you doing here?"

"I was talking to your friend Starling here—" Erin raised her hand to indicate the redhead, but she was gone. "What the fuck?" She turned and looked around, studying the dark outline of the bushes. "She was just here."

"Yeah," Arch said, and he sounded weary, "she does that."

* * *

Arch had heard voices outside, and lately he couldn't be cautious enough. He had his gun in one hand, switchblade ready in the other in case it was a demon. It was kind of a relief to step out of the stuffy apartment—Alison had turned the heat up again before going to bed—and into the cool night. It wasn't like this usually. Not even in late summer.

When he'd seen Erin outside, it was even more of a surprise. He wouldn't have been shocked to find Reeve. Man did his own dirty work, and Arch was surprised he hadn't called Alison at least. He was still working on what to say to explain everything that had happened.

"So what are you doing here?" Arch asked Erin, who was still staring off into the night, like she could catch a glimpse of Starling in the bushes and drag the red-haired girl out to prove she'd been there. Arch was sure she had been; how else would Erin have known who she even was?

"I told you," Erin said, and she sort of snapped, "I was talking to your friend Starling."

"Yeah," Arch said, patient by virtue of not having the energy to get irritable, "but I presume you were at least driving by the parking lot of my apartment building before that ..."

"Oh," Erin said, and she stopped peering at the hedgerow of bushes and trees. "Well, yeah, I was looking for you."

"Here I am," Arch said. He holstered his Glock. He kept the switchblade clutched in his palm, though, the cool plastic and metal against his skin. "Found me, you have."

"Yeah, I—" Erin stopped, her short blond hair bobbing as she angled her head at him. "Did you just quote Yoda?"

"Sort of. The actual quote is, 'Found someone, you have—" Arch felt a slight tinge of embarrassment. "I like *Star Wars*. So what?" He'd taken some heat on the football team in high school for liking geeky things sometimes, not to mention those rolled-eye looks from Alison. Didn't stop him from liking them, though.

"Reeve is looking for you," Erin said. She was at a distance, standing up the walk a ways toward the parking lot. "He's hopping pissed that you turned off your phone." She looked at him with narrowed eyes. "I told him I'd seen you up on the overpass with Hendricks and Starling."

"He's pretty mad, I take it?" Arch felt the burn on that one, too. Dereliction of duty, he thought it was called in the military. Something Hendricks would probably know. He felt a burning on that one, too, and wondered again what to do about the cowboy.

"He ain't happy," Erin said. "We got all this shit coming down, plus Tallakeet Dam is gonna start running over tomorrow." She shook her head, made a little angry noise. "I thought your God said he wasn't gonna flood the earth again."

Arch felt that tinge of annoyance for again having to explain away something that seemed obvious to him. "Despite what Reeve may think, the Caledonia River Valley doesn't constitute the whole earth."

Erin made a half-amused noise at that and coupled it with a smile. "Don't tell him that." Her expression darkened. "What the hell you got going on here, Arch? Hendricks and Starling, and ..." She looked behind her, like she was checking to see if the parking lot was clear. "Do you believe in demons?"

Arch felt the air turn colder. It was a not a question he was prepared for. He stalled. "Like fire and brimstone?"

Erin laughed. "I know, right? Crazy stuff."

Arch didn't smile, thinking of the cow-turned-demon that had hurled fire at him only a week ago. Perception changed fast. "Sure. Crazy."

She was watching him, though, and she caught it. He could tell by her expression. "Shit, you believe that stuff, don't you?"

What was the truth? He stuck close to it and started talking. "The Bible does say there are demons and—"

"Yeah, the Bible also says that the world is six thousand years old, and we've got some pretty compelling evidence to the contrary."

Arch wasn't really in the mood for a full-on, theological debate. "I'm not arguing the merits of Archbishop Ussher's chronology of the Bible at four a.m. for a variety of reasons, the least of which being I don't believe the Irishman was right and the greatest of which is that I'm too tired. You don't believe in demons. Why are you asking me about them?"

He saw her expression subtly change. He thought it turned a little ... spiteful. "Hendricks has books on demons in his hotel room."

"He showed 'em to you?" Arch felt his head reel a little at that one. He hadn't figured Hendricks would have been so dumb. Her mention of his name was more than a little salt in the wound, though, since Arch still had no plan for getting the cowboy back. Sitting around wasn't helping.

"Not exactly," Erin said, and Arch was prepared to call her out on dodging until she said something else. "But I just confronted him about them outside his motel and—"

"Wait, you just saw Hendricks?" Arch felt his body tense. "When?"

"Just a little bit ago. He was just getting back to his hotel with those two guys in suits." She blushed. "We ... uh ... had it out right there in front of them."

"Did you?" Arch murmured. He turned and fumbled for his keys, locking his door.

"Where are you going?" Erin asked.

"I lost track of Hendricks earlier tonight," Arch said, already heading down the walk toward the parking lot. "Just want to ... make sure he made it home okay."

"It's four a.m., Arch," Erin said as he started to pass her. She pivoted, and the look she gave him was incredulous. "If I were you, I might go make peace with Reeve for blowing off work in the midst of the single biggest crisis Calhoun County has seen."

"Yeah," Arch said, "I'll go do that, too."

"Seriously?" Erin said from behind him. "That's the line you're gonna give me? You gotta go check up on a twenty-five year-old bad boy that you barely know? Why the hell are you bullshitting me, Arch?"

Arch thought about looking back as he answered but decided it would be counter-productive. "I'm not ... doing that," he said, neatly avoiding repeating what she'd said, "to you. I just got business to attend to."

"You might want to attend to your job," Erin said. She was following him now into the parking lot, but not very fast. She wasn't trying to catch him. It was more like she was content to argue with him at a distance. "While you've still got one—"

He slammed the door and her words were lost under the roar of the Explorer's engine. He triggered the wipers once and goosed the gas pedal, heading out of the parking lot a heck of a lot faster than he normally would have.

* * *

Hendricks heard the squeal of tires outside his room. He was sitting there on the bed, Lerner in the chair by the window, tapping his fingers on the table. Duncan was standing by the door, staring straight ahead. He'd been doing that for a while, trying to get a handle on something, Lerner had said. Hendricks thought it was fucking creepy, but then again, he was hanging out in his hotel room with two demons with a boner for law and order of some sort.

Lerner looked up to Duncan, who stirred. "It's his cop friend," Duncan said, nodding at Hendricks.

"Arch," Hendricks said with a flash of annoyance. Couldn't they use proper names for human beings? Then again, he probably wasn't too hung up on using a demon's proper name. But of course he'd always thought they were killing machines, from top to bottom.

Also, his body and head still ached. Thinking wasn't on the top of his priorities list at the moment.

There was an insistent knocking at the door. "Open it," Hendricks said to Duncan.

"What's the magic word?" Lerner said, smiling at him with that smartass grin.

"Brimstone," Hendricks said. The mattress was soft against his ass, calling out for him to just lie down and go to sleep. It wasn't like they were doing anything else.

Lerner looked at Duncan and shrugged. "Good enough for me." Duncan opened the door.

It was Arch, sure as shit, and he jumped a little upon seeing Duncan behind the door in his purple suit, which was obvious by the motel room's light. Arch hesitated outside the door, and Hendricks could see his hand go to his holster.

"It's all right," Hendricks called out. "They're uh ..." he looked at Lerner, "... friends. Sort of."

Arch stepped inside and Duncan closed the door behind him. Hendricks watched Arch size up both Duncan and Lerner. They were both tiny compared to the big cop. "So ... who are your friends?"

"Lerner and Duncan," Hendricks said, nodding to each of them in order.

"First names or last names?" Arch asked.

"Assumed names," Lerner answered, keeping Hendricks from having to awkwardly try and guess which it might be. "In our world you don't give your name out all willy-nilly. Names have power."

Hendricks could see Arch just bristle, like he was a cat that had had a static-filled sheet of polyester run over him. "Demons?"

Duncan stared at him. It was Lerner who answered. "Yeah. And?"

Arch went a little bug-eyed, like he was gonna just wade into Duncan and start mopping the floor with him. "And nothing. Demons—"

"It's all right, Arch," Hendricks said. Though he had to admit, he wasn't sure it was. "Apparently there's a little grey area here. They're with the Office of Occultic Concordance. Law enforcement for the underworld."

"And still demons?" Arch asked. Hendricks could hear the urge to fight in the man's voice.

"You say that like it's an inherently bad thing," Lerner said from his spot by the table. Arch shot him a look that would have melted the pavement on an overpass. "I don't go killing you just because you're human, y'know."

"They're after the guy," Hendricks said, trying to insert himself back into the conversation before it got ugly. Arch had a mad-on for demons. Which Hendricks could understand, having had one for about five years himself. He paused. Still kind of did. These guys acted different, though, not like the ones that changed their faces and came at you with fangs and whatnot. He'd seen—and killed—plenty of that type. "The one that caused that massive pile-up."

"And what are they gonna do when they catch up with him?" Arch asked, surveying both Lerner and Duncan at once. It was interesting to watch the deputy try and keep his head constantly swiveling to keep an eye on them. "Pin a medal on him?"

"We don't give medals for killing humans," Lerner said with that same grin, though it went a little smarmier. "Just like you don't give medals for shooting fish in a barrel."

That one killed the conversation for a minute.

"We're going to send him back when we catch him," Duncan said after a pause. It was an uncomfortable silence, Hendricks recognized, and Arch was being damned stoic. Hendricks suspected that meant he was weighing whether or not to ventilate the essence out of Duncan and Lerner.

"Back to where?" Arch asked, and Hendricks saw him relax a little. "Hades?"

"What the fuck is wrong with you?" Lerner said with a laugh. "You can't bring yourself to say hell, so you gotta use the Greek god of the underworld's name?"

"I don't swear," Arch said, and Hendricks thought he bristled less this time. He was probably used to deflecting that inquiry.

Lerner just frowned at him, one side of his mouth up in a sneer. "True believer, huh?"

"Leave him alone," Hendricks said. "Let's talk about this syger-whatever."

"Sygraath," Lerner said and the frown went complete. "Fine."

"Why were you waiting here?" Arch asked.

"Because he was nesting next door," Duncan said, leaning against the mauve-taupe wall.

"Was?" Arch asked, and his eyes got big.

"We think he got spooked," Lerner said, dredging up some civility. It occurred to Hendricks that the demon would have been completely in place in a forties noir film. All he needed was a cigarette and for his hair to be a little more slicked back. "Someone might have tipped him we were in town."

Hendricks ran a hand over his face to scratch an itch and caught a scent of muddy stink clinging to him from when he'd been clubbed by Duncan. Whenever that had been. A couple hours ago? A lifetime ago, maybe.

"You could have called and told me you were okay," Arch said, and Hendricks looked up to see the deputy staring accusingly at him.

"Sorry," Hendricks said. "It's been kind of a blur since I got back here. I don't think I'm operating on all cylinders."

Duncan glanced at him. "You're suffering from fatigue and your body is trying to heal the cuts and bruises you've received in the last few days. Also, you're operating on a deficit of sleep."

"So, what's the deal here?" Arch said, staring at Duncan.

"He's a reader of some kind," Hendricks said. "Sees into people. Their essence."

"Yeah, they got a lady up in the hills that can do that, too," Arch said, none too amused, from the tone of his voice. "But I meant what's going on here? You're watching for this ... Sygraath together? You're working together?"

Hendricks looked from Duncan to Lerner. "Actually, they kind of bushwhacked me, interrogated me about Starling, and then dragged me back here." He shrugged at Lerner, who shrugged back. "I don't know about working together, but this Sygraath has got to go."

"He's broken the laws of the Pact," Lerner said abruptly. "In absolute violation of the Edicts of 1608, 1705 and a few other subsections. Sygraath are innocuous enough most of the time. They'll feed on death, but they don't cause it. They just savor it. You could make an argument they're making the last moments of the dying more miserable—"

"Which sounds like reason to kill them," Arch interrupted.

"—but they don't actually do the killing," Lerner said. "So we let 'em do their business. Now this one, he's crossed the line. He's killing people in a hotspot that's already hot enough to boil over. So, yeah, we want to punch his ticket." He glanced at Hendricks. "What about you, demon hunter? You want him bad enough to let us sit here for a while until he either shows up or we get another lead on him?"

"Why can't I just kill him myself?" Hendricks asked. He tried not to get too snotty about it, but he'd killed more than a few demons in his time, hadn't he? He knew how this shit worked. Plus, he'd just taken on one partner; two more was a level of ballooning that he hadn't ever figured on.

"You've been living next door to this guy for a week without even knowing it," Lerner said. One of his eyebrows popped up. "You're a hell of a demon hunter, you know that?"

"Also," Duncan added, quiet and droll as always, "this Sygraath is a greater and would likely put a fine sheen on your bones by dragging you all over the parking lot at this point. You're injured and weak and thus easy prey for even a non-fighter like him."

'Greater' was a term that Hendricks knew all too well. He exchanged a look with Arch, whose mouth was a tight line. "What do you think, Arch?"

Arch was damned quiet, and Hendricks thought that told him a lot about the cop's thought process. "You gonna throw in with demons?" He was still watching Duncan and Lerner both.

"They put up a fair argument," Hendricks said. It was true; they did have a point. He was not in mint condition for a fight with a greater, that much he was sure of.

"I don't truck with no demons," Arch said, and he was back to bristling again.

"Arch," Hendricks said, trying to figure out how to get the man to see reason, "Hollywood was a greater and he damned near rolled us even with the help of our mysterious sniper friend. Ygrusibas would've shredded us if we hadn't had Starling's help—"

"Did you say Ygrusibas?" Lerner asked. For the first time since Hendricks had met him, he looked dead serious.

* * *

Erin sat quietly in her cruiser. Funny how she'd already started to think of it as hers after only a day. The heat was still blowing, she pushed her hair back and rubbed at the tiredness in the corners of her eyes.

Arch was a good man; she had never really doubted it. Whatever he was in or up to with Hendricks, though ... it couldn't be good. Not only was Hendricks a lying, cheating sack of shit, but he might be crazy to boot.

Not only that, but he hung around the weirdest people. Who the fuck was this Starling? And could she get any more bizarre? Talking in a dead, emotionless voice about futures and shit, like one of those astrology-loving nutbags. Erin remembered some of the girls talking about that shit in school. Actually, she could have sworn Alison Stan was one of them. She always did hide some weird tendencies under that pretty, cheerleader facade.

What the fuck had Starling been talking about? Just crazy talk, surely.

Erin shook her head. "If I see that redhead again ..."

* * *

"You know what?" Arch said, and waved a hand at the three men—one man and two demons—sitting in the hotel room. "Talk it over however long you want. I got other stuff to do."

"Arch—" Hendricks said, and the cowboy started to get up off the bed. Tried, anyway. It didn't go so well and he cringed at the pain.

"You don't have to explain anything to me, cowboy," Arch said with a mirthless laugh. "Demons are real. Straight out of the bowels of Hades—" He saw that one demon—Lerner—roll eyes at that, "—and now you want to conspire with two of them to take down another. I might have thrown away my job today—"

"You didn't have to do that," Hendricks said, and this time he made it to his feet, though he was hunched a little, like an old man.

"Yes, I did." Arch didn't quite yell it, but he put force behind it. "Because I believe that demons—with the slaughters, and the accidents and whatnot—are a grave threat to the people of this town."

"They are," Hendricks said and took a shuffling step toward him. Arch backed toward the door, keeping an eye on Duncan, the one next to the door. He wasn't moving, though, just standing there.

"But now you're working with them," Arch said. He could feel the bile, the fury, rising inside him.

"Come on, Arch," Hendricks said, taking a limping step closer. "Surely even you can see that ... maybe they're not all bad?"

"Are they demons?" Arch asked and turned his head to look at the one called Lerner. He looked right back, smug. "Are they from hell?"

"That's the word," Lerner said. Still smug. Arch wanted to wipe that right off his face with a fist.

"Arch—" Hendricks said.

"Call me if you find this guy," Arch said, and fumbled for the door handle, "you know, if you and your demon buddies can't handle it."

He slammed the door as he left, indifferent to the noise it made in the night.

*　*　*

Lerner watched the cop go with little interest. He was a big fellow. Had kind of a scary look to him when he was mad. If you were human. Lerner didn't fear humans. Why would he? Most of them didn't know how to release an essence.

Lerner honed back in on the cowboy, who was standing just a few feet from the bed in his room. Which was a shithole exactly on par with the one that the unnamed Sygraath had been holed up in. At least the motel was consistent. "You mentioned Ygrusibas." He caught Hendricks's attention with that one. "How do you even know that name?"

Hendricks looked like he was just coming back to himself, and Lerner felt a little bad for having hit him earlier. Man looked like an empty shell of flesh sagging in on itself. "Because we killed—" Hendricks paused. "Because we sent him back to hell over a week ago. Whatever you call it."

"No, you couldn't have," Lerner said with a quick exhale. He meant it to sound amused, but he was in control of his facade enough to know it wasn't amusement but fear. The name of Ygrusibas had not been spoken aloud by a human in thousands of years.

Or at least it shouldn't have been.

"Yet we did," Hendricks said, shuffling back to the bed. He sat down slowly, and it made Lerner wonder if his ass was hurting for some reason, too. "Guy named Hollywood summons him up—"

"Not a real name, I presume," Duncan said. Lerner shot him a look which he thought was pretty clear. It said, *You don't actually believe this shit, do you?*

"Probably not," Hendricks said. "He comes to town with a book, kills some people on a farm on the outskirts with the intention of summoning Ygrusibas. Wreaks havoc." Hendricks adjusted his cowboy hat down, annoying the fuck outta Lerner. Why was the guy wearing a cowboy hat? He didn't even have a car, let alone a horse. Lerner looked around the room again real quick. Or a pot to piss in. "Releases Ygrusibas into a cow—"

"Whoa," Duncan said.

"Bull. Shit." That was Lerner's reaction. *No fucking way* was the other part of it, but he kept that to himself.

"More like cow shit," Hendricks said, bumping his hat back. What was up with the coat, too, Lerner wondered? "Anyway, the cow-demon starts going crazy, eats Hollywood, goes on a rampage, and Arch and I stop it before it gets out of the pasture."

Lerner didn't keep from rolling his eyes, not at this. "One of the ancients gets summoned up and two humans kill it in a cow pasture?" He faux-yawned, just to be an ass. "Yeah. Sure. You guys must be the Big Swinging Dicks of the demon-slaying scene in this fucking backwoods hell." He cast a sidelong look at Duncan and stopped. "You're not fucking serious."

Duncan was looking ahead, wide-eyed, watching Hendricks. "He believes it. And it could be. There were signs that something was seriously amiss, and it's not like we get a lot of communication about these sort of things from—"

Lerner made a low, rattling noise in his throat. "You think an ancient—" He cut himself off, because it sounded so fucking ridiculous. He stopped himself from repeating the 'You can't be fucking serious' thing again.

"It's ... possible," Duncan said with another light nod. "Things are moving fast up here. Faster than anyone back at home office could have predicted."

"Yeah," Lerner said. "Okay." He knew he wore a sour expression now, like he'd taken a sip of lemonade. And he hated that shit. No way would he believe it, though. The ancients didn't get out; not from where they were held.

No chance.

* * *

Arch pulled into the sheriff's station parking lot and killed the engine. He had that pit of dread in his belly, and it only seemed to grow as he opened the door and started toward the entrance. The night was heading toward dawn pretty quick, and he wondered—just a little—about what the morning would bring.

He grasped the cold, fixed steel handle of the door and pulled. The metal frame surrounded a Plexiglass window; there was condensation forming on the inside of it. Even though it was cooler outside now, it was still humid.

The interior of the sheriff's station was quiet, not a soul in the area behind the desk. Arch didn't quite make it to the counter before he saw movement in the sheriff's office and Reeve himself appeared at the door.

"Jesus Christ," Reeve said, and his face was blooming with thunderclouds. "Where the fuck have you been?"

"I couldn't handle it," Arch said, listening to the prepared words spilling out of his mouth. He'd gone over his options, and knew exactly where the truth would land him—up to his neck in quicksand. "I saw those bodies, that mess this morning and ..." He shook his head, keeping it low, bowed. "... I just couldn't handle it." He chanced a look up at

Reeve.

Reeve was staring at him, mouth hanging slightly open. "You couldn't handle it." He repeated it back, and Arch wondered if he'd actually stopped the sheriff's tirade before it could begin.

"Yeah," he said. "There was so much ... blood. The bodies were just ..."

Reeve ran a hand over his lip, stroking it. "Uh huh." There wasn't enough tone for Arch to tell what he was thinking. "So ... you, uh ..."

"Cut out on my patrol," Arch said. "Shut off my phone. Shut off my radio. Just went quiet for a while, went up in the woods and ... sat there."

Reeve stood at the entrance to his office and leaned a hand on the frame. When he stood like this, his protruding gut was obvious, hanging over the belt of his pants. He took a long, loud breath and sighed, then puffed his lower lip like he was thinking over something awfully hard. "We needed you today out there, Arch." His words were laced with quiet disappointment.

"I know," Arch said and gave as contrite a nod as he could. However upset he was with Hendricks—and he was powerfully upset—and the demons, he tried not to let any of this show in the moment. "I hate that I let the team down." It always came back to football for him, and he'd learned long ago that a coach more readily accepted an apology. They'd still chew you out, but it usually cut it down a little. Only a truly vindictive person would continue to harp on someone after they'd accepted an apology. "I'm sorry."

"Well, shit," Reeve said, nodding. "I can't say that ... sight this morning ... didn't send my stomach in a few different directions. Still, we had a hell of a lot go wrong today, Arch. And yeah, you did let down the team." Reeve straightened in his doorway. "But hell, you'll be paying for it later today with the rest of us." He waved at Arch, and Arch headed toward him tentatively. "Come on in. We got things to talk about."

"Oh?" Arch asked, taking slow steps toward the sheriff.

"Yeah," Reeve said, and then turned back into his office. "Just when you think the shit can't hit the fan any harder, another fucking turd splatters every-goddamn-where."

* * *

Gideon awoke just before dawn. He could see the first hints of it peeking out from behind the red curtains. He sniffed as he came to consciousness, and the smell was all burn, flesh roasted and flambéed. It wasn't a bad smell; it, reminded him just a little of cooked meat. He rolled slightly to look at the hooker. She was still there, facedown on the bed. Other than being pallid as all hell, she looked like she was sleeping in a doggy-style position, face down in the pillow. He rolled her over just to see what kind of damage his jizz could do to the human body, and holy shit, motherfucker—

Gideon rolled off the bed. He'd seen some foul deaths in his time. It was part of who he was, after all. Car accidents that rendered people wide fucking open or decapitated them. Homicides by serial killers who knew how to make the agony last. This, though—this might be one of the more grotesque things he had seen.

The hooker was burned clean through from her pelvis all the way up to her gullet. A three-inch wide trench stretched from just below her mid-throat down, down to where her vagina had been. It was seared inside, crispy and bloodless, cauterized through and through.

He'd left her hollowed out and he could see it. Her lifeless eyes were as empty as her insides now.

Gideon hurriedly dressed, peeking at the spot on the bed where his emission had burned through her. The sheets were seared and blackened, and he leaned over to look down. There was hole straight through the mattress, the box springs. He got down on all fours to look, and saw a black scar under the bed, barely visible as the sun's rays were starting to shed light through the curtains.

Gideon ran a hand into the scarred floor and felt concrete an inch or two down. A subfloor. In a bedroom? He wondered if it was meant to be soundproofing or just the lucky results of a renovation. Whatever the case, it had stopped his spooge from burning its way through into the first floor below. He didn't know where that might have ended, but it probably wouldn't have gotten him any more sleep.

When he was finished pulling on his socks and shoes, he looked around the room quickly. He hadn't brought anything with him except the rune and his cash, and those were both safely in his pockets. He opened the door to the hallway and looked out. There was no one visible, so he crept out and closed the door behind him.

He walked toward the stairs, his feet making little noise as he took care to mind his steps. He went down the carpeted stairwell and reached the bottom, about to grab the gilded handle to the front door when a voice stopped him.

"Did you have a relaxing night, Mr. Gideon?" Melina Cherry called out to him from behind and Gideon turned to see her standing in the frame of a door under the stairs, still wearing that same silky robe that was split open.

"Oh, yeah, great—uh—night of sleep," Gideon said. He had the handle in his hand. The door was right there.

"Was Colleen to your satisfaction?" Melina asked and arched her arms out, one hand on each side of the door frame. The gesture split her robe open wider, and Gideon stared at her breasts for just a moment. He really didn't see any appeal in them. They were just round lumps of skin with a discoloration in the middle.

"Oh, she certainly satisfied me," Gideon said with a nod. His hand clutched tighter on the handle. "I think I might have worn her out, though." He tilted his head toward the stairs. "She was still sleeping when I left."

"Of course," Ms. Cherry gave him a smile that was all politeness. "I hope you'll grace us with your presence again, Mr. Gideon. Colleen would certainly enjoy spending time with you in the future."

"Sure she would," Gideon said without any inflection.

"And if your tastes were to change, I or my other girl would love to help you fulfill all your fantasies," Ms. Cherry said with that same smile. "Good day to you, Mr. Gideon."

"Good day," Gideon replied stiffly. He opened the door and walked out. The air was heating up already, felt humid. He looked up and saw a sky half-filled with clouds. By the time he'd reached the bottom step of the porch he thought for sure he'd be sweating any moment now. Had to be.

He got to the car and started it up in a hurry. He looked up at the whorehouse, the faded panels and worn siding. He hit the accelerator and knew he'd have to get a new car. Soon. Real soon. He rolled the window down and stared up at the second floor window where he had spent last night. Where he'd done something he'd never done before.

Taken a human life when he was RIGHT THERE. It was a new kind of high. He was discovering lots of those lately. It was an awakening for him.

As he was pulling away, he heard the screaming start. He steered a left at the end of the street, headed out toward the edge of town. It wouldn't do for him to get caught now. Not yet. He had one last thing to do before he left this town for good.

And it was gonna be the biggest high yet.

He was sure of it.

Chapter 15

Erin killed the lights and sirens on the patrol car as she pulled onto Water Street. She could see Arch's Explorer, the doors just opening. She'd gotten the call when she was a good ways out of town but hauled ass to get there. She'd heard of the whorehouse here, but knew that Reeve hadn't ever gone after them because they'd kept their noses clean of complaints.

As she let the car drift to a stop, she suspected his days of letting it slide were pretty well over.

Reeve and Arch were getting out of the Explorer, which was an interesting pairing. She wondered how far up the sheriff's shit list Arch was sitting at this point.

She opened the door and felt the warmth of the semi-cloudy day shine down on her. The air reeked of weed. She looked down the street and saw a guy standing out on his porch with a joint in his hand. She gave him a hard stare and he put the joint behind him. Dumbass.

"I'm gonna go talk that possession charge waiting to be booked," Reeve said as he stepped up to the curb. "See if he saw anything."

"Be gentle," Erin said, "he looks dumb."

"He's smoking reefer on the street in broad daylight with two police cruisers in plain sight," Reeve said, giving her a look that expressed his annoyance and called her a dumbass all in one. "That don't exactly scream out 'brain trust.'" Reeve turned and started making his way up the grey concrete sidewalk.

Erin turned to look at Arch, who was waiting by the curb, staring up at the whorehouse like it was gonna reach down and bite him. "You make your peace with Reeve?" she asked.

"We came to an understanding, yeah," Arch said.

"Uh huh," Erin said, watching him. He looked a little shifty to her, and that was odd because shifty was not in Arch's character.

"Let's get this done," Arch said, and started up the walk.

The house was a rambling, old-style Southern home. Looked like it could have been a haunted house, even, just based on the outside appearance. It wasn't quite Addams-family style, but close. The gables were peeling even worse than the paneling on the rest of the house, but once upon a time it might have been white. A long time ago.

Arch reached the front door before her, his long legs allowing him to outpace her without any trouble. She thought about hurrying to catch up but she didn't want to seem too overeager. This was basically day two for her, after all, and she wanted to get it right.

The door was already cracked open, but Arch knocked lightly. She almost shoved him out of the way but thought the better of it. "You're too damned polite," she said and pushed it open.

There was a woman waiting in the front hall, a white silk robe laid open and her chest and belly exposed in a strip right down the middle to her crotch. Erin could see a well-groomed pubic mound, waxed like it was a spot that saw regular visits from the hedge trimmers. The woman was dark of complexion, like she was of Mediterranean extraction, and the raven hair on her head matched the minimal carpet.

"Uhh, excuse us, ma'am?" Arch sounded all tentative, a step behind her, like he was afraid to cross over the threshold without an invitation. That drew to mind the thought of vampires and demons, which she quickly dismissed once more as utter stupidity. It did set her blood to a quick boil, though.

"Come in," the woman said, and her jaw was set like it had been sculpted into place. She had a figure like a statue, too. Erin felt a little swell of envy. If she looked that good in her early forties, she'd be surprised; she'd gained ten pounds in the year since high school graduation and was doing her best to ignore it. She knew she still looked good anyway.

Maybe not as good as this lady, though.

"My name is Melina Cherry," the woman said, her expression near blank. Her eyes looked like they might have been a little puffy.

"Ma'am," Arch said in acknowledgment. At least he didn't hold out his hand to shake it. Erin checked. He was hanging just a couple steps behind her now, examining the white crown molding that ringed the walls. Doing anything but looking at the nearly naked woman in front of him. Reeve would have been gawking. Politely, jaw firmly closed and tongue reeled in, but he'd have been gawking. Ed Fries wouldn't have bothered to even try and look polite. That fat boy was a perv.

"You called and reported a murder, ma'am?" Erin asked, trying to awaken the woman out of the trance she appeared to be in.

"Yes," Melina said, focusing her striking green eyes on Erin. Erin wondered if they might be contacts, they were so incredibly bright and vivid. "One of the girls that lives here," Cherry paused, presumably waiting to see if Erin would interrupt to call her a hooker or worse. Erin didn't, just kept her lips buttoned tight and listened. "She had a gentleman caller last night." Cherry's eyes flashed. "She went to bed with him. After he left this morning I went to check on Colleen and found her ..." Ms. Cherry's dark complexion lightened for a moment, "... found her as she was."

"Dead?" Arch asked.

Melina Cherry turned and gave him a scalding, you-idiot look. "Yes. She's fucking dead, Officer. Which is why I called to report a murder and am talking to you now about her rather than the other girl that lives here that is still alive."

Erin made a mental note to ask where the other girl was but first things were first. "Where's the body?"

"Upstairs," Ms. Cherry said, pointing up the banister.

"Are you sure she's dead?" Arch asked. Erin looked back at him. He didn't seem chastened by Ms. Cherry's earlier berating. She figured Arch probably had thick skin for that sort of thing, having probably had his ass chewed a few times.

Ms. Cherry gave him a withering look. "Yes, I'm sure," she said, her voice below freezing.

"All right," Arch said. "One of us should go look at the body."

"Yeah," Erin said with a nod then turned back to Melina Cherry. "One thing first. Where's your other employee?"

Ms. Cherry gave her an insincere smile. "You mean the other girl that lives here? This is just a boarding house, you realize."

"Of course," Erin said, rolling her eyes. Ms. Cherry pretended not to notice, but her own eyes narrowed marginally. "Where is she?"

"She didn't see anything more than I did," Ms. Cherry said.

"Still," Arch said, "we need to question her."

"Lucia," Cherry called out, tilting her head toward the open parlor just to their left, "come here." She smiled, a little more warmly now. "Lucia is new in town, hasn't been here for more than a few weeks. She's already quite popular, though ..." Ms. Cherry turned her head as a woman appeared at the entrance to the parlor. "Lucia, these officers want to ask you some questions." Cherry smiled insincerely again. "And since they haven't bothered to introduce themselves, let me just go ahead and handle this by reading you their names off the name plates on their uniforms. This is Officer Harris," she pointed to Erin, "and Officer Stan." She turned back to the entrance to the parlor and Erin turned with her.

The woman standing in the entry to the parlor was taller than she was, with pale skin. She wore a tank top under an overshirt and tight jeans, and looked like she might have just gotten dressed. She wore no makeup, and her eyes were downcast but blatantly green, maybe even more vivid than Ms. Cherry's, from what Erin could see.

And her head was fire red, glimmering in the glow of the morning sun peeking through the windows of the whorehouse.

"Starling," Erin whispered.

* * *

Lerner let a long, slow exhale cause his lips to sputter against each other, making a THBBBBBBT noise. It annoyed the shit out of Duncan, he knew, but he did it anyway. Besides, Duncan was trancing against the wall, taking a listen to the things going on outside of the motel room. The cowboy looked like he was ready to pass out on the bed.

"I think I need to sleep," Hendricks said, slurring his words.

"You shouldn't have taken those painkillers if you wanted to stay awake," Duncan said from his spot on the wall. His suit clashed with it horribly, the colors wrestling for dominance of Lerner's sight.

"I didn't see him take any painkillers," Lerner said. He hadn't. And he'd been watching the cowboy pretty close.

"He did," Duncan murmured, eyes closed. "I saw it."

"Maybe if you fuckers hadn't aggravated my injuries, I wouldn't have needed them," Hendricks said. He was slurring worse now. "Do you know what it feels like to have broken ribs?"

"No," Lerner said. "I don't have any ribs."

"Right," Hendricks said, and nodded. His cowboy hat was beside him on the bed, and his eyes were fluttering.

"I don't think he's coming back," Duncan said from beside the door. Lerner looked over at him and Duncan went on. "He's gotten wind of us. It's only the reason he'd mask himself. That means he won't come back here."

"Unless he's trying to bushwhack us," Lerner suggested. It could happen. It had happened before to their people. No one really loved being policed, after all.

"You're thinking like he's a fully-formed criminal mind," Duncan said with a shake of the head. "He's not. He's evolving right now. Awakening." He paused, closed his eyes again. "Something's going on across town. Lots of agitation."

"Another ... incident?" Lerner asked. He glanced over at the cowboy. Hendricks's eyes were closed now.

"Another dead body, yeah," Duncan said.

* * *

"No, no," Melina Cherry said as Arch stared at her. "Her name is Lucia."

Arch was desperately uncomfortable. The whole place smelled heavily of perfume and was decorated on the inside in high Southern style. He supposed it was all to make the johns feel better and more comfortable, but it was having the opposite effect on him. He had a sense of what this place was supposed to be like—the brothel had been here since he was a kid, after all, and his teammates had come here in high school—and this wasn't quite it. He imagined it smokier, like a speakeasy, a place where illicit dealings happened in a glamorous setting.

"Right," Erin spoke up, nodding. "Lucia." She turned to "Lucia" and pursed her lips. "We could use a word."

Arch stole a glimpse at Lucia again. She was Starling, there was no doubt in his mind about that. He'd seen enough of the woman, even in the dark places she usually appeared, to know what she looked like. This was surely her, though her eyes looked different.

Plus, she had an actual expression on her face. Lips quivering, eyes darting a little tentatively from Arch and Erin to Ms. Cherry. Arch would have guessed she looked a little ... intimidated. That was certainly new.

"Anything you have to say to her you can say in front of me," Melina Cherry said. She didn't move, but Arch had a mental image of a mother thrusting herself in front of an attack on her baby.

Or a criminal trying to keep an accomplice from getting rolled by the cops. That was probably more likely.

Evidently Erin saw it that way, too. "We're not here to investigate any unrelated crimes that may have taken place here," she said, focusing in on Ms. Cherry. Arch could see she was trying to be reassuring. "We only want to talk about the murder."

Ms. Cherry seemed to relax at that. "Why don't you go take a look at the body? We'll wait for you here, and you can talk to us however you'd like afterward."

Arch caught Erin's look back at him, and he could tell she was thinking the same thing. "Ma'am, we can't leave the two of you alone right now."

Ms. Cherry rolled her eyes. "I am a pillar of this community. I'm not going anywhere and neither is Lucia." She must have caught their hesitation, Arch thought, because she immediately backed down. "We'll follow you up the stairs and wait outside the door." Ms. Cherry held up her hands in a show of surrender. "We are willing to cooperate in any manner possible." Her face hardened. "To make sure justice is done for Colleen."

Arch looked to Erin as she looked back at him. "Fair enough, ma'am," Arch answered for both of them. This time he couldn't tell what Erin was thinking.

Arch took the lead, walking up the carpeted stairs and ignoring the white French insignias that were stenciled on the walls. What were they called? He couldn't remember. Flower something. He kept his hand on his holster even though he knew he was heading up to see a body. It was unsecured scene, after all, so technically he could have been running into anything.

"Just stay a couple paces behind me," Erin said to the two women. Arch couldn't bear to think of them as anything other than women. He didn't want to consider their jobs, because it wasn't the sort of thing he cared to dwell on. He knew plenty of others willing to cast more than a few stones their way, but he didn't do that sort of thing. Mary Magdalene had walked their path once upon a time, after all.

Every step Arch took up the stairs made him feel the nerves more and more. He took a quick breath and let it out slowly, blowing it out quietly between his lips. When he reached the top of the stairs he took careful steps, as though any squeak of the floorboard would wake the dead. If that happened, he'd have bigger problems than breaking the news to Hendricks that Starling was actually a woman of the night in some sort of disguise.

He frowned. She'd always seemed stronger than a normal woman to him. He kept himself from glancing back at her, didn't want to blow her cover with her employer. Something about this whole thing was awfully bizarre, though. Nothing about Starling had ever seemed coy or shy. She hadn't ever blinked away from him like she did downstairs.

But then again, he'd never had a conversation with her in the brothel where she apparently worked, either.

Arch reached the door. It was open just a tad, and he reached out and pushed it further with his elbow. He could hear Erin just behind him, now, could almost feel her breathing down his neck. He inched inside one slow step at a time.

As soon as he was clear of the frame he took a step to the left and just stood there. What was waiting on the bed was every bit the horror he was coming to expect since the demons had come to his town. He knew the girl on the bed; she'd been a freshman when he'd been graduating. Colleen something.

"Damn," Erin said from next to him, standing in the middle of the door. "Colleen Hudson. Her daddy works at the mill."

Arch nodded. She was all burnt up on the inside from what he could see, like she'd swallowed a cup of molten lava and it had all bled out of her. He wanted to cover her up, though there wasn't much left of her that was improper to be shown, but he knew that'd interfere with the crime scene. "I ain't never seen nothing like this," he said.

"It's kind like she got blowtorched," Erin said. "From the inside." Her voice was hollow and she sounded to Arch like she was somewhere else.

"What's that on her mouth?" Arch asked. He started to take a step toward her, but Erin's hand on his shoulder stopped him.

"It's a gag," Erin said, and she only met his eyes for a second. "He gagged her so no one would hear her scream."

Arch stared back at the body for a moment before turning away. He'd seen about all he could stand of this. So many dead yesterday and now another one on the pile. This one wasn't even close to human in its execution. More demons. Maybe the same one, the … Sygraath. They'd found that burning stuff on the pavement, after all.

Arch wheeled around and looked again. She wasn't Colleen anymore, that was certain. Her face was ashen and her eyes rolled back. If her mouth was gagged, and something burned her from the inside … His eyes roamed the corpse, and he cringed as he did it. Not because of the gruesome state of it—though it was—but because he was looking at a naked woman who wasn't his wife.

She was not burned at the neck, not really, but all the way through the chest and down to her pelvis. It seemed obvious to him, though he was hardly a coroner. There was a black, burnt strip on the bed next to her and he lowered himself to his hands and knees so he could see that it had carried under the bed.

Another strip of burnt-out wood. Something glimmered in there, like oily liquid, and Arch knew. He knew.

It was the same guy.

* * *

Gideon took the car onto the bumpy dirt road and braced himself with every shock. He needed to stay off the highways now, and he'd figured out the back roads, the ones between him and his ultimate goal. He'd found another route after that, one that would lead him out of town via some old, scenic highways. They'd carry him to Knoxville, and from there he'd be able to rent another car and head north. Maybe to New York. He had a good feeling about New York again.

He turned the A/C down as he pulled up in front of the farmhouse again. He stepped out into the morning heat and looked up. The dark clouds were coming again, and that wasn't bad. Storm coming to a head but still some sunshine making its escape before it got blocked. He could smell the rain in the air.

He liked it.

He turned the handle and didn't experience the disorientation this time when he stepped inside Spellman's storefront. He decided that it must have been some sort of conjuring that Spellman had done here, that he wasn't actually in a farmhouse in Tennessee. He could feel the shift this time as he crossed the threshold. Most people wouldn't notice that. Fewer would care. Spellman probably moved shop with the hotspots, but he didn't really have to "move" anything. Not literally, anyway.

The smells and sounds were still muted from the cage room to his left, but he could detect them this time. Gideon ignored them; now didn't seem like the moment for him to take interest in the misery of others, not when he'd learned just how amazing causing said misery could feel.

He walked down the hall, listening to the echo of his shoes against the floor. He came around the corner into the dining room to find Spellman sitting there, hands folded, as though he were expected. "I told you midday."

"I know," Gideon said. "I'm not here to pick up yet. I just figured I'd wait here until it's done."

Wren Spellman's eyes watched him, a little smile perched upon the man's thin lips. "You have nowhere else to go."

Gideon shrugged. "I could go shopping in town, but ..."

"No, you can't, "Spellman said with a knowing look. "You're lying low because of what you've done. Refuge will cost extra."

Gideon smiled. "Money I've got."

Spellman's smile matched his own. "Indeed you do."

* * *

Erin hadn't seen anything like Colleen Hudson's corpse before, not ever. Not in all the year's she'd slaughtered animals, not in the time she'd spent on the internet looking at pictures that were designed to gross her out, not anywhere. It was disturbing in a way, all the more so because she could not figure out how the hell it had happened.

She was hardly a forensic pathologist, but it looked like Colleen had

had some molten liquid poured into her vagina or anus, and it had just dribbled down and opened her up. It was hard to tell without stepping up and getting closer, but that seemed like the sort of shit that would require something elaborate to carry.

"This gentleman caller," she said, making herself loud enough to be heard out the door. "Was he carrying anything with him when he came in?" She talked to direct her voice out into the hall, but her eyes never left the body.

"No," Melina Cherry called back. "He wore cargo shorts and a t-shirt, a pair of tennis shoes. I doubt he had anything with him, why?"

"Just checking," Erin said, lower this time. She was already back to thinking about the body. She looked sidelong at Arch. "What's your friend doing here?"

"I don't know," Arch said, voice low. "I didn't know she worked here."

Erin paused, waited a second. "Does Hendricks know her from here?" She watched Arch freeze and started to ask him something else, but there was a noise out in the hallway.

"Reeve, maybe?" Arch asked. He looked a little relieved, like he might have been spared the question he didn't want to answer. She'd hit him with it again later, even though she was beginning to wonder if it even mattered at all anymore.

"Hello?" A voice from the door caused Erin to turn. It wasn't Melina Cherry, nor Lucia or Starling or whatever she called herself. It was a woman in middle age, blond hair that was too blond to be natural, dressed in a tweed skirt and suit jacket. She was smiling, look in the door as if there weren't a burned-out corpse just over Erin's shoulder. "How do you do?" she asked and took a step into the room. She was wearing black shoes, expensive ones, high heeled, and they clicked on the maple floor. "My name is Lex Deivrel. I'm Ms. Cherry's attorney." She proffered a business card, waving it in Erin's face.

"Well, that's just fucking great," Erin said, and she didn't even care who heard it.

* * *

They'd done a bank transfer because it was easier, Spellman had said. Gideon didn't care. He had plenty of money and if everything came out like he hoped it would, he'd be able to replenish the coffers and more after today. Not that he cared about that part; he just liked to be comfortable, even though he usually ended up in the lower rent neighborhoods.

He went where the death was, after all.

Now Gideon was just sitting in the chair and Spellman was across from him, staring at him blankly. Really blankly. Like there was no one steering the ship, actually. "Pardon," Spellman said after a moment, the light coming back into his eyes. "You're talking to a shell I use to conduct business. I'm presently working in the ... back room, let's call it."

"Yeah, that's fine," Gideon said. He wasn't looking for someone to entertain him. He was just building anticipation for the big event anyway.

* * *

Lerner and Duncan had left Hendricks sleeping. Why bother the poor guy? It wasn't like they needed him anyway. They headed toward the disturbance Duncan had mentioned, Lerner at the wheel, Duncan next to him with his eyes closed, directing him.

"This whole thing has got me thinking," Lerner said. Duncan grunted, a low noise that indicated he was listening, so Lerner went on. "If left to their own devices, without us to ride herd on them, would every Sygraath out there eventually start scrounging up their own meals?"

Duncan made a hmm-ing noise. "The world is a little more peaceful in the last few decades than it has been before."

"And the murder rate in the U.S. is at a forty- or fifty-year low," Lerner said, feeling himself warm to the subject. These were the kind of discussions he loved to have, but Duncan was all too reluctant to participate. "Fewer war deaths worldwide this decade than in decades past. Fewer plagues. Longer life expectancies."

"I've heard tales about Sygraaths gone bad as far back as the 1600s," Duncan said. "Which means there were probably more before that. This isn't something new."

"No, but the state of the world might be changing them," Lerner said.

"Less death means less for them to feed on. Just like scarcity of food makes wildlife migrate. A starving man will do desperate things, right?"

"They're hardly starving," Duncan said, still with his eyes closed. "Chicago alone last year had some four hundred plus murders. Plus the normal mortality stuff couple with larger overall populations."

"But you know what I mean," Lerner said. The A/C was blowing in his face.

"Rarely."

"I'm wondering if this guy is pushed to the edge by societal change," Lerner said.

"Most human societies would view fewer murders and deaths as a good thing."

Lerner sighed. "But a Sygraath wouldn't, and that's the point. Now he's sparked his own little habit and doing some seriously fucked up things to hit his high. I mean, really," Lerner said, "who knows what he's capable of?"

* * *

Erin was still trying to absorb what was going on with the lawyer when Reeve came in. They'd already moved back down the stairs into the foyer, and Deivrel had the madam and her hooker in the parlor. She was standing in front of the door holding court like she was guarding the passage. The place still stank of cheap perfume, and Erin was trying to decide whether she was more sick of the smell or the lawyer who'd been politely but firmly rebuffing and steering them for the last five minutes when the door opened and Reeve came breezing in.

"Turns out it wasn't just possession, but also a probation violation from one of my favorite repeat offenders," Reeve said as he strolled in. He stopped when he realized there was someone standing before him that wasn't expected. "Well, shit. There goes my day."

Lex Deivrel still wore the uncaring and cold smile of someone who was putting on a face for their audience. "Well, Nick, I hope it was that dead body upstairs and not me that did it."

"Lex," Reeve said, making a clicking noise with his mouth, "every time you come to my county, it seems like hell rides in behind you. I didn't see you park your pale horse out front."

"Oh, Nick," Lex said, and Erin could hear the slyness, "from what you say about me behind my back, you don't think I ride a pale horse, you think I ride a broom."

"Can't argue with that," Reeve said, staring her down. "You giving my deputies problems with their duties?"

"Just trying to make sure my clients are given the fairest treatment possible," Deivrel said, her fake smile not so much as flagging. "There's a lot of room for them to be wronged here, you see."

"Yes, well," Reeve said, "I can see where they might be concerned with that, being hookers and all—"

"Why, Sheriff Reeve," Deivrel said in utter shock, "that's an unsubstantiated allegation."

"Oh, it's well substantiated," Reeve said without amusement. "It just hasn't been proven in court."

"Which is the guidepost you should use in your conversations with my clients," Deivrel said coldly, "Lest you find yourself on the wrong end of a slander suit."

"Do you get a percentage of the recovery on something like that?" Reeve asked, and ran a head over his balding head.

"Of course," Deivrel said with that same faux smile.

"I knew I should have been a lawyer," Reeve said under his breath. "All right, well, the crime scene unit from Chattanooga ought to be here soon—seeing as they have to take the regular roads, they can't fly straight here on a broom," he gave a nod to Deivrel, who just smiled. "Why don't we move this on down to the station house so we don't have to do this on the front lawn while the mercury is heading toward ninety?"

"I'd rather not," Deivrel said, and Erin got the impression that she was a wall, standing between her clients and Reeve. "It's going to rain again soon, anyway. Cool the whole town off."

"Your 'rather' and mine are about to come in conflict," Reeve said and looked sideways. "I need to consult with my deputies for a moment. I also need you and your ... 'clients,'" he said it with enough differentiation that Lex Deivrel scowled at him, fake smile gone in a second, "to step outside. Away from the crime scene."

"Fine," Deivrel said, and her smile came back. She recovered quickly,

Erin thought.

"Deputy Harris, Deputy Stan," Reeve said, and beckoned to her and Arch, "a word, please." He nodded to Deivrel. "You ladies, too. Let's get out of here."

* * *

Lerner and Duncan were parked just down the street. It was easy to see when the house started to clear out. The big black deputy came out first—Lerner was bad with names, but hadn't Hendricks called him 'Arch' or something? Yeah. The cowboy's girlfriend was next, pert little blond, followed by a woman wearing nearly nothing, a lawyer—Lerner could smell that for himself—and a redhead. "Hello," he said. "Look who we have here."

"Coming out of the whorehouse, no less," Duncan said, eyes opened. He was wearing a frown. "I can feel her."

Lerner looked over at him. "Really? Are her tits real or fake?"

Duncan ignored his classless remark. "She's definitely there. Not like last time at all."

Lerner stared at her, dressed just about the same as when last he'd seen her, save for an overshirt. "Well, well, well. This is getting more and more interesting."

"You think so?" Duncan asked, eyes closed. "Because for me it's taking a turn into WTF territory."

"Pffft," Lerner said. "Stop trying to talk like the human kids. WTF. Just say 'what the fuck' like a man."

* * *

"Arch," Reeve said once they were off the porch. Dark clouds were accumulating in the sky, but the sun was still backlighting them. Arch could feel the heat, and the rain would be nice to help cool it off. "I put that pothead in the back of your car. Mind taking him to the station for me?"

"Sure," Arch said then frowned. He and Reeve had hashed things out—sort of. This seemed like a peculiar peace offering, though. "I'll get him down there, booked in, and head back."

"No," Reeve said with a shake of the head, and he stepped closer to Arch. They stood on the lawn, a good twenty feet from where the two ladies—Starling and Ms. Cherry—waited with their lawyer. Erin was hovering just a few feet from them, keeping her eyes on the porch. "Listen, you've seen a lot these last few days. Why don't you take the rest of the day off?"

Arch felt a curiosity burning now. "Really?"

"Yeah," Reeve said, and he was all sincerity as near as Arch could tell. "No one ought to see the shit we have these last few days. Just go on home, get your head on straight, spend some time with your missus if she has the day off," which she did, Arch vaguely recalled, "keep your phone on and close by. I'll whistle you up if we run into a shitstorm." He looked up. "Which we probably will if those fucking idiots from the TVA don't get down here to start sandbagging the river soon."

"I'll get this taken care of," Arch said, gesturing toward the car. He could see a man in the back. Even from where he stood, the fella looked mighty sullen. "Thank you, sir."

"Don't mention it," Reeve said, waving him off. "Now get that taken care of, will you? And don't go disappearing on the way to the station house." The sheriff wore a grim smile as Arch looked back at him. "I won't be as forgiving a second time."

Arch didn't really find much to say to that, so he just started back to the car. The lights were still flashing on it, and he couldn't remember if he'd left them that way or if Reeve had turned them on to justify his diagonal parking job, but either way, he was taking up a good portion of the street. He made his way around the back of the car and stopped when he saw a sedan parked less than a hundred feet behind his Explorer.

It was the demons.

* * *

Erin watched Arch walking toward the car as Reeve started coming back toward her. "Where's he going?"

"Back to the station with the prisoner," Reeve said. "Come on, we got work to do."

"Doing what?" Erin asked. "Trying to slink past some fancified lawyer so we can question a couple hookers about someone who died in a way that's pretty damned impossible based on what they've told us?"

"I can hear you," Lex Deivrel said, her arms folded as she stood on the edge of the porch, looking down at them. "I've warned you twice now, Nick. Any further prejudicial comments by yourself or your deputies toward my clients and—"

"Yeah, yeah," Reeve said, "day in court, et cetera. I got it. We'll play nice." He turned to give Erin a look but ended up smiling through his admonishing glare.

* * *

Arch strolled over to the sedan, glancing around at the run down, ramshackle houses up and down the street as he did so. There were still gawkers out, but none of them were smoking anything funny, at least. Gawkers were just a normal part of life in a small town. Rumors about what had happened at the brothel were probably already burning up the phone lines in Midian.

"Gentlemen," Arch said as he strolled up to the window of the sedan. The quiet one—Duncan, he thought—was just sitting there, waiting for him, already had the window down. Like he was ready for a conversation. The mouth of the operation, Lerner, was looking across from the driver's side.

"Good day, deputy," Lerner said with a wink. "Another tragic victim of the bad influences on your lovely little burg?"

Arch felt like reaching through the window and knocking the smug right off his face, but he didn't. Instead he went for an alternate topic of conversation. "Where's your new best friend?"

"I assume you mean your pal Hendricks?" Lerner said, still a little smug. "He's sleeping it off back at his motel. Your boy's in a lot of pain. Maybe he should find a less hazardous occupation."

"Someone's gotta keep a watch on what your kind is doing 'round here," Arch said, and after he said them, he wished he could shove the words back into his mouth.

The irony didn't seem to be lost on Lerner, and the smug smile stayed fixed where it was. "Heh. The more things change, huh?"

"Hendricks is fine," Duncan said in a soft voice, changing the topic of conversation. For some reason, Arch believed him when he said it. "Though he should take it a little lighter on the painkillers."

"You talk to him about it," Arch said. He didn't want anything to do with that conversation lest he have to involve it in some way with his job.

"You mind telling us what's going on here, Officer?" Lerner asked. The smugness was reduced but not gone.

Arch sighed. Why not? "Dead woman in there. Looks like she got burnt up by some demon's ... uh ... emission."

The smug vanished off Lerner's face in a heartbeat. "You're fucking joking."

Arch glared at him. "I assure you I'm not."

Lerner let out a low whistle. "Oh man, looks like our old Sygraath learned a new trick." Lerner paused, like he was doing it for comic effect. "And tried it out during a trick."

Duncan didn't laugh. "That's not funny," he said. Arch had to agree.

Lerner sighed. "Whatever. We've still got a Sygraath off the chain here and presently untraceable."

Arch cast his eyes toward the house. "You don't think he's gonna come back to the scene of the crime, do you?"

"Unlikely," Duncan said in that quiet way he had.

"We think he's planning something big," Lerner said. "He's probably laying low until then."

"Something big?" Arch asked. "Bigger than the mass murder yesterday morning? Or the traffic pile-up yesterday afternoon?"

"He didn't do the mass murder," Lerner said with a shake of the head. "That was a group of Tul'rore. We sent those back the night before last."

Arch frowned. "*You* did?"

"Yeah," Lerner said, like it was no big deal. "We got that taken care of for you." He smiled. "See? We're not all bad."

Arch wasn't quite ready to concede that just yet. "I gotta go drop some parole violator off at the station."

"Watch out for the lawyer," Duncan offered helpfully as Arch stood up, his back cracking as he removed himself from where he'd been leaning down to talk to them.

"Why?" Arch asked. "Is she a demon?"

"Possibly," Duncan said evenly. "Though not as many attorneys are demons as you might think. I just meant be careful because she's a lawyer."

"Not every evil thing on earth is done by demons," Lerner said, and he was lecturing Arch now, which Arch found plenty annoying. "It's not like there's a shortage of morally vacuous humans on this planet."

"Yeah, yeah," Arch said and started back toward his car. "Tell me something I don't know."

* * *

Gideon sat at the table, thinking. It was what he spent most of his time doing when he wasn't enjoying a death. There was nothing on the horizon, sadly, but that was all right. It was understood. He'd accepted that death just didn't happen here with the frequency it did in cities. So instead of dwelling on that, he was trying to—gently—relive some of his greatest hits.

Surprisingly, they were all from the last few days.

It came as a shock when he realized it. He'd hated this town, after all, and how frustrating it had been for him. It was stifling, the lack of death for him to enjoy. Like starving.

Like starving in the middle of a buffet, though. That's what he'd figured out here.

All he had to do was take matters into his own hands. And not masturbationally speaking, either, because he'd been doing that for years, obviously. No, he had take his destiny in his own hands, go after what he wanted. It was an important lesson.

Now he was a hunter. Now he didn't have to wait for the satisfaction to come to him, he could seek it. And it was more thrilling than any of the other deaths he'd felt.

Spellman's empty vessel was still across from him, staring blankly into space. He'd been like that for a couple hours now. It didn't bother Gideon; it was like being in a room with a doll. Which Gideon hadn't ever done, that he could recall, but it didn't bother him.

There was a stirring, and Spellman's hand moved. Something was in it, something he could see. It was a red silk bag, tied at the top, and big as his head. Gideon knew it hadn't been there before, and it was embroidered with gold stitching on the sides. He wondered if he was paying extra for that fanciness, then realized he didn't care.

"It is done," came Spellman's quiet voice, pushing the bag across the table toward him. Gideon grasped it like it was water and he was in the middle of a desert. "It still requires a few trifling components in order to activate, but it should be no challenge for one such as yourself."

"Additional components?" Gideon felt the urgency rising within. He needed to get off. Soon. "What components?"

"The heart of human," Spellman said, ticking it off on his fingers, "some blood, a scream. You should be able to get it all from one person, actually."

"Where am I supposed to ...?" Gideon looked at the bag. He hadn't killed anyone before, not in the way that would pull screams and a heart from them. Not blood, either, really. "I'll have to get my hands pretty dirty for this."

"As though they were clean before?" Spellman asked, with a twinkle in his eye. Gideon got the feeling there was a double entendre thrown in there somewhere. "There will be security guards where you're going, and they'll be human, of course. Naturally, they will be no match for a greater such as yourself."

"I have to kill them myself?" Gideon took a breath and felt a tightness, as if his essence was heating his breath to expand within him.

"Now, now," Spellman said with that same glimmer in his eyes, "think of how much of a growth experience this could be for you. Especially after all the self-discovery you've had in the last few days."

Gideon looked down at his pudgy hands. The incense smell in the air grew stronger around him. It could be fun, couldn't it? It wasn't like killing that girl last night hadn't been a joy. This could be better, even, because he could make it last longer, make it more painful. It'd be like foreplay. With tremendous ejaculation involved. "All right," he said and pulled the silk bag up as he stood. "All right. I can do this."

"Of course," Spellman said with a smile. "Now ... I'll need to do another bank transfer to cover the cost of this ..."

"Do I have to wait for you to do that?" Gideon stared at the bag in his hands, and he found himself wanting to do nothing more than add the last components and place it where he wanted it to go. He wanted to get the party started. Now.

"I can handle it," Spellman said with a vague gesture of his hand, "if you're in a hurry."

"Please," Gideon said, turning to walk out "I've got business to attend to up in the hills." He carried the silk bag at his side, and it bobbed with his motion. It felt kind of heavy to him, like he was carrying something of great importance. Which he was, he supposed. The next stage in his growth, in his awakening. Soon he could take the next step, and move on.

All he needed now was a blood sacrifice.

* * *

Hendricks was floating peacefully in the water when heard the knocking at his door. It was a recurring dream for him and it usually turned into a nightmare. This time it was different. It hadn't yet turned into a horror story when the thumping jarred him out of it.

He came to with the comforter mashed against his face. It kind of smelled, like feet or body odor or both. He realized as he woke that his legs were hanging off the edge of the bed, that he had not in fact been in the water, nor anywhere near it.

There was another thumping at the door and he realized it was closed. Lerner and Duncan weren't anywhere around, and he wondered for a moment if he'd hallucinated the pair of them. Demons that were out to help people? Bullshit, his common sense told him as he rose, wiping the drool off his chin.

He still felt the fog as he staggered to the door. He flipped the lock and opened it without even thinking about who might be behind it. It was only as it was swinging open that he considered it. Too late by then.

An unfamiliar man waited just outside, dark clouds behind him covering the sky. Hendricks wondered if he was a Jehovah's Witness, and was trying to think of a polite way to say FUCK OFF when the man spoke.

"Good day to you, Mr. Hendricks," the man said with a bow. He looked to be in his fifties, grey hair. He looked awfully alert, though Hendricks thought he might have been drawing an unfair comparison since he was still swimming in the wash of his own head. "Are your friends Lerner and Duncan still here?"

"What?" Hendricks asked. He really did feel like he'd just gotten pulled out of the wash. Since that had actually happened to him at one point in time, he knew it was a valid comparison.

"Lerner and Duncan?" the man asked again. "They're not here right now, are they?"

"No," Hendricks said, and he felt the weight of the sword in his coat. His gun was on his hip. "Who are you?"

"Ah, forgive me my lapse in manners," the man said with an abbreviated bow. "My name is Wren Spellman." His eyes glimmered, as though he had a secret. He put a finger into the air, and red sparks shot from it as though it were a firecracker. "I've come to talk."

Chapter 16

Erin's frustration tolerance was being tested to the point of ridiculousness. She was convinced that Lex Deivrel was, in fact, a demon, if such a thing existed. The blond lawyer had a perpetually smug smile, and it was driving Erin to the point where she wanted to just slap it off the woman's face. She'd grown up with three older brothers and had no compunction about doing such things. Outside of the lawful consequences, of course.

Reeve, fortunately, was taking a more patient approach. They stood under dark skies, and it looked like the rain might cut loose at any moment. The road shimmered from the humidity, and it was getting past midday now. The crime scene unit from Chattanooga filled the street, and they still hadn't managed to get Cherry or Lucia's statements.

Erin reconsidered that helpful bit of face punching but doubted it'd do much other than land her in jail. And civil court, probably.

"We're going to need to talk to your clients sooner or later," Reeve said to Deivrel, "and we're gonna do it at the station." He'd been on and off the phone with the TVA all morning, trying to manage their flood response. In addition he'd fielded calls from the Highway Patrol regarding the mess on the freeway and also the crime lab's initial report. Reeve was a busy man. Erin felt a little sorry for him.

The smell of the body in the house was wafting out now, the heat of midday causing it to ripen. It just smelled burnt to her, an appalling odor. She would have covered her nose, but for the fact it would have made her look ridiculous.

Instead, she sat there and listened to Reeve dicker with Lex Deivrel as she looked down the street. Just past the crime lab van she saw a familiar sight. It was the sedan that was parked outside Hendricks's motel room, and the two guys that were with him were sitting in it.

* * *

Lerner and Duncan were still sitting outside the whorehouse, staring at the goings-on and had been for hours. What else were they going to do? "Laywer looks like she's cockblocking everything," Lerner pronounced with a note of sympathy. They had lawyers to deal with in their own work, though fortunately not as frequently as human law enforcement had to. The Pact from whence their authority was derived had a variety of interpretations, and lawyers tended to find lots of devils in the details of it.

"Deputy Harris has seen us," Duncan said, calm on the outside, but Lerner could hear the alarm in his voice.

"That's the little blond, right?" Lerner asked. "This could be good or bad, I suppose. For Hendricks, I mean; not likely it'll have much effect on us."

"She could make herself a pain in the ass," Duncan said, about as succinctly as Lerner himself could have put it.

Lerner sighed. "Let's hope she doesn't, then. I'd hate to have to—" He stopped as Duncan's head snapped up, eyes wide open. "What?"

"Someone just threw up a conjuring," Duncan said, mouth hanging open when he finished talking. "A big one—loud, showy but without any substance, at Hendricks's motel room. Someone's with him there, now, and they want to get our attention."

Lerner sighed again. This was not going to look good to Deputy Harris, taking off after she just noticed them. Probably seemed suspicious. He started the car anyway, put it into gear, and executed a three-point turn on the street to take them back where they came from.

* * *

Arch unlocked the door to his apartment and set his keys on the table just inside. He paused as the cool air hit him, and listened for a sign that anything was moving in his home. Not a sound. This was getting to be usual.

Alison sat there, on the couch, swallowed up by the boxes rimming the white walls. She was dressed in one of her halter tops with a pair of jean shorts that had been cut ragged. Her hair was all done up, he noticed.

When she turned to look at him, she wore that same aura of indifference, that cool, unemotional look that had become so common on her lately. He wondered if she was suffering from PTSD. They'd been through something traumatic, after all. "Hey," he said, casually as he could.

"Hey," she returned, without much in the way of enthusiasm. She was seated without anything in her lap. The TV remote was on top of the entertainment center, and he hadn't even hooked up the cable yet. What had she been doing? Just sitting there? "I thought you were working again."

"I was," he said with a nod, taking a few tentative steps toward her. "Reeve sent me home. Figured I'd, uh … seen enough, I guess."

"Oh?" She asked it with no more seeming interest than she'd devote to a coupon circular. "Nothing new going on, then."

"Actually," he said, almost regretful to spoil her image of the town back at peace, "there was another murder this morning." He figured it'd get some reaction out of her, but she didn't even blink.

* * *

Erin watched the sedan do its turn in the middle of Water Street and drive off. She wondered if it was because she'd seen them that they were taking off? She thought about going after them, but a peal of thunder overhead caused everyone to look up, and the first droplet of water hit her on the cheek.

"Goddammit," Reeve said. "Can we please take this show on back to the station?"

"Aiming for a change of venue?" Deivrel asked, the same insufferable smile on her face. Erin still wanted to punch her.

"Aiming to not get soaking wet," Reeve replied, hitching his thumbs in his belt. Erin couldn't tell if he was doing it for some kind of effect or if he was holding up his pants under his gut.

Lex Deivrel seemed to ponder this. She'd been stonewalling them all morning, had come up with fifty different excuses thus far. "All right," she said finally. "Back to your station. But my clients come in my car." Her smile broadened. "Which seems to be blocked in by a crime scene van."

"Oh, Jesus," Reeve said. "I'll take you in one of my squad cars—all of you. And you can watch to make sure I don't say anything out of line."

"I'm afraid my clients would be insulted by a ride in the back of a police car," Deivrel said with a smile. "They're not criminals, after all."

"Sure," Reeve said, deadpan, "there but for the grace of a prostitution charge or twelve, go I. Or you. Probably more likely you."

Deivrel's smile grew colder. "We can wait."

"Oh, for fuck's sake," Reeve said. "Two of you with me—in the front seat, if need be, and one of you can ride with Deputy Harris." He chucked a thumb at her. "You pick the arrangements, but I've had enough of this stonewalling shit, Lex. You got no ground to stand on here because I haven't charged your clients with anything, they're probably not guilty of anything I'd charge them for, but that is gonna change rapidly if you don't stop fucking with me and help me get their goddamned statement on paper!"

Deivrel didn't flinch, didn't change expression one whit, just froze. "Fine. I'll ride with you and Ms. Cherry. Lucia can ride with Deputy Harris." She shot a look at Erin that was malice wrapped in razor blades. "Talk to my client about anything other than the weather and I'll make sure it ends your career."

Erin started to say something but Reeve held up a hand to shut her up. "I think we can live with that." He looked back at her. "Right?"

"The weather," Erin said, looking up in time to get hit in the face with another drop of rain. "Got it."

* * *

Hendricks wasn't sure how to feel about Wren Spellman, at least not until he frowned at Hendricks, waved a hand at him and produced something that looked like a cured cow's bladder he'd once seen when he was younger. "Drink this."

"Are you fucking kidding?" Hendricks retorted. Stranger shows up to your hotel room, tells you to drink something. Sounded like the perfect setup for him to be roofie'd. "No."

"Suit yourself," Spellman said with a shrug. "But it'd cure what ails you. I just feel bad for you, sitting there, looking like hell. I can tell some people have been less than gentle with you of late, and coupled with what

I'm reading of your past," his eyes flashed blank—like, white—for a minute, "I'm just feeling a spot of pity. Like I should help you." Spellman pushed the bladder thing toward him, held out in a lightly spotted and wrinkled hand. "Drink this. You'll feel better. Promise."

Hendricks took the thing, not really sure why. It was kidney shaped, seemed kind of like leather, like something you'd see in a fantasy movie when the characters would drink on a long journey. "What is this?"

"The container is a cured cow's bladder, as you might suspect," Spellman said, talking with his hands. They came up in a looping gesture that turned into a palms-up shrug. "What's inside is a tonic tinged with certain ingredients that are ... otherworldly, let's say." Spellman grinned. "It'll heal your injuries in the course of about thirty seconds. Call it a sample."

"Uh huh," Hendricks said, and stared at the bladder. "Why?"

"I told you, pity," Spellman said. "Also, marketing. I have a store out in the country. You should come see me sometime if this works for you." He held up a hand to his lips. "But don't tell your friends," he said in a whisper that felt ... shrouded, somehow, like it had been breathed right into his mind.

Hendricks stared at the bladder, pondering if the Percocets he'd taken were still fucking with him, and how hard.

"Ah, here we go," Spellman said mildly. "About time."

"About time for what?" Hendricks asked, looking from the bladder to the unassuming man in the Nehru suit. Vaguely, he heard something outside, like tires squealing. He listened closer and heard car doors slamming then watched as Spellman gently opened his door for him.

"Let's keep them from knocking down another door, shall we?" Spellman said. "I hate to cause any more expense for the owner of this motel. Concern, you know, from one business owner to another. It's tough enough out there without someone cutting into our margins."

Lerner and Duncan came up seconds later, and Hendricks just stared at them as Lerner paused on the threshold, a rough look on his face, peeking his head inside like he was afraid he'd get whacked in the head or something. He had something clutched in his hand and Hendricks stared at it. It was a little cylinder that was an inch longer than his hand on the top and bottom, and he kept it by his side.

"What the hell is that?" Hendricks asked as Lerner scanned the room and stopped on Spellman, who was now standing by the table in the corner.

"Baton," Lerner said and stepped inside. "Used for breaking shells. Who is this?" He pointed the baton at Spellman.

"My name is Wren Spellman." The mystery man bowed to Lerner. "I'm here with some interesting information, as evidenced by my rather obvious attempt to get your attention."

Duncan followed Lerner into the room a moment later, and Hendricks watched him. He wondered if Duncan's suit had always been so purple. He couldn't remember. "He's clean," Duncan said. "It's just a screen."

Hendricks waited to see if anyone would explain what that meant. They didn't, so he asked. "Screen?"

"Empty vessel," Lerner said. "Someone's communicating through 'him' from somewhere else." He waved at Hendricks. "Now take a seat, kid, and let the big boys talk, huh?"

Hendricks stifled the urge to pull his sword and show Lerner how the big boys reacted to consecrated metal, but Duncan gave him a sympathetic smile so he didn't.

"You seek a Sygraath named Gideon," Spellman said, hands neatly folded in front of him, same pleasant smile perched on his lips. "I am here to tell you where he's going, what he's going to do, and when he's going to do it."

"Why?" Lerner shot out immediately. Hendricks was wondering the same—once his brain translated it through the fog he was in. He figured he was on about a five second delay, but his head was so fuzzy it wasn't really possible to be sure.

"Because," Spellman said, "his plan is no good for my business interests in this area."

Lerner seemed a little suspicious at that. "How is it bad for business?"

"Because," Spellman said with little emotion, "he's going to blow up the dam that holds back the Caledonia River." Spellman made a helpful hand gesture to illustrate. "And when that dam breaks, everyone in this valley—including my potential customers—will all be washed away."

* * *

Gideon pulled up outside the gate at the end of the dirty road. His car was really struggling at the end, and by the time he reached the guardhouse with the gate, he was worried it wasn't going to carry him much further.

That was all right, though. One of the security guards probably had a pickup truck he could use. He ran a hand over his smooth cheek, scratching his flesh. He'd just need to ask nicely.

There was a yellow and black striped gate barring his passage. He suspected it was metal, but it really didn't matter in any case. It was starting to rain, so he stepped out of the car just as the security guard was stepping out of the guardhouse. It wasn't really a house so much as a six-by-ten-foot booth, roughly. Looked a little like a tollbooth to Gideon, like one of the ones that dotted every off-ramp around Chicago.

Gideon felt his shoes splash in the first puddle he came to. It drenched his sock. He felt the cool water wash down into his shoe, soaking him all the way to the toes. It was a sensory discomfort for him, but little else.

The booth had an overhanging awning that stretched a couple feet out from the roof, and Gideon felt the volume of rain soaking his t-shirt lessen as he stepped under it. "Ugly day out," he said to the man who was coming out of the booth to greet him. The guy had on a khaki uniform and a polite smile, but Gideon had a feeling it wouldn't last long.

"You look lost," the security guard said. Like he'd had this happen before.

"I could use some directions," Gideon said, stepping closer to the guard. The guard didn't flinch away. Probably figured he'd have time to go for the gun on his belt if Gideon tried anything.

"Where you heading?" the security guard asked.

"Not far," Gideon said and reached for the man. He had him gripped by the time the guy's hand got anywhere near his holster. He broke the security guard's arm, snapped it and jammed it hard so that the bone tore through the skin. The guard let out a scream, and it was sweet. He pushed the man down and looked in his eyes. He could feel the fear coming off him as he held him down with one hand. "I think I'll go straight for your heart. Have you heard what the quickest way to it is?"

Gideon found out. Turned out, it wasn't through the stomach. It was through the ribcage.

* * *

Erin sat in awkward silence with Starling—Lucia, she was constantly correcting herself—in the passenger seat. The redhead wasn't saying a word, and she was tempted to let that rest. Tempted. "So," she said, breaking the silence, "you want to talk about the future again?"

There was a pause, and it was almost painful. When Lucia answered, it was with a quiet confusion. "Excuse me?" She talked in a deep Southern accent that sounded nothing like Starling's blank, unaccented speech had.

Erin wondered if she was being punked, or if this girl had some sort of multiple personality disorder raging inside her. She'd seen that shit on a movie before, and it was just about as crazy as what was happening around her lately. "Oh, you're gonna play like you don't know what I'm talking about, Starling?"

Erin watched Lucia go paler than her usual self. "Who's Starling?"

And Erin got the feeling she meant it.

* * *

"Shiiiiiiiiiiiiiiit, fuck, damn," Lerner said. Spellman had spilled it, really, answered the follow-up questions, and it smelled real enough to him. Based on Duncan's expression, he felt the same. "A whole fucking town gone under. How's he gonna do it?"

Spellman gave a sympathetic nod. "He has a conjuring that will damage the structure enough to break the dam open, I think, with the increased pressure from all the rain that's been falling."

"Well, goddamn," Hendricks said in a little whisper.

"I'm afraid this one's all on Gideon, actually," Spellman said to Hendricks.

"And the guy who gave him the fucking conjuring," Lerner said, hot enough that he would have let the air out of Spellman right here, if he hadn't been a fucking screen. "Why didn't you give him a fake if you're so concerned about saving your damned business?"

Spellman shrugged lightly. "I have a guarantee. He ordered a product, I delivered it. Whatever happens to him after that is entirely out of my hands. I just wanted to make sure he didn't leave a bad review on Yelp."

Spellman looked almost apologetic. "Those things will hurt sales faster than—"

"Oh, fuck off," Lerner said, and he started to pace. "You put a bomb in the hands of a psychotic Sygraath, and now he's—" He shot a look at Duncan. "Come on, let's get to the dam."

"I can't see him," Duncan said in a soft tone.

"I fucking know that!" Lerner said. "I need you to read the map and tell me where to go." He snapped his fingers and made for the door. He caught sight of Hendricks heading toward him and held out a hand. "Not this time, junior. Sygraath's a greater; he'll pop your head off and drink your blood out like you're a growler of ale. Sounds like he's getting a taste for it, too."

"You need all the help you can get," Hendricks said, and he staggered and swayed as he took a couple steps.

"I need help from someone who can fucking stand up straight," Lerner said, and he knew he'd snapped at the cowboy. He didn't care. He had shit to do, humans to save, status quo to maintain, and some wobbly demon hunter wasn't getting in his way. "Stay here and sleep it off." He shot out the door and headed for the car.

He could hear Duncan pause in the threshold behind him. "Drink it," he said, and Lerner wondered what he was talking about. But he didn't wonder long because Duncan was out behind him a hot second later, and Lerner already had the car going. They peeled out of the parking lot as fast as the wet tires on the watery road would allow.

* * *

Arch heard the phone ring as he sat silently on the couch next to Alison. It was his personal cell phone, he could tell by the plain tone. Not that he had a different or fancy tone for his personal one, it was just a different default ringer. He looked at Alison apologetically, but she still wasn't looking at him. She was just staring off into space, had been for the last fifteen or twenty minutes.

"Hello?" he asked. He hadn't checked the number first.

"Arch," Hendricks's voice came over the line. He sounded frantic but slurred. "We figured out what the Sygraath is up to."

"Great," he said, giving his wife an apologetic look that she didn't even notice and getting up to walk toward the bedroom. "What now?"

"He's gonna blow up that dam you showed me the other night," Hendricks's reply came. "Flood the whole town, feast on all the souls passing into the ... I don't know, afterlife or void or whatever."

Arch felt his eyes slide back and forth, real slow. "When?"

"Well, he's already up there, I think, so—"

"On my way," Arch said. He didn't even have to think, it was just instinct. "I'll pick you up on the way, so you better be ready." He hit the end button and ran for the door. "Gotta go!" he called to his wife as he passed. He had no idea if she even noticed he was leaving.

* * *

Erin took the long way back to the station. She'd wanted to avoid some of the roads that were starting to flood over, figuring that with the rain coming down they'd be bad again, so she'd gone up and caught the interstate on the far edge of town and was following it back to the Old Jackson Highway exit. The rain was constant, pelting the windshield as her wipers squealed in a steady rhythm to keep it clear enough for her to see.

She'd settled into an easy silence with Lucia, and was still trying to work out in her head if the girl was lying, nuts or actually telling the truth. The latter seemed crazy, but she was a dead ringer for Starling, and—

Erin stopped at the light at the top of the exit ramp as she heard tires squealing to her right over a crack of thunder overhead. Pulling out of the Sinbad's parking lot was the sedan that those two peckerwoods who had been parked outside the murder scene were driving. They blew down the Old Jackson Highway in one hell of a hurry, violating the speed limit as they headed toward the hills—the opposite direction from where she was supposed to be going.

She took a long breath, trying to decide what to do. Unconsciously, her hand reached down to the switch for the siren and lights and she flipped them. "Hold on," she said to Lucia, whose face was a mask of uncertainty as Erin jerked the wheel to the right and headed after the sedan.

*　*　*

Hendricks stared at the thing in his hand. He had some doubts about drinking out of a cow's bladder.

"It's been boiled," Spellman said, watching him. "You needn't worry about cow urine. Not that it would harm you in any way if you did drink some."

The dude had seemed to go blank for a few minutes after Lerner and Duncan had left, with Duncan exhorting him to drink it. He wasn't sure why, but he trusted Duncan. Sort of. "How did you know I was thinking that?" he asked Spellman.

"It was written all over your face," Spellman said mildly. "Or somewhere." He went blank again, like someone had cut the power to him.

Hendricks started to move toward the door. Arch would be here in minutes, and he needed to be outside. If Lerner and Duncan could handle this, fine, and all the better, but … if they couldn't …

He grunted in pain as his ribs screamed at him. "Fuck it," he said. There was no way he'd be ready for a fight, not in his present condition. He'd limp into a greater and get his head popped off like a cork, just the way Lerner had said.

Hendricks pulled the stopper out of the bladder and upended it, chugging it down. He caught movement from Spellman out of the corner of his eye, like someone turned the power on to him again. He looked pleased. Unsettlingly so.

*　*　*

Lerner had shot off on a back road at a ninety-degree angle, tires skidding across gravel. He could hear the heavy thunks and tiny plinks of rock hitting the car, and wondered how much it would cost to fix it at the body shop. The accountants would have his ass in a sling for that. Maybe literally.

Duncan was reading the map next to him, and his usual calm was gone out the fucking window. "Uhhhhmmm … it looks like there's a turnoff up ahead …"

"Left or right, numbnuts?" Lerner asked, gritting his teeth as he felt the traction slip on a curve.

"Right, I think," Duncan said.

"You *think*?" The rain was pounding the windshield, trees were zipping by outside. They were blurred by the lines of water falling down the windows.

"Yeah," Duncan said. "This map ... I'm not sure how accurate it is."

Lerner felt the car slalom around a lazy S-curve and tried to keep from jerking the wheel too hard to compensate. "Lovely."

"It might be easier to read it if the car wasn't bumping all over the place."

"You're just eighteen different kinds of fucking helpful, aren't you?" Lerner asked. He kept going, though.

* * *

Erin saw the sedan make the turnoff toward the lower dam and followed. Lucia was still sitting pale next to her, and she tried to give her a reassuring smile. They were ahead far enough that they might reasonably be able to claim they didn't see her coming up on them with sirens wailing and lights flashing. She needed to get closer.

The brothel thing could wait. Right now she had her teeth into something else, and oddly enough—and she did kick herself when she thought of it this way—it felt like her future depended on catching them.

* * *

"Get in the car!" Arch called out the window as he slowed down. Hendricks was already in the parking lot, running through the wash. Arch was pretty sure the parking lot had dried out yesterday after the rain quit, but it was already back to flooding. Bad sign for the town. Maybe an omen of things to come.

Arch watched out the open window as Hendricks hustled toward the Explorer, splashing all the way and holding on to his hat. His black drover coat seemed to be keeping the rain off him, but his black cowboy hat looked like it was soaked and drooping just a little after being out for only a few seconds. It was a gully-washer, no doubt, and he hit the switch to roll the window up as Hendricks opened the door, jumped in and slammed it shut in seconds. The cowboy took his hat off and shook it toward the floorboard. "Let's go," he said, and Arch obliged, gunning it.

* * *

Gideon had gotten the guy's heart, but he was so caught up in the moment that he hadn't bothered with a scream. By the time he remembered he needed it, the security guard was already dead. Double damn.

He threw the body into the woods with ease, like he was Cubs fan tossing a baseball. It landed about ten feet from him, in some underbrush, with a cracking noise. Not like it mattered. The guy wasn't going to feel it anymore anyway. Gideon hadn't even caught his name as he passed through.

He'd saved him for later. Stored away that pain, that screaming agony in his essence. He'd never done that before, preferring to pleasure himself right when he got them. It was a curious feeling, a churning, constant arousal inside.

He flipped the gate switch in the guardhouse, got back in the car and started up the road again. He could feel the pleasure from this kill welling up inside him, stirring. He was already rock-hard, but he didn't have time to satiate himself, not now. His erection caused his cargo pants to tent, just a little, as he sat in the rental car and pushed his foot to the pedal. The engine in the sedan whined as he started up the hill's incline. He could see the dam out his window.

There were more souls coming, and soon. He could almost taste the anticipation of having so many of them to chew on, to savor. He'd have a feast of them to satiate himself with, and he could jerk off for weeks on what he'd get once the dam went down.

* * *

Lerner hit the brakes when they got to a guardhouse. There was a fence blocking them from going any further, and the gate looked strong enough to at least fuck up the front of the car, if not stop them. Lerner wasn't all that sanguine about trying to bust through. When he saw the security guard come walking out, he suspected he might not need to.

Lerner slowed the car and crept it up to the gate. Stared down the slate grey hood as the rain washed over it, and rolled his window down halfway. Big, heavy drops of water drenched his left arm and started to soak the pleather interior of the door panel.

"How y'all doing?" the guard asked by way of greeting. An awning above the guardhouse was shielding him but not by much. His security uniform was already showing signs of dampness.

"Anyone come through here lately?" Lerner asked. "Anyone who didn't have permission?"

The guard just sort of frowned at him, like he didn't get asked penetrating questions by total strangers every day. "No. You're the only ones to come through here in hours. All the employees go up to the top of the dam; we just block the bottom because the Department of Homeland Security says we gotta." He shrugged. "Terrorists, y'know."

"Oh, fuck," Lerner said. He could see the dam up ahead, barely, in the distance, through the rain, over the trees. He put the car in reverse without even bothering to roll the window up or say so much as Thank you to the guard, who was looking pretty damned confused at this point.

"He wasn't lying," Duncan said, "and he didn't have any kind of gap to indicate he was being fiddled with."

"I figured that out on my own, genius," Lerner snapped. "Clearly this Gideon bastard is going to the top of the dam." He smacked the wheel lightly, careful not to do it any harm. Which he could, easily. "Why didn't you steer us to the top?"

Duncan stared down at the map, concentrating on it like it contained the secret to all existence. Lerner had read in a human book once that the answer was forty-two. It made about as much sense as anything else he'd heard. "I don't know how to read a map. I just followed the road that led to Tallakeet Dam—"

"Well, find another one!" Lerner exploded. "Fuck," he breathed as he finished his one-eighty and saw flashing lights of blue and red blurring as the windshield wipers cleared the rain and another torrent covered it again.

***

"Got him boxed in," Erin said, almost to herself. The rain was coming down hard now, and she wasn't looking forward to getting out in it to write this ticket. But part of her was.

"What if he runs?" Lucia asked. Erin glanced at her; the girl looked terrified. And she really did look like a girl right now, not a woman, damned sure not a hooker. She looked like a scared girl, no more than twenty-two. Older than Erin, sure, but ... fearful. For whatever reason.

"They only run on *COPS* and in movies," Erin said. She said it with enough feeling that she saw Lucia relax a little. She had a little of the perfume smell from the whorehouse on, and Erin had to admit the fragrance was kind of growing on her. Maybe she'd ask what kind it was later.

***

"It's Deputy Harris," Duncan reported, matter-of-factly.

"Yes, I fucking know it's her," Lerner snapped again. He could feel his essence bulging him at the seams. He did not have time for this shit, not now. Maniac on the loose, what did you do? Lerner shifted the car into drive and gunned it. The sedan slipped a little as he darted to the right and went off the road.

"Home office is going to be pissed," Duncan said. Lerner could hear the strain in his voice, and did not give a single flying fuck.

"Let them come do this job," Lerner said as he slid on the grass just off the road. He cut it close and watched his driver's side mirror smash into Deputy's Harris's as he blew past her and skidded back onto the road.

Lerner caught a glimpse of Harris as he went past her window. She looked appropriately shocked, he thought.

The redhead in the passenger seat, though? Not so much. Lerner tried to decide whether that should worry him or not, and figured he'd just say fuck it all and deal with it later.

***

Erin watched the sedan shear off her driver's side mirror with enough shock that it'd rival whatever the hell Tallakeet Dam generated in a day.

"He ran," Lucia said, calm as dead. Like she was Starling.

"I saw that," Erin said, shaking as she put the car in reverse and floored it backward. She whipped around and saw the sedan's taillights disappearing into the curving trail, dropped the cruiser in gear and took off after him.

* * *

Gideon had forgotten the scream twice more at the top of the dam. A couple engineers were surveying cracks or something on top of the dam, watching the water roll over the top. He'd heard them scream, sure, had felt them churn as they died.

But he'd forgotten to catch a scream into his red silk bag of conjured goodness. He didn't see anyone else on top of the dam, and he wondered how far he'd have to walk to get another. At least there was a good reason why he'd missed that last one. Something totally unexpected.

His essence was just churning now, and his skin was burning up with the heat of the souls he'd stored up. He'd never waited this long before releasing before. He hadn't even known he could. Usually his hand went straight to his cock when death approached. That was the advantage of staying in his own apartment all the time, just watching at a distance. He was always ready for death's approach and the gratification was instant when it arrived.

Here he'd felt something new, and as he tasted the acrid smoke on his tongue from what he'd just found out, he had to reflect ... it was pretty cool. Definitely something he could use in the future. The fear and terror had been so worth it, even though it had scared the hell out of him at first.

Not as bad as that second engineer, though. Not even close.

Water was running over the top of the dam. It was big enough for a two-lane road, Gideon figured. He wondered if there had been one here at some point; it looked like there had been, faded lines under an inch of water that washed from the reservoir side to his right down the face of the dam at his left.

He had a good two or three hundred yards of walking to get to the other side of the dam, and he'd left his car behind for obvious reasons—he didn't want it to get washed away when he set off the conjuring. Still, in the mad rush he figured he'd be able to sit on top of the dam—what was left of it—and savor the death for a while before anyone came looking for him. It'd feel good to take matters in hand once more. Let some pressure out of the system.

His shoes splashed as he walked and the ripples from the current washing down and over the face of the dam was mixed with the impact of the rain coming from above. Down below, some four hundred feet he could see the sluice gates open, the water churning white as they drained the reservoir as fast as they could. Gideon glanced back at the water streaming over the top. Not nearly fast enough, apparently.

All he needed now was a scream. Gideon breathed deep, smelled the fresh air as a thousand raindrops hit him in the face and head, and over the rush of the water he could hear a car in the distance.

He turned and saw headlights. He peered through the haze of the falling rain and realized he knew that car. It was a cop car, the one he'd seen outside his motel. The cowboy got out of the passenger side, looking fresh as a daisy. A hell of a lot better than when last he'd seen him. The black cop got out of the driver's side, and both of them looked serious.

Gideon just smiled. He wouldn't have to walk very far for that scream after all.

Chapter 17

Hendricks got out of the Explorer first, before Arch had even parked it. He just felt good, revitalized, like his body was all in working order again and he'd gotten the best night of sleep he'd ever had. He couldn't remember feeling this good even in the Marines, when he was at the top of his physical conditioning. His boots hit the puddle as the Explorer parked just past the sedan that the Sygraath—Gideon—had had parked outside his motel room when last he'd seen the fucker.

The rain was coming down in sheets as he started to run down the road toward the dam. He could see Gideon out there, just staring at him. He didn't wait for Arch because he didn't need to. Hendricks pulled his sword as he went, and he felt fucking invincible. Whoever this Spellman guy was, he knew his shit.

"Wait up!" Arch called from behind him. Hendricks heard him and estimated he was at least twenty paces back—a couple seconds, maybe. He didn't slow down because there wasn't time.

A wind buffeted Hendricks, but his hat stayed on and that was all that mattered. He kept his grip on the sword as he ran. Gideon just stood there, and Hendricks could have sworn—yes, that fucker was smiling.

"I'm going to wipe that goddamned grin right off your shit-eating face," Hendricks said, low and menacing, when he was only about ten paces away. He did not give a fuck that Gideon was a greater. Up close, the dude looked like his vision of an internet troll—bald, overweight and dressed like he should never leave the house.

"You're going to die screaming," Gideon said, and Hendricks was kind of amazed at the high pitch of his voice. The demon wasn't small, but his voice made him sound a lot less intimidating.

The rain just poured on around them as Hendricks closed the last steps between them.

* * *

Lerner jerked the handbrake and sent the car into a skid. Like some shit right out of *The Fast and the Furious*, that's what it was. Lerner had seen those movies on cable. They were mindless, but so was everything else that humans watched, and he had a lot of downtime between jobs.

He heard the gravel rattling on the undercarriage as they kicked up rocks. He kept the car from fishtailing, though. They'd hit a switchback, a sharp damned S-curve going back up the hill toward the top of the dam, and it taxed his driving skills. He would have considered it a minor miracle that he'd made the turn, but his people didn't believe in miracles.

At least not for them.

"How much longer?" he shouted at Duncan.

Duncan took it well. "I don't know. Five minutes? Ten?"

"You suck at reading maps," Lerner said bitterly.

"I'd rather stick to reading," Duncan said. Lerner knew what he meant by reading, and it wasn't *Fifty Shades of Grey*. Though instruction in the best uses of whips and chains was occasionally useful in their work.

Lerner jerked the wheel as they came around another bend in the road. The rain was just slamming them now, making him drive half-blind. Which was an easy formula for disaster in these conditions.

As they came around the corner, Lerner caught a glimpse of the top of the dam. It was hard to see, but someone was up there. No, two someones. Then he saw a third.

"Looks like our cowboy showed up after all," Duncan said. Lerner didn't have to look to see if his eyes were closed; they were. "And his cop friend."

"Well, I'll be a son of a bitch," Lerner said. He really wasn't, though; he didn't even have a mother.

* * *

Erin was a couple turns back from them, she was pretty sure. She'd catch glimpses of them here and there as she went, and it wasn't like this road had any turn offs. They were racing up the curvy fucking path to the top of the dam, and it was as direct a route up into the hills as you could get without climbing up at a near ninety-degree angle.

"Ummmm," Lucia said from next to her. She spared a look for just a second as they hit a straightaway, and the hooker was green in face. She was holding real tight to the Oh shit bar, and Erin sent them around another corner in a skid. Lucia bounced in spite of her seat belt; she was just too small for it to hold her effectively. Erin sympathized; she had the same problem.

"Yeah, I know," Erin said, spinning the wheel back to the left, "your lawyer will probably call this coercion or scaring the witness or some kind of shit like that." She white-knuckled the wheel, and the car felt like it was perpetually an inch from sending them both over the edge. "I'll take complaints later."

"Who are these guys?" Lucia said, almost hiccupping as she spoke. Like she was gonna heave.

"I have no fucking idea," Erin said, the frustration bleeding out as she floored it down a straightaway. Rain washed over the windshield. "But I'm damned sure gonna find out."

* * *

Arch watched Hendricks do the windup as he came at Gideon. The cowboy wasn't moving nearly as slowly as he had been when Arch had last seen him; it was like he wasn't hurt at all. Arch would have wondered if he'd been faking it, but he'd seen the bruises. And if he wasn't mistaken, Hendricks now had both eyes open and looking absolutely normal.

He didn't have time to wonder, though. Hendricks failed to lead with his sword and took a body blow from a backhand Gideon threw out just casually. The cowboy went flying. He landed a few feet away, almost skidding over the edge but catching himself just in time.

Arch felt a frown take hold on his face. He had his gun drawn but knew how little effect it had on these things—and that was just the lessers. He tried to remember how much impact Hollywood, the last greater he'd faced, had shown from bullets. He had lost an arm to a big rifle.

"One of you is gonna scream for me," Gideon said in a high voice. Arch thought he had a northern accent, but didn't know enough about northern accents to place him. "Which one of you wants to volunteer?"

Arch raised his gun, a Glock 22, filled with sixteen .40 caliber bullets, drew a bead on Gideon's torso, and started to fire.

* * *

Lerner took what he hoped like hell was the last curve. He blew past a guardhouse like the one he'd seen at the bottom of the dam doing about sixty, shooting up the hill with the pedal mashed to the floor. The road was straight from here anyway.

"The party's started without us," Duncan said, and Lerner knew he was reading. The engine was revving like it would blow any minute.

"I hope our friends," Lerner slung the word friends like it was toxic, "last until we get there. I'd hate to see the guest of honor rip through them and get done with what he needs to do before we get a chance to intervene."

"Don't forget the party favors," Duncan said. Lerner hadn't forgotten. Their batons didn't do shit against greaters.

That was what the bag in the trunk was for.

* * *

Hendricks took the impact on his shoulder and rolled out of it as best he could. Gideon hit harder than most demons, and he wasn't even really trying, Hendricks didn't think. The wet splashing noise he'd made as he landed coupled with the sudden rush of water down the neck of his shirt was a rude fucking awakening.

Arch stood off with Gideon gun raised while the demon said something about screaming. Hendricks could have heard him over the rain but he wasn't paying any attention. He was too busy going for his own gun.

Arch started firing and Hendricks tried to match him. He had a 1911, made by Colt. He'd heard the story in the Marines about how it was actually designed by legendary gunmaker John Browning for the U.S. Army in the wake of the Spanish-American war. It had some hard-hitting rounds, big .45s. Bigger than what Arch carried, anyway.

But not as many bullets. He blew through all seven rounds in the magazine plus the one in the chamber about the time Arch was hitting his stride. Hendricks had a spare mag and changed it out quickly, fumbling a little from where he still lay in the water.

When he had the slide safely locked back into position and ready to fire again, he looked up. Gideon was just standing there, a look of discomfort on his face, like he had gas and nothing more troubling than that. It turned into a smile as Hendricks was getting to his feet and holstering his gun. He tightened the grip on his sword.

"Okay, boys," Gideon said, grin showing some crooked teeth, "now that you've fired at me, let me return the favor."

And he opened his mouth and blew fucking fire at Hendricks in an eight-foot jet of flame.

* * *

Erin was on the sedan in the home stretch, saw it crest the ridge at the edge of the dam road and disappear from sight. She could see a couple cars parked up there—one of them was Arch's Explorer, she noted with surprise. "What the fuck?" she whispered.

"Another cop up here?" Lucia said, like she was looking for affirmation.

They were seconds behind the sedan in cresting the top of the hill. The road dipped down at a low angle after that, leveling out where it met the dam. The sedan had stopped in the middle of the road just in front of them and the two guys were already out, already running onto the dam where something—she squinted—what the fuck—?

There was Arch, she realized in a flash, with his back to the two guys getting out of the sedan. Just a few feet in front of him was another guy, a pudgy one, but it took a second to realize he was even a guy because he had a jet of fire coming out of his mouth that stretched out toward the steep edge of the Tallakeet Dam. At the end of it, jumping sideways toward Arch and rolling, kicking up water as he did so, was a man in a black coat and a cowboy hat.

"What the ..." Lucia whispered in quiet awe as Erin hit the brakes, stopping the cruiser behind the sedan they'd been chasing like it was life itself only a moment before. "What IS that?"

"Holy fuck," Erin said in raw shock, a cold, clammy feeling crawling over her skin as she watched the fat man breathe fire again in a long, blazing line at Hendricks, who was scrambling to avoid it. "It's a fucking demon."

* * *

Gideon was boiling over, the hot desire unspent and burning out of his mouth in the form of flames. He could spray it in a jet, he'd figured out with that engineer, and had seared the man to ashes from the waist up.

The rain was pounding as he unleashed it aiming for the cowboy, his motel neighbor. Served the demon hunter right; he was clearly looking for a fight.

Now he had one.

Gideon had never been a very physical person. Most Sygraaths weren't. They lived in isolation, didn't deal with people. Now Gideon had no idea why. It was so good to touch, so good to kill while you were up close. He'd always known being closer made it more intense, but this was taking it to new heights.

He chased the cowboy along with his breath of fire. He could hear the rain hissing and turning to steam as it hit the flames.

The cop kept shooting at him, but he shrugged it off. Like pinpricks, they were. The noise was the worst part.

Then a gun roared from somewhere behind the cop, up on the hill, and he felt a hell of a lot more than a pinprick.

* * *

Erin heard the shot crack down from somewhere behind her, watched the fire-breathing demon stagger from the hit. The jet of flame that had been following after Hendricks stopped immediately as the tubby bastard reeled, arms pinwheeling from the impact.

Erin stared at the scene taking place through her front window, then blinked to make sure it was really happening. It was.

She threw open the door and shouted, "Stay in the car!" to Lucia, who was watching wide-eyed through the windshield herself. Erin pulled the keys as she got out and stormed around to the trunk to pop it open.

Ka-ching.

The department had lived a little larger in the days before the recession. That was in the heyday before the budget cuts came, eliminating overtime along with some necessary equipment and training. That was before Erin's time, but because she spent her days in the office with the sheriff, she got to hear about it. Ad nauseum.

The good news was, some of those one-time expenditures from the heydays were still good five or ten years later.

Like the AR-15 rifle that the sheriff carried in his trunk.

Erin snugged the stock against her shoulder and clicked the red dot scope on. It produced a little circular targeting reticle in the middle of a square display. It looked straight through into the magnifying scope just beyond on the top rail of the rifle, giving her a nice 4x zoom on what she was looking at. It didn't have the power of whatever that person was shooting from up in the woods, but it'd spray some hurt, she figured.

And it'd be better than sitting in the car waiting to see if Arch and Hendricks survived their encounter with some fire-breathing creature from hell.

She didn't want to think about how Hendricks had been right—and not crazy—about this one thing. She didn't have time for it right now. She felt the stock against her shoulder, cranked back on the charging handle and palmed the forward assist for good measure. Then she thumbed the selector switch to three-shot burst and ran down the hill toward a fight she damned sure didn't understand—but instinctively knew which side she was on.

* * *

Lerner was hanging back until the rifle shot echoed and Gideon staggered. Even a greater could get knocked down by enough force, and whatever that person was wielding looked like it had the oomph to do the job. Lerner had been shot before, by handguns, mostly, and he didn't like the sensation. He wasn't a greater, though, because those fuckers could shrug off a pistol shot like it was nothing.

He saw Duncan across the hood. Duncan spoke first. "You get to the trunk, I'll—"

"Okay," Lerner said, and Duncan was already in motion, drawing his baton as he charged at Gideon, who was falling back a couple steps from the impact of that shot.

Lerner fumbled with the keys and slapped the right one into the trunk. He would have wished for an auto open, but his hands were shaking so bad he probably would have crushed the key fob anyway.

* * *

Arch still had a couple rounds left when the roar of a big rifle up on the hill was followed by Gideon nearly falling over. He looked back, instinctively, since the bullet had probably only gone about two feet over his head on the way to the demon. He couldn't see anyone up in the woods, but that was the point of a rifle, right?

His eyes fell down and he saw a couple things in quick order—the first was Erin Harris with an AR-15 and a mean look in her eyes. She was just stepping onto the dam when he saw her, and he wouldn't have wanted to be in her way.

The second thing was a blur as Duncan shot past him, that peculiar-colored suit flapping in the breeze as the demon launched himself at Gideon. A baton popped in his hand as he went past, snapping to a three-foot extension like a miniature sword, and he brought it down on Gideon's skull like he was an old-time lawman clubbing a protestor.

* * *

Erin watched as one of the suits she'd been chasing closing on the demon. He produced one of those spring-loaded batons and hit the thing in the head with it, causing the demon to stumble again and shake his head. He didn't look pleased.

She came up on the sedan she'd been chasing as the other guy, the driver that she'd gawked at as she watched him smash her sideview mirror, opened the trunk and snatched a big black gym bag out of it. She started to tell him to stop, but he moved faster than anyone she'd ever seen, leaving the trunk open and her in the dust as he ran off across the dam toward the melee.

Erin cut across to the side of the sedan's hood and got behind it. She'd seen that flame and didn't really want to be on the receiving end of it the way Hendricks nearly had been. She parked herself there, pulled up her gun, looked through the scope, and waited.

* * *

Hendricks was getting up as Duncan came into the fray. He pushed off the flooded surface of the dam and brought his sword up as Duncan rained a hell of a blow on Gideon's head. If it had been a normal skull, the crack he heard would have been bone splitting open.

As it was, all Gideon did was shake it off, take a step back, and blow a bellow of flame that sent Duncan into the air, on fire, and past Hendricks over the edge of the dam. Hendricks felt the wave of heat overcome him, and he flinched away.

It caused Hendricks to whip his head around to watch, involuntarily. Duncan shot past him like he'd been hit by a car, a ball of nearly unrecognizable flame as he plummeted four hundred feet down the sheer surface of the dam.

* * *

Lerner saw Duncan go over, was close enough to feel the heat. There was a hiss as the falling rain turned to steam and obscured his view.

Lerner felt some additional heat, though, a burning rage down deep. He started to drop to his knees in the mist of steam, grabbed hold of the zipper on the black gym bag in his hand, and he started to tug on it.

A jet of flame shot at him, lighting its way through the mist. Lerner rolled to dodge. The fire came at him so fast that he lost his grip on the bag as he evaded, throwing himself hard left. It only took a moment for him to realize he'd gone left when he should have gone right, and he fell off the dam just the way Duncan had gone. He snagged hold with one hand and dangled there by his fingertips while the flames roared over his head.

***

Arch saw Lerner go over the edge just a few seconds after Duncan. His first thought was that if the OOCs (or whatever) had sent their A-team, this whole thing was going to end badly for everyone but Gideon.

He didn't dwell on that thought too long, though, instead popping the switchblade he'd been carrying in his pocket for the last couple weeks and charging at Gideon. The demon was focused on spraying the edge of the dam with flame, which was forcing Hendricks to dodge again; the fire was separating him from the cowboy.

Arch ignored the rain pelting him in the face and each splash of the water soaking his pants legs as he ran at Gideon in a tackle. Any second the demon could turn back, and Arch had to do some damage first.

How had they killed the last one? The heart, that was it. A blazing light in the chest of Ygrusibas—that cow-thing. He'd stabbed it himself, watched the thing burst into flames.

Arch bent lower for a tackle. He was going to hit Gideon right in the gut, blade first. Then he'd cut up, see if there was a light in him like there had been in Ygrusibas.

Then Gideon turned right at Arch, and Arch saw the light. But it wasn't any sort of inner light, the beating heart of the demon.

It was Gideon's breath of fire, hitting him squarely in the face.

***

Hendricks saw Arch disappear into the flames as Gideon swept around to counter the cop charging at him. Hendricks had been stuck in place, separated from Arch by the flames as Gideon chased him with the fire. He'd seen what it had done to Duncan, and getting hit by it was not on his priority list.

But when it hit Arch, Hendricks felt the cold, clutching fear wrap itself around his stomach and pull down like he'd had a weight tied to his gut. His knees felt like they wanted to buckle, and he could feel his jaw drop.

The fire blazed, pouring out of Gideon's mouth, billowing like an orange cloud that was tall as a man and just as wide. Arch was swallowed up by it entirely.

Hendricks could feel the anger course through him, and he raised his sword. He charged as he heard another thunder crack of a bullet whipping down from the hills at the same time a burst of gunfire came from behind Lerner and Duncan's sedan at his right.

* * *

Erin watched Arch disappear in the mammoth burst of flame, swallowed up by the demon's breath, and it took her a second to catch her own. She'd known Arch for years. Since long before they'd worked together.

Everyone knew Arch. He was the local hero, the guy every other guy wanted to be in high school, and the one every girl wanted to date.

Plus, he could have been a real dick, but he never was. He'd stayed humble, and though he wasn't a social butterfly, he never talked down to anyone like he was better than them, never got pushy about his faith, even back then, and was always decent to everybody. Even those jealous, racist fucks who said shitty things to him for being a black man dating a pretty white girl.

Erin pulled the red dot scope up and centered it on the demon's face. She could barely see it, through the hiss of steam. She could feel the heat, even from here, and she pulled the trigger and let a burst fly just as the big gun up in the hills opened up again.

* * *

Hendricks saw one of Gideon's arms go spiraling through the air and he thought, damn, whoever was at the business end of that fifty cal rifle was a pretty fucking good shot. Not Marine Force Recon good, but pretty fucking good.

Not that it mattered, because Arch was almost certainly still burnt to death.

Hendricks let that thought fuel him as he came at Gideon. The fucker had killed the one guy who he'd confided in. Five years he'd been doing this. Five years he'd submerged himself in it, in over his head every goddamned day.

Sure, he'd talked to other demon hunters, but rarely. Arch was the first person he'd connected with, other than Erin, since he'd started down this road.

Hendricks let his feet splash across the flooded surface of the dam as Gideon staggered backward, the flames in front of him dissipating into steam as another three-shot burst of rifle fire pelted him in the chest. He raised his sword and slammed into the demon, burying his blade into Gideon's belly and following with all his weight a moment later.

His momentum hit the demon while he was already off-balance. Hendricks saw the sword slide into the demon's fat gut as his pudgy face registered surprise. As his shoulder hit Gideon, he felt himself leave the ground and they both fell back, over the edge of the dam, and Hendricks felt a splash as they hit the flooded reservoir below and began to sink.

* * *

Lerner pulled himself up on one arm, an easier feat for a demon than a human, he knew. Dangling over the side of the dam, picturing the drop that Duncan had just taken, it wasn't something he wanted to ponder too long. As soon as the flame vanished over the side, he started to reel himself up using his wiry arms.

Water was sluicing over the edge, the overflow of the reservoir running over the dam and raining down on him. Lerner cursed it, cursed Sygraaths, cursed his fucking job and cursed the home office for sending him here. As he came up over the edge of the dam, water pouring onto his face, he cursed Duncan, too, for being a brave, dumb son of a bitch and doing what he'd done.

The black bag was still sitting there, just a few feet away from him. Lerner pulled himself up as Hendricks hit that fucking shitbird Sygraath with the sword, plowing into him and knocking him into the reservoir. Lerner could barely see it from behind the wall of steam that Gideon's flame breath had made. Lerner had a feeling it was pointed at someone, and that meant said someone was dead. Duncan might have been able to survive that shit—maybe—but a human? No way.

Then the smoke started to clear, and Lerner saw who was at the middle of it. It wasn't until he saw the state of them that he whispered, "Son of a bitch." And he almost forgot to finish pulling himself up over the side.

* * *

Erin was standing there, stunned, the rain dotting the end of the scope as she watched Hendricks plunge a sword through Gideon and then tilt with him into the reservoir. It wasn't exactly a long drop, maybe a foot or two, but because of the steam from Gideon's attack on Arch they disappeared within a second. It took her a second more to realize that what she'd seen was real, not the product of the steam or the drops of rain gathering on the scope.

She heard movement behind her and turned with the AR-15 to cover the approach of whoever was coming.

It was Lucia, her bright red hair wet, and her white tank top soaked to match. Erin lowered her gun then turned back to the edge of the dam, where she'd just seen Hendricks go over. The steam was starting to clear, but something in her mind flared before it did—

She spun back around to Lucia and stared at the girl's eyes. They weren't green anymore, they were dark, indescribable, shadowed. "What the fuck?" she whispered, all thoughts of Hendricks and Arch momentarily forgotten. "Who are you?"

"Starling," the girl answered and walked past her like she hadn't even seen her. "Follow me."

Erin turned to watch the redhead go, beating a steady path to the edge of the dam where Hendricks had disappeared. And she would have followed, but the steam finally dissipated, and she caught a glimpse of Arch, crouching down, his uniform top seared and burnt, nearly gone—

But his skin was flawless, drops of rain beading on it and running down his muscles like he was some model posing for a photo shoot instead of man who ought to have just burned to death.

* * *

Arch hadn't even felt the fire as it surged around him. He'd looked down as it blazed and watched with almost absent interest as it burnt his uniform shirt to embers that flaked off, melted the radio that was clipped to his shoulder into plastic slag that ran off his back like droplets of rain, burning holes in his pants as they fell.

He was on his knees, not from the impact or the heat, but because he'd reacted by dropping down. It was a natural position for him, the same one he adopted as he prayed his prayers each night. Just as he'd done every night since he was a child and had learned to pray and speak scripture.

He had murmured one as the orange fire of hell had nearly blinded him—with its light, not its heat. "I sought the LORD, and he answered me; he delivered me from all my fears." Then the flames disappeared, and he started to stand, his eyes still blinking away the light of the blaze.

* * *

"Out of the way, Shadrach!" Lerner called as he pushed past Arch. He shouldn't have been surprised the cop was still standing. He'd seen this kind of thing before, once or twice.

That didn't matter at the moment, though. Lerner peered over the edge of the dam into the reservoir. The water was right there, in front of him, and Hendricks had already disappeared beneath the dark, rippling surface, sunk from sight.

Lerner felt a presence next to him as he started to jump in. He caught a glimpse of red hair and thought, *Son of a bitch, it's the hooker,* before he plunged into the cold water.

* * *

Erin halted after watching the man in the suit and Starling both jump into the water after Hendricks. Arch was standing there on the edge of the dam, looking in, and looking like he was still trying to catch his breath.

"You all right?" Erin asked as she came up behind him. She had the AR in her hands, cradled, pointing it down the dam automatically, her finger off the trigger but ready in case she needed it.

"I'm fine," Arch said, but he sounded a little dazed. She couldn't really blame him for that; it wasn't like being immolated alive was an everyday thing. "Where's Hendricks?"

"He pushed that—" she stumbled with the word, "—that demon-thing into the water. Tackled him in, I guess."

Arch stared into the black water after him, and Erin wondered for a moment if he was going to jump. "Damn," he said finally.

"What?" she asked. Hearing Arch say damn was like hearing Reeve drop the c-word; it didn't happen, at least not in her presence.

"I don't know how to swim," Arch said.

* * *

Hendricks could feel the cool water seeping into his coat, saturating his shirt and flooding his boots. Gideon was right there, in front of him, he could feel it, even as the world went weightless around him.

Gideon tried to hit him, but his blow was reduced in power, slowed by the water. It felt like a hard slap and that was it. Hendricks smiled, a hand anchored on the hilt of his sword. He pulled it hard to the side across Gideon's belly.

Air bubbled out and the water warmed around Hendricks. He knew he was getting somewhere and even in the frenzy of the water bubbling around him he could swear he heard Gideon scream.

Hendricks ignored another ineffectual blow from the demon and turned the sword right, then pulled it up. The blade sawed its way up to where the demon's sternum would have been and stopped. Hendricks could barely see him in the water, and the light from above seemed to be growing ever dimmer.

There was a low thrumming all around him, mechanical and steady. It was audible somewhere around the level of his heartbeat.

Hendricks felt hyperaware, time slowing down as the water flooded into his nose and mouth. It was just like this the last time, too, that drowning feeling, except this time he wasn't helpless when he plunged into the water. He didn't stagger into trouble by accident, dragging an innocent person with him.

He'd pulled Arch in with full knowledge, and he'd gotten the man killed.

Hendricks ripped the sword through Gideon even harder, and he felt the heat wash off in waves as the water bubbled up around him. He'd been in Ygrusibas at the end, felt the flames of hell licking at him. They were real, he knew that much, wherever they came from, and they were hot enough to boil the water around him if he didn't find the heart soon.

Gideon hit him again, a punch that didn't even make him blink. The mighty demon, reduced to something that felt comically like a slap fight. Gideon clearly hadn't been in any fights; if he had, he'd have grabbed Hendricks around the neck and just crushed his throat. He had the strength for it.

Hendricks stared down at him, and Gideon flailed his remaining arm at him one last time. Hendricks ignored it and tugged once more on the sword. He brought it diagonal this time, and broke through where the ribcage would be on a human.

Where the heart would be, if Gideon had any such thing.

The effect was immediate; the water turned from warm bath to scalding hot in an instant, and Hendricks felt his skin start to sear. This was it: he was going to burn too.

Just like Arch.

But at least he'd taken this fucker with him first. And before he could drown the town.

* * *

"What's that?" Erin asked, her eyes catching on a red silk bag. It was pretty and stitched, and floating in the rapidly rising water that was running across the dam.

Arch seemed to stare at it with unblinking eyes as it washed to the middle of the dam. "I think it's ... it might be that thing that Gideon—the demon guy—was going to use to blow up the dam."

"He was gonna blow up the dam?" Erin said, blinking. Holy shit. She didn't say it, just thought it. What the fuck was going on here? She didn't say that either. She just watched as the red silk bag washed off the front of the dam, making its long drop down the sheer face before she or Arch could even move to stop it.

* * *

Gideon felt the blade cutting into him, felt it and fought back. He was slow, though, from the wounds, and from the water holding him back from using his full strength. He could feel them sinking, here in the depths, and as the sword cut through his chest, a dim feeling of awareness that came over him, even as he tried to lash out at the man in the black coat.

He'd felt this feeling before. A thousand times. Ten thousand times. But from the other side.

Death.

When the blade tore through into his heart—the beating central nexus of his massive essence—it didn't kill him right away. No, just like a knife to the heart—or a heart attack, he thought ironically, remembering that guy a few days earlier—what was his name? The first one that he'd felt die here in Midian?

It was like that. Agony in the chest, a sick feeling spreading through his limbs. He lost control of his hand first, and with a last spasm it went limp. He could still feel the heat rising off his body, like blood flowing to his extremities in one last burst.

Gideon drifted down and looked up to the face of the cowboy. He was missing his hat now. Didn't look right. Not like the time he'd seen him in the parking lot.

It was the black hat that sold the look for Gideon. Without it, this guy just looked human. He realized that now as he stared him in the face. Before, he'd been a demon hunter. Now he was just a guy.

A guy who'd killed him. But still just a guy.

There was anguish at the thought of his long life being squandered. All those years and he'd never awakened to what he had in the last few days. It could have been so much better if he'd known. He could have had so much more if he'd just pushed beyond what he'd always been told.

But now it was too late.

He wanted to rail against it, would have if he could have moved his arm or his legs. But he couldn't. The heat was rising, the cowboy hanging over him like death—real death, finally—and dark wings sprouting up on either side of him.

Gideon was going to burn, he didn't have any illusions about that. He was lifeless, but the life hadn't quite fled yet. When it did, it would be a spectacular burst of hell's fire that would flash-boil the water around him for twenty feet.

And maybe—just maybe—he could burn the cowboy up as he went.

One last one, for the road.

Show him who death really was.

* * *

Hendricks felt strong hands grabbing his arms, dragging at him as he hung there in the wash. In the river? Water had flooded into his nose and mouth, was drowning him now, just like it had last time, and he was ready. Oh, Renée

, how he was ready.

One last death, and he was settled up. Not really, but it was as close as he was going to get in this life.

He wanted to fight against the hands that had him, but he couldn't. He thrashed, but they were far too strong, both of them, and he was far too weak, and his lungs were crying for air, and—

When his head broke the surface, it felt like had the last time he'd been pulled out of the water. He hadn't wanted to come back then, either, but he'd been at peace—or something close to it—when he had. Now he was kicking and screaming as he was lifted up onto the concrete, sputtering and spitting the water out of his nose and mouth.

Hendricks landed on his forearms and knees, and he felt it when he did. He rolled to the side shortly, then to his back, and felt water tap-tap-tapping him on the face as he lay there, spent.

"Hendricks?" The female voice was lighter than the last time. He knew it, too. Not because it sounded like something born of infinity and familiarity, but because he'd heard it before. Whispering in the night. Urging him to fuck her.

He opened his eyes to see Erin leaning over him, an M-16 in her hands. And he could have sworn he saw Arch just behind her shoulder. "I'm not married," he whispered as he looked at her. "Not anymore."

* * *

Erin stared down at Hendricks, a little surprised by his first words after Starling and the guy in the suit had fished him out of the water. "Uhm … that's good. It looks like you were right about there being demons, too."

"Heh," Hendricks said, still looking up at her like he was dazed. "I guess I'm not a fucking liar after all."

"No," she agreed, "just a fucker."

* * *

Arch stared down at Hendricks over Erin's shoulder, and finally saw Hendricks's eyes alight on him. "Arch?" the cowboy said.

"I'm here," Arch said. He was still feeling more than a little dazed himself. And cold, the rain beating down on him with his shirt gone and all.

"Where are your clothes?" Hendricks asked. "Why do you keep losing your clothes?"

Arch sighed. He really didn't have an answer for that.

* * *

Lerner stood on the edge of the dam closest to the reservoir. The redhead was next to him, watching Harris and Arch hanging over Hendricks like he was dead. They were all wrapped up in each other, but he was watching the redhead.

He'd seen her at the whorehouse, at a distance. Her eyes were normal, then. And Duncan could read her just fine.

Now, her eyes were dusky as all hell. Indeterminate color. And he was looking real hard, trying to figure it. This wasn't some shit he'd seen before, and he'd been on the job a long time.

Which meant she was something new? Or something that predated his years of service?

He kept watching her, and she kept watching the little scene playing out in front of them.

* * *

Hendricks almost felt well enough to get to his feet. Almost. Arch threw him a helping hand and he took it, and the cop pulled him up. He ran a hand up his own face and up to the top of his head before he realized something was missing.

"My hat," he said.

* * *

Arch saw it drifting toward the other edge of the dam. He went toward it at run and caught it before it went over the edge. He looked down—all the way down—and took a quick step back. It wasn't a plunge he thought anyone could easily survive—human or demon.

* * *

Hendricks felt the smooth felt of the wet hat as Arch handed it back to him. He dumped it out and set it back on his head, felt it settle just right. The brim drooped from the effect of the water, but that had happened last time, too. It dried out in time.

"Thank you," he said to Arch. "I can't …" He stopped before his voice broke.

* * *

Erin heard the quaver in the way Hendricks spoke, and while part of her said to stay back, another part urged her on, and she placed a hand on his back, unasked. It felt right. He made a slow turn around to look at her, and she caught sight of something in his eyes. A pain in the depths, something she'd never seen all the times they'd been together.

She leaned in and kissed him. It just felt right, too.

* * *

Lerner was still watching the redhead watch everything unfold. She was a cool customer. Beyond cool, actually. It wasn't until the cowboy kissed Deputy Harris that the ice queen melted, just for a second. But when she did, it was obvious as hell to him. Him and no one else, because she only wavered for a blink before she went back to her normal even self.

But he saw it, the flash of it, for the half second of existence it had. Saw it and recorded it in his mind for later. He knew that emotion. He'd felt it himself only a few minutes earlier when he watched Duncan go flying off the top of the dam.

Rage. Pure, hate-filled rage.

* * *

"This is a beautiful denouement," Hendricks heard Lerner say as he broke off his kiss with Erin. Her lips were soft, and moist. He was still dripping wet and could feel it as he stood there, his clothing absolutely soaked under the weight of his coat. His sword was on the ground where he'd let go of it when he got thrown out of the water, and he stooped to pick it up and sheathe it. "But I need to go check and see if my partner survived his plunge off the dam," Lerner finished. "Adios." The demon sketched a rough salute to them and started off toward the sedan.

"You owe me a mirror," Erin said. She didn't sound angry, more weary. She was still clutching an M-16 in her hands. It took him a second of staring at it to realize it was probably an AR-15. Cops didn't carry M-16s.

"Bill me for it," Lerner tossed over his shoulder without looking back. He stooped to pick up a black gym bag that was still resting on the surface of the dam, two or three inches of water running around it. It didn't so much as move until he picked it up. "Better yet, bill your boyfriend," Lerner went on, holding the gym bag in his hand like it weighed nothing. "I did just save his life, after all." Lerner got into the car without once looking up and backed up off the dam in the sedan with a little more speed than Hendricks would have thought safe given the location.

Hendricks looked at Arch, who was still standing there, shirtless, the rain coming down around them. He met the cop's gaze, and neither one of them said anything for a minute. "Need a ride home?" Arch asked him, finally.

Hendricks thought about that for a minute then looked at Erin. There was something in her eyes that told him what he needed to know. "Nah, I think I've got that covered," he told Arch.

"Shit," Erin said, snapping her fingers. She let the rifle in her hands sag. "I'm supposed to drop Lucia—I mean Starling—off at the station."

Something about that prickled at Hendricks. He looked around the surface of the dam. "Hey, wasn't Starling here just a minute ago …?"

"Son of a bitch," Erin said. Hendricks agreed with part of that assessment, anyway. The dam was empty from side to side, except for the three of them. Hendricks peered at Erin's patrol car, parked just a little closer than Arch's cruiser. It looked empty. "Man," Erin said, "Reeve is gonna have my ass for this."

"Why?" Hendricks asked, frowning. "What does the sheriff have to do with Starling?"

He could see the pained look on Erin's face. "That's … kind of a long story."

"Tell me on the way home?" Hendricks asked, and felt her wrap an arm around his waist. He put his around her shoulders and they started back along the dam, side by side. The rain had slackened, finally.

"Yours or mine?" she asked. And he didn't have an answer for her. Not right away.

*　*　*

Lerner made his way back down the winding hill road almost as fast as he'd made his way up. This time, he didn't even have a cop in pursuit; something more important was at stake. The shift of the car's transmission as he revved up and down bothered him not at all. He almost tuned it out as he raced around tight corners and taxed his wet tires well past the point he knew he should have.

He knew he was home free when he hit the last straightaway, knew that the guardhouse was ahead less than a mile. The Caledonia River was running to his left, the source up over the dam somewhere ahead of him. He kept one eye on the road and one on the water as he drove like mad.

It was the eye on the road that eventually found him. Lerner hit the brakes as he approached, squealing the sedan to a stop and jamming the PRNDL switch into park without bothering to even pull his keys out of the ignition. He had the door open and was half out of it when the naked figure rushed in front of his headlights and opened the passenger door, sliding into the front seat.

"You scared me almost worse than hell," Lerner said as he got back in the car.

"Occupational hazard," Duncan said. He looked like he was shivering, but he wasn't. He was shaking. "We won, of course." It wasn't even a question.

"Yes. *We* did," Lerner agreed, and put the car in reverse. He turned around so he didn't accidentally back into a pine tree while he pulled the car about. He liked that Duncan didn't ask what he meant about the we thing. "The redhead came back."

"Did she?" Duncan asked. Lerner could see the puzzlement. It was just barely there under Duncan's almost inscrutable expression. "I didn't ... I couldn't see her there. When I looked."

"I figured you wouldn't," Lerner said, nodding to himself. He was driving slowly, now. Crisis passed. He took a breath and let it out. "When she was the hooker coming out of the whorehouse, her eyes were normal, some human color, and you could read her, right?" He didn't need to wait for Duncan's nod, but he did. "The same girl shows up on the dam, her eyes are some dusky hue I can't place, she looks ... just different and feels off—and you can't feel her at all." He smiled and looked at Duncan. "You ever heard of anything like that before?"

Duncan didn't answer at first. That was a bad sign, Lerner thought. "Maybe," he said finally. "But ... it's been a long time."

"I was thinking it had to be something old or something new," Lerner said, still nodding.

"Real old," Duncan said. He paused. "You know, if those humans hadn't been there—"

"Don't ..." Lerner said. "Just don't. We're OOCs. We don't do team-ups."

"You know we're here for the duration," Duncan said, and Lerner heard a little hint of something. Emotion. "Till the hotspot goes."

"I know."

"There could be worse things than having—"

"If you say 'friends,' I will kick your naked ass right out of this car and make you walk back to town," Lerner said.

Duncan didn't say anything for a moment. "I was going to say allies." He let that hang for a minute, but Lerner didn't reply. "That suit was one of my favorites," Duncan said. Now he sounded like he was whining. As much as Duncan ever did, anyway.

"It was ugly," Lerner said, and caught the faintly—very faintly—scandalized look from Duncan. "You're right, of course. Not about the suit. But we're gonna be here for a while. Maybe we play nice." He didn't smile. "They've got an in on some power—some thing—that we can't place, with that redhead. That's worth keeping an eye on, wouldn't you say?"

Duncan didn't say—at first. Finally, "We should definitely keep watch." Lerner couldn't disagree with that.

* * *

Erin pulled the cruiser into the parking spot in front of Hendricks's motel room. They sat there for a minute in silence. They'd talked, on and off, on the drive down from the dam. Erin wasn't sure she understood the whole demon thing, really, but Hendricks had shed a little light. Basic stuff. Every question she asked left them in silence, though, for a few minutes while she processed the answer and honed in one which was the next best question to ask.

She hadn't run out of them, that was sure.

The hot air was blowing out of the car's vents, and they were both still soaked. The sheriff's cloth seats were drenched, and Erin had a suspicion that it was liable to leave a mildewed stink once it dried that would be just as obvious as the missing mirror. The hot air blowing out of the vents helped a little, though they both still shivered occasionally as they sat there in the parking lot.

"You want to come in?" Hendricks asked. Tentatively, like he wasn't sure.

What the hell did he think she would say to that? He wasn't married, he wasn't crazy, and her head was swirling like a martini someone had just spun a swizzle stick in. Plus he was some kind of big fucking hero demon slayer who'd damned near gotten himself killed to save the whole town. She wasn't sure what the proper protocol even was in this situation; whether she should run screaming away from him or just throw her panties at him. "Sure," she said.

They got out of the car and drifted toward the door. At least the rain had stopped, though every step caused another ripple in the giant puddle that was the parking lot of the Sinbad motel.

He paused at the door and rummaged in his pocket before producing the key—along with a handful of water. "Guess I'm lucky I didn't lose this," he said.

"Guess so." She tried to laugh, but it was a halfhearted effort at best. She stared at him. He was a hero. Saw Arch go down and just charged right at the demon knowing that it could turn him to ash. She wanted to say something of that sort to him, but he was fumbling with the keys, and she didn't know how to say it.

So she kissed him. Long, slow. Her hand ended up on his chest, she felt the muscles under his wet shirt. She knew she was past running away, even as fucked up as things had gotten, and she wanted to throw her panties at him but something—some damned something—was holding her back, so she just kissed him until he broke it off.

She tried to go in on him again, could hear the door squeak on its hinges. She caught his lips and felt him press back, but only for a moment before he broke away again. She grasped his shirt in her hand, squeezing it and trying to pull him close but he stopped her. "Wait."

She caught her breath as she paused, lips inches from his. This was what she wanted, right? He was good at it, they had fun together. She'd seen what he'd done, who he was, right? This was what was supposed to happen next.

It was what always happened next.

She held there, though, dripping, in the open door of his motel room, staring him in the eyes. He stared right back, and she could watch him think. It was still cute, but something nagged at her. She waited for him to say something, get something out or off his chest before he resumed kissing her the way he always had. He already knew how to get her started, get her wet, even after a couple of weeks and just a few times. And this time, she was ready. She should have been ready. It was like makeup sex, right?

Except it wasn't, she realized, and after a moment of staring into his eyes she realized he felt it, too. It was the anchor that was holding him back, keeping him from leaning in and kissing her the way she was so sure he would. She suddenly felt the burn of shame, and she started to pull away but he caught her hand. "Wait," he said. "Don't go."

"I ..." She thought of a thousand excuses, then a million of them. None came out. "I should go." That was what came out.

"Stay," he said, and he said it like he'd said "wait"—like he was taking a breath. With hope and purpose, and there was no rejection in it. "Stay," he said again, and she realized she wanted to.

"What ..." She realized, as wet as she was, soaked from head to toe, her mouth was bone dry, like the dust. "What would we do?" It was an answer she didn't have. She had a hint of it, though, and now she wanted to see what he'd say.

He didn't say, not at first. He just licked his lips, like he was buying a minute to compose his thoughts. She gave it to him and waited like he'd asked—maybe *because* he'd asked—and he finally said, "Why don't we just ... talk ... for a while?"

She thought it over for only a second before she answered, with her gut instead of her head. "Okay," she said, and followed him into the room. And he shut the door behind them.

* * *

Arch opened the door to his apartment like he always did now, tentatively. He listened and heard movement somewhere in the bedroom. He shut the door behind him and tossed his keys onto the table. Fortunately they hadn't been in his shirt, or he might have had to beg a ride with Erin, too.

Alison emerged from the bedroom, wet hair draped over her shoulder, a white terrycloth bathrobe clinging to her figure. She didn't look surprised to see him, he thought. Then he took a breath. "Hey," he said, low-key and casual, while he took a minute to gather his thoughts.

"Hey," she returned to him. She lingered in the short hallway between the bedroom and the living room, a good twenty feet from him, and made no move to get closer.

"How are you doing?" he asked, lamely, he knew. He was searching for something to say—anything, really—to postpone what he knew he HAD to say.

"Just got out of the shower," she replied quietly. Like she did everything lately. Since—

Since he'd—

Arch crossed the distance between them and fell to his knees like he had when the fire had come at him. He'd thought in that moment that his life was over, had been almost certain of it. He'd prayed, sure, had cited scripture, absolutely, but he'd left one thing undone.

He reached up and took her hands in his. "I'm sorry for the way things have gone lately," he said. "I'm sorry for how bad things have gotten, how distant I've been, how much I've … I've let you down by not talking." He saw a flicker of emotion in her eyes. "I'm sorry I've let things outside our house take me away in the hours I needed to be here and own me even during the times I was here with you."

She didn't say anything, just watched him with a stricken look, and he went on. "I'm sorry I failed you as a protector and let those animals violate our home. I'm sorry I let them lay hands on you." He clutched at her hands, held them in his, and looked up at her. He wasn't welling up, though somewhere down there it felt like he should be. His voice was thick with emotion. "I'm sorry I've failed you as a husband, and I'm sorry I haven't been here for you in any capacity at all. I will change," he said, with certainty. "God as my witness, I will. I am your husband, and I will start acting like it again."

He could see a little waver from her now, a twitch of her lips. He brought her hands to his mouth and kissed them, then rubbed them along his face. He could feel the smooth skin against his cheek, feel the softness of her palms, could smell the—

Smell the—

He froze, her hand against his face. "It's all right," she said finally, and he looked up at her. She stared down at him and the coolness was gone. She looked a little warmer at him, still a bit reserved, too, but warmer than she'd been since the day she'd been attacked. "It's all right, Arch. We'll get through it." She gave him a hint of reassurance and rubbed his cheek. "It'll be okay." Her wet hair hung limp over her shoulder, spotting the white robe where it dragged. "It'll all be okay."

He said nothing.

"I'm going to go get presentable," she said, and brushed his cheek again. "And maybe," she said, "after I'm done, we can spend some time together like a husband and wife should." She paused, and he looked up in her eyes. "If you'd like?"

Still he said nothing, but after a few seconds, he found it in himself to nod. She smiled and withdrew her hands. Slowly, gently, and without taking her eyes off of him. She smiled all the while, that same gentle, lightly happy smile. She disappeared into the bedroom again, and he heard the closet door open as she rummaged for something to wear.

As soon as he heard her clacking the clothes hangers together, he fell onto his haunches. He sat there, eyes unfocused, staring at white walls of the apartment. He felt the hard linoleum floor under his buttocks through the seat of his pants. He could taste something in his mouth, something bitter from where he'd put his lips to her hands and smelled—

Arch drew a deep breath and let it out slowly. She hadn't asked about his shirt. He was before her, shirtless, begging her forgiveness and she hadn't said a word about it. He'd thought when he came in maybe she was too distracted, but she hadn't said anything even before he launched himself at her in apology.

And now he knew why.

He held his hands up to his nose and sniffed again. They smelled of gunpowder from where he'd shot his Glock, over and over at Gideon while trying to stop him. It was distinct, it had a tang that hung in his nose, an aroma that couldn't be mistaken.

When he'd held Alison's hands up to his nose he'd smelled gunpowder of a different kind than was on his. Sharper. Stronger. As if from a gun that had far more power—and powder per cartridge—than his piddly handgun.

He heard the clack of the coat hangers moving in the closet as she stood there—like she always did—trying to figure out what to wear. The same old Alison.

But to his ears, every time the plastic hangers clacked together, he heard the roar of a sniper rifle barking down from a hill above him.

Where his wife had stood, raining hell down on his enemy from on high.

Return to Midian, Tennessee in

CORRUPTED
SOUTHERN WATCH
BOOK 3

Coming Summer 2014!

Author's Note

If you want to know as soon as I release a new book (because I don't do release dates - there's a good reason, I swear), visit RobertJCrane.com to sign up for my mailing list. I promise I won't spam you (I only send an email when I have a new book released) and I'll never sell your info. You can also unsubscribe at any time. You might want to sign up, because in case you haven't noticed, these books keep showing up unexpectedly early. You just never know when the next will get here...

I also wanted to take a moment to thank you for reading this story. As an independent author, getting my name out to build an audience is one of the biggest priorities on any given day. If you enjoyed this story and are looking forward to reading more, let someone know - post it on the site you bought the book from, on your blog (if you have one), on Goodreads.com, place it in a quick Facebook status or Tweet with a link to the page of whatever outlet you purchased it from. Good reviews inspire people to take a chance on a new author – like me. And we new authors can use all the help we can get.

I appreciate your support and thanks for reading!

Robert J. Crane

About the Author

Robert J. Crane was born and raised on Florida's Space Coast before moving to the upper midwest in search of cooler climates and more palatable beer. He graduated from the University of Central Florida with a degree in English Creative Writing. He worked for a year as a substitute teacher and worked in the financial services field for seven years while writing in his spare time. He makes his home in the Twin Cities area of Minnesota.

He can be **contacted** in several ways:
Via email at cyrusdavidon@gmail.com
Follow him on Twitter – @robertJcrane
Connect on Facebook – robertJcrane (Author)
Website – http://www.robertJcrane.com
Blog – http://robertJcrane.blogspot.com
Become a fan on Goodreads – http://www.goodreads.com/RobertJCrane

Other Works by Robert J. Crane

The Sanctuary Series
Epic Fantasy
Defender: The Sanctuary Series, Volume One
Avenger: The Sanctuary Series, Volume Two
Champion: The Sanctuary Series, Volume Three
Crusader: The Sanctuary Series, Volume Four
Sanctuary Tales, Volume One - A Short Story Collection
Thy Father's Shadow: A Sanctuary Novel* (Coming Summer 2014!)
Master: The Sanctuary Series, Volume Five*

The Girl in the Box
Contemporary Urban Fantasy
Alone: The Girl in the Box, Book 1
Untouched: The Girl in the Box, Book 2
Soulless: The Girl in the Box, Book 3
Family: The Girl in the Box, Book 4
Omega: The Girl in the Box, Book 5
Broken: The Girl in the Box, Book 6
Enemies: The Girl in the Box, Book 7
Legacy: The Girl in the Box, Book 8
Destiny: The Girl in the Box, Book 9* (Coming Spring 2014!)
Power: The Girl in the Box, Book 10*

Southern Watch
Contemporary Urban Fantasy
Called: Southern Watch, Book 1
Depths: Southern Watch, Book 2
Corrupted: Southern Watch, Book 3* (Coming Summer 2014!)

* Forthcoming

Printed in Great Britain
by Amazon